THORNS OF WAR

THE SMOKESMITHS
Book Two

JOÃO F. SILVA

First paperback edition May 2024

Edited by Sarah Chorn

Proofread by Edward Crocker

Cover Design by MIBLART

Interior Illustrations by CyberOni Arts

Published by João F. Silva

www.joaofsilva.net

For the oppressed.
Because the violence of the slaveowner
isn't morally the same
as the violence of the slave
trying to end that violence.

Read a Free Prequel Novella

The Usharian Empire rules the Known World with an iron fist. Imperials protect their world from the tainted hand of the Deceiver, but he is back with an avatar capable of breaking the Empire and grounding humanity into ash.

JEHA is a sentinel of the Empire, willing to fight and die for kinship and duty.

AGOR is an imperial general. Disgruntled by the darkness he sees seeping into everything he loves, he makes his move.

MATALA is a young smokesmith who sees his courage tested as Ushar burns.

ALAMAKAR is the world's most powerful man, but even strong blood ties can hold him down and tear him apart.

As the Deceiver threatens the Usharian Empire's heart, fiends walk the streets of the capital. Men and monsters clash in a battle fit for gods. And the smoke follows them.

My novella 'Ruins of Smoke' is a prequel to The Smoke-smiths series, and it was a finalist in the 1st iteration of the Speculative Fiction Indie Novella Championship (SFINCS). But the best thing? It is available for FREE to all my mailing list subscribers. In fact, this short story isn't available to anyone else. You can read it completely for free.

CONTENTS

AINISIAN OCEAN
ADLO
AINIS
EVORIS
MOSENDE
MUNZI BAY
ALARKAN
HELERONDE
THE KN

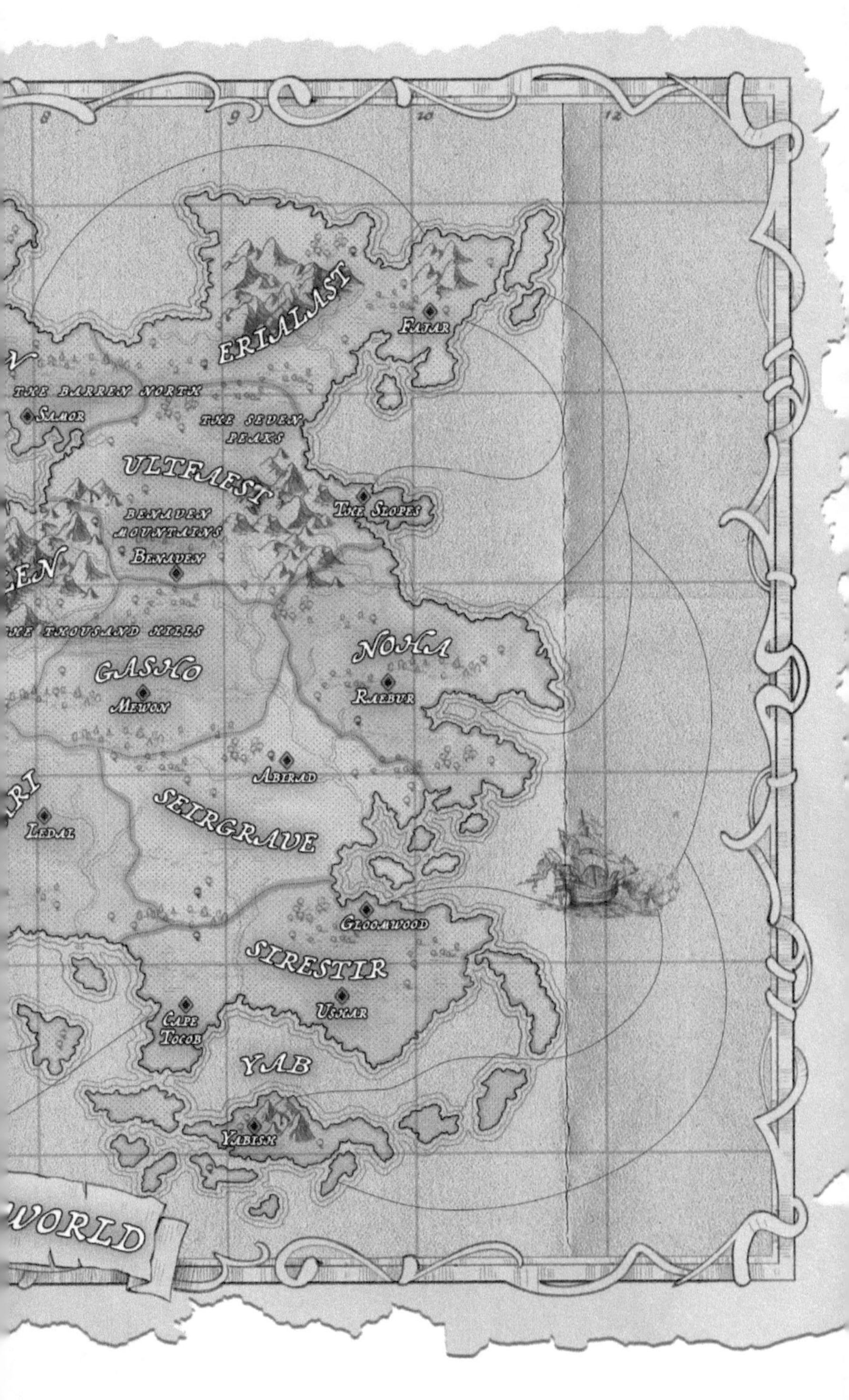

8
9
10
12
ERIALAST
FALAR
THE BARREN NORTH
SAMOR
THE SEVEN PEAKS
ULTFAEST
BENAVEN MOUNTAINS
THE SLOPES
BENAVEN
EN
THE THOUSAND HILLS
NOHA
GASHO
RAEBUR
MEWON
ABIRAD
RI
SEIRGRAVE
LEDAL
GLOOMWOOD
SIRESTIR
USHAR
CAPE TOCOB
YAB
YABISH
WORLD

Shadesgrowl
Marcruncher
Bloodsleuth
Hearthspear
Mossback

Lantern Horn

STORY SO FAR

The Crimson Wars ended ten years ago when Orberesis broke the world with the power of his orb. He destroyed the beasts that plagued humanity and pulled a new continent from the depths of the ocean. But he doesn't remember how.

Orberesis still has the orb but can't get it to work. With a legion of devout followers who believe he is God Himself at his back and with his best friend Tavanar, Orberesis manages to become a major advisor of Doemus, king of the powerful Two Nations. But Orberesis hides crippling headaches and nightmares, even from his staunchest follower Solvi. After all other remedies have failed and after several assassination attempts by the elite of the Two Nations, he gets fixated on a power-enhancing elixir found across the world, in the very continent he lifted from the depths of the ocean during his miracle.

On this new continent, Gimlore, a single mother turned crime boss, starts the settlement of Heleronde, where she finds a new home for her children Tinko and Thata, and for her old brigand mates Edmir, Nork, and Nosema. She dreams of finding the stability she never had and of growing a criminal empire, but when she welcomes a foreign ambassador of the Two Nations in a prospective business deal, she discovers the kingdom plans to seize her town and steal the elixir she produces. Gimlore won't go down without a fight, so she reluctantly allies with veteran lawman Keryon to keep the town safe from invaders.

Gimlore discovers soldiers of the Two Nations have started a camp next to her town and are trespassing on her lands. She ambushes them, but it goes awry when her right-hand man Edmir is caught and killed. Keryon saves her and burns the enemy camp to a crisp with his smokesmith powers, and she realises she can't win by herself.

Knowing the Two Nations will retaliate, Gimlore requests the help of Rednow, the leader of the Leeth, the world's most feared mercenary army and a smokesmith. After a botched job in the nearby kingdom of Gasho, he and his commanders Merey, Tellwoon, and Zatak flee, penniless, by the skin of their teeth. To make matters worse, Rednow is plagued by the voice of his dead sister.

Gimlore's request is Rednow's last chance to feed his army for the winter and retire in peace before he passes the torch to the younger generation. In lieu of gold, Gimlore offers part of her lands as payment, giving Rednow a place to finally retire in peace after the battle.

Orberesis travels with a fleet to secure the elixir. During the journey, Tavanar discovers that Orberesis can't actually control the orb and tries to hurt him for lying to him. The orb activates, protects Orberesis, and sends Tavanar overboard. When the fleet of the Two Nations arrives in Heleronde, the settlement town turns into a battleground against Rednow's mercenaries. Gimlore and Keryon infiltrate the ships to stop the cannons from destroying their town and to capture Orberesis.

Keryon burns the main ship. He and Gimlore chase Orberesis but are held back by Solvi. Keryon defeats her, and Gimlore goes after Orberesis. In a scuffle, she steals his infamous orb, the source of his power, but it falls on the ship's deck, shattering and creating a beam of blinding light which reveals the Old One, an ancient god, who was manipulating Orberesis all along through the orb. As Rednow is about to die from using his smokesmith abilities too much, he discovers that the voice of his sister was in fact the Essence, another deity, who kept him alive but took his arm as payment. She reveals an ancient feud between her and the Old One and tells Rednow he must be the one to help her now that the Old One has awakened.

With Orberesis presumed drowned, his ships destroyed, and his troops defeated by Rednow, Gimlore goes back to her town, where the townspeople thank her by volunteering to rebuild her tavern. Gimlore has found a new trusted partner in Keryon and a new mentor in Rednow, who is now retired after nominating Merey to be the new leader of the Leeth. With Solvi captured, she rebuilds the town completely and asks Rednow for a safe way to turn her children into smokesmiths.

CONTENT WARNING

Besides the typical things you might find in an adult epic fantasy book, such as swear words, violence, light torture, blood spilling, references to alcoholism, and other strong themes of mental health (or lack thereof), this book also contains a scene in which a character experiences the loss of their child. If you want to know which chapter of the book this scene takes place so you can read without fear of being triggered, you can check it out on my website.

ONE
BACK PAIN

GIMLORE

Gimlore lounged in her bedroom chair and stretched her arms over her head, elongating her back. For the Gods, she wasn't even that old, why couldn't she have a few days of good spirits now that the kids were away?

As if teasing her, her back spasmed. She bit her lip and frowned, swallowing the pain. Leaning forward carefully, with a hand supporting her lower back, she picked up a bottle of cerro wine from the bedside cupboard. A hefty one, this was. She took a drag and let the liquor slide down her throat, providing her the buzz she sought.

Everything in her life was better, but ever since the children had left, she had found herself turning more to the bottle. Nothing to be concerned about, of course, but she did notice the tendency, which meant others must have as well.

"They could at least come visit..." she muttered. "Ungrateful bastards."

"What did you say?" Keryon asked.

"Nothing."

The Warden hummed, his eyebrows climbing higher. He gave her a sly smile in return. "Sure, Madam."

Now that they were fucking, she wished he would drop the formalities.

She shook her head. *Why am I fucking him?* Maybe *he* was the reason her back hurt so much.

The floorboard creaked as she moved to get dressed. A loose white shirt, casual brown pants, and knee-high mud boots. "I'm off to see Pie," she said.

"Send him my regards."

"I will send him your morning breath, how about that? So much more delightful," she teased.

Keryon sighed and shook his head. Gimlore smiled and walked out of the room.

If the old Maiden's Hall had a beauty that was an acquired taste, the newly built tavern was nothing short of magnificent. It stood solidly in the swamp, looming above all other buildings. Not even the new town hall was that imposing. The lumber was freshly milled, the rooms were far larger, and it could host twice the patrons.

Ah, she thought, *so much room to store ale, wine, and all the black powder I might ever need.*

The bar counter was long enough to host about forty patrons banging their fists for a refill. The old scent of spilled liquor absorbed into the wood was gone, though. Now it only smelled of proper cedar.

She tapped her knuckles on the counter and two mirrored heads popped out of the kitchen window, one of them covered by a red bandana. "I'm going to the Town Hall, boys."

"Yes, boss," Nosema said, his gaze shifting back to his brother Nork and their kitchen.

Gimlore stood there for a moment watching Nork and Nosema cut potatoes, carrots, onions, and other vegetables that would go into the stew. Their focus was unrivalled, as though nothing could stop them. Held by their trained hands, the knives moved cleanly through the vegetables.

Maybe I should find myself a hobby as well. Something I can immerse myself in.

But what? She was many things already: a mother, a landlady, and a businesswoman, among others. All of those were work though, and someone in her line of work didn't get to where she was by spending her days painting, or writing, or singing like a stupid nightingale.

She shook her head and left the Maiden's Hall only to be flooded by the sound of progress. The bustle of the construction workers pulling their wagons loaded with timber was overwhelmed by fish merchants doing everything they could to entice the passersby.

"You, asshole!" a merchant shouted at a shaggy fellow. "Buy this bass and I won't tell your wife where I see you every day."

The poor man hurried onwards, and the merchant laughed before the shouting resumed. When Gimlore passed by, they quieted.

"No insults for me? No threats?"

"Not for you, Madam," a toothless fishmonger said. "Never for you!"

"I can take a punch," Gimlore said. "But I suppose I might also punch back."

The fishmonger smiled. "Precisely, boss."

The rest of Heleronde looked different now that caravans of refugees were all too common. Droves of them came, carrying their packs. They looked pale, as though they had lost the weight that used to fill their clothes on their journey there. She made sure to be the first one to welcome them with water, some soup, bread, and a contract to work for her in the marshes in exchange for the right to a small plot of land to build a shack. They were eager, and she didn't blame them. These were better conditions than many had ever had in their miserable lives.

She kept walking towards the Town Hall, which was no longer the old shack it had once been. Now the façade was made of sturdy wood panels, but it was still devoid of any fine details since it was meant to convey its purpose as a building where important business was to be conducted by important people. She would rather have these meetings in the Maiden's Hall, since people always ended up spending more on wine, but things had escalated, and she was more of a general than a barmaid these days.

She walked in, her steps announced by the creaking of the humid floorboards. Pie and Keryon had previously decorated the walls as well as the rough wood boards allowed. Mementos of their past lives were nailed to the walls, and a strong motif of plants and herbs seemed to be everywhere she looked.

"Keryon is supposed to be the Warden, and yet this place looks like it could be your bedroom." Gimlore raised her voice. "Don't be surprised if I don't like to come over often."

Pie snorted as he glanced at her. "I could almost say the same for that filthy tavern of yours."

The man's long beard was tidier now. Instead of his typical wizard-like apparel of white robes and goggles, he looked like a desk man—someone who people owed taxes to, but who would send others to collect for him. While Keryon was indeed the Warden, he was more suited for the physical and violent tasks. Pie was better at keeping records and administering what other matters needed to be handled in the Town Hall.

Gimlore sat across the desk, which she had paid for, and looked around, stopping only when the muscles in her back spasmed. "Tell me: how much richer am I this month?"

Pie sighed. "It's not that simple, Madam."

"Please, don't be afraid to talk down to me," Gimlore said with a smirk.

However complicated things were, she *was* richer. The false god had probably drowned somewhere, and the people had rallied behind her to rebuild the town back. Everyone worked twice as hard to make their dreams a reality.

"Well, the ships have been our main source of income. We've spent a considerable amount of gold in the construction of the harbour, but we've been able to sell the mossback serum to the kingdoms of Mosendel, Ainis, and Vaerghulen. We've invested significant sums of the gold from those deals in building our defences. The eastern walls are still under construction, but the stonemasons should have them ready in the next few months."

"What about the watchtowers? I said I wanted those."

"Patience, Madam. Everything we're building here takes longer, and our gold reserves are being drained as soon as they are replenished. I'm not a miracle-maker."

Gimlore rubbed her chin. "So, we still need *more* gold?"

Pie shrugged. "It's a perpetual cycle. You *always* need more money. It's just the nature of the business. But we're doing very well, Madam. My laboratory is replicating the elixir at a very decent rate, and emissaries from mainland kingdoms keep begging us for it. We can use that to haggle with our existing clients and raise prices every once in a while."

"Don't haggle too much or they might think invading is a better idea," she said. "We can't afford another siege, even with walls and watchtowers."

Pie got up from his chair and paced around the room. "That's not a concern at the moment. The word has spread that we defeated the Two Nations, and the other kingdoms are all drooling at the prospect of taking over. And they know we have the elixir, so we can very well use it ourselves. No, that's not what I'm concerned about."

"What *are* you concerned about?" Gimlore frowned. She wasn't used to seeing Pie in a thoughtful mood. He was usually quick to give her accounts of the progress in the city and, more importantly, of her finances.

"It's about that other topic, Madam. Related to the elixir. You asked me to... procure scholars and wisemen such as myself... from other kingdoms."

Gimlore smiled as she thought about it, but it faded as she wondered what the problem could be. "I asked you to bribe them, yes. To help you study the elixir and produce more of it in fewer hours. It's called maximising production. I remember. What's wrong?"

Pie swallowed. "Well, as you can imagine, even with the bribes, it wasn't easy to convince many of them, but it was even harder to bring them all over here. It was a painful journey, no matter where in the world they were from. Some of them... didn't quite make it all the way."

Gimlore sighed. "Well, that was to be expected, but it doesn't seem like reason enough for you to be apprehensive. What else is happening?"

"Oh, it's just that the ones we managed to bring over here haven't been very... cooperative. They want more gold than was promised."

Gimlore frowned but remained silent, looking for any rogue sounds she had missed. It was muffled, but there it was. A scream coming from somewhere under the building. A trap door, perhaps? That was new. "Who's extracting information from them?"

"Foloi is, Madam."

Gimlore brought her hands to her head and grimaced. "Well, that explains why they've been so uncooperative. Foloi is a brawler. He's no questioner."

Pie stood firm, feet planted on the floor and chin held high. "I won't let you talk down on him, Madam. I know you and him used to be together, but he's with me now, and I won't let you challenge his work ethic."

"Oh, keep him forever, please. I really don't care. I'm just saying he's not the right man for the job, common past or not. Let me have a crack at it. Where's this trap door?"

Pie shook his head and shrugged. He knew damn well he could say whatever he wanted, but her word was still law in Heleronde, especially after she had defeated the bastards from the Two Nations. Well, Keryon and Rednow had done most of the work. It had been a collaborative effort, but she was the face of it, and that was all that mattered. She needed to be the face of hope for these people, even if she had more than a few crooked bones in her body.

"Help me move the desk," Pie said.

They both moved the desk by two paces to the left, and Pie picked up the large Ainisian rug, revealing the trap door to the newly created basement. With her back aching, Gimlore squatted slowly and picked up the hook to open the trap door.

"Back problems? I have some herbs for that, Madam."

"Oh, fuck off."

Was that who she was? After decades of pain and trauma, she was now being offered medicine for pain, like a decrepit old woman. As much as it pained her to admit it, though, accepting it was not completely off the table.

Gimlore made her way down the makeshift ladder that led to a small cave dug under the building, and Pie followed her immediately. "Why did you build this cellar, anyway?"

"I wish I could say we dug this to hide smuggled goods or to stash imports away from your watchful eyes, but it was just for this, actually. I thought we needed to incentivise them to talk, without having people hear it."

"Well, you should have said so earlier. I would have come to help you."

"Oh, I know how busy you are."

Gimlore looked back at him as the muffled screams grew louder. "You didn't want Foloi to see me, did you?"

Pie scoffed a little louder than necessary. "Nonsense. I don't know why you would think that."

Maybe it's because I knew Foloi for far longer than you did.

She opened another door to a damp, dark room where three blood-soaked men knelt in line. Foloi stood with his neck bent, the room's ceiling too short for him. His beautiful mace-like fists were swollen, almost as much as the faces of the men in front of him.

Foloi frowned, eyeing Pie with a fury. "What in the underworld is she doing here?"

"It's so nice to see you too, Foloi. Where's the warm welcome for an old friend?"

Foloi scowled, looking away from the kneeling men, brushing past her and Pie. "Friend? We used to fuck, that's all. Isn't that what you always made sure to tell me?"

Gimlore swallowed, no response at the tip of her tongue. She had said that on numerous occasions.

Foloi climbed the ladder to the town hall, leaving them there with the men grunting in pain. He had done the questioning all wrong. Yes, violence always worked, but there had to be a way out for them. A viable alternative. They had to see her now as the beacon of light in their miserable lives.

As she was considering what to say to the scholars, she noticed the mud was especially thick in the floor of the dug-out cavern. Some of the cavern walls were even moist, riddled with tiny, flowing water streams.

She brushed that aside to the back of her mind and remembered everything Madam Mazi had told her all those years ago about persuading people to do as you please.

"I'm terribly sorry for what has transpired, gentlemen. Oh, so terribly sorry. My friend has hurt you badly, has he?"

TWO
SMOKE CLOUDS

REDNOW

Heavy rain battered Rednow. Its constant sound was loud enough to muffle the voice of his dead sister, a conduit still employed by the Essence to communicate with him. These downpours were common in Alarkan, and sometimes almost a relief to wash away the dreadful layers of sweat that built up over his skin.

He remained still, focused on himself, hearing only the rain. Then he opened his left eye, and sighed.

"You're not meditating, are you?" he asked the kids.

One of them—Rednow never knew which one was which—shook their head.

"And why is that?"

"We want to fight, Uncle. You said we could be smokesmiths. So, teach us!"

Relentless, they were the most athletically gifted children Rednow had ever trained. The training allowed them to set a goal, to release their energy, and to channel all their frustrations into something useful. But they hated meditation.

"Very well," Rednow said. "But if you're going to fight, I'm going to be quizzing you on the core principles of smokesmith training, so I hope your memory is fresh."

One of the children nodded—maybe Tinko—and the other mimicked the first as they both promptly adopted fighting stances. Rednow took a while before he allowed them to start. They looked like their mother, with high cheekbones, dark features, and wavy dark hair. Each of them carried the bamboo sword Rednow had made for them. The cane was green enough to last a while, but these two were already so strong he would soon need to make more.

"Start."

The children lunged at each other like veteran warriors. Their swordsmanship could still be much improved, of course, but their agility, their focus, and their tenacity were things Rednow didn't even need to teach. They had been fighting pretty much in the womb, Gimlore had told him.

"What's the first principle of being a smokesmith?"

"Smokesmiths..." one of them said mid-hit, "must be trained in hand-to-hand combat first and... foremost."

"They need to learn timing," the other offered. "Proper technique, and quick finishers."

Not bad. They listened. "And how important is herbalism?"

"Argh!" The bamboo swords collided, and the children grunted as they attempted to speak. "Smokesmiths must study it. They must know the difference..." one said, dodging another blow. "Between the herbs they burn."

"Good. And what are the most commonly used herbs?"

"We've gone over this a thousand times, Uncle!"

Rednow smiled. "And you will go ten thousand times more if I feel like it. You agreed to my terms, so answer the question."

"Tinko can answer," Thata said.

Thata frowned as they parried a blow from their sibling. Both their breaths were running wild now, but to fight maintaining that speed while wasting breaths with words was truly spectacular, especially for children this age. What a shame their healthy lungs would soon be filled with nothing but putrid smoke. That gave Rednow pause.

"Answer!" he insisted.

"Nebelshu Quicksilver is the most common. Stained Delve. Bone Bush."

"You forgot one," Rednow cautioned, eyebrows raised.

"Belleaf," Thata said, a smirk building on their face as their sibling grimaced.

"Aha! There it is." When those two put their mind to something, they just didn't give up. *Let's see if they remember beyond the basics.*

"What's the third principle, then?"

"That's easy, Uncle," Tinko said. "Almost as easy as defeating Thata!"

"No need for arrogance," Rednow retorted. "What is it?"

"Knowing the science must mean knowing its consequences."

"That's good, that's good. It's probably the most important rule. Inhaling the smoke increases blood flow, heart rate, and body temperature. That's why you two need to be in peak shape if I'm going to test the smoke on you. What happens if you succeed with smoke in your lungs, then?"

"Our lungs expand," Thata said, their sword grazing their sibling's hair just by the forehead.

"We become faster," said Tinko, pushing Thata back with a front kick. "We heal faster too. Our muscles and our bones get stronger."

Rednow nodded. "And what happens if you *don't* succeed?"

They both stopped fighting and looked at Rednow, uncertainty painted all over their sweaty faces. Rednow took them both in, arm around their shoulders, and ushered them over to the little hut. He looked them in the eyes. "If you don't succeed, you die."

"But we won't die, Uncle. You promised Mother you'd keep us safe. And we trust you."

"Besides, no one breaks promises to Mother."

Rednow broke into laughter, the seriousness of his lesson vanished. He laughed long and hard like he hadn't in a long time. He'd never thought he would have reasons to laugh again, but these two were exactly what he needed. They kept him busy, meaning the Essence was less likely to bother him.

"Sit. Let's finish the lesson."

The children abided. Each of them grabbed a towel to wipe the rainwater and sat in front of him, legs crossed and eyes wide. Rednow saw so much of himself in them. That eagerness to learn. To grow. To show others what he could do. If only people could hold on to this innocence and grow old with it, without being tainted by life.

He cleared his throat and pushed those thoughts out of his mind. "Beginners like yourselves have little control over the smoke, but even less on how the smoke changes *you*. Besides the basics, your bodies can change."

"What about you, Uncle? You have mastered the breathing techniques to hold the smoke in."

He nodded. "Of course. I had to. And so will you. But even more important is knowing how much smoke to take in at a given time. That brings us to the end of this lesson. Now, I had something special planned for you two."

The children glanced at each other in surprise. "A present?"

Poor kids had been working for him for months. Their hands had calloused from the hoes, the swords, and the axes. They had learned every other task he'd demanded without ever complaining, because they believed it was part of the training. So, it was time to reward them with the *real* training.

Rednow produced two small satchels from his side pouch and threw one at each of them. The kids picked them up, still confused about what was happening.

"I'm a one-armed old man with too many mossbacks to feed, and too little time left to teach you what I need. Let's get to it, shall we?"

Their eyes glistened with excitement, and they could no longer sit as their gaze switched between the satchels and him, as though they were hoping he would confirm what they already knew.

"Yes, yes. Those are *your* herbs. It's going to be a gradual process. Let's start by seeing if you have any tolerance at all. Remember everything I've taught you so far, is that clear?"

"Yes, Uncle!"

It was the middle of the night and the smoke of the Quicksilver still danced in the air in tiny threads until it faded into the night sky. The children had coughed more than Rednow thought they would the first time, but much less so than he would have anticipated the second time. If they were to become smokesmiths, they'd do so *his* way. Not through the barbaric smoke chambers the monarch bastards employed to weed out orphan children and urchins of the sweat provinces.

"Take it easy. We have time," Rednow said. "You're both doing well."

The kids nodded, as though they were now undisturbed by the small breaths of smoke they inhaled from the burning herbs. "I think I feel something now," Tinko said.

"More awake?"

The child nodded. "Yes. Is that a good thing?"

"It can't be bad. You are both building up tolerance. I'm not going to have you die on me."

"How long is it going to take?" Thata asked.

Rednow frowned. "As long as required. Now, take another whiff. Very small one, though."

The kids did as he asked, and Rednow thought it was going rather well. He had been younger than this when they'd turned him into a smokesmith. At the time, his body was asked to choose between perishing or holding firm in a breath or two. This way, slower and more steadily, their chances of surviving were much higher.

"While you wait out the smoke, I might as well tell you more about the herbs, yes?"

"We already know everything, Uncle."

Rednow frowned. "What?"

"This is the third time you're telling us all of this. We are prepared, Uncle. We'll stay strong and control our breaths. We know Twisted Twins makes the smokesmith invisible. We know Ominous Kas gives monstrous strength, Stained Delve stretches the limbs, and Bone Bush creates a snake-like constrictor of smoke."

Rednow scoffed. "I'm only repeating myself to make sure you really get it in those hard heads. But here's something I haven't told you yet."

"What is it?" Tinko asked as they inhaled some more of the belleaf-drenched Quicksilver. "I bet you've told us, already."

"Some smokesmiths develop their own personal ability no matter what herb they burn. That's the case of your mother's friend, Keryon. He is able to set the smoke on fire and control its movements. He decides when the smoke is ignited and how much of it burns. It's a rather terrifying ability. I couldn't do it if I tried."

The children went quiet, taking that in. "Are we going to get special abilities too?" Tinko asked.

"That remains to be seen. You must learn how to control the smoke first, don't you think?" Rednow chuckled.

The child's eyes narrowed, concentrating on the smoke above their head. For just a second, the smoke wavered, before adopting its normal flow. Tinko let out some of the smoke they were holding in. "I did it! I told the smoke what to do!"

Rednow blinked, unsure if that had just happened or if the children were pranking him. How could this be? Even when he had turned into a smokesmith, it had taken weeks for him to be able to control a thread of smoke like that.

He was about to say something about the child's unparalleled feat when it was paralleled by the sibling, who was now looking at their own smoke thread and making it waver slightly. Dumbfounded, Rednow's mouth hung open. It was near impossible.

He cleared his throat. "That was... very impressive."

The children took that as a sign of approval and, for the next two hours, the sky became a cloud of herbal smoke. Despite Rednow's constant warnings against it, the children started competing. When Tinko was able to make the smoke waver once, Thata managed it twice, a feat that was ultimately equalled by Tinko as well. Into the little hours of the morning, they kept like this, slowly becoming smokesmiths before his very eyes. As the time passed, and Rednow's eyes started to threaten to shut for the night, the Essence's everlasting presence kept him awake.

The Old One is back, Rednow. You must do something!

If he could shut that voice of persistent insanity forever, he would. She had taken his arm in exchange for his life without asking permission. She had also turned his sister into a martyr, and now used her voice and her image as an avatar. Rednow had never touched the red sword after that, and it sat in a chest in the corner of his room. Why should he? He had students to teach now, mossbacks to raise, and crops to grow. That was all he needed.

DO SOMETHING!

He jumped, then took a moment to consider it. What was he even supposed to do?

"Go away," he muttered, too quietly for the children to hear. They were still busy, sitting a few feet from him in the hut's little porch, building up their tolerance to the smoke and learning the craft by practicing over and over, just as he had all those years ago.

"I'm at peace. What more could you want to take from me? Just leave me alone," he whispered to himself.

⸻

"Watch your back!" Rednow shouted.

Tinko listened and jumped into the smoky air. The white fumes followed the child like a hound, tracking their every step. Their every move. But Thata was on their toes and emerged from below with a long cut of the wood sword that Tinko timed and parried with ease.

"That's why some smokesmiths prefer daggers or knives instead of swords," Rednow said. "Swords have a longer range, but they're much heavier. It fits my fighting style, but it might not fit yours. Perhaps a sword isn't right for you, Thata. You're still a little too slow."

Thata gritted their teeth and lunged forward, the bamboo sword now swinging faster and faster, impossibly so. Thata pressured Tinko, forcing them to step back and allowing little time for a reaction. An unexpected cloud of smoke gathered above Thata. Tinko faltered and tripped, scared of the sight, falling on their back with Thata's sword at their throat.

"What was that?" the fallen child bellowed, defeat burning in their eyes. "Thata cheated!"

Rednow found himself wordless once more. That smoke cloud formation was something he had never seen. Something he had never expected. It could only mean one thing.

"That cloud of smoke... was a special ability," Rednow said, wrapping his head around the thought. "Thata has an ability by the looks of it. We don't know what it is and what it does yet, but we still have plenty of time to find that out."

"No, Uncle! I want to know what it is now!"

The disappointment in Thata's eyes almost made Rednow go back on his word, but that was something he couldn't do. The children were learning too much and too quickly. Could he really trust children this young to bear the responsibility of a power this great? When he had agreed to train them, he imagined the training would take months, maybe years. Never only a few weeks.

He shook his head. "We've got to take it easy. You know that."

Thata's eyes dropped to the muddy earth, and the child nodded. Tinko had jealousy written across their face, and Rednow tried to imagine what was going on inside that young mind. They were used to sharing everything to a point where their identities almost blended, as though each of them was only half a person and they needed each other to be complete. Unless twins went their separate ways, there was always a co-dependency. When one proved to be more successful than the other, that was sure to drive jealousy and fiercer competition from the other.

He wrapped Tinko's neck in an armlock and used his knuckles to scratch the child's head. "What about you? Come on, what's with that face? You never know, we might discover you have an ability of your own too."

Tinko wrestled their way out of Rednow's playful grapple and a hint of a smirk appeared on their lips. "One that's better than Thata's, Uncle. You'll see."

Rednow sighed. "You know I get all fired up when you two are competing, but there are limits to things. You've done more than enough already for such tiny humans."

"What else are we supposed to do around here?" Tinko asked.

Thata nodded. "Yes, Uncle. Mother used to let us play with the throwing knives and greasy bombs, but you say that's not for us."

"You have the smoke now. Thankfully for the two of you, there are still plenty of herbs left. So, practice. Become accustomed to your smoke and your herbs, and develop your fighting style. Remember to hold your breath, but never be too greedy with the smoke you want to inhale, or you'll end up like me and my tattered lungs."

The kids waved Rednow off like they had already heard that at least one million times. He chuckled. *Like I was any better than them at that age.*

THREE
SECOND CHANCES

KERYON

Keryon walked through Heleronde, his Warden badge reflecting the rare glimmer of sunlight. His boots squashed the mud, and he sighed as it splattered back onto them. You just couldn't keep anything clean in this town. All that time spent polishing the boots only for them to be completely ruined by the mud the moment he stepped outside.

If he said that out loud, Gimlore would surely tell him he was being ungrateful, and that the whole point of having boots is to walk through mud with them.

He shook his head. She just didn't get it.

The industrious bluster of the town surrounded him. The shacks were doubling both in number and height. The sheer amount of refugees they were taking in was initially a concern to him, but none had caused any trouble yet, in contrast to the old residents. Those were a different story entirely. He was just happy he didn't have to breathe in any smoke to get the town's problems solved.

Not yet, at least.

This meeting could prove tricky, so he kept his satchel well supplied and the bottle of belleaf oil with the cork cap half-twisted for faster use, just in case. It wasn't every day that he met his own kind, but because they were like him, he had to be extra careful. Gimlore had worked so hard to protect Heleronde, and Keryon himself had bled for the woman and the town as well. He had vowed to protect it, hadn't he? And he was willing to break many things if he had to—arms or legs—but not vows.

The town folks didn't care much that he was the Warden, but he saw their side glances and heard the murmurs of the fishermen pointing at him discreetly.

"How's the wickplate season going?" he asked, to show he was aware of their gossiping.

The fishermen exchanged glances and one was shoved forward to answer for them. The man looked uncertain but didn't stutter. "Uh, it's good, Warden. It's good. They're gutting a few of them right now."

Keryon smiled, eyeing the man and his companions. "It's time we start using those plates for armours now that we are building an army. I'll send someone over to trade."

The fisherman nodded and rushed to get back to his mates while Keryon continued to walk to the main wharf that Pie had ordered built. They needed to accommodate larger ships to haul the elixir and unload anything they needed.

A large vessel was docked to the wharf. It wasn't as big as one of the two marvels of engineering that he'd helped commandeer from the Sirestine fools, but large enough to take dozens of people on a long journey.

He waited there. There was no need to speak to the captain or the deckhands. Still, he kept a hand in his satchel, just in case. Why did it always frighten him to meet others of his kind? Not all of them had his morals, but being a smokesmith shouldn't need to be a scary endeavour. There were plenty of good-hearted smokesmiths, weren't there? He just hadn't had the chance to meet that many, was all.

He heard the commotion first and a group of men and women—probably around ten or twelve in total—were now walking the gangplank towards him. Keryon was never the best at first impressions. Gimlore had found him insufferable at first and he suspected she still thought that now. But if he posed too friendly, they'd think him a fool and question his authority as the Warden. Balance was key.

"Good morning to our newest guests. Welcome to Heleronde. I was made aware of your intention to come over a week ago."

The smokesmiths looked at each other, confused. Was it his accent?

"We thought Gimlore was a woman," the one in front of the group spoke. He had long hair and a beard, and looked more like how people thought mythical wizards or druids should look like. He was all skin and bones, but with a menacing presence to back them up. "I'm Ferkin."

Keryon grimaced. "I'm not Gimlore," he said. "Gimlore is my... she's the founding mother of this settlement town, if you will."

"And what a town this is," a woman said from the back of the group. She looked bigger and stronger than Keryon. "Watchtowers being built, a stone wall in the works too. Not bad at all."

Keryon let that comment hang in the air for a little longer than he would have liked. How to explain the source of their wealth? They had surely heard about the mossback elixir, so he had to be very careful about what he said, especially after promising Gimlore he would weed out those coming over for the wrong reasons.

"Well, what can I say? People work hard. There is much to be done, but also plenty of opportunity, which is why you are all here, I reckon."

Ferkin stepped forward and swung his long hair to his back. "We just want to be our own masters. No more serving."

"Like me, then."

"You're a smokesmith?" the large woman asked, a deep frown in her face.

"Oh, come on. Don't tell me you didn't notice the satchel," Keryon said. "You probably saw it all the way from inside the ship, madam."

"Don't you *madam* me. I'm Chona. Just Chona."

"Good, let's all get acquainted, Ferkin, Chona, and the rest of the gang. All here for a new life and no masters. Let's all take a walk and I'll get you set in the best inn in town, which has just been refurbished. It's called the Maiden's Hall. The safest place I can think of."

Keryon wiped sweat from his forehead as he drank wine from the cup. While the rest of the smokesmiths were resting in the rooms Nork and Nosema had prepared upstairs, he sat at a table with Ferkin and Chona while a group of farmers played cards exceptionally loudly at the table next to them.

"This isn't what I would call a cosy home, but it'll do for now," Ferkin said.

There was something about the man that Keryon didn't like. The way he spoke as a matter of fact, as though his wishes were commands, or as if he knew something others didn't. Keryon would have to probe some more. For the sake of the town and even *his* own sake. If these smokesmiths decided to attack, it was him and Rednow against this whole group of veterans, and the old man barely ever showed his face in town these days, so it would be all on him. For better or worse.

"I'm aware of the challenges that smokesmiths face starting new lives. We dedicate our existence to the masters at such a young age. It's not easy to start over. Many of us never even get that privilege. I'm aware of how hard this transition will be."

Ferkin nodded. "Your awareness is well appreciated, Master Keryon. And we thank your wife for the arrangements she went out of her way to make for us today."

"Oh, she's not my wife, she's..."

"When are we going to meet her?" Chona chimed in. "From the stories I've heard, it seems like we could be great friends, her and I. I heard she went on with that Sirestine fucker face to face. Told him to go fuck himself and sent him into the underworld, did she?"

Keryon sighed. Everyone always forgot *he* was the one who defeated Solvi and nearly brought her over to their side. "Yes, she did that. I trust you and Gimlore will be fast friends. I haven't known you for long, but it seems like your temperaments are... somewhat similar."

Chona smiled and swallowed at least half a cup of wine.

"So, you are here now. Have you thought about what you're going to do?"

Ferkin cleared his throat. "Well, I don't speak for the rest of them. I am going to set up my own herb and flower shop. I heard there are exotic plants here that the lords of the mainland would love to get their hands on. If I can ship it to them safely, they'll pay fortunes."

"Wait a second..." Keryon said. *The sly bastard...* "*I* own an herb shop and it's already a struggle. I'm not sure there's room for yet another one."

Ferkin feigned surprise with an overly exaggerated raise of his eyebrows. "Do you, now, master Keryon? What a coincidence that is. Two smokesmiths. Two herb shops."

Ferkin left the implication hanging in the air. Had Keryon been wrong to ask Gimlore to give these smokesmiths a chance? He needed to show her they could be good people, but it was starting to seem they were more trouble than they were worth.

"Interesting, indeed. There are plenty of job opportunities here, but none better than being part of the Warden Patrol. Working under me, that is."

"How is that different from working for a master?" Chona asked, now chewing on a delicious-looking piece of calf meat still warm enough to produce a thin cloud of steam.

"No resemblance at all. I'm no master. I just happen to be in charge, but you'll find that *being in charge* is a very loose concept in these parts. I hold no absolute power of any kind. I just patrol the city and make sure the people are safe. Now, the Warden Patrol will eventually become an army and I'd be *extremely* interested in requesting your services. You all have battle experience, so why not help the town folks by protecting them, or helping them protect themselves?"

Chona nodded at the suggestion and exchanged looks with Ferkin. "You seem like a kind fellow, Master Keryon," the bearded man said. Keryon still couldn't quite place his accent. Where could he be from? "It's a most honourable proposal."

"I accept," Chona said. "I'll join the Warden Patrol."

"Really?" Keryon was taken aback. It seemed like the woman was just as impulsive as Gimlore. Maybe they could really end up being friends. "Just like that? No questions asked?"

Chona shrugged and chewed the meat some more. "What else should I want to know about? Money? This is my retirement plan, so if you give me a bed in a room with no leaky roof, and keep me fed, there is nothing else I need."

"Very well. I will contact you with more details." Keryon didn't know what else to say to Chona, so he turned to Ferkin, who remained calm. Keryon noticed he hadn't touched the wine at all, something Gimlore always said was *very* suspicious. "I take it you will go on with your original plans, then?"

Ferkin gave him a curt smile and nodded. "I'm afraid so. I have no interest in pursuing anything remotely related to the art of war or combat anymore, to be frank. All I really care about are flowers and plants. Maybe I'll discover a new kind of wine, who knows? The possibilities are endless out here."

"They truly are." Keryon had to bite his tongue not to spit out a healthy dose of snark. "I wish you nothing but riveting success."

By success, he really meant the business dying and the man knocking on his door, begging for the opportunity to be in the Warden Patrol.

He took another sip of his wine and assessed Ferkin. Was the bearded man playing a role here, or was he truly nothing but peaceful these days? Funny how Keryon still expected to find war in the eyes of men built for it, even when they claimed to want only peace. He watched Ferkin's eyes for any signs of deceit, observed his hands and feet for any nervous movement, and looked for sweat covering his skin. The man showed no signs of trickery or ill-intent.

Keryon smiled and let out a breath. Maybe some men really wanted no trouble. It was about time *he* got some peace as well. He chugged the rest of the wine and got up.

"I'll let you rest. I've got some other things to oversee."

"We won't hold you back, Master Keryon," Ferkin said, extending his arm. Keryon grabbed his hand, shook it, and took off with a nod.

He walked out of the Maiden's Hall and onto the street. The old building had smelled like dampness and rats, with doorways too narrow to walk through and barely any natural light, as though it was haunted. The new version of the Maiden's Hall looked much more like a proper tavern, thank the gods, but it was good to be out of that place and get some fresh air.

When he arrived at the Town Hall, he failed to find Pie or Foloi, which was odd, but they weren't who he was there to see, anyway. He pulled out an entire chunk of meat and a loaf of bread from his bag and walked over to the jail area.

The incarceration facility was simple enough, with three damp cells locked by steel bars from floor to ceiling. Two were empty while the third had a measly woman sitting down on the cold floor, hugging her knees. Her blonde hair was long and dishevelled, covering most of her face.

"I brought you some food," Keryon said, his tone as flat as he could make it. "How have you been?"

Solvi looked up at him, only now aware of his presence. She stood and slowly grabbed the bars, eyes fixed on him. Keryon shivered and took an instinctive step back, even if she posed no threat inside the cell with no smoke to inhale. It pained him to see her like that, caged like an animal, but Gimlore had been right to keep her behind bars. She was just too volatile to be trusted out of bounds, and her allegiances were outright worrying, even if Keryon suspected his trips to the town jail had already started to bear some fruit. Perhaps Solvi was starting to realise just how deceived she had been all those years with Orberesis.

Instead of replying, Solvi merely opened her mouth and Keryon swallowed as he lifted the loaf for her to take. She picked it up and chewed. It was always up to him to turn this interaction into a conversation rather than a monologue.

"The town has grown quite a bit over the past few weeks already. I never thought that was possible. Can you hear it from here?" he asked. "People are happy. There is peace. There are more refugees coming. Things are all going well."

Solvi hummed as she continued to chew the bread, though her face revealed nothing.

Let's see what you think about this, then.

"Do you want to know who I welcomed to town today?"

She showed no reaction, but he wasn't discouraged.

"A group of twelve fully trained, battle-tested smokesmiths. Just like me. Just like *you*."

Solvi's jaw ground to a halt for a second and she looked at him as though asking for confirmation.

Keryon smiled and nodded. "That's right. Twelve of them. They're looking for a fresh start. They're retiring here. Some of them will be joining me in the Warden Patrol. They've abandoned their masters."

He let that sink in for her.

Solvi swallowed the bread and nodded. "That's good," she said.

Two words. Better than last time. "Maybe one day you'll join me in the Warden Patrol as well. How does that sound?"

Solvi gazed at the shackles binding her wrists.

"Ah, yes. I'm confident we'll remove those eventually. But it will take time. We just need to play it safe. I'm sure you can understand. I'd be willing to take the risk and have you shadow me for a bit, but..."

"The woman..." Solvi said, her eyes narrowing.

"Madam Gimlore, yes. Don't blame her, though. She's just trying to do what's best for everyone."

Solvi slumped even further, taking the meat and the bread into the cell and reverting to her seated position.

Keryon sighed. How could he help her if she refused to help herself? He could only imagine the divide of worlds taking place in her head. She had held such strong beliefs for such a long time. The world that had emerged from that evening had been fruitful for everybody except her. She had lost the only person she had cared about, so now she had no strength left. No passion. No life.

Perhaps I can probe a little deeper.

"He is probably dead," Keryon said. Solvi's face turned into a snarl as she covered her ears. "It's true and you know it. We've had divers, sailors, and farmers look anywhere he could have gone, and they all found nothing. I am willing to admit something strange might have gone on. People don't just disappear like that, but think about it, he most likely dr—"

"I'm with child," Solvi said. Her face narrowed and she started crying, tears flowing down her cheeks, leaving Keryon paralysed. "His child. I know it's early, but I can feel it."

Keryon swallowed and cleared his throat. He kneeled by the bars next to her, and looked her straight in the eyes. "It doesn't matter if he's dead. We'll take care of you and the child. I will make sure of that."

Solvi's puffy face turned to him and nodded, hugging her legs.

Fuck.

Keryon walked out of the jail at a hurried pace, his mind spinning. Gimlore would hate this. She would find a way to get rid of Solvi just as she had always wanted to. But now she was pregnant, and it wasn't the child's fault both parents were dangerously delusional.

As he trod the muddy ground with quick steps, someone behind him cleared their throat.

Keryon turned to see who it was, his hand touching the satchel, ready to burn herbs.

"She's a lost cause, that one," Tavanar said. The man leaned against the Town Hall building with arms crossed and his long dark hair pulled back. "It's true and you know it, Warden."

"Were you spying on me?"

Tavanar smiled and shook his head. "I was just passing by. But what I said is true, so you're going to have to choose. Where does your loyalty lie, Warden? With your madam and this town, or with your smoke-breathing kind?"

Keryon gritted his teeth. *This joke of a man.* He had no powers of his own and yet here he was, antagonising him. "My loyalties are clear. Yours, however, I am not too sure about."

"Mine? I made it very clear I'm no longer interested in following Doi or this woman around. They're lunatics. I'll find my own path. You'll see."

"In the meantime, here you are, wasting space that could be used for people who actually work. Wasting my time. Find a job, will you?"

Tavanar's eyes shot fury at him, but he left it at that and walked away as he burned inside like a candle.

Keryon sighed. Perhaps wishing for peace had been a tad naïve of him.

Four
To Rise

Orberesis

It was dark everywhere, but the cold and the drip, drip, drip of the water had become almost a part of his being. Orberesis' head ached, and he couldn't tell where he was or how long he'd been there. He tried getting up and realised his muscles hurt and he was soaked. As much as he looked for light, there wasn't any in a place like this. It could only be a catacomb or a cavern of sorts.

Exerting more effort than he probably should, he clung to the rocky wall and pulled himself up to his feet, which made him dizzy. He had to explore and find an exit.

A gurgling sound emerged from his right. He looked, but still couldn't see anything in that unforgiving darkness.

The gurgling returned, bringing a hint of light with it this time. A strange yellow light with a blue tint was coming from under a small pool of water. He had been right. This was a cavern of sorts, but the light was coming towards the water surface at full speed, brightening the closer it got. Orberesis was able to see more details of the rock bed that made the cavern, but it was the little pool in the middle that drew his attention the most.

Quickly and with no warning, the light emerged from the water and onto the surface. It was like the horn of a bull, but lit from the inside.

Orberesis recoiled in fear as he noticed what creature possessed such a horn—a slimy monster, with slithery grey skin and dark buttony eyes. It was bipedal, but with a tail, as though a human and a tadpole had given birth to a gruesome offspring the size of a giant.

The creature looked at Orberesis. The light of the beast's horn made him squint first and then crawl a few steps back until the cold cavern wall touched his elbows. He couldn't back up any further.

The beast eyed him, and then another light emerged from the pool. And another. There were three of those beasts sharing the cavern with him. They didn't seem to speak to each other, but their lights flickered at different paces, lengths, and intensities.

They're sentient, he realised.

How could this be? He knew about bloodsleuths, shadesgrowls, mossbacks, and hearthspears but he had never even heard about a creature like this, so it must mean he was in a dream. He was already too used to those, every one worse than the last. These creatures didn't approach him. They barely took notice of him, continuing to flicker their horn lights in ways that made him dizzy.

Don't worry, they won't harm you.

Orberesis flinched and recoiled again at the booming voice inside his head. "What are…" And then he remembered the Old One. The parasitic deity that had clung on to him for good and ill. Mostly ill. He had promised to make Orberesis a real god, but this seemed all too far from divinity.

They're my friends, Doi. They're harmless. To you, at least.

"What are they? And where the fuck am I?"

Is that how you treat those who took care of you and brought you to safety? How ungrateful. You will stay in a safe place as we plan our next move. And just as I said, they are my friends who have been in hiding, for far too long.

Orberesis hated how the Old One always spoke in riddles, leaving him with more questions than answers. He wished he could abandon the deity, but it was too late, especially as it lived inside him now that the orb had been destroyed.

"Explain," Orberesis said with gritted teeth. "I'm sick of your games."

We are under Alarkan, boy. The continent we brought from the depths of the ocean, remember? Under that town the ants call Heleronde. There is a complex cave system where my friends, the Lantern Horns, have lived in hiding. They've got enough water, and they can hunt the mossbacks for food. It's too humble a life, but they're used to the suffering.

"Lantern Horns…" Orberesis took another glance at the creatures. They looked far less frightening now than they had at first. "They saved me?"

My rescue message reached them in time.

"I've never seen anyone like them. They can't be real."

Ah, and what is real, Doi? You're right, though. They are from... another realm. I was able to save some from their perilous existence many years ago, and I've been hiding them here for generations, so they're loyal to me. They're thankful. But they long for their families and their clans, who are still on the verge of death. We must save them—you and me.

Orberesis frowned. He still didn't understand why the Old One cared about these creatures, or why *he* of all people should care.

I sense your doubt.

"I *am* doubtful. Where are the things you promised?" Orberesis probed. "I'm seeing none of it!"

The Old One roared, and a tingling pricked the back of Orberesis' head, as though it was coming from the inside.

The booming voice took a more sinister tone. *I need you, Doi. But you don't command me. It's best you don't forget that.*

Orberesis contorted, his body moving in broken motions, out of its own control, according to the Old One's will. Arms flailed, and his legs twisted from side to side. It was as though he was outside his own body, leaving him terrified.

If you want to see it so bad, I will show you.

Orberesis' vision blurred. He thought he was about to fall asleep after losing control of his body for a moment, as though all the nerves and muscles had shut themselves off.

There was a light in everything he saw, and it slowly darkened until he was floating in an endless night sky with no ground under his feet, no land anywhere in sight; only empty, dark space sprinkled with stars, controlled by the Old One. It made him nauseous, as though his brain had been laundered with the uncaring touch of a washwoman. He hardly had time to appreciate the beautiful light.

Then he started dropping into a tiny dot that grew at every second. Not a dot, but a world. A small one. No, it was massive. Then Orberesis stopped.

Do you see it? This other world?

Orberesis tried to focus. He could barely see anything with his eyes hazy or think about what he saw. He certainly couldn't muster a response. That was how the Old One preferred it, no doubt. Orberesis found himself conflicted by the sheer panic he felt, and the marvel of seeing a world as closely as only gods could.

It was a round like a ball of dough, with the seas and the land easy enough to spot. He had even been able to spot the moon. So, this was how worlds looked from the outside. Knowing there were *other* planes of existence out there made him tense up as he considered the implications.

I found this world many millennia ago, just after I discovered Temporal Exploration. A new world, and with creatures in it! But something is strange about it. It's locked.

"L-locked?" he somehow was able to muster.

Yes, locked to the star. There's one side in perpetual light and another in darkness. Do you know what this means?

The fog in his brain was so thick he wanted to cry. He wished he still had his father, or Solvi and Tavanar. His father was dead, though, and Tavanar had tried to kill him. Now he was alone, trapped between dreams, illusions, and realities he couldn't understand.

One side is a scorching hot desert that burns forever and the other is nothing but cold darkness where nothing grows in the absence of light. There is a balance between the burning heat and the freezing night, but it's thin and shrinking. There are too many Lantern Horns and not enough space for them. So, we will have to make room for them here.

"I don't care!" Orberesis said, crying. He truly didn't. All of this hurt more than he could fathom.

Suddenly, he was rushed towards the planet, thrown at it like a pebble. The Old One again. Diving towards this new world, he fell straight into that space between the darkness and the light. He drew closer until he could see them in the distance: Lantern Horns, some grown, some tiny. Entire civilisations of them. But then the planet shook, the earth cracked open, and flaming lava poured from underneath their webbed feet, catching dozens of them. The bowels of the planet spat out combinations of hard and molten rock. The oceans tumbled, and giant waves formed, swallowing the coast and everything in their wake.

Do you see it now, Doi?

"S-see what?"

DO YOU SEE HOW THEY SUFFER? HOW CAN I LET THEM SUFFER?

Orberesis' head pounded like a thousand hammers, but he could see the Old One's point. An entire civilisation of these Lantern Horns being wiped out of existence in a world distant from his own. They were at war with their own land, and he was the only one who could help. "You mean to have them live with us?"

Why not? There is plenty of space, isn't there?

Orberesis thought about it. All the unused land. All the miles and miles of stretching forests and lakes that belonged to kings and queens who didn't even know what to do with it. Sprawling mountains everywhere, endless oceans. There was definitely space.

"If I help you to do this, will you stop hurting my mind? Will you keep your promise?"

The Old One laughed. *I always do, Doi. You just might not know it. Consider it done. Now, help me! It's time for us to rise. Time for them to be made free!*

"How do I do that?" Orberesis asked. "I need your guidance."

Of course. I wished it was easy, but it isn't. I have the same enemies as I always did, and they're no less active than they used to be. We must handle them first before we can bring about the change that is necessary.

"Who are these enemies?"

You've met a few, if I recall. And they'll be on your toes once again, like the pests that they are.

Orberesis, too, had enemies. He thought about the woman. Gimlore, was that her name? And her little bunch of swamp rats. Just thinking about them made his temper flare. He needed to show them he was a god after all, that he was ancient power personified, not just a charlatan!

"Fine. What do I need to do?"

The Old One laughed.

RISE UP! RISE UP LIKE YOU DID TEN YEARS AGO. RISE UP AND FREE THEM!

Somehow, Orberesis' temper was ablaze. He was thirsty for revenge, hate flowing in his veins. He gritted his teeth, tired of the Old One and being kicked around like a rock in the dirt. He closed his fists, tensed up, and rage he didn't even know he had stormed inside him. It was festered by the Old One but created by those who had ruined his young life all those years ago.

His father burning. His friend betraying him. All the false devotion. He would show them.

Orberesis roared, and ripples of energy pulsed from within, tearing the very fabric that held the world together. He roared, and the earth cracked open. He roared, and the skies roared back. Mountains rose in the form of lava, making room for him, no longer afraid to take up space.

He was back in Heleronde now, floating in the air like the divine being he was. Everyone would see it too. The world under him crumbled and shook.

This time, his memory didn't fail him. He remembered everything.

He waved his right arm and the water caves of Heleronde burst open, water and rock flung upon the air. He waved it again, and all the debris was thrown into the town, landing on roofs and roads alike. He waved his left hand, and the trees were pulled out from the earth. His ire continued, now stronger than ever.

This was true power. True divinity.

He rose again, settling well above the peasants' heads, and opened his arms as the earth shifted, swallowing the land as they all knew it. Another flail of his right arm and the earth was made bare, roaring even louder than he did. Fissures cracked the ground open and shifted the continent's geography entirely.

That was good, Doi. That was very good.

Maybe he didn't always like the Old One, but this surge of power was irresistible. He needed more.

On the surface, the townspeople struggled with the elements thrown at them, running like the cockroaches they were whilst everything they had built was on fire.

The Old One laughed again in a way that Orberesis had already learned to tolerate. It seemed like the deity was making a mockery of him, but his power was undeniable.

This is really good, Doi. You used my power well, he said. *Now, the Lantern Horns can come out to play.*

FIVE

GUILT

REDNOW - GIMLORE - SOLVI

*H*E'S HERE, REDNOW! THE OLD ONE!

The Essence's voice in his mind was all Rednow could think about. It affected every thought he'd had, like a constant inebriation he just couldn't shake off. But what was he supposed to do when the land rippled under his feet? When rivers of lava crossed his farmlands and roasted his mossbacks alive?

The children!

"Pick up your satchels! Quickly!"

The kids didn't need to be told twice. They picked up their smokesmith satchels and weapons of choice: a short sword for Thata and a pair of daggers for Tinko. Rednow entered his little hut, careful not to let the earth swallow him, and looked for two things he just couldn't part with. The first he found easily. The bag with the scriptures Rebma had written was stored carefully under his bed. The other was harder to find. He hesitated before he sought it out.

Shit.

He didn't want this, but he had to do it. He lifted his mattress and grabbed his old red sword by the scabbard, struggling to fasten the belt around his waist with just one hand.

"Help me," he told Tinko. The child did it promptly, and he nodded in appreciation. "Let's get to safety!"

Rednow and the children started running but a big grey beast emerged from the little creek that Rednow used to water his crops. Standing in their way, the monster devoured a mossback, tearing chunks of the poor animal with sharp teeth.

"Hide!" he whispered, waving at the kids to take cover in the tall grass.

But it was too late. The creature saw him and started running towards him. The beast was too fast for them to outrun, and too strong to defeat with raw power. Rednow unsheathed his sword, and the red tint glistened in the sunlight.

Where are you now that I need your help?

Of course, the Essence didn't reply.

Next to him, Tinko and Thata adopted fighting stances and Rednow cursed himself. He didn't want any of this. These children were too damn young. "No, no! You two run away and call for help. I will stay back to hold off the beast."

The children didn't listen. Tinko and Thata charged towards the creature just as it charged at them.

"Wait!" he tried to shout, to no avail. Then he caught a whiff of smoke and noticed thin threads following the kids. When they reached the creature, Tinko and Thata went their separate ways with a two-step move. The beast hesitated, unsure of who to chase, then ultimately chose Thata.

Tinko turned back, faster with smoke in their lungs, and reached the creature, stabbing it repeatedly in the back.

The monster howled as it fell to the ground, dead. Its horn continued to emit flickering lights before going dark.

"That wasn't so bad, Uncle." Tinko stood victorious, with a foot resting on the beast's head. "But what is happening?"

Rednow could barely muster a reply, recognising in himself a panic he hadn't felt since he'd seen his parents slaughtered in front of him. He had allowed himself to feel too safe. Too peaceful. He should have known ignoring the Essence wouldn't solve anybody's problems. And now, he had been rescued by children young enough to be his grandchildren.

Rednow knelt as the land continued to shake. "Listen, kids. This is serious. We need to survive this, you understand? No more heroics!"

Thata frowned. "But Tinko killed one and I didn't get to!"

Rednow almost backhanded the child but caught himself. "This isn't a game. We need to find our way to safety. To town. Let's go."

There they went, the three of them, carrying nothing but their clothes, their satchels, and their weapons. As they made it past the initial marsh, another three of the horned creatures appeared, setting their dark, beady eyes on them, and immediately changing course to fight them. There wasn't even time to run.

Rednow burned some of his Ominous Kas and unsheathed the red blade again.

If I die, at least I'll die protecting them.

If I die, will you take my other arm?

Still no answer from the Essence.

He breathed in a whiff of the white fumes and his lungs burned. The buzz from the smoke grew to his head, bringing relief and confidence. Rednow knew who he was when he held in the smoke. He was the Blood Collector, and soon enough, these beasts would know it too.

"We need to make our way to the town, so fight if you need to, but don't stay behind!" he bellowed.

The children nodded and ran alongside him like seasoned warriors. Rage burned even stronger than the smoke inside him, and Rednow gritted his teeth. He enhanced his arm and legs, stabbing the grey creatures who weren't so large compared to this monstrous form of his. The children used agility to their advantage, often cutting through and using each other as bait for the other's final blow. By the time the beasts hit the floor, dead, both children were already a dozen strides away.

But there were more and more of them, and even with no weapons other than claws and teeth, they were strong and fast for their enormous size. Rednow observed some of them using their tails to jump farther as well.

Rednow and the kids ran through the woods, always watching where they set their feet. But that was a journey often made on the back of hearthspears, not on foot. Rednow cursed himself for having chosen to live so far from everybody else, and with no mounts to ride on top of that. The children's lungs wouldn't be able to hold for that long. Meanwhile, the beasts kept on coming, their horns flickering. Were they... communicating with flashes of light?

This was a bloody sentient race!

Rednow jumped at the throat of one. With a single motion, he cut the horn clean off and the light faded, gooey yellow liquid oozing out of the stump.

"Argh!" Tinko held their leg. Their feet had been caught in a vine and now the ankle was busted. "I can't walk, Uncle!"

The despair in the child's face propelled Rednow to action. He would die for these children if destiny required it. "Here, jump on my back and hold tight. Can you do that?"

Tinko nodded. In that smokesmith form, the child's weight was no issue at all, but Rednow was more concerned about the child's grip in case he had to fight. About a dozen horned creatures stood in front of them now, and when Rednow tried to change course and turn to the left, he realised there were more. Same to his right and where he had come from.

It's like we're being chased by experienced hunters.

Rednow let Tinko sit on the muddy ground. "Do not move. I'll get us out of here."

"You can count on me, Uncle," Thata said, sword raised and eyes locked on the enemy. Rednow would be oozing pride if the situation wasn't so dire. How did it come to this? These beasts had come from nowhere, and if their numbers were any indication, they'd destroy the entire town. Rednow wished he didn't have to count on Thata, but the truth was he needed any help he could get.

The horned monsters charged at them.

Rednow drew in the smoke and willed for a full transformation that would surely be his end. Brutal, long limbs with claws tore up his clothes. Spiked, hardened skin and bones made him stronger than any of the beasts while his long legs gave him a considerable height advantage.

He charged them, doing his best to keep an eye on Thata, who also fought, using the smoke in their lungs. Rednow's arm flail knocked three of them down to the ground, but he needed kills, not knockouts. He needed them to stay down forever, so he dug at them with his talons, ripping yellow flesh. He felt a weight on this back: a sharp pain, incisions into his hard skin. The bastards were clawing him, biting him.

Rednow shook them off. One, two, three of them held on to his arm, shoulders, and legs, so Rednow cut them down with his talons.

"Uncle!" Tinko shouted. Rednow glanced at the child and saw the panic in their eyes as their sibling Thata lay flat on the muddy ground, a beast about to take their life. Tinko's panicked face became branded in Rednow's mind.

No. No.

If he were just half a second too late, Thata would die, so Rednow ran to save the child from certain peril. Curse that monster!

He burned his lungs for more speed. More strength. It didn't matter, he just had to save Thata!

Praying to the gods his worst fear didn't come true, Rednow charged into the monster, nearly tearing it in half with his claws. Pain shot through him amidst the chaos of battle, taking him a second to gather himself again.

Did I save the child?

Glancing back, he saw the one thing he didn't want to see: a droplet of blood dripping out of Thata's mouth as the child held their hands close to their chest, inanimate, with eyes blank. Rednow snapped the neck of the other creatures, but that was too little, too late.

Tinko howled in pain, a primal scream of a very specific kind of loss with which Rednow was too familiar.

Thata's wound was too deep and large, especially for a child that size. Tinko slowly shook their sibling but to no avail. Thata's eyes had an empty gaze now, and the body moved like a dead weight in response.

Rednow wanted to cry.

He was powerless. He was useless.

Rage and frustration bubbled up inside him. In that moment, nothing short of destroying the world could fill the hole in his chest. The beasts kept on coming towards them, so he couldn't even stop for a while and see to Thata's last few breaths. He couldn't even grieve, lest he lose the other child as well.

"No!" Tinko bellowed for their sibling, the raw pain of losing half of themselves coursing through them.

Kneeling by their sibling's corpse, the child bobbed, slowly shaking Thata's lifeless young body to try and revive them, no longer caring about the carnage taking place around them, no longer caring for their own life. Tinko's eyes were wet, eyebrows curved widely in shock, mouth gaped in terror. They had not only been twins, but almost like halves of each other.

Rednow cursed himself. Another broken promise. Another person he cared about dead on his watch. He was cursed and useless. A child!

"Are you happy now?" he asked the sky, but the Essence still didn't respond. "Are you fucking happy?!"

"Uncle?" Tinko asked, their eyes wet, red with a mix of the sweat and their sibling's blood.

The child's innocent face brought Rednow back to himself. Not all hope was lost. He could still save this one.

"Jump on my back! Now!" Rednow commanded, and the crying child swallowed and wiped their tears, determination showing on their face. This kid would go places. As long as Rednow didn't let them die.

"There you go. Now hold tight," he said, though his mind was spinning with rage, and it wasn't only directed at the grey monsters. *I fucked up. I fucked up bad.*

Rednow ran like the monster he was, crashing through the marshlands, charging everything in his trail, be it horned monsters, bushes, or trees. He would get to Heleronde, no matter what.

And he would save Tinko.

. . . .

Gimlore fell to her knees as the land beneath her wavered. The dirt that made up the walls and the ceiling of the cellar crumbled, and bits of land fell around her. She hurried to the exit. *I'm not letting myself be buried alive in here.*

Her thoughts went to the children as well. At a time like this, she was thankful they were with Rednow of all people, but that didn't mean they were safe. She needed to get to them soon. A loud, squashing sound emerged from behind her. She glanced back and saw what looked like a giant fish head emerging from the floor. It was grey, with gills and a slimy skin, dark eyes and a large yellow horn that lit up the entire cellar better than the torches.

What the fuck is this?

She stabbed the head with one of her knives until it was no longer moving. "Something must be happening."

"And we need to get out of here!" Pie said. "The cellar is collapsing."

Both hurried out of the cellar, climbing the wood ladder that led up to the surface and bringing the captives behind them.

As soon as Gimlore had time to look around through the window and see what was happening to her town, she saw Foloi lying flat on the floor.

She raced to him and knelt by his side. "Foloi?" She nudged him, but he didn't respond. Then she saw the vicious wound in his gut, and her heart sank. No, it simply couldn't be true.

"No!" Pie uttered a loud bellow, holding his mouth with one hand, arms trembling in fear.

What the fuck is going on? She checked for Foloi's breathing anyway as Pie cried out, unable to face the lying man. *He's not breathing.*

Foloi was gone.

Gimlore leaned back; powerless, guilty. There had been so many words left unsaid, so much friendship thrown to the mud because of her pride. And now she'd never be able to apologise. She *had* cared for Foloi despite him thinking otherwise, but he only thought that because she made sure to tell him.

You stupid, stupid woman. She had always appreciated how he had played his role in her schemes for years, always showing loyalty. For him to go like that, something must be horribly wrong. She wasn't even sure she had time to mourn. Whoever—or whatever—killed Foloi might still be out there.

"We need to go!" she said. The scholars ignored her and scattered in all directions, but she couldn't give chase.

Grabbing Pie's arm, she rushed from the Town Hall's building slowly, to avoid getting thrown into the floor by the shaking earth. If she stayed inside that building for another minute, the entire place would collapse on them.

The picture outside the window was even worse than she had imagined. She barely even recognised Heleronde. Hills and mountains of rock and lava exploded from underground. Most of the shacks in the town's western quarter had been destroyed, and the sky was painted in shades of red and grey, thunder building up.

She froze, paralysed not by fear but powerlessness. She had tried so hard to build this town and then rebuild it again, and now it was utterly destroyed. All the nasty things she'd had to do, throats she'd had to slit, it had all been for absolutely nothing. She found her hands trembling as she slowly realised that she was no longer in control. She had no idea what was happening, but she needed to find out.

"I'm sorry, Pie, but we need to find somewhere safe," she said without looking at the big man. When she finally did, she saw there was a giant grey monster towering over him.

Before she could react, the beast lifted its thick, long arm and shoved its claws in the back of Pie's neck.

The burly man grunted, gurgled, and spat out blood, his body falling to the ground.

No! Not again!

Instincts kicking in, Gimlore produced a few more throwing knives from her belts and threw them accurately at the beast. The monster was too strong. He tore out one of the knives that had landed in his forearm and threw it back at her, as though it wanted to show her it could do that, too.

Gimlore took a few steps back, hesitating to part with Pie's body.

Shit.

She had never expected this. Her thoughts went to the children. Were they safe outside of town with Rednow? Her heart sank just thinking about it.

She caught a hint of smoke lingering in the air as Keryon stormed in. He ignited the smoke and burned the horned beast behind her like a dragon of the ancient tales. She shielded her face from the smoke and the ashes.

"Are they dead?" He glanced at the two bodies, his face sombre.

Gimlore could only muster a nod. "What is going on?"

"The false god. He's here. And he brought these beasts with him."

Gimlore's rage flared, and she gritted her teeth. "Where is he?"

Keryon pointed upward and into the sky. "There."

When the earth shook the first time, Solvi thought it was just an earthquake, but the second time, she knew it had to be him. Had he felt her presence? Had he come for her?

The ground roared and shattered. She dodged a falling piece of the cage's ceiling that fell on the floor. Minding the seed that the Highest One had placed inside her, she kicked the bars that kept her imprisoned. Without a proper foundation, they collapsed, allowing her to escape and save herself and the Highest One's blessing.

She peeked outside the jail building, chaos on everyone's faces. Hundreds of grotesque monsters were destroying the town and slaughtering the people, who ran for their lives even though there was nowhere to hide. Spilled blood and primal screams made up the terrifying atmosphere.

She looked at the dark sky and saw him.

There he was, the Highest One.

Part of her wanted to shout, call for him, announce her presence and tell him what a gift she had for him. But upon seeing him like that, with eyes set sharply and arms wide open as he floated in mid-air, she realised he didn't look like himself. He barely looked human.

Of course, he doesn't. He's a god. She shook herself. Glancing around the streets, she looked for something to cover herself. Luckily, one of the fallen men had been wearing a dark rain cloak with a hood.

Perfect.

She undressed the dead man, put on the cloak, and pulled up the hood to cover her long hair. Could she get her herbs back? No, that would harm the baby. She needed to survive these dreadful beasts and escape. This continent was nothing but a pathetic attempt at a utopia, no matter what that man, Keryon, had tried to tell her.

But the Highest One had shown himself to be so cruel as well…

Doubt had seeped in and was taking root far deeper than she could admit. Why had the man treated her so well? She had tried to kill him. She had tried to destroy all those he cared about, even if she was protecting her own master. But God Himself had also been good to her. Oh, so good. He had been ink on paper, a rose garden in spring, sweet sugar on her tongue.

Shaking off her thoughts, Solvi snuck out of the ruined town and headed to the harbour. There were many row boats and sailboats of all sizes. After choosing a small one with a modest sail, she jumped in, pulled the ropes, and tried to figure out how to release the ropes to steer the vessel to where it needed to go. Once the sail was out, dragged by the wind, she untied the ropes that bonded the fragile boat to the wharf, and it left just as the storm was picking up.

The Highest One was doing all he could to destroy this town, but why hadn't he done it before? Why hadn't he looked for her first? Why had he been gone for so long all these weeks while Solvi withered in the damp cage? Surely, there would be an answer. This was God Himself! The evidence was clear as he had performed another miracle, it was just that this time, he had done so in a fit of wrath rather than attempting to save humanity.

She would sail to the mainland and get herself sorted. She still had friends in the Two Nations, didn't she? King Doemus and other faithful servants of the Highest Lord. They would welcome her with open arms.

Solvi took one last glance at the town as a huge column of smoke emerged from it, mixing with the dark clouds. It wouldn't be long until there was no town left. She couldn't risk getting caught in the destruction. Not when that would put her baby at risk.

⋯⋯

Gimlore stepped out of the destroyed town hall building and faced the sky. "Come here, you bastard! Come get me!"

She must be losing her mind, but she didn't care.

But the noise of the ground roaring, wood cracking and fire burning muffled all of her shouts. She wiped the sweat from her forehead and looked around. Where was she needed the most first?

"We need to get to safety. This is not a siege. This is a bloodbath," Keryon said.

Gimlore grimaced, her confidence evaporating. Keryon was right, but *where* was safety? She saw more carnage to the west side of the town, with Pinesy somewhere in the distance, tending to a large man lying on the ground.

Rednow! But that means...

"Don't tell me..."

She raced towards them, a bad feeling taking hold of her heart, spreading like a disease with no cure. Before she could reach them, a massive crack split the ground between them, leaving a more than thirty foot wide chasm where the muddy road had been. "Pinesy! Are they alright?" she bellowed from her side of the chasm.

Pinesy looked at her, hesitant, and Gimlore saw uncertainty in his face, a pit in her stomach draining her guts and squeezing them.

"Pinesy?" she pleaded. She just wanted to hear three very simple words. *They are fine.* That was it.

The pinehead had his hands around Rednow's chest, so she looked around him for the children. One of them hid behind Pinesy, looking around with a dagger in their hand, a fountain of tears pouring from their eyes. Tinko! Gimlore had never seen them cry like that. Not in many years.

But the relief of seeing Tinko alive wasn't enough to fill the inner carnage her body was undergoing from the anticipation and fear. Her hands trembled and her heart fluttered. She needed to know.

"Pinesy, where is Thata?" she bellowed.

Pinesy shook his head.

Gimlore's legs trembled, and she collapsed to her knees as her world ended.

All the noise faded. All the chaos and the horrific, mangled destruction no longer meant anything. She imagined Thata's fragile body lying on the muddy ground, shrinking, hardening up. Her baby, dead. All the innocence gone, grounded into nothing but memories. It should be impossible for children to die before their parents.

She found herself empty. It was too awful to think about, but nothing else mattered.

This is on me. On me alone.

Gimlore went from paralysis to being dragged by the arms by someone. She lost her sense of self and her vision blurred. She didn't know if she had even produced any tears. It was as though she had died inside.

Maybe she deserved to die.

Someone was saving her, taking her away from all the madness and death. Maybe Keryon, or somebody else? She didn't check.

Time became a blur, but she saw flashes of lightning hitting the ground, and fire creeping up into houses and trees.

This must be the underworld.

SIX

SADNESS AND SORROW

REDNOW

Rednow touched his leg, and pain shot through his body. He grimaced, gritting his teeth with every breath. Despite being half nude and with his clothes in tatters because of his transformation, the cursed red sword was still next to him, and he still had all three of his other limbs.

I'm either lucky or a fool.

The sunlight was too much for his eyes, and the smell of sea salt mixed with the rocking of the waves was enough to make him nauseous, though he doubted there would be any food in his stomach.

"What is this?" he croaked, his throat dry and hoarse.

A tiny hand stretched to offer him a mug with water. It was that pinehead fellow that always hung around Gimlore. Rednow drank it slowly, letting the water coat the insides of his throat. He should be better, but a coughing fit left him paralysed, as though his lungs desperately wanted to be out.

One day, I'm going to die from this.

The pinehead eyed him. Besides the shaggy head of curls that was common to all their kind, he had fair skin in greenish undertones. His bright eyes were also not too different from the other pineheads Rednow had travelled with before. On the fellow's other side, Tinko slept heavily and undisturbed by the rocking of the sea.

A wave of sadness and sorrow washed over him upon seeing the lone child. There were supposed to be two of them, twins, always up to something. Not just one. He'd lost orphan children before, when he was the leader of the Leeth. He'd raised them, and might as well be their dad, but this felt different. Losing someone else's child was a million times worse.

He let out tears as he thought about the wasted potential of Thata. *Such a bright future, thrown to the underworld. And it's all my fault.*

Rednow drank more water and cleared his throat multiple times until he felt like something close to a normal man, which was hardly possible now that he'd had his heart ripped from his chest.

The pinehead didn't seem too worried about talking to him, but he surveyed Rednow with his eyes, seemingly understanding what he was going through.

Rednow put down the water and looked around. Grey clouds covered the sky, thick enough to make him question whether it was early morning or nearly evening. The gulls were loud, flying over them in droves, hunting for fish. Beyond the sky and the gulls, there was only blue. A sea that extended beyond the horizon and carried the vessel they were in crashing through the waves.

"What is this?" Rednow whispered to avoid waking up Tinko.

"A ship," Pinesy said in a hoarse voice roughened by an age he didn't show.

"I know that, but who's navigating it?"

"My cousin."

That didn't narrow it down one bit, given that all pineheads called each other cousin. Since they lived in parallel with human civilisations, they had formed a close bond with all their kind, calling themselves cousins even if blood didn't tie them directly.

Rednow sighed. They were on a ship navigated by pineheads, but Rednow couldn't see anybody else in there. He glanced at the deck where they sat and saw nothing but a few crates, barrels, and miles of rope tightening this and that, or tying bits and bobs to the mast. It was a small ship overall, probably no longer than twenty strides.

"What happened in Heleronde after I passed out?"

The pinehead glanced at him again, his face expressionless. "Many people died. Town was destroyed. Everyone got separated."

"And you saved me and the child?"

The pinehead nodded.

"For that, I'm thankful," Rednow said. "I assume Alarkan has fallen, then?"

"I didn't stick around to find out," Pinesy said. "I needed to save you. And Tinko."

"Do you at least know what happened to the others?"

A hole grew in Rednow's chest, already expecting the worst. He had lived in Heleronde only for a few weeks and had not left his hut often, but it had truly been the place of his dreams. It was warm, and there had been no pressure. There were no kings or queens demanding tariffs, no cutthroats pillaging or tribal lords fighting for their turf.

Pinesy looked to the sea. "We got separated. I don't know what happened to them."

Rednow nodded. Uncertainty was still more comforting than confirmed desolation, at least. For a moment, he let the wet, salty breeze wash his hair and beard, finding he had no strength left to do anything else, much less protect anyone or even himself. It was ironic how he had never been defeated in battle but now felt as though he had lost everything.

I hope Tellwoon and Merey are well.

Hours passed with him thinking of Thata wielding their short sword at Tinko, and then he spent even longer thinking of the child just lying there in the mud, hazy eyes open and lifeless. An image that would be forever stuck to his mind. His own guilt was undeniable—the child had died because of his clear neglect.

"Where are we docking?" he asked Pinesy.

"I am not the captain."

"I need to send word to the Leeth when we dock. I'll summon them and we'll take back Heleronde. It will take time, but they're reliable."

"We're not going back to Heleronde," Pinesy said matter-of-factly.

Rednow furrowed his brow. "Why not? Do you want to just let those beasts take the land? We need to fight back."

"She doesn't want you to do that yet," the pinehead said.

Doubt lingered between them until Rednow broke the silence. "Gimlore? I'm sure she has her reasons, but we can't possibly sit still."

"Not Gimlore. *Her.*"

Me, the Essence said.

Rednow jumped as the voice appeared in the form of a caress at the back of his mind. There was nothing tender about it.

Rednow snarled.

"*You*? Where were you when I needed you?" he hissed, then turned to Pinesy. "And how do *you* know her?"

The pinehead's determined look didn't waver, and the man didn't even flinch while maintaining his silence. Rednow saw wisdom in his bright eyes.

Where was I? WHERE WERE YOU? I'm not your slave, Rednow. Where were you when I told you time and time again the Old One was back? That you needed to help me defeat him? You did nothing but ignore me and pretend like swordplay was all that mattered in the world. This is not on me. You could have been the herald of doom, but you chose to be silent.

Rednow closed his hands into fists and gritted his teeth but found no reply. On the one hand, he was stuck with the Essence in a deal he had never agreed to, being told what to do and how many things depended on him. On the other hand, this much had been true. He could have warned Gimlore. Why didn't he?

"What does the Old One have to do with this?"

"It was the Old One's new host who destroyed Heleronde. And freed the shadowlings," Pinesy said.

Rednow frowned. He had blacked out before he had seen any of that. He didn't even have the chance to see just how badly the town had been destroyed. He glanced at the pinehead, who clearly knew more than he would ever tell. "Orberesis?"

Pinesy nodded.

Rednow cursed. They should have dealt with him earlier. They should have tirelessly chased him instead of sitting comfortably and assuming he'd drown. They'd all been naïve fools.

They were naïve because of your silence, Rednow. WAKE UP!

Rednow cursed the bloody Essence, who made him want to tear into his own head just to get rid of her. "I'm well awake, you old hag, but I'm not your slave, either. I read the scriptures Rebma wrote, but they explain none of this. Why didn't you help us? Heleronde was destroyed. People died…"

I don't have the strength. All I can do in this state is guide you. You're my avatar. You're supposed to be the one helping me, helping the world.

"If you want me to help you, you need to tell me everything. I need to know."

The silence was only broken by the gawking gulls and the thrashing of the wind in the ship's sails. Then the Essence returned.

What must you know?

Rednow took a deep breath and allowed the wet salt lingering in the sea breeze to soothe the sting in his lungs. There was no healing for old smokesmiths, but the sea was as close as he'd ever find. There was so much he needed to know. He knew little of the old gods and their quarrels. But he needed to know what his role was in all this.

"What is it that you need me to do?"

You are different, Rednow. You're the one with enough power to do my bidding. So, for now, you need to run away so that you can defeat him later. If the Old One kills you, he'd be killing me too. He's still gathering his strength, not at his strongest, but neither am I.

"But what is it that I must do? Surely, you know! Enough of all this deceit!"

Rednow thought he spotted Pinesy flinching. The pinehead could hear him, but he could not hear the Essence, though he somehow knew what Rednow was doing, that he was not talking to himself. Pinesy understood Rednow wasn't insane.

You must rally my supporters. And others like you.

"How do I find them?"

"I'll help you with that," Pinesy said.

"How do you—?" Rednow started but the Essence interrupted him.

My brother and I are destined to fight. There will be periods of peace, but the war will continue, just like it has. It will never stop.

Rednow swallowed, and his throat ached. He was the newest pawn in an ancient, eternal war between two gods that feuded every few generations. He barely understood anything.

He glanced at Pinesy. *And there are still many secrets to be unveiled.*

"And who are these shadowlings you talk about? The horned beasts that he summoned."

In the time of the great collapse, the kind the Old One calls Lantern Horns faced extermination in their own world, the Essence started. My brother found them and tried to save them by bringing them here, to this world. The shadowlings didn't settle here well, and the humans tried but there was never peace. The Old One didn't care. He would have brought all of them if it wasn't for me. He will if he manages to get rid of me.

"Why does he want it so badly?"

I ignore his motives. But he created the death of man, of trees, of the world. He crafted each death with his own hands. He stopped the wind from blowing, and the trees withered. Even the moon turned her face away. I locked him up in the orb because of it, but now he has escaped his prison and seeks revenge and to accomplish the plan I didn't let him finish. His thirst for power and control might just devour him too, if we're lucky enough. That's how you can stop him, Rednow.

Rednow sensed pain and the longing in the Essence's voice, tickling the back of his mind. It was mournful and full of sorrow. A grief that never went away just as her duty never had. In that moment, not even his own familiarity with grief was enough to understand everything the deity had gone through, facing the death of entire generations of friends and allies, and being forced to see them perish, time and time again. If even gods were destined to suffer like that, then what was he supposed to hope to accomplish?

"I'm just a man," he whispered.

The Essence scoffed. *Just a man? Your former adversaries would disagree. I've always said people can often be compared to metals. To me, you're like lead. It's the heaviest of the seven metals I created. It's grounded. It's a very stubborn metal equally known for its durability and resistance to change.*

Rednow smirked. Those could have been words straight out of Rebma's mouth. His eyes welled up again as he remembered his sister. The time he had spent with her and the Leeth would forever be engraved in his memory.

"With Heleronde destroyed, I should go back to the Leeth."

NO! the Essence bellowed. Rednow wasn't going to be silenced, though.

"There is a place there for Tinko. You took one of my arms. There is no more fighting I should be doing. I'm only a teacher now. I've got to take care of the child. How can I defeat a god while I do that?"

Nonsense! You can and you will.

"How?" he bellowed.

"Enjoy the breeze," Pinesy said, his tone flat and nonchalant. "Tomorrow you'll learn.

SEVEN

DIVINITY

ORBERESIS

P ower flowed through Orberesis, filling every muscle fibre, bone, and trace of his skin with divinity. He floated just like the Old One had in his past nightmares, but ever since the parasite had showed himself, there had been no more pain. No more migraines or any kind of nightmare.

If this is the price to pay, I'll gladly pay it, he thought, and the Old One laughed in the back of his mind.

From around a hundred strides in the air, he saw the full effects of his new-found power. Rock had risen from the bowels of the earth, the rivers forming and stretching anew between them and the sea. The ramshackle town was destroyed, and its people cowered like cockroaches, scrambling for survival.

They reminded him of those who had hurt him. Bakers who'd rather feed bread to the rats, or cobblers, merchants, and tanners who let him freeze in the winters. Fishmongers who didn't bother with gulls stealing their fish but were ready to chop on his hands when he did. They had all hated urchins like him. This was just the beginning, and soon the kings of the world would find out his divinity was no farce.

You could do so much more, Doi, the Old One said. *When we get stronger, you will see.*

He didn't really mind having the parasite listening to his every thought, given everything else he received in return. He lusted for more waves of the power, but found the well drying up, and his energy fading.

"What's happening?"

We must go back, Doi. Don't worry, we'll return.

Orberesis didn't want to go anywhere. He wanted to stay there, where his power was real and the effect was tangible. In there, the miracle hadn't just been a fluke. He now remembered everything.

Unwillingly, his body slowly made it down, his bare feet touching the mud. That single touch made him falter and lose his composure, his energy draining. And from down there, the aftermath of his rage didn't look as impressive. The Lantern Horns feasted in the chaos, but humanity had its guts hanging out, and blood soaked the mud everywhere he walked. Were there any humans left alive?

Well, they can't say I didn't warn them, he thought, thinking especially of Gimlore and her threats. He had come for her and what she loved, but everything felt empty and grey now, in the aftermath. Orberesis realised that wasn't the town, but him.

Why did I do all this?

Because, together, we will create better worlds and better futures, Doi.

Orberesis nodded, but the emptiness was still there. It had grown, if anything. He needed to find someone alive. Anyone, to soothe his growing guilt. "Where are the prisoners of war?"

Doi...

Orberesis snarled. "I asked where. Are. The. Prisoners. Of. War! Don't forget you're a guest, because I could still very well deem you an intruder."

The Old One laughed louder than he had any right to do. Orberesis imagined the parasite sitting down with a drink in his hand, the widest of smirks painted on his lips. But the real Old One was now only found when he looked in the mirror.

You can investigate. For now.

Orberesis walked towards the rubble, a few dozen Lantern Horns joining him.

"Oh-dah-On!" the creatures grunted to the best of their ability. They couldn't speak, but their horns flashed wildly at shifting intensity and speed. "Oh-dah-On!"

They were calling him Old One, he realised.

Orberesis had wanted to be a king and had dared to be a god, someone to be revered and worshipped, but he had thought about ruling over men and women, not these foul beasts. He winced as they came closer to him.

What was left of the town was now just rubble and debris. Cracked wood still burned. Charred timber lay scattered across the mud, hindering his walk.

There weren't many humans left, and those that had stayed behind had their faces bloodied and their arms dirtied by mud and soot. They had their arms bound in shackles and were under the surveillance of the Lantern Horns, whose flickering horn lights made him dizzy.

As he passed by them, Orberesis searched for familiar faces. The tall, blonde man or that woman, Gimlore. No success there. Perhaps she was among the victims, somewhere.

"Gather all the bodies. I need to find someone," he said.

The Lantern Horns blinked their lights and seemed to understand what he said, as many of them started moving around the ruined town.

They're not here. The Old One seemed to understand who he sought.

"How do you know?"

I just do, Doi. I'll let you search, but we have much to accomplish. This was just the beginning.

Orberesis scowled, and shook his head, though he acknowledged the Old One was probably right. He approached a group of weeping town folks who kneeled in the mud, their eyes fixated on the ground beneath them, their bodies shaking.

It was a feeling Orberesis understood all too well—the fear and the pain of being utterly helpless, filled with pure despair and not a single sliver of hope between here and the horizon. His mind travelled back to his father and his brutal killing.

I hope one day you can be someone better than I am, he had said. *Something better.*

Back then, Orberesis hadn't understood what his father meant. Now, he understood. It didn't matter how much he thought his father was a good man if the rest of the world thought he deserved a cruel punishment. Could Orberesis still be a good man? Probably not. That was long past him. His father had tried so hard to redeem himself and be good that he had ended up burned alive like a hog.

When I first bloomed, I thought I was beautiful. But all the flowers around me withered, the Old One whispered in his mind, now in a softer tone.

Orberesis did not reply and continued to make his way through the groups of survivors until he stopped and kneeled in front of an old woman with a skin withered by the sun, denouncing the many years of hard labour. "What's your name?"

The woman took her time, glancing at him, and it was as though her eyes were piecing him, judging him deeply, which was unsettling. "Eshof," she finally said.

"Who's the leader here?" he asked, pushing past the terrible emotions he had just felt. Not even the Old One could pretend he was liked by anyone now.

"No one that I know of. You killed everyone we had," the woman said. Her voice was steady, with the resolution of someone who had lived long and seemed to have nothing left to lose. Nothing left to fear.

One of the Lantern Horns made its way toward her, ready to force its claws on her, but Orberesis stopped him. There had already been enough killing. He raised his voice, addressing all the survivors. "Who's the leader here?"

The imprisoned men and women raised their heads and exchanged glances among themselves, searching for a leader. None of them said it, but many of them looked at two dark-skinned men. Just like the others, these two had dishevelled hair caked with mud, sweat and ash, though one of them wore a red bandana that protected most of his hair from the filth. They were the same height, the same built and looked... identical. Twins.

"Are you the leaders?"

They looked around and shook their heads. "No."

"Interesting. Then why is everyone looking at you?" The twins stayed silent, so he insisted. "What are your names?"

They looked at each other and shared one of those intimate glances where no words were needed. Then they both faced the ground and remained silent, as though they'd rather face death than say anything at all.

These two are interesting, he thought. "Keep an eye on them. Don't let them out of your sight."

"They're Nork and Nosema! They used to work for Gimlore!" an old man shouted, only to be met with murmurs.

"Traitor," the others around him whispered. "Motherless bastard".

Orberesis smiled and faced the man. "Is that so?" his gaze shifted back to the other two. Maybe that meant Gimlore was dead. One could only hope. "And what is your name, old boy?"

"Fanan," the toothless man said.

Orberesis cared little for the man, but if he was going to rule over these people, they had to start seeing him as at least an ambiguous figure. Yes, he could destroy when provoked, but he rewarded those who were loyal. He turned to the closest Lantern Horn and pointed at Fanan. "Remove his shackles."

The Lantern Horn hesitated but did as he asked. Fanan beamed as he caressed his own wrists where the shackles had been. "Thank you," he said.

Orberesis smiled. *Let them see I can be merciful too.*

The Old One giggled in the back of his mind. *I was lucky to be picked up by you, Doi.*

Orberesis smiled at that. Maybe that was who he was, after all. The aftermath of his rage had left him empty and craving something like empathy or comfort. It was something he had never had, something he had always lived well enough without. His father wanted him to be a good man, and he had tried to be one, until the world had decided that he, too, must be shoved down into the mud.

Orberesis was done being shoved down. He was going to rise, instead.

EIGHT

A WAY BACK

GIMLORE - SOLVI

Gimlore tried closing her eyes, but the pain did not abandon her. It was still there, in every fibre of her, deep in her core. She followed Keryon out of the ship, making sure her face was undetectable under the hood. He grabbed her hand and almost had to drag her. His pull was the only thing keeping her going. He was the only one she had left.

She followed him first through the maze that was the pier of Munzir Bay, riddled with dangerous-looking sailors at the end of a day's worth of labour, ready to spend the coin, ready for debauchery. She had dealt with the likes of these before, but she wouldn't need to lift a finger this time.

"Let's find a place to settle for the night," Keryon said. "I grew up around here. I know a place we can go."

The Warden looked at her first, then at the long-haired man who travelled with them. Tavanar looked even gloomier than she did. He had thought Orberesis' powers were a fluke, but now it was clear he could control the divine powers after all. Gimlore didn't understand why Tavanar was still alive and travelling with them at that.

Gimlore only wanted to find Tinko and cradle the child, bring their little head to her chest. She knew it was selfish. She'd never had motherly instincts, but now she that had lost Thata, guilt tore at her from the inside. No decent mother would let her children die. Or let herself get separated from the only child she had left. She was barely able to hold herself together now that Thata had passed. She wasn't sure she could survive losing Tinko too.

The bustle of Munzir Bay was almost deafening, but it was still better than being stuck in her own mind. She let Keryon guide her and listened to the shouts of the merchants who scrambled to sell the last of their stock, while cobblers and tinkerers packed their knickknacks for the day. It all reminded her of Heleronde, in a way, without the mossbacks and the humidity.

Keryon guided them through what looked like the main street, where pedestrians and shadesgrowls pulled carts, and wagons travelled both directions. The more they walked, the more Gimlore noticed the atypical, yellow-coloured bricks of the buildings, in a style she hadn't seen before. The alleyways became narrower and darker as the sun dipped past the horizon.

Keryon halted and banged his fist three times on an odd oak door marked with a tree. They waited in silence until an old man's voice greeted him. "Why are you here?"

Not the warmest of greetings.

"I need help," Keryon said. "For the three of us."

"I told you not to come back." The door opened and revealed a small brown-skinned pinehead with hair just as shaggy as Pinesy's.

"It's just for an evening," Keryon said.

Gimlore had never seen the man that meek, but then again, she had never been that quiet herself. People did desperate things when desperation called, when they were thrown against the wall. They did what they had to do, even if that meant rekindling old flames, digging up old grudges, or facing their fears.

The pinehead's face remained impossible to read, but he took a step back and urged them in.

"Thank you, Lorans," Keryon said as they all stepped inside. "Truly."

"Don't thank me yet. Wait until you hear how much you'll owe me after this."

The house seemed stuck in time, with most of the furniture looking at least three hundred years old, and the walls painted with a kind of old chalk, with no wood or exposed brick in sight. There were strange items scattered around the house, some that looked part of the decoration and others that made Gimlore wonder if this Lorans fellow had a hoarding problem.

The pinehead took them to the next room, where four people became a crowd. If Gimlore wanted, she could touch the low ceiling, but the height was not an issue for a short pinehead.

They all sat on an intricate Mosendi rug, and Keryon kept his eyes on Lorans, waiting for their host to sit with them. Tavanar remained just as quiet as she did, unsure what the etiquette was for such a strange situation. The pinehead ended up sitting down with them in the end.

"Why did you come back?" Lorans sounded exasperated.

"I didn't know where else to go," Keryon said. "You heard what happened in Alarkan?"

"Maybe I did."

"We lost everything."

Those words lingered, as though each syllable, word, or sentence had a personal vendetta against her. She had lost *everything*. All those years of pain, and now she had no gold, no elixir, no town, no tavern, and worst of all, one child was gone forever.

She wiped her tears away and took a deep breath to keep the composure. For the gods, that was hard. She didn't even know the whereabouts of the child she hadn't lost. She gripped her own knees hard, an urge to slap herself taking over.

How did I let this happen? Grinding her teeth and lost to her current surroundings, she decided she had to chase Tinko and make sure they were alright.

"I see," Lorans said. He was lively for a pinehead, with a more expressive face than Gimlore was used to, and certainly a wider vocabulary than Pinesy ever used. "But I can't help you."

"I need more herbs. We need to get back and fight!" Keryon said.

Both Tavanar and Gimlore looked at him and furrowed their brows.

"Are you insane?" Tavanar said. "You want to fight *that*? How would you go about it? It's not bloodsleuths or marcrunchers we're talking about. Those are creatures that do not belong in this world. My best guess is Doi pulled them down from the underworld, somehow. Speaking of whom, how do you intend to fight a man who can destroy the world just by flailing his arms?"

"Shut up, you bastard. You were licking his boots for years before he got rid of you," Gimlore hissed, earning a grimace from Tavanar but also his silence. He knew she was right.

Lorans cleared his throat. "Well, my friend. It seems like you and your... companions don't see eye to eye on what you want, so I'll give you some time to figure it out."

Keryon bit his lip and nodded as the pinehead walked into the next chamber and closed the door behind him.

"Who the fuck is this? And what are we doing here?" Gimlore whispered. "I need to find my child!"

Keryon eyed her. "I'm glad you've finally come to your senses, but an hour ago you were paralysed by grief, so I took us to safety. Lorans is an old friend, a herb merchant with vast contacts around the world."

"He doesn't seem to like you much," Tavanar pointed out.

Keryon shrugged. "We had a falling out when I decided to go to Alarkan with... Pie, to set up the herb shop."

Keryon slowed down as he mentioned his old friend. Gimlore noticed the pain in his words. He didn't want to show it, but he was hurting, perhaps as much as she was. Keryon was also grieving his friend.

Tavanar cleared his throat. "Sorry to interrupt, but I see no reason we should go back. Everything we had there is gone. We must assume everyone we knew is dead. Going back is not just hard—it's a death sentence. We should take some time and figure out what we'll do next."

Gimlore was in for a fight, even if it was just a verbal one. "It's easy for you to *assume* everyone is dead when you didn't *know* anyone. Feel free to leave, then. Why are you with us?"

Tavanar swallowed. "I have nobody else and you spared my life. I'd rather stay with you."

She slowed down, staring at him. "If you're going to stay with us, it's best if you learn rather quickly who's in charge."

"Gimlore," Keryon said. "*No one* is in charge now. Let's focus. You don't want to fight back?"

"Of course, I fucking do, but how exactly do we do that? You're a smokesmith, but neither of us are. And how do you fight back against a man, god or not, who summons thousands of monsters and can break the world with a finger snap?"

No one had an answer for her. "See? That's why I'm in charge. You have good intentions, but planning isn't your forte."

Keryon frowned and his eyes dug into hers. They'd talk about this later. "So, what do you suggest? I must avenge Piesym."

"And I need to make sure my child is alive."

Even if Tinko faced the dangers of the world, at least they wouldn't be direct targets of the manic bastard. But there was still Nork and Nosema for her to worry about. There was also Eshof and so many others... She had no way of knowing whether they were alive or dead.

Even if she went back to assess the losses and tried to rescue those left as prisoners, she would be seen from miles away at sea, and the enemy would crush her before she even had the chance to moor the boat. But with Tinko, Rednow, and Pinesy unaccounted for, and the Leeth army still too far north, there were no real options.

She was truly, desperately fucked.

Think. Think. Think.

"If Tavanar says Tinko is alive, we should try to find them. Regroup with Pinesy and Rednow before we do anything else," she said.

"And how do you intend to find them? Only the gods know where in the Known World they might be. It's quite possible you might find yourself spending the next twenty years looking for them. It's better to regroup and gather some resources first, before anything else."

Gimlore mulled it over. "Tinko and Rednow were with Pinesy. Your friend Lorans is a pinehead. We can ask him for help. Pineheads can always find each other."

"Sure, I can ask Lorans to contact his cousins. But that doesn't change the fact they could take months to respond, or not respond at all. There is no guarantee Pinesy has other pineheads around. If no one else knows his whereabouts, they won't find him unless he wants to be found."

Gimlore nodded, sighing. "Why would he not want to be found?"

"I don't know. I'll ask Lorans to contact his cousins anyway, but we better think of a second plan in case we don't hear back."

"I take it inaction isn't really an option? We could just sit tight." Tavanar scoffed.

Keryon shook his head. "Lorans won't allow us to stay here forever. Even if we pretend it's not our problem, Orberesis won't be content with just destroying Heleronde. He has the power to conquer nations, so I'm guessing he has a plan. He will venture further; we just don't know where. Perhaps he'll come right here, in which case we should take our leave as soon as possible."

Gimlore nodded. She had thought the same.

"Then why not strike at the heart of the problem?" Tavanar asked.

"What do you mean? The *problem* is Orberesis, and he's in Alarkan. We can't strike him. We already established that."

Tavanar shook his head. "I don't mean attacking him. I mean the Two Nations. They allowed him to thrive in the first place and sponsored his invasion of Alarkan. King Doemus is a true devout follower of his. Doi might be powerful, but without the backing of a real kingdom, he won't go far. If we could travel there, get inside the palace, and convince the King we're on his side, at least we'd have access to the resources we'd need to find our friends. We could then figure out how to flip the situation to our side with sabotage or something like that. Or just get out of there in the dead of night."

Something lit up inside Gimlore. *Could we?* In theory, yes. She had plotted sabotage missions before. All her life, really, but never at the heart of a kingdom. In this case, there would be too many unknown variables, too many things she couldn't predict. She had never even been to Sirestir, and she would loathe having to rely on Tavanar, but she had to admit having the resources to find Tinko sounded appealing. "What's your plan?"

"Wait. You can't possibly be alright with this." Keryon's frown had deepened. "It's far too dangerous, no matter how good it sounds. Your last risky plan only worked because you had me."

Gimlore nodded. "I still do, don't I?"

Keryon cleared his throat, and Gimlore thought she saw a hint of embarrassment in his face. He said nothing else.

"Listen," Tavanar said. "I was there with Doi the entire time. I met King Doemus and his advisors. I was their general! I'm not sure the King has caught wind of what happened in Alarkan, but I don't see why he wouldn't believe whatever I'd have to say. He'd welcome us and give us lodging, I'm sure. If we were to ask about the resources to find our loved ones, he would help. He says yes to anything that has to do with Doi."

Gimlore had to admit that sounded interesting. At least it was better than wandering aimlessly, asking people across the world if they'd seen an old man, a pinehead, and a child. "And how do we get there?"

"Many people join the processions to Ushar to see God Himself. They come from all across the world. There are hundreds of thousands of people in these. I say we take a ship not to Ushar but somewhere near, then join one of these processions, at least at the tail end of the pilgrimage. I can wear a hooded cloak, and we pretend to be devoted pilgrims. Once we're inside the city walls, I can get us to the palace. I lived in that city my whole life. Once we're in the palace, I pull the hood down and I'm a general, as far as they're concerned, bringing news of God Himself and his efforts to conquer Alarkan from the savages to the king."

"Everything about this idea is terrible," Keryon spat.

Gimlore considered this and gritted her teeth at hearing just how the people of Heleronde were perceived. "If Orberesis has in the King a faithful follower, and he's destroying and occupying Alarkan after we destroyed the Two Nations' army, then it's possible Ushar is in utter chaos, isn't it? Wouldn't local lords be unhappy about that? Try to seize power and blame the King for putting too much faith in Orberesis? What if we get there, and the King has been hanged for failing his people?"

There was just too much uncertainty.

Tavanar shrugged. "I can't answer that. The kingdom was already weakened before Doi got there, and he made it even worse. The King is an absolute fool and a devout follower of his, so what you're saying is not impossible. I know it's a risk, but I think it's our best shot. The King knows me and thinks me an ally. I could go back to him, claim I survived the battle, and say you two are also devout followers who found me, and saved me, but your loved ones are missing. He might even reward you! If we get there, and the city is in peril, we can always get on the first ship out of there, and we will have wasted nothing but the time it takes to arrive."

That got her thinking. "Assuming everything goes as you said, could *we* take over the kingdom? It's a fucking gambit, but perhaps with the forces of a kingdom behind us, we could fight Orberesis."

"Are you seriously considering this? I'm not getting involved in more power scuffles. For the gods, we're just three people!" Keryon said. "And they must have smokesmiths. I don't want to have to kill any of my own people."

"Then don't!" Gimlore snarled. "I'll call the Leeth now and pay them once we're in the palace. I'll pay them enough gold to hire them for fucking eternity!"

Keryon shook his head. "You'll pay them? With what gold? We lost everything! You're not thinking straight. I don't see *any* of this working. It's madness! The journey from here to Ushar is also a long one, even if we take a ship. Orberesis could conquer the whole world in that time."

"What else do you suggest we do, then?" Tavanar asked. "I don't think we could... take over the Two Nations. No, that'd be too ambitious. I only see an attempt at doing that ending one way, and it's not favourable. But getting inside the city shouldn't be hard, and neither should be getting the king's help. Once we're there, finding whoever we need to find won't be hard. I haven't done much to prove my worth, so please trust me with this. Let me help."

Keryon sighed and rested his hands on his lap. Gimlore could see he didn't like the ideas but had none of his own. The truth was, whatever they decided to do would probably be either too cowardly, or too reckless and dangerous, with vastly terrible consequences. That seemed to always be the way with her.

Amidst the silence, she considered her options. Maybe she could go back to the steppe and bushwhack travellers like a bandit. Then it dawned on her just how much she had aged since then, with only the pain of her loss surpassing the pain at her lower back. And she no longer had Edmir, Nork, or Nosema.

For the gods, I could use some wine right about now.

The silence was broken by sighs, and Lorans fiddling about with his trinkets somewhere in the other room. What was the pinehead doing here anyway, and what was all this junk?

"We're fucked either way," she concluded, and both men nodded in agreement.

The lack of decent options left Tavanar's half-assed excuse of a plan almost sound like an amazing idea. She remained silent, thinking of Tinko and Thata, her flesh and bones. But now there was only Tinko. Gimlore just wanted to hold her child for a moment, tell the child everything would be alright, even if it wouldn't. Didn't she have that right?

Tavanar's plan was the only option they had, as terrible as it was. Gimlore saw Keryon and saw Keryon's probing eyes assessing her. She shrugged lightly at him without breaking eye contact, and he resigned, settling with a sigh.

"I would need a lot more herbs," he said as he walked towards the door. "And proper clothes. I'll ask Lorans to contact his cousins about finding Pinesy."

Gimlore nodded. "While you're at it, do you know where I can find some throwing knives?"

⋯⋯⋯

Solvi hugged herself as she continued to walk. She had been on the run for what felt like years, though she knew it was only weeks since leaving Alarkan, and around four months after she had first landed in the dreadful continent. She had only eaten enough to satiate the deepest of hungers. With no weapon and no energy to hunt anything, she was at the mercy of kind strangers.

She walked slowly, with her right arm extended, and whispered, "Please. Bread. Water." Her throat was dry, but she still felt the child kicking inside, her belly now visible beneath the loose cloak.

Her sailboat had landed in Kifell beach just a day after deserting Alarkan, and it had taken her weeks to walk through Mosendel's cerro fields to Munzir Bay, the trading capital of the southwestern most country in the world. The city was mostly built in the typical solid yellow bricks made from the stones found in the region. The city walls, the docks, and the watch towers had all been built with those massive bricks centuries ago. With a quick glance, Solvi saw guards armed with crossbows on the towers and the walls, wearing red and yellow uniforms. The seagulls gawked above her. On the beach, under the ridge she walked towards, the fishermen shouted at their apprentices.

Her stomach growled. *I must find a way out of here.*

Each step just brought more pain, and she considered herself someone who *knew* pain well enough that she had no need for any more of it.

Solvi kept walking, and a few hundred strides ahead, her nose picked up the scent of something sweet and comforting that made her mouth water. She didn't want to draw any attention to herself, but for the gods, she *needed* food. The closer she got to the source of the scent, the easier it was to figure out what it was that smelled like that—honey-roasted bread, a Mosendel specialty. She got off the main path that was parallel to the beach and was overwhelmed by the luscious smell as a baking tray of about fifteen loaves cooled by the window of a shop, oozing the sweet aroma. She stood there, under the parapet, wondering if she should steal one for herself.

For the child, she reminded herself.

A broad man with a furrowed brow appeared on the window and glanced at her, then at the bread. "You were going to steal it, weren't you?"

Solvi looked at herself and realised she looked like an urchin. Her dark cloak was covered in Alarkani mud and her face must still be covered in soot. "No, I wasn't," she lied.

The man's face changed, and he sighed. He looked to both sides and, when he didn't see anyone, he grabbed a loaf and threw it in her direction. "Don't tell anyone. And don't come back," the man said.

Solvi grabbed the bread and held it like the most precious thing she had ever had. Her mouth watered, and she couldn't resist biting into it right away.

It was the sweetest, most pleasant thing she had ever eaten. She chewed it fast and took a second bite while the man watched from the window. He then removed the tray inside and started closing the shutters.

"Wait!" Solvi said. "Please!"

"I already gave you one. I can't give out more!"

"No, thank you. I'm looking for passage to the Two Nations, good sir."

This is what it came down to: the good will of a stranger. A man Solvi would have scowled at in any other circumstance. How powerless she had become, especially now when the baby needed her. She was good at surviving, at least, and now she wasn't surviving just for her own sake. She would do what she had to.

"The Two Nations?" The man frowned. "Why would you want to go there?"

Solvi scrambled for an excuse as she chewed on the bread. "Family. My family is there."

The man noticed her belly and considered her words. "Last I heard, the Two Nations were in peril. The King let himself be fooled by a false prophet, ordered for trade with other nations to halt and the like. There isn't much trading happening between us and them. And now, with the troubles in Alarkan, I'm not sure a ship is where you'll want to find yourself."

Solvi swallowed, bit her tongue, and reminded herself the man had been kind to her. She glanced towards where Alarkan would be. Of course, she couldn't see it from there. Even if there was clear sky, the smoke threads wouldn't be big enough for Mosendel to see, but trading vessels must have been there and passed the word.

"What happened in Alarkan?" she probed. *Let's see how much he knows.*

The man shrugged and shook his head. "I didn't hear any more than you did. Anyway, if you really want to get to the Two Nations, you should try your luck at the port. Maybe there's a vessel there booked for Ushar. But for the love of the gods, be careful. The harbour is no place for a young woman like you.

Especially not one with child. I would have a word with your family for letting you out on your own like this..."

Solvi nodded her thanks and removed herself as the man shut his window. To the harbour, then. She took her time to savour whatever was left of the honey-roasted bread and when it was gone, she wished she could have another one. She looked around and saw the tall masts of the ships in the horizon in what could only be the harbour. Flocks of seagulls flew above it, circling it and gawking, certain of a fresh meal to come.

The harbour of Munzir Bay was just as she had imagined. It was large, with more than one hundred ships moored there, and thousands of men of all shapes and sizes buzzing about like ants, each with a task to complete. Some carried barrels to be loaded onto ships, certainly cerro wine fermented from the cerro fields just northwest of Munzir Bay. Others carried ropes, fishing lines, and some used shadesgrowls to pull carts loaded with caught giant wickplates, which would be gutted and have their coveted plates stripped soon enough.

There were women as well, but most were men. Solvi grimaced at the realisation. She had always hated men, with a few exceptions. The face of the Highest One flashed in her mind. He had shown her kindness and courage when all she had was utter despair. And Keryon, the man who had discovered her light still flickered, even in pure darkness. He had believed in her without asking for anything in return, but he was the Highest One's enemy.

He must be dead now, anyway...

Solvi remembered his comforting words before the town was destroyed. Keryon had promised to look after her and the child, but Solvi had left. Should she go back and seek him out?

No, there was only one thing to do now.

When she walked through the harbour, she squinted to see the flags on the ships. They were all from different places, but none of them were from the Two Nations. As she looked at the flags, sailors and fishermen called out to her.

"Come here, sweetie," one said, squeezing his lips into kissing sounds.

"I'll show you a good time!" another whispered as he got up from the crate he sat on.

It took Solvi every bit of inner strength not to respond. If she'd had the herbs and wasn't carrying a baby, she would have slit their throats in a heartbeat. Before that, she would have played with them, though. Stabbed them, cut their fingers off, and then decapitated them, and impaled their heads on spears. Perhaps she would have written "human rubbish" on a little plaque under it.

Now she was defenceless, though, and carrying an even more defenceless being in her womb, so she had to bite her tongue and hurry up.

Then, she saw it, waving in the sea breeze. The flag had the red half with a blue shield engraved in it, and the blue half with a red anchor, symbolising the unity of the Two Nations of Sirestir and Yab. A smile crept into her lips. Soon, they would see her, and they would bring her to Ushar, where she would wait for the Highest One to arrive.

Then why did she take her time? Her feet didn't seem to move, as though she was stuck to the wharf. If she went, she would see the Highest One again, and she'd be surrounded by his followers. If she stayed, she could look for Keryon and live her life in peace, maybe build something new, and find the respect she had always craved. No longer obeying the orders of scummy men.

The child moved within her, as though they wanted to be consulted for a decision on their fate. Solvi smiled and caressed the belly.

What should I do, young one? Tell me.

NINE

OF KINGS AND FOOLS

GIMLORE

All those miles of sea, and then of nothing but grass, dirt, and mud had given Gimlore time to plot everything in her head a million times over, but how prepared could she really be for what could only be described as a suicide mission?

Before they left Munzir Bay's loud fish markets, she had sent word to Merey and the Leeth through Lorans that Rednow was unaccounted for, along with her child, and the pineheads couldn't find them anywhere. She had hoped Merey's respect and loyalty to Rednow would make her willing to help, even if there was not much coin involved.

She had also written about her plan to infiltrate Ushar's Palace of Brilliance.

What a fucking stupid plan. I must be insane.

She had grown tired of Tavanar, the sound of his voice, and the way he had lowered his guard around her and Keryon, spending all his time telling them all about his childhood in Ushar, or how he never got caught once inside the city walls.

"... and then I jumped to the roof below and the guard was left scratching his head. That's when I knew I was one of the best at it."

Good for fucking you.

She smiled at him. Keryon sighed, as bored by Tavanar as she was. Why would they speak when Tavanar could talk for the three of them?

The steppe had turned into bushland, then into forests and hills. After that, there were only cerro fields. Sirestir had always claimed to produce the best berries the world had ever known, and if her tongue had any say in it, they were damn right about that, even if she preferred the liquid form of the berries, well-fermented and boozy.

The plants were bright red as poppies or spider lilies, but taller, reaching her height. There were not many farmers around—it must be a few weeks short of the harvesting season. She had bushwhacked Ainisian troops in Mosendel and battled in the steppes of Shari, but never in Sirestir, so she had no idea when the harvest was supposed to be. There was so much of the world she hadn't seen, but she was fine with that.

If she could give up the world and get Thata back, she wouldn't hesitate.

It had been weeks—too long—without her child, and as badly as her lower back ached, it was nothing compared to the hole in her heart she hadn't even tried to fill. It was still a bloody open wound and she still bled from it. Badly. She told herself she had deserved that constant, burning pain. Some days had always been darker than others, but ever since the day Orberesis took Thata from her, the darkness had festered, climbed up her through the wound, and sat comfortably inside her.

"How long until we reach the city walls of Ushar? We should join the pilgrimage now," Keryon said, cutting off Tavanar's blabbering.

"Should be there by the end of the day by the looks of it," he said after drinking from a waterskin Lorans had supplied. Gimlore picked up her own. In all her years, she had never seen such a thing, and she had no idea people still used these for anything when a flask or a bottle would do. This was something of the past, perhaps a relic.

Tavanar pulled his hood up as they slowly merged into the massive caravan that occupied the main dirt road to Ushar, tracking the cliffs that led to the Yabbish Strait. She could almost see it from there, far in the horizon, the main island of the Yab archipelago, where warm waters attracted wickplates and fishermen made fortunes after catching them by the dozen.

The caravan was made up of poor farmers and other vassals who were fed up with their lords and kings and had seen in Orberesis the promise of something more. They saw him as one of their own, someone who inspired them to strive for more, dream for more. Gimlore had long been thinking about the orb, the powers it had given Orberesis. She wondered how in the underworld the bastard still had those powers when she had shattered the artifact. She would probably never get an answer.

Keryon was cautiously talking to one of the farmers that rode alongside them.

"They say he isn't there, that he sailed to Alarkan, but Ushar is still a holy place for us, so we go there. If we see him, all the better," the man said. His ratty clothes were crafted from used burlap, stitched back over and over by someone with sloppy needlework. "They say the air smells fresher in Ushar since he has risen. I want to feel that for myself."

"Will you still have a job when you come back?" Keryon asked.

The man's eyes found a target far in the horizon, and he swallowed. "My lord doesn't take kindly to his vassals running off. At least thirty lashings are to be expected. Rat stew as well. It's worth it, though."

Keryon's eyes shifted, and Gimlore could see the hurt in them. He had fled his own old masters as well. "Maybe you don't need to go back at all," he said.

The man scowled. "And where do I go? Do I become a beggar, or a thief? No other lord will take me."

Gimlore opened her mouth to suggest Heleronde, but she stopped herself in time. Just a few months ago, her town would have welcomed men and women of any background, as long as they didn't bring any trouble, but now the dream was dead. The utopia had never grown much beyond all the dreaming.

She swallowed, and the emptiness spread inside her.

"What a fool I've been," she muttered.

They stayed on the road for a few more hours, until the cerro fields gave way to a large city spread across the horizon, built on hills between land and sea. Ushar. Gimlore could barely see it yet, but her mind scrambled to find a way to complete their plan. They needed to get inside the walls first, and then inside the palace, but they had no idea how well guarded the city was after the King had ordered so many of his soldiers to help Orberesis conquer Alarkan.

"Do you see that?" Keryon whispered as he leaned towards her. "There are no guards or soldiers posted anywhere near the city. Their defences are in shambles. Tavanar was right."

Gimlore nodded, but she was still unsure just how right the man had been.

They reached the outside of the city walls in time for Gimlore to dismount the shadesgrowl, land on her feet, and stretch her legs and back. For the gods, that was painful. Surrounded by the pilgrims, she eyed the massive gates. "What now?"

Tavanar shrugged. "Now, we pray they open."

She gritted her teeth. "Fucking *pray*? Is that the best you can come up with?"

Keryon strutted to one of the pilgrims that were closest to the gates. "Aren't they going to open it?" he asked, feigning total ignorance. "What are we to do?"

The farmer smiled in a toothless grin. "Don't worry, friend. They always open the gates for the pilgrims. Once every two hours."

"And they let in everyone?"

"Not everyone. Only the first one hundred or so. We better make sure we're at the front, right?"

Keryon smiled and gave the man an appreciative nod.

Gimlore sighed. How did he do this? How could he stay so composed, so patient, and so... kind, after everything they'd lost? That was another reason to keep him around...

When the time came, a loud metallic sound came from the giant gate, and the chains that held the pulley system started stretching and opening it. The pilgrims rushed forward, pushing and shoving to get ahead. Gimlore, too, did her best to stay at the front, making good use of her elbows to navigate the fiery crowd.

Just how desperate she had become, now forced to wait on the kindness of the guards of a city she had never been in, just to have the tiniest chance of saving those she cared about, before she could even think about revenge. She had seen pain and sorrow, but this was almost a humiliation of a kind she had never felt, not even in the orphanage, before Madame Mazi took her in.

"No pushing!" one of the guards shouted.

The more the guards said anything, the more the pilgrims forced themselves inside the walls. Gimlore was being pushed from all sides, bodies touching her legs, arms, back, and chest. She couldn't move at all. Panic settled into her.

What if I don't make it inside?

What if she fell, and the mob trampled her, stomping her to death?

Gimlore tried to force her way into the front, and shake off those dreadful thoughts, but she got separated from Keryon and Tavanar, who were about three strides ahead. The guards shouted at them to walk slowly and keep the distance, but none of the pilgrims abided by their words. Slowly, the gates started to close and Gimlore was still slightly short of getting inside the city. She wrestled with the crowd, panic surging within.

I need to get in. Now.

She hated herself for it, but in that crowd, it was everyone for themselves. Flailing her elbows, she clasped her hands into fists and started using them. Hopefully, no one would notice where the hits were coming from amid the chaos. The pilgrims gasped and screamed, as apparently others were doing the same as her.

She didn't want to hurt these miserable people, but she *needed* to get in. At least she wasn't stabbing them. One more elbow to the right and a shove to the left and she was able to squeeze herself in moments before the gates closed with a loud boom.

She stopped, hands on her knees, panting. Sweat covered every pore of her skin. She hadn't realised just how suffocated she had been in there.

"Are you alright?" Keryon grabbed her right arm. "Have some water."

Gimlore grabbed the waterskin and chugged its contents without thinking twice. She had taken so much for granted. Her life in Heleronde. The respect of people. Her position of power. Her wealth and status. Now she was scrambling like the rest of them, back even lower than when she had started.

"What am I even doing here?" she whispered to herself, struggling not to let the emotions take over. "I should just give up."

"The Gimlore I know would just tell me to fuck off and strut around without another word. We'll be alright."

She almost wanted to laugh at that. The *old* Gimlore. Not the current one.

They walked slowly through the cobbled streets of Ushar as she fought back the surge of utter despair that had assaulted her earlier. This was the new normal.

"What is this…" Tavanar frowned. "It looks even filthier than last time. And that's saying something."

Gimlore was tempted to agree. Heleronde was a grimy place, but it was supposed to be, as a settlement town built over a swamp. Ushar, on the other hand, had the old buildings and wide roads only found in ancient cities, but it seemed like it had also been plagued by famine and death, with beggars crowding the streets. The cobbled stones had moss and grime, and the painted brick walls were stained and dirty. Not a single resident looked happy. Several small scuffles broke out as they walked, and there was no one around to stop them.

Where are all the guards? Or the smokesmiths?

Orberesis had only brought infantry soldiers to invade Heleronde, so there should be other garrisons in the capital. Yet all she saw were only a few guards posted in strategic locations, most of them paying no mind to what the city folks were doing. With this free range, of course, people got drunk and caused trouble. Cutthroats and pickpockets were aplenty, and children ran around stealing food from the street vendors.

The city had turned into a complete shithole. And she was the fucking queen of shitholes.

"Goodness, me…" Keryon said, watching a child running down an alleyway to evade three grown men. "Right. We're inside the city. That wasn't so bad. What about the palace?"

"The easiest way in would be to just walk in and announce my presence," Tavanar said.

"That would also be the *riskiest* way," Gimlore hissed. "Shouldn't we try to get more news first, just to be safe?"

"There is no trace of invasion or rebellion, so all in all, we can assume Doemus is still the king of the Two Nations, and the fool knows me as God Himself's best friend. I can only assume it's safe for us to make our way into the palace and gain his trust."

Gimlore didn't like this plan at all. She scratched her hair trying to find a fault in it, but the truth was she was depending on luck and other people, which made it hard to plan things. How the fuck could she come up with good plans when she didn't have resources, contacts, or knowledge of the people she was dealing with? It was like being blindfolded, thrown into shark waters, and told to swim to shore.

She had lost control all those months ago, and it would be a while until she would get that back. She turned to Keryon. "What are your thoughts?"

The Warden remained thoughtful, glancing at the steep, cobbled slope that led up to the Palace of Brilliance, then turned to Tavanar with piercing eyes. "What if they ask you how you got separated from the bastard? If they suspect your betrayal, you will be placing both of us in danger."

Keryon had as many doubts as she had, but what were they supposed to do? Waiting for the Leeth could turn to months, and there would be no guarantee that Merey would agree to help. That's it. They were fucking outcasts. They had no one else to ask for help. Whatever they had to do, they had to find a way to do it themselves.

"My friend." Tavanar smiled, though Gimlore doubted Keryon would consider the sleazy bastard a friend. "I've been telling lies for a living since I could talk, so I'll just keep weaving in lies with the truth. I'll tell them our armies were defeated and that Orberesis went missing, but that I managed to escape imprisonment because of the kindness the two of you showed me. He's a fool. He'll buy it."

Gimlore mulled that over. There were still many things they couldn't predict, but there was no other way. It was either that or trying to climb the walls herself, and risk having a hundred city guards waiting on the other side when she finally got over her back pain.

Shit.

"And if he doesn't?"

Tavanar shrugged. "Then we're fucked."

Gimlore sighed. "Is this plan the best we could come up with? I fucking hate it."

Keryon nodded. "I've never been much of a gambler, but it seems as though our luck rests on the shoulders of one of the least trustworthy people I'll ever meet. Delightful."

Gimlore scowled. She was thinking the exact same thing.

"Let's go?" Tavanar asked. If he was nervous, he sure didn't show it.

They climbed the slope, which got steeper as they went. It was a deceivingly long climb, which made it the perfect place for a palace. By the time invaders got to the top, they would already be tired. Two guards stood over the inner walls by the gate that connected the enormous palace to the rest of the city. Unlike Ushar, these inner walls were clean, and the guards posted there had much cleaner uniforms than those in the city.

"State your business or leave," a burly soldier said, as though someone had dared interrupt his daydreaming.

"Don't you recognise me, you fool?" Tavanar croaked. "Take a good look at me."

The guard shuffled and swallowed but ultimately said nothing.

Tavanar took another step towards him. "I'm general Tavanar. I've just covered thousands of miles from the battlefield in Alarkan, and you cannot even recognise me."

The man's eyes widened as the implications seeped in. He stood upright and opened the gate with no further delay. "My apologies, sir. I don't know what I was thinking. Who are these two, if I may ask?"

"I'll have a word with your superior," Tavanar said, a sly smile building. "These are the heavenly gifts that saved my life and brought me to safety. The least I can do is show them some appreciation."

"Yes, sir. Of course," the guard said, his eyes dropping to the stone floor as the three of them entered the palace.

"Not bad." Gimlore had to give it to him. At least he could act.

The inside of the palace was nothing like she'd expected. Unlike Enoris, Ledal, or any of the other palaces she's seen during her bushwhacking years, this was more like a city within a city, with several smaller buildings stretching away from the main one. There were small gardens decorated with ponds, immaculately clean tiled passageways, and neatly trimmed grass leading up to the palace. The guards up there wore full purple armour built from the shells of the wickplates, which was said to be as resistant as full plate armour, but much lighter.

A short man wearing white robes slowly emerged from the main building and headed toward them. "General Tavanar! What a pleasure it is to see you. And two guests. Wonderful. Who should I announce?"

Gimlore was about to say her name when Tavanar cut her off. "I will go in and introduce them myself."

The servant didn't like that. Gimlore saw the man was trying hard to conceal a snarl. "Ah yes. Certainly, General. It's just that there is a certain protocol we must follow."

Tavanar walked forward with the confidence of a long-lost son returning home to his parents, which made Gimlore more nervous than she wanted to be. This was what trusting people was, right? Though, from her experience, when foolish men acted confidently, there was almost always no reason for them to be confident, and that was fucking worrying.

Even so, Tavanar strutted on, passed several rows of guards, and crossed a massive room with high ceilings, with Gimlore and Keryon on his tail. At the end, two figures stood. A man and a woman, but Gimlore was too far away, and the backlight shining from the stained-glass windows was too strong for her to see how they looked.

"Keep your eyes down as you approach," Tavanar whispered.

Gimlore gritted her teeth and walked with her head down, like a hog lining up for slaughter. *For the Gods, I hate this.* Never again, she had promised. Never again would she obey any monarch's rulings. And here she was again, about to do just that.

Think of Tinko, she told herself. *Fight for Tinko.*

Tavanar stopped, and Gimlore and Keryon stood right behind him.

"My king, it's good to see you again," Tavanar said. "We have much to discuss."

"That we do," the man said. His voice was raspy and hinted at a sickness of some kind, though those three words were filled with meaning. She glanced at the monarch, but it was the woman next to him that drew her attention. Gimlore's eyes widened after she covered them from the sun with her hand.

No. It can't be.

Next to King Doemus was Solvi. The woman wore the dark robe Gimlore had first seen her in, but now her belly was protruding. Gimlore's mouth was agape. *And she's fucking pregnant.*

Her heart fluttered and all her hopes died in that moment. Tavanar may have fooled the King otherwise, but not with Solvi standing by his side.

It was all over.

"How did you..." the words left Tavanar's mouth, mimicking what Gimlore would have asked herself. "What is..."

"I wish I could say it's nice to see you," the dreaded woman said. "But I'm more surprised than anything."

A rage started to consume Gimlore. Keryon. He had *insisted* so many times that the woman be kept alive, all for his fucking morality. Gimlore had decided to go against her own better judgement and imprison her instead, and now here was the blonde hag again, a massive fucking thorn in her side. If Solvi had been left dead to rot in the marshes, they could probably have got away with Tavanar's plan. Now, all hope was gone, and she would never see her family again.

"Let's find out what you came here to do," Solvi said, looking directly at Keryon. "And don't you even try to ignite your herbs. I'm with child, yes, but I'm not alone."

Several men and women dressed in black appeared from a door behind Solvi's left side. Smokesmiths.

They were doomed. Completely and utterly doomed.

Ten

The Quarry

Gimlore - Keryon

The first lashing was the worst, but that didn't mean the second and the third were much better. Gimlore had been on the receiving end of all this pain, but she was no longer a young woman. She couldn't take it as well as she had when in her twenties. Before she'd had the children.

Tinko.

The child was all that held her together and prevented her mind from collapsing, though she suspected she was already close to the dreaded breaking point. The lashings stopped suddenly, and the man delivering them stepped away. Looking back in between gasps of pain, Gimlore could hardly see anything in that dark underworld. All she knew now was the damp cold of the stones, the scorching sting of the whip, and the smell of blood lingering in the air.

Her own blood, of course.

She was utterly alone in that cell now. Not even a shit bucket had been given, and her hands were tied against the stone wall in shackles that tightened the more she pulled.

Someone waltzed in, and the dark wooden door closed. The sliver of light that lit up the cell in that instant wasn't enough for Gimlore to see who it was. The pain was bad, but she stayed up like that, her body shaking. Whether from the cold or the pain, she didn't know.

"Solvi has told me about you." The King's voice was calm and collected yet sombre. "She mentioned your little utopia in the swamp. Said you were playing queen of the mud."

"F-fuck... Off," Gimlore managed to say between gritted teeth, and drool came out. She'd probably regret this, but this excuse of a man would not have her kindness, no matter what state she was in.

"Ah, yes, she also mentioned your filthy tongue," Doemus said. "You know, before I was made king, I was a scholar. I'm still one, as a matter of fact. I spend whatever time I can studying. History, for the most part, but also culture, mythology, and religion. I'm deeply fascinated by it all. So, I like to consider myself an expert in these matters, even if I'm not well-suited for other things like ruling or marriages and things of kings, truth be told. There is one thing that has never been carried out successfully in history. Care to guess what that is?"

Gimlore spat onto the floor. *There you go, you fucker.*

The King was in the mood for a lecture. "It's *rebellion*! Imagine that. There has always been unrest—mobs rising against their rulers. But no any attempt at a full-fledged rebellion with the purpose of overthrowing the regime has *ever* worked. Do you know why?"

Gimlore spat again, but that didn't deter the King.

"Because sooner or later, people like you realise that they need people like me. Poor folks *like* being told what to do, what to think. They like the stability, even if there is pain that comes along with it."

"Fuck that," Gimlore spat. "And f-fuck you."

She had, for ten years, lived on the fringes, away from the world of kings and queens squabbling for power. She had removed herself from it all and hadn't been the only one. Thousands of others had joined her, victims of the pain caused by the wars of these rulers with the golden spoons. Sure enough, here she was again, being tortured due to the orders of a fucking king, which proved her point entirely. The pain didn't allow her to reply, though, which seemed to only invigorate the man. His voice picked up.

"With that being said, what makes you think you are different? That you can just... opt out of a sacred arrangement between vassals and lords, kings, and subjects, that goes back thousands of years? You think you do, but you don't get to opt out, no matter how long you sit on the mud and claim it's your land."

"Yes, I do," she could only whisper. "I did just that."

She took the king's silence as annoyance at first, but then he pressed on.

"And your punishment for thinking you're entitled to that is proportional." He let the words linger as the blood flowed down her legs. "Surely, you knew it would end like this sooner or later, didn't you? Do you perhaps think this childish idea of *freedom* is better than having a stable system that allows for wealth and the development of civilisations? Such short-sightedness. Is all that excitement more important than safety? Is feeling alive more important than... living? This is why peasants should stay in the mud, where they belong."

Gimlore almost laughed. She would have if every heartbeat didn't carry swathes of pain throughout her body. A grim smile formed on her face. She did what she could to clear her throat even though she hadn't had as much as a sip of water.

"Of course it fucking is."

The King scoffed. "You say that because you don't know what is coming after this."

⸻

Keryon spat blood. He'd expected this. The worst of all worlds, being closed on in a cell like that again.

There was no smoke being injected into it, but since the day he was made into a smokesmith, being trapped in dark rooms was as bad as dying. His naked feet were wet from the cold stones of the cell, and his ankles bruised from the shackles. He steadied his breath, but breathing hurt as well now that his back had been split open by the whip. He was light-headed, his mind hazy, flickering between visions of Pie's dead body and the corpses of other loved ones taken from him over the years.

I will not succumb to it.

Hope was his only vessel in the darkness. If he held on to hope, then maybe one day everything would fall into place. It was easier to accept the madness and the rot, but true strength could only appear in moments of hardship. He held firm, forcing his legs to keep him standing straight.

This had been his first time getting whipped. Quite the message from King Doemus, sending the torturer first just to punish, without even asking any questions. Keryon hadn't thought the man a warmonger or a bloodthirsty animal, but his own experience with monarchs had never been great to begin with. Now, he couldn't let that go. No one could torture him and humiliate him and get away with it.

Light shone through the door, and he closed his eyes. Blood got in, making it even harder for him to see properly.

"I didn't want things to turn out this way." Solvi's brisk voice echoed in the cell. She hadn't tried to lower her voice and spoke without hesitation.

Keryon only scowled. No use wasting his energy.

She remained silent for a moment, long enough to let Keryon imagine the guilt she was feeling.

"I know you treated me well when I was a captive. You brought me food, water, and blankets whenever I needed. But you also promised me freedom and happiness, and I can't help but feel those were lies."

"They... didn't have to be."

Solvi swallowed before she continued. "I'm sorry you must go through this. You can believe me. It was the King's decision, not mine. I wanted you to know that."

He scoffed. She didn't want to dirty her conscience.

"Now you understand your little utopia is dead, don't you? It was always destined to," Solvi said. There was a hint of hesitation there, as though she wanted to be told otherwise. Maybe there was still hope for her. For all of them. "Things are back the way they always were."

Keryon slowly moved his neck to face her. Pain shot through him, as if a new lashing had just been delivered. He opened his mouth to speak, but there were few words he could muster. "One day, you will see it," was all he had the strength to say.

"Why are you still trying to persuade me? I follow the Highest One! He destroyed your little town. He wiped out your future. Don't you understand? Didn't you see that power? He is God Himself!"

"All.. his promises... Lies," he whispered. "Illusions."

"I won't let you talk about him like that!" Solvi said, and yet her voice said otherwise. Her words stumbled and wavered. As if she *wanted* Keryon to prove her wrong. As though she wanted to be saved.

"One day, I will show you," he croaked.

"Show me what?" Solvi raised her voice. "Why do you do this? Why do you still show kindness? They've whipped you until your legs crumbled and you still act as though we're friends. Why?"

Keryon smiled. "Not blood. But... you and I... are the same."

Solvi's eyebrows rose, but she shook her head. "You know nothing about me! I'm not like you. I have faith in the Highest One. And I'm bearing his child."

"Protect the child... from him," he whispered.

Solvi hesitated. "I'm leaving. Me coming here was a courtesy. My debt to you is paid, if I—"

"I don't care... about debt. For you... and the child... Stay away from him."

That should do it. That should stoke the simmering coal of doubt in her mind.

She would see it one day. She would understand. He would make sure of it.

"You are to be transferred out of here soon, to a more... permanent facility." Her words dripped with regret. "Have you heard of the Uzundar Quarry?"

The air was hot but there was no humidity at all. Gimlore's fingers swelled from the heat, and every time she swallowed, it was like rough wood sliding down her throat. Her skin was dry and blisters were forming as the shackles bit into her ankles and wrists. She had never seen such a scorching place all her life. There was not a single cloud in the blue sky, and without as much as a tree to use as shield from the sun, she would have no refuge.

It was her versus the sun, and the sun was winning.

Gimlore marched, along with Keryon, Tavanar, and a dozen others, escorted through a rocky patch of desolate land by a handful of captors who looked unfazed, as though the sun wasn't trying to murder everyone. She had imagined wearing short clothes would be appropriate in there, but with her skin already burning, she realised some form of clothing might be needed to keep her alive. She was glad they'd allowed her to keep a white robe of sorts, which was now, of course, already covered in dirt and dust. There was no mud in such a place. How could it be that there seemed to be no wind at all either, or even a breeze?

"I take it Solvi didn't appreciate your betrayal?" Keryon asked Tavanar, but he didn't reply. Didn't even acknowledge the question.

The bastard looked even worse than her, with eyes nearly shut, dark rings around his eyes, and head down facing the ground as he walked. He'd likely never faced that kind of punishment before. Gimlore no longer saw a trace of misguided innocence in him, or the bravado that he'd had when lunging into the Palace of Brilliance like he owned the place. Now he looked... broken and reminded her of Edmir, or how Nork and Nosema used to be before she found them.

They kept going like that for far too long with hardly any breaks. The waterskins were long gone, and Gimlore wanted to be anywhere else. The lashings had been the worst she had felt lately, but she had endured far worse in her youth. This? It was an even worse form of torture.

The others continued in line with their captors, who barked orders in a Sirestine accent that Gimlore hardly understood. The terrain was harsher than the weather. At every step, her bare feet hurt and were pricked by wicked little plants that seemed to find a way to drain the soil around those rocks. They walked for another hour or so, heading northwest, with their backs to the sea. If the Two Nations were known for their merchant ships and fishing towns, this was far from it. And yet, the path they walked looked like it had been carved into the dirt for centuries, already part of the landscape from all the prisoners who had stepped foot in it.

Finally, the soldier who led the convoy of captives yelled some words in Sirestine, and they stopped, forcing Gimlore to halt as well. They were at the edge of a cliff. Gimlore blinked and focused her eyes again.

No, not a cliff. There was the fucking quarry, a hundred strides below them. Hundreds of miserable people worked, backs bent forward, with tools in hand, and always under the close supervision of whip-wielding soldiers or guards who also carried swords in their scabbards.

Gimlore grimaced as she saw the misery in it all. The groaning from the prisoners blended with the sound of the steel tools hitting the stones. Flint and limestone, by the looks of it. By the depth of the quarry, humans must have been tearing at these stones for thousands of years, still going strong. Some poor bastards carried the boulders in carts while others pulled and pushed the little wagons away, to take the extracted product to the nearest stone masons.

The Uzundar quarry was large enough to host an entire city, but it was all in the open and barely had any shadow or place to rest. The prisoners below didn't seem to stop, and most looked more dead than alive, with their skin darkened by the sun, and their frail figures slimmed by the back-breaking work.

"The oldest quarry in the Known World," Keryon said.

Gimlore scowled as she glanced at her future. "It looks more like the underworld."

ELEVEN

THE ANCIENT ONES

REDNOW

Rednow didn't think himself a complainer, but that journey had been tiresome even for him. According to the maps, the distance wasn't the issue, as Vaerghulen shared a long border with Mosendel. The issue had been making their way through the mountains when the border had already been crossed. As harsh as the mountains were, he missed their cold, crispy air.

"Are we there yet?" Tinko asked.

Pinesy only turned his face and shook his head. "A little more."

Tinko sighed but they kept walking. It had taken Rednow long enough to recover from the mayhem of Alarkan's invasion. He had lost track of how many months it had been, but he still dreamt about it, and the poor child did as well. He glanced at Tinko through the corner of his eye. The kid had lost their sibling, and who in the world knew where their mother was?

Probably desperate to find them, if she's even alive. Tinko also looked slightly matured compared to when Rednow had been training them, but their evening practice was only half-serious now, as though Tinko no longer had the drive to become a smokesmith without Thata.

"When are you going to tell us why we're here?" Rednow asked. He meant to ask that of the Essence, but Pinesy was their apparent guide to wherever they were supposed to go, and he seemed to know as much as the deity did.

"Soon," he said.

Climbing the rocky slope wasn't hard for the pinehead. It was as though he had lived in them all his life. As used to the mountains as Rednow was, but he was not young anymore, and it still hurt every time he breathed.

After just another hour of climbing the southwestern edge of the Thousand Hills, Pinesy stopped and told them to set up camp, which meant no more than a small fire and a few blankets over their backs for extra warmth. Their dried meat and week-old bread was running low, so he hoped they would reach their destination soon enough. With the three of them sitting by the fire, Rednow stretched his hands. "I need to know, Pinesy. If the Essence isn't going to tell me, you must."

I'll explain.

Rednow nodded, waiting for the deity to say their piece.

I've explained to you how all these years ago, I've been fighting my brother. But I wasn't always alone. Before the humans there were the Ancient Ones.

Rednow frowned. He had always assumed the Ancient Ones were an older human civilisation, one that had built entire cities, ports, and ships, before being wiped out of existence.

They came to my aid. I lent them my powers: the herbs that grow in my soil, and its smoke. They fought alongside me for many years and we defeated my brother. I sealed him in the orb and those you call the Ancient Ones hid the artifact until... well, now. I had never had such devoted followers. They built their cities according to me, to... let me flow, prosper and thrive.

Then the humans came much later, when I was already ill and bound to that sword. And humans weren't worshippers. They didn't care about deities like me, so they destroyed some of the architecture built in my name, and the Ancient Ones continued to lose the gifts I'd bestowed upon them. With the Old One gone and no real enemy to fight against, humans started fighting each other, so the Ancient Ones did the only thing they had to do. They left.

"What does that have to do with us being here?"

Because you're going to ask for their help.

Rednow's eyes widened. The Ancient Ones were... alive? This had to be nothing but ridiculous nonsense. The Ancient Ones were said to be able to fly like birds, to possess the strength of marcrunchers, and the wisdom of immortal kings. But they were gone. They had abandoned humanity, hadn't they?

They abandoned humanity for the reason I mentioned, but they're our only hope of defeating the Old One, Rednow. We must harness their aid one way or another.

"But if they are alive, how has no one laid eyes on them? It's impossible for them to have stayed hidden for these many centuries."

Of course, but you've seen them. There is one standing in front of you at this very moment.

Rednow's eyes drifted from the fire to the figure opposite to him, Pinesy. The small pinehead's eyes gave nothing away, but Rednow's eyes widened as he understood, his mouth agape. He should have known. He should have guessed, given how much Pinesy seemed to know about the Essence when she lived only in Rednow's head. "Pineheads are... the Ancient Ones?" He could hardly believe it.

"We used to call each other the Builders once," Pinesy said. "Not Ancient Ones nor pineheads. Builders."

The silence that hung between them let Rednow consider all of this. Tinko looked at him, confused. The child was used to Rednow speaking to himself, but now Pinesy seemed to be involved in the conversation.

"Uncle?"

Rednow shushed Tinko and patted their head, turning back to Pinesy. "But... then you didn't abandon humanity. There are millions of you."

There are those who adapted to the new world, and those who clung to the old ways.

"Most of us adapted, so we live with humankind. We accept that the world is different," Pinesy said. "But there is a sect that thinks us heretics and accuses us of dirtying our kind, of lowering ourselves and abandoning the Essence."

The flames of the fire reflected in Pinesy's eyes, but Rednow thought he saw a flame burning deep in them too. "You don't think that's true, do you?"

Pinesy shook his head. "We've kept our word. We remain faithful to the Essence. I wouldn't be here if I wasn't. And we haven't fought. We've dedicated ourselves to helping others and helping our own. *They* were the ones who abandoned everyone and think themselves superior."

Rednow could hardly understand what Pinesy had seen, what he had lived. "And this sect of Builders is hiding here in the Thousand Hills, closed off from the rest of the world?"

Yes, Rednow. They're like children to me. I care about them, but they are stubborn. They don't want to work with humans, or with their long-lost cousins.

Rednow sighed and slumped. He had never been much of a diplomat. Rebma had always been his voice of reason. How he wished she was here. She had the silver tongue to weave everyone in her favour and could have probably made sworn enemies fall in love with each other.

"They won't listen to me, then. I'm not only a human. I'm one of the worst humans in the world according to anyone you ask. The Blood Collector. Children have nightmares just thinking about me."

Tinko scoffed. "No, they don't. The stories aren't true. You are not evil, just a little crazy."

Rednow smiled, affectionately elbowed the child, and faced Pinesy again.

"Either way, how am I supposed to convince them to help us against the Old One and Orberesis?"

They will have to help us. They'll be doomed too if they don't.

Rednow nodded. "Are you alright with this? I owe you for saving me and the child. I don't want to do anything that hurts you."

Pinesy looked at Rednow for a moment, as though he had found something surprising in his words. He retracted slightly and shrugged, shaking his head. "It must be done."

The next morning, the journey continued, and they walked for what seemed like days without leaving the same ridge. Rednow didn't dare ask how Pinesy knew where his cousins were, but he showed no hesitation and barely looked back. Tinko, on the other hand, looked bored to death. If it hadn't been for the occasional bloodsleuth, shadesgrowl, or marcruncher tracks they'd spotted along the way, Rednow would've probably had to carry them.

"How far are we?" Tinko asked again.

Pinesy always answered the same thing. "Almost there."

Along the way, and mostly to make Tinko feel normal again, Rednow continued to train the child in the arts of fighting as a smokesmith. Besides all the theory about what herbs to burn and how to incorporate the smoke into combat, the child had become quite proficient.

"Charge at me again." Rednow's voice was calm and collected. Up in those mountains, the air was thinner, so it was good for Tinko to get used to it. Lung capacity went a long way in being a smokesmith. Pinesy watched them, sitting cross-legged by the bonfire he had just set up.

Tinko rushed in, with a thread of smoke tracing their movements. The child was agile and in great shape. They moved with a precision that should be impossible in someone that young, their shaggy locks now dropping over their face. One dagger first, which Rednow dodged, and another, which he parried with ease.

"Use the smoke or you'll never be able to hit me. I've got fifty years of fighting experience, maybe more. You won't catch me off guard with a dagger or two."

The child gritted their teeth and charged again. Rednow smiled as he saw smoke coming from the pouch in Tinko's belt as the belleaf oil kept the herbs simmering slowly. Tinko became faster, each step a forward charge towards Rednow's left side, where his arm was missing.

Well thought.

But Rednow could still wield a sword more efficiently with an arm missing than most could with both, so that wasn't going to be a problem. Rednow extended his red blade to meet Tinko's dagger, but there was only smoke where the child had stood. Tinko's figure had been there, hadn't it? Rednow's eyes widened, and he turned just in time to parry Tinko's daggers, already less than a foot away from where the back of his neck had been.

Rednow could barely find the words. "Fuck me... When did you learn that?"

"Learn what?"

"*That*! You used something... An ability. You misdirected me. You goaded me into my left and appeared behind me as though you'd never been in front of me in the first place."

"I guess so." Tinko shrugged.

"That's an ability, child! So, you have one just like Thata did. But yours is obvious," Rednow said.

He sheathed his sword and pulled the child into a feigned chokehold. For the gods, he was happy for the child! In the middle of all the rot in the world, there could still be moments of joy. "Your ability is using the smoke as misdirection."

Tinko fought their way out of Rednow's hold but when they finally escaped, a smile was drawn in their lips. "I want to train more, Uncle!"

Rednow would do almost anything to keep that smile as wide as it was now.

For hours, they trained. The child's energy seemed to have no bounds, which forced Rednow to be much more active than he'd like. It was good for both, though. It helped Tinko move beyond their grief, but it also helped Rednow clear his head when everything else in the world seemed dreadful.

Pinesy shot him a glance that said it was best for them to leave it at that, so he halted the practice and told Tinko to extinguish the flames. "Are we going there now?"

Pinesy nodded. "We're outside their sacred refuge."

Rednow frowned. If they were right outside, why wait? He kept the question to himself, though. The pinehead must be stepping on many of his long-held beliefs just to do what needed to be done. He could have ignored the call and survived, but he had listened to the Essence and saved their lives. The least Rednow could do was respect it if he needed more time.

They packed their belongings and walked another hundred strides until Pinesy stopped in front of a very thin gap between two enormous boulders. There was nothing special about it; it was just big enough for an adult man to squeeze their way in.

"We have to get inside. I'll go first," Pinesy said, squeezing sideways through the gap.

Tinko followed him quickly enough. They were both smaller, so the gap posed no challenge, but Rednow was bigger. He tried squeezing through, but it took him several attempts. Why were they going to that cave in the first place? Pinesy had said they were close to the Builders' refuge, but somehow Rednow hadn't ever considered they may be living in a cavern.

He made his way through, rock scratching his back and chest as he moved in sideways. He continued like that for another thirty steps with much difficulty until he reached the end of what looked like the entryway to this hidden haven.

On the other side, it was as though they had been transported into another world. The rocks formed a large open-air pavilion of stone, with impossibly large statues carved meticulously over what Rednow could only imagine had been centuries.

Numerous long, wood bridges hung from side to side of the mountains, criss-crossing multiple times and at different heights, connecting the sides like a city suspended in the air. Under, at the bottom of the valley that separated the foot of the ridges, a small river flowed fast. There was no rock ceiling, as though the gods had conspired to create a closed, rocky fortress only they could access from the skies.

The rock walls were riddled with hundreds, perhaps thousands of little, rather deep alcoves, which Rednow realised were houses, chiselled away by hand over the years. Almost all of them had rope ladders leading up to the very top of the rocks, which stood about two hundred strides above Rednow's head.

"It's an entire civilisation, hidden in the middle of nowhere," he mumbled.

They are the Builders, after all. The Essence's voice was soft but he felt a burn every time it came back to him. If only he could mute it forever...

They walked slowly in a ridge much too narrow for Rednow's comfort. His feet almost reached the edge. The hidden city had been built beautifully and blended into the environment, but it was clear enough it hadn't been built with the taller humans in mind.

The sound of his struggles to keep up with Pinesy and Tinko on the ridge that led to the main rocky platform brought small heads peeking out of the alcoves.

"They spotted us," Rednow said. "I'm sorry."

"It must be done," Pinesy whispered, though Rednow wondered if that was for Rednow or himself.

It wasn't easy, but Rednow found his way to the platform and, once he stood on it, he realised just how far above the surface level he was. It must have been about three hundred strides above the river that flowed beneath. Then Pinesy stopped there, overlooking his old cousins.

"What now?" Rednow whispered.

"We wait."

Soon enough, a group of Builders made their way out of the alcoves, though it took them longer than Rednow would have imagined. And none of them came armed. They looked utterly confused as to what was happening. They had every right to be, especially if they hadn't seen humans in hundreds of years. The group stopped about twenty strides away from Rednow. They were pineheads, no different from the ones he was used to seeing. There was nothing special about their appearance. Some had lighter skin, others darker, but they were all about the same height, with curly hair in heads shaped like a pinecone, and eerie, unsettling eyes.

"What is the meaning of this? Who are you and how did you find this place?"

"The Essence brought us," Pinesy said.

Murmurs answered. Some of them nodded, others shrugged and shook their heads.

"Impossible," said the Builder who had spoken before. He had blonde hair and wore a neat white robe with golden highlights and trimmings, making him stand out against all the others who wore more grey, brown, and other earthlier colours. "You abandoned the Essence. Why would she call to you?"

"We didn't abandon anyone." Pinesy's face went serious, and his eyes were fixed on the blonde-haired Builder. "But you can ask her yourself."

A gust of wind swept them and whistled as it hit the stone.

"So dramatic," Rednow muttered.

Children, I recognise your faith. I feel your devotion.

Even though the words of the Essence weren't spoken aloud, he could tell by their face they had heard them. They exchanged glances, their eyes widening. Slowly, they all kneeled, though the man in white remained sceptical. He took his time and knelt on only one knee. "You brought humans to our temple," he said. It wasn't a complaint, just something he didn't seem to expect.

You must all rise again, Builders. The Old One is back.

The white-robed Builder nodded, and his peers mimicked him. "I've felt it."

The world needs you.

To that, there was no answer from the one who seemed to be their leader. He looked at Pinesy first, then at Tinko, and then at Rednow. The pinehead's gaze lingered on him, and his contempt couldn't be more obvious, but Rednow did not look away.

"They're smokesmiths." the Builder said. "I can smell it."

"What of it?" Rednow couldn't help himself. He had always hated monarchs and people who thought themselves above the rest. As far as he was concerned, this one wasn't different from the others.

"You're *fouling* our temple," the Builder croaked.

Rednow sighed. "A thousand apologies for that. It's who we are. Smell and all."

The Builder moved towards Rednow. As he did, his feet left the ground and he started floating until he was ten feet above ground.

"A thousand apologies, you say?" His voice boomed, echoing in the rocks. "A thousand apologies aren't enough to make us forget what humans did to us. To the world! Look at us, we are all that's left!"

Rednow's eyes were wide and his mouth agape. Never in his life did he think this would be possible. So, it was true! The Ancient Ones could fly.

Please, Arkan. I need you. I need you, more than ever.

The Builder flew back to the ground and landed with the grace of a divine being. "You may stay for one night. We will hear you because the Essence is asking, but I make no promises."

Something told Rednow he had a long night ahead.

TWELVE
PROTECTED HAVEN

ORBERESIS - REDNOW

Orberesis settled, but he could feel the Old One moving inside his mind now. He picked up on the restlessness, the desire to break out and sow chaos. He wished he could have better accommodations in Heleronde, more than a handful of chairs and a poor excuse of a bed, but the Old One didn't care about comfort. He was only driven by his pride and his goals.

We need to find her, Doi. Now, or she will grow stronger.

"Find who?"

My sister.

Orberesis nodded. "She imprisoned you in the orb, didn't she? She sounds powerful."

The Old One stirred in rage, and Orberesis' vision blurred, as something tore at him from the inside, twisting his mind. It was pain, but what was Orberesis if not pain made flesh?

You're lucky I need you, the Old One said, releasing him from his grip.

Orberesis gasped, but his lips turned into a smirk. "And you're lucky I don't kill you by killing myself. You need me as much as I need you, parasite."

The Old One grumbled but seemed to accept that.

"Now, tell me about your sister."

She used to rule the earth. She created things and I took them away. That was always how it worked. Last time I faced her, she won. But not this time. With you as my vessel, we can accomplish much! But we must get rid of her. The sooner we do it, the better.

Orberesis walked to the broken window of the pathetic wood shack he was in—which looked like a tavern of sorts—and took notice of all the Lantern Horns beneath. He still hadn't got used to them. They were vicious and had already started to build their nests and homes over the rubble. Every day that passed, there seemed to be more of them.

"And where is your sister?"

I can take you there. Take us there. And we can bring our Lantern Horn friends for company. Temporal Exploration is still mine. She hasn't stolen that from me.

"You said you'd teach me," Orberesis said, irritation abound. There were moments of great power when he *was* like a god, but there were also moments, like now, when he felt more human and powerless than ever. What had he accomplished for himself besides getting rid of his illness? He was feared, but not respected or adored. Revenge was a sweetness that only lasted until his hunger appeared again. He needed more power. If he was to be a god, he needed to know *how* to be one.

The Old One scoffed. *You still see the world as a physical reality. You're not aware that even that has been tampered with.*

Orberesis frowned. "What do you mean *tampered with*?"

Do you remember the void beyond? That empty space just over the horizon? Watch it. It's like a waterfall at the very end that throws sailors and vessels into the underworld. That's where I made my home. There's so much beyond this plane.

Orberesis gritted his teeth. "I said no more fucking riddles."

As you wish.

The air around Orberesis wavered. He thought he would lose his balance but found himself floating again. His vision blurred and the reality of that room—of that world, of that plane—faded into a never-ending darkness that extended to the infinite. The space around him was like a big dark sea. He could only see mysterious dark materials and starlight hanging above him. Orberesis moved in slow and calm motions, as though still in his mother's womb, as glittering stars faded into the nothingness, into the everything.

"Where am I going?" he asked, though it hardly mattered, as long as he found himself in that blissful state.

Try to hold on to that feeling. Don't let go. Our lives change, it's only natural, but the void stays the same, doesn't it? The serenity is... addictive.

Orberesis did what he could to hold on to the feeling of being utterly relaxed and worriless. But holding on to that feeling forced him to be thoughtful, to think about holding on to it. A slight itchiness appeared, but he didn't know where to scratch. His jaw locked and he gritted his teeth.

Hold on to it, Doi.

He did, but the pressure mounted as though he was being torn, his limbs separated from his body. At first, he flexed his muscles, bearing the load of whatever that force was, no longer feeling that addictive silky smoothness of floating in the void. Now his heart pounded against his ribs.

He screamed, but there was only silence in the void. He was tired—so tired—and needed to rest, to let go of the pleasurable moment that had turned into nothing but pain.

He released himself and wondered if the universe was going to end in a cascading explosion. His mind rushed back into itself, light flashing before his eyes, too fast for him to see. He was starting to fade, a heavy dizziness taking hold of his body; the Old One controlled his mind.

Then it stopped.

Instead of being in a torn wood shack of sorts, he was somewhere else: outdoors, in a mountain range, somewhere.

Temporal Exploration isn't easy. You see that now, don't you? You are beginning to learn the commitment needed to transcend the boundaries of reality. This reality, at least. And as you approach these boundaries and probe them—poke them—you feel it, don't you? What it's like to have a foot in one world and a hand in another?

Orberesis was still recovering, and his vision was still blurred. He could see the environment, but still couldn't walk properly. He could hardly think straight. "What... have you done to me?"

Me? You did it to yourself, Doi. But I'm glad you did.

Orberesis swallowed, unable to even talk back. The Old One had used Orberesis' bodily strength to get him wherever he wanted to be. The bastard had nearly drained him out. He had manipulated him.

The parasite chuckled in Orberesis' mind. *Come on. You and I are one. We need to act as one. I had to bring you here, for both our sakes.*

Orberesis steadied himself, leaned against a cold boulder, and closed his eyes. It was disorienting but, somehow, he had travelled a great distance by using his... mind? That should count as a divine power, shouldn't it? Even if at a steep cost.

The longer you can hold on, the more of them we can help.

"Th-them?" The words hurt.

Orberesis squinted and saw them in the distance: hundreds of Lantern Horns made their way up the mountain, heading to where he stood, treading ground as though it was nothing.

·····•·••····

The night had been spent in what could only be classified as silence. Rednow's initial impression of the Builders was that they were a talkative bunch, but that had turned out to be a complete lie. They had remained silent as though only silence and peace were appropriate answers to a plea for help.

He glanced at Arkan, who claimed not to be the Builders' leader but acted like he was. "Will you hear me just this once?"

There was not as much as a hint of understanding from the fellow, which made Rednow's blood boil. He wondered if that was precisely what the Builders were trying to prove—that humans were prone to harsh emotions and couldn't be trusted.

"I wouldn't be here if I had any alternatives," he insisted, but the man didn't move from his meditative stance. Rednow had learned that the Builders spent their days meditating, engaged in prayers and in readings of what they called the Essential Flow.

Wait a second...

Rednow went back to the bag he always brought with him—Rebma's bag. He opened it and pulled out parts of Mother's Memories. *Let's see what they have to say.*

Rednow was a rather poor reader, studying never having been his forte, but he did his best to read out loud parts from what Rebma had called *scripture*. It was everything the Essence had told her about the past and even things of the present. He saw Arkan's eyes slowly widening, realising he wasn't jesting or pretending.

"How could you know all this?" Arkan asked.

Rednow smirked as he closed the bag but took time to reply. Let him sweat for it. "I learned this from the Essence herself."

"So, you're not just the vessel? You know the commandments and the doctrines too."

Rednow couldn't say he did, but he nodded anyway, as that seemed to make his host more agreeable. All he wanted was a chance to be heard, even if he had no clue what exactly the Builders, who hadn't fought in centuries, could stand to offer.

Arkan faced the floor in front of him, frowning. "I'll hear you, then. Tell me your story, smokesmith."

Rednow could hardly contain the smile. It was fun, this diplomacy thing. Of course, in this case it was fun because the other party was a group of peaceful, zealot hermits. He drew a heavy breath.

My story…

He pointed at the stump where his left arm had been split clean by the Essence. "This is the price I paid for my life. The Essence kept me alive to fight the Old One."

Arkan remained silent, so Rednow continued. He grabbed the hilt of the sword and slowly pulled the blade halfway out of the scabbard. "I have had this sword since I was a young boy. Can you feel it?"

Arkan nodded. "The Essence."

"Yes. For better or worse, she chose me. And I need help. If we allow the Old One to rise again, the world is doomed, humans and Builders alike. I'm not proud of a lot of what I've done, and I'm sure others will feel the same way, but it's the truth."

The Builder's eyes pierced him, as though he was trying to ascertain the worthiness of Rednow's soul. "And how would we help? Fighting is against our doctrine."

"You used to. I can see you still train your youth."

"The training is part of our prayer."

"But it used to be exactly for this, didn't it? You and your people fought on the Essence's behalf, and now she needs you again. I know you are deeply connected to her, more than the others are."

"That's because we seek the connection to her in everything we do. It's our purpose. It's the very reason we exist. And to abandon her in such a way…" Arkan seemed to be in pain, as though he didn't understand how the humans could have abandoned the Essence. "When we built the ancient cities, we did it in a way that preserved the Essential Connection. Long rows of trees accompanying buildings. Canals providing water to every city corner. Gardens at an arm's length. Flowers in every window, and vines climbing up the brick walls to breathe life into the world and into humanity itself. But you cared little for it. You drained the canals and cut down the trees for firewood. You built prisons where temples once stood. Palaces that hosted hundreds now belong to greedy men. How can this be?"

Rednow sighed and shrugged. He hadn't been alive that long ago, but he had seen it depicted in paintings, tapestries, and palace ceilings ironically now owned by the monarchs who ruled the world with an iron fist.

"Humankind is imperfect. It has many flaws, Arkan. I know it. And it has committed grave sins." He looked at Tinko, who practiced sword forms in a corner. "But we mustn't let the children pay for their parents' mistakes. We mustn't let the powerless pay for the mistakes of the powerful."

"Ah, but that's what humans do. That's what humanity is all about, Rednow."

It was hard to argue with that. He swallowed and paused to think for a moment. What else could he offer?

"It doesn't have to be. We can count on your guidance and your enlightenment. You can bring back the old ways and teach it to the humans who never had the chance to learn them. I've led men and women all my life, and I know they rally behind you when there is something to fight for, something to believe in. I'm asking for that to be you. Together, we can change things."

Rednow only half knew what he was saying. He had always considered himself faithless, and he deeply despised the Essence, the only deity he knew. He hadn't quite forgiven her for impersonating his sister and chopping his arm off. But, for better or worse, he definitely needed the Builders if he was going to help anyone. "What if I want to fly like you? Can you teach me?"

Arkan scoffed. "Teach you? Before flying, one must undergo the Internal Flight."

Rednow frowned. "Alright. Can you teach me that?"

"It cannot be taught. It's something that cannot be explained with words."

Rednow didn't understand and Arkan must have seen that, since he started gesturing, as though it helped. "It's a thought pattern... almost half a dream. It's untranslatable. You'll know it if you are ever lucky enough to experience it."

Rednow nodded, still waiting in silence for a longer reply about his plea for help.

Arkan sighed. "I'll consult the rest of the sect, and I'll let you know. We're all concerned about the Old One's return, though I must warn you I'm not the leader, so even if I possess an inclination to fight, many of my cousins might not."

Rednow stood. "I am not here to force anyone into anything."

By the time he left the Builder's company, he felt a strange empathy for Arkan. He wasn't the kind of man Rednow had expected. He had presumed Arkan to be arrogant and overzealous, but the man was completely devoted to his people, and that level of devotion sometimes required a firmness of mind that appeared to be stubbornness from the outside. Rednow had been in those shoes as the leader of the Leeth and it had been no easy feat.

When he settled in front of Tinko and watched the child train with their dagger, viciously cutting the air, he realised he would probably have had the same reaction as Arkan if the roles were reversed. He almost saw the ghost of Thata mirroring Tinko's movements in the dance of battle. Rednow had lost one of the children, and he wasn't going to lose the other.

"Your form is sloppy." That was only half true, but the child was antsy, so Rednow wanted to encourage a calm mind. "Take a deep breath and run through it again."

Tinko paused, then nodded. Everything he had just learned over the last few months loomed over him. He'd had no idea the Builders existed. He hadn't known pineheads were the Ancient Ones, or even that the Essence was a real deity, worshipped by living people.

Without warning, his legs trembled as the earth shook, forcing him to his feet.

HE'S BACK! HE'S HERE!

"No, this can't be," he whispered to himself, his eyes immediately darting to Tinko. He unsheathed his sword. "Tinko, come here!"

"Uncle..." Tinko's eyebrows rose and Rednow could almost feel the child's tears coming out. There was still too much trauma. Last time the earth had shaken like that, Tinko had lost Thata.

He caught Pinesy's knowing eyes and then those of Arkan, who scrambled to coordinate his people. The man's eyes fell on Rednow, if just for a second, before rushing to find others. *You did this*, Arkan's eyes said. *You brought war to my people.*

"You must take shelter, Pinesy," Rednow said, his gaze shifting back to the child. "The Old One is here."

Pinesy shook his head and stood his ground whilst another thunderous shake almost sent them back onto the ground. "No. This time, I will fight."

When the first shadowling broke through the little crack that led to the Builder's sacred haven, Rednow raced towards it, his fear of falling down the ridge all but gone in the moment. His belleaf oil quickly burned through the herbs in his satchel and it didn't take long for a thread of smoke to surround him.

With the red sword in hand, Rednow ran like the monster he was. And the smoke followed.

Thirteen

Hope

Gimlore

The sun had barely risen, but the men with the whips were already out, shouting at everyone in sight, keeping them in order, preparing them for a new day. Gimlore could hardly stand. Her bare feet had blisters and layers of cuts from the rocky ground. Her arms ached as though she'd been asked to carry logs all day. Worst of all was her back. She kept the lashing scars covered under a ragged shirt, but when she had spent all day standing, moving, and hauling heavy rocks into wood carts, the pain shot in all directions—down into her buttocks and thighs, but also up into her shoulder blades, shoulders, and neck.

Worse than that was the void in her soul, which was still growing in the absence of her child, as was the guilt of having let such foul destruction even take place.

And today she had to do it all over again.

She groaned. With her head still in the dirty sack she had been using as a pillow, she embraced herself, tucking her knees in before the foremen came for her. She shivered. How could a place that was so bloody hot during the day get so chilly in the night?

Around her, the other workers—or rather, prisoners—started getting up, moans and complaints aplenty, but they were already into motion, slowly heading to the main working area of the quarry yet again. They were completely resigned as they marched to the sound of the whip overhead, from the slightly bushy hill where they were allowed a meal at the end of every day to the pit of despair that was the Uzunar Quarry.

Keryon made his way up as well. "Let's go."

Gimlore just couldn't make herself get up. Why would she? She'd lost one child, maybe even another. Her wealth was gone, all her possessions were destroyed, and the land that was rightfully hers was occupied by fiends from the underworld. All of her loved ones were either dead or damn near it. Every skirmish and every battle she had fought had been in vain. And now she reckoned she was in the worst possible place people could be in. A place that didn't discriminate between men and women, adults and children, and boys and girls.

As though they were trying to prove her point, a pair of older women marched past with a young girl almost glued to them, desolate eyes covered in dark rings. She gave Gimlore a glimpse of her attention before quickly marching on.

"Come on. We *have* to go." Keryon was impatient, but that was to be expected when they all knew what would happen if the foreman had to be called into action. "What are you doing? Come on!"

"You go ahead. I'll be out in a second."

He bent down and grabbed her by the arms. "I'm sorry for doing this, but it's better if it's me doing it and not them." He picked her up and threw her over his shoulder.

Gimlore hadn't the strength to resist. She let Keryon carry her on, and her eyes welled. She had been stripped of everything that made her what and who she was. If it wasn't for Keryon, she would be getting dragged to the lashing pole right about now.

One of the foremen scoffed as he looked at her. Once she was in the quarry, they would make sure she worked.

And she did.

With hammer and chisel in hand, she got to know flint and limestone like she had hardly ever known anything. She dropped the hammer once and the foreman almost stepped in to lash her back, so she hurried her pace. Another time, the hammer had failed to hit the chisel and hit her left index finger instead, quickly turning into a swollen red mess—not that the foremen cared. They were quick to use the whip. Any mistake or slip up, and the whip would come flying, inevitably followed by a snap and a scream.

I've lasted this long. I can survive this, too.

Survival meant doing what she could to stay alive—to avoid the whip. Even if her entire body hurt, and her mind was sluggish, she had to survive by avoiding the whip.

Over the course of days, or perhaps weeks, she embraced the white dust from the chiselled rocks covering her hands and figured out the optimal rhythm for the hammer to hit the chisel.

Not too slow, or the foremen would notice, and she wouldn't survive the whip. Not too fast, or she would wear herself out too much, and the whip would come again. Little by little, that pace became part of her as though she was being chiseled as well.

The days went by in a blur.

Sometimes her mind would play tricks on her. She would look at someone's face and see Edmir or Foloi. At night, just before she fell asleep, she would see Thata and Tinko after she closed her eyes. Blood all over them. Blood all over everyone.

Keryon also struggled despite his ability to mask it and tolerate the pain. Tavanar... he had had his share of lashings. She learned that the more lashings one got, the slower their recovery would be, which would only earn them yet more lashings until they were too weak to work and ended up getting disposed of.

If things were the way they used to be, she would probably take care of Tavanar, but now she couldn't afford to put others before her. Because of the whip. The damn whip and her fear of it.

She couldn't take it anymore.

As soon as Keryon fell asleep, she got up and walked through the tiny, improvised camp, illuminated only by the moonlight. It was cold, but not cold enough to make her shiver yet. The rest of the prisoners were fast asleep. A handful of them snored as she sneaked past.

The guard responsible for watching this batch of prisoners was looking the other way, marching back and forth. If she was stealthy enough, he wouldn't see or hear her move. Heading to the tent where the other guards slept, she slowly and carefully sneaked in. Her hands drifted to the ceramic bowl where they kept the potato stew that they served the prisoners.

Fuckers. There's still so much left over and we're all hungering.

She pulled a spoon from her belt and ate a spoonful of the porridge-like stew. Another. And another. And another. That would probably be enough to satiate her, and they wouldn't notice it.

Once again, she exited the tent and made her way back to the little encampment. Every time the guard looked towards her general direction, she lay flat on the dirt, aided by the darkness and the hard bush that was scattered all around. As soon as he walked the other way, she snuck back into the camp.

"Where were you?" Keryon whispered as quietly as she'd ever hear him. There was urgency in him. Concern, even.

"Went to get some food. I was hungry."

"You know it's too dangerous. You can't do that."

"Well, I just did. And I've done it multiple times already."

Keryon swallowed. "I know this is hard. It really is. But we need to be patient and wait for the right moment."

"*Patient?*" Gimlore's question was harsh, her eyes narrowed. "When the fuck will the right moment be?"

"If I knew that, I would tell you, wouldn't I?"

"I'm only doing what I can to survive. If I eat more, I can wake more rested, I get less tired from those fucking hammers, and I can actually get my brain to function, to think of a way to get us out of here."

Keryon sighed. "We don't need that. We wouldn't get far during the night if we escaped. This is the middle of nowhere.

There are no trees to hide or rocks big enough to take cover behind. They would see us fleeing. We wouldn't last an hour."

"Then I'll use the hammer and cave their skulls in. Or something like that. Now let me sleep or we will be poorly tomorrow."

Keryon was fuming. There was much more he'd still wanted to say, surely, but she always seemed to have the upper hand whenever they argued. *That's something I'm good at, at least.*

The evenings after a day's work were the only solace she had, but they were short, and it wasn't like she got along with any of the people there anyway. She reckoned a lot of them *deserved* to be in there, though the same could perhaps be said about her, as she had stolen plenty and killed more men and women than she could count. That hadn't been why they'd brought her there, though.

A big group of prisoners gathered around the pot. The men keeping guard would pour a scoop of the same old potato stew every day and leave them alone, though one of them would always keep guard.

"...And then I slammed the hand into his head, and he fell overboard," a wiry fellow that went by the name of Tooth said.

The nickname was appropriate as he only had one tooth left in his mouth. The others laughed at the man's stories and misadventures. Even Keryon grinned, his hands hitting his knee with joy.

Gimlore couldn't laugh. Every time they gathered for the meal, she'd sit with them, but she never smiled, as though that would be betraying the memories of the fallen. She'd lost not only people who meant everything to her, but the very place she had founded and everything she'd worked for. How could she laugh? She kept to herself instead. Survival against the whip.

All that time alone with herself made her realise she was desperate for a sliver of control. She couldn't stay content with an unknown future in the hands of people even crueller than her or laugh just to pass the time.

I've always been obsessed with power and control, and always end up with nothing. Maybe they're right. Maybe choosing to submit to this new life is the only way forward.

Outside the quarry, she could seek power and control through money. It was the only thing everyone respected and agreed on, Madame Mazi had taught her. But in there, she was hopeless, and surviving was hard enough. Her instinct was to assert her dominance and show she was better than the laughing bastards. She would steal their food and eat it, but she had no army to back her, not even enforcers. And Keryon, he was too naïve. Too full of good intentions and illusions that people could change. He had insisted on keeping Solvi with them when she should have been killed. And because of that, they were in this predicament.

"Why do you never speak? Never laugh?" he asked her one evening. "Not even with me."

It was hard for her to explain why she hated everyone. The prisoners hadn't locked her up or whipped her in the back, but laughing and pretending they weren't half-dead was like disrespecting her pain.

"I know you're suffering," he insisted.

"Then let me."

"You don't have to," he said. "I too struggle with the shackles I grew up with. This is bringing back all sorts of dreaded memories, believe me. But choosing to embrace the pain isn't the answer."

"Then why do you side with them? Over me?"

Keryon looked at her for a moment and Gimlore's eyes welled. His face was all she could see in the silent darkness. Tears poured out. She seemed to do a lot of that these days, all shame gone. After cleaning them up properly, she seemed to breathe better. Her body was no longer so tense.

"I'm not siding with anyone, much less against you. I'm just unwilling to part with what makes me who I am. They can punish my body all they want, but they'll never break my mind. If I change who I am because of them, then they will have won. I can't let go of myself; do you understand? I can't let go of who I was before we landed here. They want to kill me, but I am not dead inside. And neither are you."

Sometimes, she wished she was. She took a deep breath and continued to wipe the damn tears that didn't stop coming. Guilt, and shame, and fear took over her again. Keryon was right.

Fuck.

"I thought I'd always be alone, abandoned by everyone," she whispered. His face was close to hers. And what a handsome face it was. The only solace to be found in that underworld. "I thought... I had to relinquish all concepts of right and wrong. In fact, I don't think I ever learned the difference between them, truth be told. And then you showed up and made me question everything I believed in. Even now, you still do. I always felt guilty around you, like I could never deal with people that aren't as... *tainted* as me. I still do. With tainted people, everything is easier, I know how to treat them. But with people like you, I haven't got a clue."

"Gimlore, I don't—"

"Shh. Don't say anything. I think this is the first time I've been honest with myself in a long time. I want to remember it."

They stayed there for a while longer. Their bodies didn't touch, but it was as though they were one. Her tears dried up and she wiped her eyes again, unsure if she would regret what she had just told him.

"I was just going to say you're not as tainted or corrupt as you think. You're not beyond repair. I know that for a fact, and I will prove it. I will make it so obvious you will see it for yourself."

Promises had always been cheap. But she was eager to find out.

The next few days were more of the same. Gimlore and the others chiselled limestone and flint, hauled the rocks in carts to be delivered to the stonemasons, and then rested with some more potato stew.

Not even a fucking bonfire.

Her contempt for her captors had only grown during her time in the quarry. Not too far from her, Keryon talked with a few of the men and women with whom he had recently become friends. They were agreeable enough and didn't make waves. They looked at her respectfully, though Gimlore wondered if that was just because of Keryon. She wished she was like that, like him, able to act like a normal person, to sit in the twilight when the world was on fire. Any hopes and dreams she may have would be terrifying as she would have more to lose yet again.

She got up and walked slowly outside the camp and glanced down the ridge. The sun was setting, and the twilight of oranges and purples left her nostalgic. One quick step forward and it would all be over. She had already failed Edmir, Foloi, and Thata. She had all but abandoned Tinko, Nork, and Nosema as well. Even Rednow and Pinesy. Her loss was so profound she could hardly breathe anymore. It was as though the entire world was crumbling, like the dark of night was growing, approaching and being sucked deep into her chest.

One step...

"What are you doing?" a voice broke through her thoughts.

Gimlore turned around to face a small girl, no older than nine or ten years. She took two steps back and searched for whomever usually took care of this girl. "I'm just appreciating the sunset. What do you care?"

"You were thinking about killing yourself, weren't you?"

Gimlore's brow rose. How could a child so young already know about these things? Growing up in a prison camp did that, she supposed. "What I was thinking is none of your business. Tell me, what is a young girl doing in a place like this?"

"Working."

Insolent little shit.

"I meant *why* you're here." Her voice was harsh. "Were you caught doing bad things?"

The girl shrugged. "My ma killed some people. And my da got angry, so he beat my ma. But my da had killed more people than my ma. He had no business beating her. So I killed him."

Gimlore took a better look at the girl, and even though they looked nothing alike, she thought that story wasn't too different from what had happened with her growing up. Except Gimlore had found Madame Mazi to mentor her while this girl had only had a bunch of hopeless degenerates to idolise. Her gaze jumped from the child to Keryon, and then back to her. "Quite the adventurer, aren't you? What's your name?"

"Hope," the girl said. In her thick Sirestine accent, it sounded more like Rope. "And you?"

"I'm Gimlore."

"You were looking at that feller over there. Is he your husband?"

Gimlore sighed. "It's not like that. And which one is your ma?"

Hope shook her head. "Died last year. Now the other older women always give me a bit of their stew."

"You do look quite skinny."

"Can I sit out with you?"

Gimlore swallowed. "Nah. It's best for you if you stay clear."

"Why?"

"I'm not good company these days. And I'm no example to young girls like you."

"I'm not looking for examples. But I saw you sneak in at night to get more stew. I want some of that too."

Gimlore took one step closer towards Hope and kneeled in front of the child. "Did you tell anyone?"

Hope shook her head. No emotions showing. "No. I won't tell if you bring me next time."

This little shit. I get all the risk with no reward. She's good...

Gimlore smiled. She reminded her of her own children. Except her own knew well not to mess with her. "I'll see what I can do. But be careful, child. Like I said before, I have my reasons to be here, and I don't think I'm an example for you. I'm capable of terrible things."

Hope narrowed her eyes. "Nah. You wouldn't hurt me."

"I might if you don't shut your mouth."

Hope laughed and so did Gimlore. "I like you," the child said.

Those three words left Gimlore stuttering. She couldn't muster anything to reply. And the little shit had laughed!

PRISON OF FLESH

REDNOW

Rednow slashed the throat of a shadowling, but more were on their way to face him. A smelly, orange liquid poured out of them, but Rednow had his smoke to shield him. He inhaled slightly more of the fumes and felt his body surging, making him tower above them all. The Essence wanted him badly. Needed him. So, she had to look after him, even if that cost him another arm.

FIGHT! She urged him.

The earth shaking wasn't enough to destroy the mountains that surrounded the Builders' haven, entirely carved in the rocks. The Old One would have to tear out the mountains from their foundation before it was all destroyed.

Rednow smirked at that, as three more shadowlings made their way through the gap in between the rocks. In that moment he understood why the Builders had chosen that specific place to build their refuge.

Rednow stabbed two of them, chopping off the head of one and forcing the others back. "Good. They're retreating."

"No, they're not. Look up!" Pinesy pointed at the sky, at the very top of the mountain walls. A few shadowlings had climbed there from the outside and were now making their way down.

Shit.

Dozens of them now, maybe hundreds.

Rednow glanced around, but the Builders were hidden in their coves. They had vowed never to fight many years ago, but this was for their deity, so he could only believe they would stay true to their faith and put their training to use. He had to trust Arkan to protect his people, or their entire city would be wiped out and the Essence would never be able to stop the Old One.

"What should I do?" Pinesy asked as he used a short sword to stab a creature more than twice his size. "We can't keep holding them off. They're almost down here."

Without the Builders, the best Rednow and Pinesy could do was contain the small entrance and prevent the shadowlings from breaching or jumping into the river below in the hope it would deep enough to carry them back to safety.

"I'll fight too, Uncle." Tinko's words came with the confidence of someone who had seen too much. Not even Tellwoon or Merey had that intensity when they were that age.

Rednow couldn't erase the memory of Thata's dead body in the swamp, which they had to abandon. He couldn't put the child at risk again, but the growth had come so naturally...

"Fine." Rednow cursed himself for saying that word the moment it left his mouth, but going back was hardly an option.

"Pinesy, if you can hold it in here, Tinko and I can try to deal with the ones coming from above."

"Aye," Pinesy nodded, and his focus became the invaders. Their sharp teeth and talons crept up, trying to sneak into the village through the tiny crack between the rocks.

Rednow ran and took another whiff of smoke from his burned Ominous Kas herbs. He held it in longer this time. Dangerously longer. He had no idea how he would survive another battle as a smokesmith, but he would. Not for the Essence—for Tinko.

His legs and feet grew to three times their normal size. His thighs thickened and so did his torso. His lungs expanded, and he took in even more smoke. Spikes grew out of his arm and legs, and his fingers became weapons with claws. His entire skin turned purple, a sign of the strain it would put his body in for days after this if he survived.

"Let's get them!" he bellowed, with a voice that was barely his own, but one he recognised regardless. The monster within him. The Blood Collector.

Tinko nodded, smoke shrouding them. Each stride a quick one. "I'll be careful, Uncle. I promise."

They jumped straight at the area where the first few shadowlings had landed, next to one of the wooden bridges. Rednow picked up one of them by the throat and threw it down to the creek below. Without waiting to see if the shadowling had crashed into the rocks, he lunged at the others and tore at them with his claws, ripping pieces of their skin as though he was ripping weeds from the soil at his home in Heleronde.

A home he no longer had because of them.

He was the embodiment of rage, and even the shadowlings hesitated to come at him now that he was twice their size. They thought Tinko would be an easier opponent, but the child had been practicing misdirection and moved far too quick for them to catch. Like a shadow, Tinko moved through the monsters methodically, their daggers wasting no movement, landing just deep enough to cause fatal wounds.

Five of them tore at Rednow, biting into his flesh, claws clinging to his skin. He squealed in pain. Even with a skin now tougher than leather, it would still be far too hard for him to survive those fangs.

He looked back, hoping for assistance. Somehow, he had almost expected to see Merey and her troops at his back, with Tellwoon fighting by her side. But none of them were there. He had given up the Leeth and now had to fight this on his own. Pinesy too, struggled to contain the shadowlings. Some of them went past him, and others pushed him back so that more could enter the haven.

What do I do now? Another shadowling clung on to him. *I can't call for a retreat. There is nowhere to retreat to and no one to have my back.*

"ARKAN!" he bellowed.

A group of Builders left one of the rock-carved alcoves. With Arkan ahead, about six of them carried long spears three times their height. They wore studded armour, inlaid with gold and brown trimmings over green underclothes.

They jumped off the platform.

Rednow's mouth gaped. Arkan must be out of his mind.

But instead of falling to the river, they soared like giant, wingless eagles. Four of them flew in formation, towards the frontline of the battle where Rednow and Tinko fought the beasts, while two others went on to help Pinesy.

The flying Builders dove in without landing. Rednow could hardly believe his eyes. Like birds of prey using their claws, they stabbed the shadowlings with their long spears, and the odds definitely flipped in Rednow's favour again. He thrashed, slashed, and tore at the enemy with fury.

Let them come.

Rednow and the Builders would slaughter the bastards.

As though to steal any hope he may have had, Rednow's lungs started to flare. Breathing became twice as hard, but he still fought. He twisted the neck of another shadowling and slowly started finding them a lot less demonic than he had originally thought, even if they were beasts of the underworld.

Rednow couldn't say much. What was he, if not a different kind of monster?

As though they had sensed the odds of the battle turning, the monsters kept coming in droves. Dozens of them poured from the other side of the walls, keeping Rednow's claws busy with tears and slashes.

Perhaps the only way to end this is to go outside and stop them from coming in.

But how would he do that? He was on his last legs. On his last lungs. He wasn't even supposed to be alive.

Arkan and the flying Builders continued to handle the shadowlings well enough, but the creatures quickly realised they could wait for the downward stabbing motion of the spears to grab them and yank them down, forcing the Builders to crash or let go of the weapon.

Two Builders fell this way almost at the same time. Their bodies were left behind in the carnage as Rednow continued to wreak havoc in the enemy lines. Arkan howled in pain for his fallen cousins, and it hit Rednow right in his heart. He could nearly feel that pain himself.

What are they trying to accomplish?

They came after me, the Essence muttered. *That means they came after you. But they don't know yet that you're my avatar.*

Rednow roared and pushed forward again, flailing his arms.

There was no point speaking to them or taunting them. He was already the bane of their existence, the last being they'd see before they returned to the underworld.

Through the corner of his eye, he noticed Tinko holding their own. Beads of sweat lined their forehead amid heavy breaths. They were still a child after all, as bright as they were in the end.

"Fall back," Rednow told the child. "Take some rest now that the Builders are here."

"No, Uncle," they said between gritted teeth. "I can keep going."

How could the child keep going like that if even Rednow was already reaching the limit of the smoke he could inhale? As much as it felt like they were winning, the shadowlings never ceased to come down from those bloody rocks. He couldn't keep going for much longer, and the Builders weren't enough to handle it.

"Atarakni-mor!" Arkan shouted as he stabbed another creature with his spear. The snarl on his face was now evident. Rednow didn't understand the language, but he saw a man of peace being forced to give up what he had believed was right to save his people.

Another twenty-odd Builders came out of the chiselled holes in the mountain walls, flying to what was now a battlefield littered with bodies. Rednow could barely walk or move without tripping in a dead shadowling. The fuckers were persistent, and their strikes showed no hesitation.

With more Builders in the air, Rednow's job was easier on the ground. He flailed his arms, stabbed with his claws, and crushed their throats. Still they didn't avoid him. His breathing worsened, and he tasted blood in his throat, the worst possible sign of his inevitable future.

I'm going to die here today, he thought. No pity, no regret. But Tinko...

"Arkan," he bellowed to get the man's attention. "Take care of Tinko if something happens to me."

Arkan seemed as though he didn't even understand the request, like he couldn't fathom losing Rednow in battle. Ultimately, a glance of recognition finally settled, and he locked his gaze to Rednow's for a moment, nodding.

If Rednow were to die in a place like this, killed by a combination of the beasts and the smoke, at least he would die a good death. A proud one.

You're not going to die.

The Essence spoke in Rebma's voice, sending shivers down Rednow's spine yet again. How dare she? "How dare you use her voice again?"

As Rednow was preparing to snarl at the Essence, Tinko slipped on a dead shadowling, and their misdirection trick failed. For a moment, the child was exposed, their back to three creatures.

No.

"NO!" Rednow lunged forward and placed himself between them and Tinko, covering the child's back. One last surge of strength.

One breath.

One jump.

One death.

This time, he *knew* it was his death. The smoke had been too much for him. His brain fogged and his vision became too hazy. The sense of battle halted, as though it had been removed from his brain. But he was still... conscious. Why wasn't his life flashing before his eyes?

Everybody fears death, but why? What is it about dying that they fear? They are presumptuous in assuming life is all there is. That there is nothing awaiting them after it.

Thoughts and spoken words meshed, and Rednow struggled to understand what was real and what was his imagination. Perhaps that's how the underworld worked, confusing people until they went mad.

You inhaled too much smoke to protect that child. You knew you were going to die, and yet you did it anyway. You did not fear death. In all my moons, it's rare that I see such a display of devotion, choosing my smoke, my Essence as the way to go.

What? Rednow thought. That wasn't it. He just wanted to protect Tinko. He wasn't faithful to the bloody deity.

Suddenly, light emerged all around, but Rednow couldn't see in front of him. He couldn't move. He could only be dead. So, what in the underworld could this be?

Here. Rise, my faithful avatar. I'll strip you of your prison of flesh.

No. No. NO!

Rednow couldn't feel it, but he still did, somehow. His inert body was now but a bag of flesh and bones. The Essence had been right. He couldn't control it any longer. He couldn't see. He couldn't hear, smell, or even feel any touch.

There was no pain, either.

And yet, he knew exactly what the Essence was doing to him. First, the skin in his back ripped open. His muscles tore like fabric, and then in sharp, violent motions, both skin and muscles around the ribcage were stripped away, leaving only the bones and everything they were meant to protect. Lungs, heart, and all of his organs collapsed into smoke, leaving only the bone structure intact.

Little by little—or perhaps that was all a fraction of a second, he had no sense of time any longer—he shed off the rest of it. His arm, then his chest, and then his belly, all the way down to his feet. No skin. No flesh. Just the bare bones.

This will not be as bad as you think.

The skin of his face was stripped off, but there was no pain. It was akin to peeling a grape. One by one, the other bits of him were off, and he was nothing but a pile of bones that somehow held firmly together, stronger than ever.

Aware of the horror of his new condition, he was too overwhelmed to react.

What have you done to me?

At least he could still think, though part of him hoped this was no more than a nightmare. It couldn't be, though. They were never this vivid. This definitive.

There you are! The Essence said, excitedly. *Rise, Rednow!*

Not that he had a choice. He tried moving, but his new skeleton self struggled. And then the smoke returned.

His old friend. His murderer.

With the smoke surrounding him, Rednow was lighter than a feather. He was air, and wind, and smoke.

To control the smoke, you have to be the smoke. Which you are now. My true avatar.

A mix of rage and panic settled in him. He hadn't wanted or chosen any of this. Even his death had been stolen from him twice already. Could he even feel *anything*?

Once he thought about it, he realised he couldn't. He was as blank as an untouched canvas. Essence was the painter, ready to paint him in her light, to the dance of her inevitable brush.

What have you done to me?

I used your dwindling corporeal energy to turn you into a higher being. A Smoke Rider. The first in centuries. And my new avatar on top of that.

Rednow didn't understand. He didn't know what a bloody Smoke Rider was supposed to be. All he knew was he didn't want it. Any of it. Especially not being her avatar.

And what do I do now? Where is everyone?
Where you left them.

Rednow focused and reality came back. Everything was different now. Everything seemed too feeble. Everyone looked so fragile. Or maybe it was he who was stronger. *What am I to do?* He wondered.

Protect.

Rednow saw them all under the cloud of smoke that kept him safe. There was terror in their faces. Even the shadowlings had stopped to look at him. They must think him even more of a beast of the underworld now.

He floated to where his pile of flesh was, to where Tinko was. Everything physical was easier now. He wasn't constrained by the physical boundaries of the world. He found in himself a strange strength, as though he had a new pool of power from which he could draw. The shadowlings could feel it too and hesitated in making a move, so he took his chance.

"LEAVE NOW OR FACE MY WRATH," Rednow bellowed.

He must have sounded like a demon.

The shadowlings weren't put off by his threat and resumed their attack.

"What do I do?" he whispered.

Be the smoke.

Rednow didn't really know what he was doing, but it felt right to summon a gust of thick dark smoke to surround them and cover the entire top of the walls. It was strange, as though he was choking the shadowlings with his bare hands, as though every inch of smoke was part of his body.

The Essence laughed. *In millennia, no avatar has ever tried something like this. You are an interesting one.*

The beasts gasped, choked, and dropped from the rock top. Hundreds of them. With no time for the Essence's patronising remarks, Rednow controlled his smoke to close the tiny gap between the rock walls where Pinesy and three other Builders had struggled to keep off the shadowlings.

Step away. I'll handle them, he said, realising the words came out differently now.He had no mouth, no tongue, and no vocal cords, so how could he speak like this? It didn't make sense. Pinesy and the others seemed to understand him well enough, as though his voice had appeared in their minds.

He shot another wave of dark smoke into the shadowlings, who gasped and couldn't escape the trap. The smoke was poisonous to anyone who wasn't a smokesmith, and while the creatures might be from the underworld, they still needed air to stay alive. By replacing that air with the smoke, he shot death upon them.

He was no longer a monstrous man but a true monster indeed. One capable of delivering thousands to the dirt in just minutes. He looked for more shadowlings, but there was nothing but corpses. The ones that had survived were now running from the smoke and out of the Builders' haven.

I am nothing but peril. A man turned into a weapon. Why couldn't you just let me die?

In these trying times we face, even peril is necessary, Rednow. I knew you would be strong enough to become a Smoke Rider. I knew you could defeat the shadowlings with the snap of a finger. Only you could become my avatar.

If Rednow had all that power, he felt absolutely nothing, like he was neither alive nor dead. He was nothing but consciousness loosely tied to a pile of bones.

I don't want this.

No? You can fly. You are the smoke. You can do anything. But I'll tell you what. If you defeat the Old One, I'll let you die in peace.

There it was again. A lifetime of running away from monarchs and lords only to find himself half-dead and utterly dependent on someone or... something crueller than all of them combined. He didn't care what Rebma believed and what she thought—she had been manipulated by the Essence. Rednow would remain vigilant.

He would be himself.

Fifteen
Smoke and Bones

Rednow - Keryon - Nork - Solvi

Rednow would take time to adjust to this new life, with no physical needs but also no pleasures, no real senses in the human way. They had nearly lost the battle against the shadowlings, the last of the creatures already gone. The next time the Old One came, though, he wouldn't fail. In front of Rednow was a sacred refuge littered with bodies and a scattered crowd of pineheads who stared at him intently. And they weren't the only ones.

"Uncle?" Tinko said, eyes watery. Their face covered in soot and ash. "Is that you?"

It is me.

The child flinched upon hearing Rednow's words in their mind. "How did you do that?"

I'd tell you if I knew how, I swear it. Now, listen to me. Things will be fine. You are already a fine smokesmith, and now it looks as though I'm a little more than one. We will be fine.

"What are you, then? A smoke skeleton?"

Somehow the child's words brought a melancholic feeling that Rednow knew wasn't real anymore. But he still cared for Tinko, Smoke Rider or not.

Something like that, he said before turning his attention to Pinesy, who glared at him wide-eyed.

Take care of Tinko, would you?

The pinehead hesitated but nodded. "I promise."

Not everything about moving around without a body was terrible. Long gone were the aches from a lifetime of beatings. He could be one with the air; his thoughts were quick to become actions without a single physical constraint.

He looked for Arkan and eventually found the leader of the Builders looking as exhausted as Pinesy, with a gash across his face. The man dropped his spear, and bowed all the way down, his forehead touching the ground. "All hail the Smoke Rider. All hail the avatar."

Rednow had expected horrified looks on people's faces now that he was a skeleton wreathed in smoke, but no one seemed bothered. It was as though they weren't horrified by the skeletal appearance, just surprised to be seeing a Smoke Rider again, which made him wonder just how many Smoke Riders there had been all those centuries ago, when the Builders were still a civilisation.

Rise, Arkan. Please. I'm no deity. I'm still Rednow, for better or worse.

Arkan nodded and straightened himself again. "As you wish."

Thank you for helping us. I know the resolve it took, and just how much it cost you to do so. I'm sorry about those who fell. Are there any badly wounded?

The leader of the Builders nodded and waved for Rednow to follow. They entered a rocky alcove of surprising depth. From the outside, the man-made caves looked small, but Rednow could now see a complex cave system connecting them inside the rock, which impressed him even more. Just how many centuries had it taken to chisel that much stone and carve a system like that?

Arkan took him through a few caves that resembled palatial hallways and into what looked like a training ground adapted for an infirmary. Some of the injured had flesh wounds or broken bones, but those would be mended in due time. Others, though, were in more critical condition. A man had a stab wound to the abdomen and another a sharp gash in his chest, his ribcage exposed. They would probably not make it.

Please step away.

The Builders who took care of their fellow cousins looked at him, as though noticing Rednow for the first time, but also as though they didn't quite understand what he meant. Ultimately, they abided by his words without protest, and Rednow realised just how fragile the poor fellows looked. One snap and their lives would wither. One shake and their hearts would stop beating.

Slowly and after everybody besides him had cleared the space, Rednow brought a thin thread of smoke to the injured Builders' nostrils. They coughed at first as they took the smoke in, but it didn't take long for it to reach their lungs, and for the traces of the Essence to be transported in the blood. Their hearts showed some strength with that, so he kept the smoke going towards them, mixed with air.

The Builders didn't shy away and still weren't surprised, as they peered from the doorway. They'd seen this before, Rednow supposed.

One of the injured pinehead men coughed again and blood hit the ground.

Shit.

This poor man would probably die, Rednow thought. Not everyone could become a smokesmith, after all. If Rednow failed to turn the man into one, would he be his killer? It was his smoke, his poison... Still, Rednow didn't give up. He stared at the small, shaggy-haired pinehead and his wounded body, hoping that he lived.

All he could do was keep the smoke active and cross his now fleshless fingers. People almost never considered themselves superstitious or spiritual, but that was only until something they really wanted ended up in the hands of luck and fate. Then, they would pray to gods in which they didn't believe. They'd kneel in tears and practice all sorts of rituals. Rednow had seen it all: farmers hoping for rain, soldiers begging for their comrades to live, and sailors who just wanted to see shore again. The harshness of life often ended up being the gateway to faith. And life was harsh for most.

The Builders, though, were unfazed. No prayers or pleading. No hearts on their sleeves or emotional displays. They were stone-faced and in control of their emotions.

Despite the smoke, the injured man's chest stopped moving up and down, his eyes blanking and losing focus. It hit Rednow as though he'd known the man all his life. Why did he always put himself in this position? One of saving others and bearing their pain?

Rednow was aware of the fallen faces of the other Builders who watched from afar, now that the first of the injured had failed to resist the smoke ailment. They were stone-faced, but Rednow knew they had high hopes for him. He was everything they believed in, and couldn't let the second man die, for their sake as well as his own.

He continued to pay attention to the process. Thin threads of smoke that he could control with a thought danced around the man's face, waiting for each breath, slowly threading themselves with the air the man breathed. Steady was the way. It once had been a strenuous process for Rednow and too much of a last resort, but now that he had no need to burn the herbs and the smoke was easier to control, he was more hopeful.

The smoke continued to flow through the man's nostrils. After a while, he opened his eyes. Rednow brightened and walked towards the man, taking hold of his hand. The Builder coughed but opened his eyes, looking at him before they shut again.

Easy, my friend. I'm making you a smokesmith. Can you speak? What is your name?

"Y-yes," the man said, his voice raspy. "Foran is my name."

You're tougher than most, Foran. And my appearance doesn't scare you, either. I'm glad.

The man's face softened, and the initial horror dwindled into a mix of concern and pain. "I-I was stabbed."

You were, and you were badly wounded. But look at you now, already conscious and talking. And almost no reaction to the smoke.

Foran's face lit up and he looked around him, as if just now realising there was smoke surrounding him. His eyes widened. "I survived the smoke?"

The wound hasn't gone anywhere. It will take time to heal. But with the smoke to aid you, you will be fine.

The man nodded.

Rednow could get used to this. If only his new existence could be to solely focus on helping dying soldiers survive by becoming smokesmiths. He scoffed at his own silly thoughts. That would never be possible. Those were illusions only fools would consider. As long as he was the Essence's avatar, she would make sure to play him like a pawn.

Rednow kept some smoke focused on slowly repairing the man's health and walked towards the entrance of the improvised infirmary, from where Arkan and the rest of the Builders watched intently.

No sign of the enemy?

The Builder shook his head. "No. They've fled."

Relief flooded him, but it didn't last long. First, he saw all the blood splatter and the bodies of fallen Builders. And the many more bodies of the Old One's shadowlings littering the haven the Builders had chiselled for themselves. How could he be relieved? Then he looked at his own hands and arms. He was a bloody skeleton that could float in smoke.

How do I get my body back?

As though twisting a knife already lodged in his back, the Essence ignored him. She had her own motives. *We can't rest, Rednow. We must do something quickly before he gains his strength.*

Rednow didn't want any of this, but now he was in the thick of it. He was the bloody avatar. His chances of escaping the Essence and avoiding whatever plans she had for him were slim at best. That realisation hit him harder than seeing the first man dying under his care, harder than Thata dying on his watch. Amid the cloud of despair in his mind, he could hardly get any words out. Should he just accept it, go with it? Or fight it?

He found himself still too weak, and too ignorant. Powerless. *What would you have me do?*

You must call to all those who share my Essence. To all the smokesmiths.

Keryon dozed off, even with the Tooth snoring in the distance. It was all he did these days: sleep, work, and try his hardest to remain himself without letting this trauma define him as well. He wasn't a savage. He would show Gimlore and the rest that hope was possible. They just needed to be patient.

He looked out as the damned woman attempted to steal a few spoonsful of the stew again in the dark of night. This time, however, she had the pesky girl, Hope, with her, as though she was teaching the child her mischievous ways. Against his better judgement, Keryon stood on guard duty. He wouldn't let any of the Sirestine bastards get a hold of her, not after everything she had gone through.

I couldn't keep her from the whip.

He watched her in the distance, like a fox preparing to hunt her next meal. Maybe it was the heat, or he was just nervous for her, but his forehead had produced countless beads of sweat that he had to wipe away with the sleeve. She was in her element doing this, so he let her. This was her way of feeling useful, he reckoned, even if her instinct had been to feed herself first.

Someone stirred in their sleep, and Keryon wished he could be asleep as well, but his stomach was already growling again. Maybe she was right—maybe they needed to eat more than their daily rations.

Come on. Don't linger for long.

He clasped his wooden spoon in case he needed to use it as a weapon. He would be more than capable of defending himself with it, but the problem was they wouldn't get far in a place like that, not without his herbs.

A sensation tickled the back of his mind, which gave him pause.

What was this?

Then a voice spoke in his head, and he froze. *SMOKE-SMITHS,* it said.

Keryon recognised Rednow's raspy voice and northern accent immediately. But how was he...

My name is Rednow, and I'm a smokesmith. I'm reaching out to all the smokesmiths of the Known World. The Old One is back. You may know him by many names from old tales and legends you may not even know were real. The Deceiver is one of them. Father Time is another. He is going by the name of God Himself, using a Sirestine man named Orberesis as his vessel. Every day, he drains this man and grows stronger. I was in Alarkan when the Old One rose, already with thousands of his shadowlings. Some of them have already made it as far north as Vaerghulen, where I am now. Soon, the shadowlings will reach you, all of you, for that is what the Old One desires: to make the Known World his, with the shadowlings doing his bidding.

Keryon gasped. They had already reached Vaerghulen! That meant Rednow was alive, and then... Maybe Tinko as well. And Pinesy!

He glanced at Gimlore and had to control his urge to tell her. While Rednow's message was troubling, there was also a sliver of hope. It was something to hold on to. Gimlore needed that more than anyone. He was about to sneak his way to her when Rednow spoke again.

We face a threat we haven't in generations. Smokesmiths must unite. We must fight the Old One together. Join me. We need as many smokesmiths as we can. Come to the Thousand Hills of Vaerghulen and I will find you. If we don't, we won't be here to see tomorrow.

The Thousand Hills were too far from Sirestir. Keryon clasped his hands into fists and punched the dirt as powerlessness took root in him again. He couldn't be patient. He needed to do something *now*. This had been enough prison for a lifetime.

Gimlore lay in her improvised cot, and Keryon flinched. He had been so immersed in thought he had missed the grass around him move as she made her way back.

"Did I spook you?" she asked playfully. "You're losing your touch."

With no time to waste, Keryon told her everything Rednow had said, and she heard it all without uttering a word. When he was done, her face remained thoughtful. "I'm glad he's alive. But how the fuck did he manage to speak into your mind?"

"I always sensed he was different," Keryon admitted. "Not many smokesmiths have the willpower to leave their masters when they have nothing else in a world that hates and fears them. And he did that."

Gimlore swallowed. "And he also survived his arm getting chopped off after the fake god invaded. I was always lost for words as to how he could have done such a thing."

Keryon shrugged. "A man of mysteries."

Gimlore scoffed. "He is the kind of person I want looking after Tinko."

Keryon could almost hear the pain in Gimlore's trembling voice, or her saying "even though he let Thata die". He was sure Gimlore would ask Rednow about that as not much else had occupied her mind these last few months. She hadn't forgotten any of it yet.

"We must find a way out," he said.

Gimlore shook her head. "We are hopeless. This is the new world for us. A hopeless one."

Keryon smiled. "And yet, you've been around that little girl called Hope, isn't it?"

Gimlore punched him in the shoulder and turned the other way.

He had to get to her, somehow. "We need to find a way out. For Tinko," Keryon risked.

Gimlore turned around, looked at him, and wiped the tears. Keryon could practically see the pain in her face. Both of them knew it wasn't over yet, even if they were to get out, but it tended to mould people differently. They still had to unlearn everything the whip had taught them, even if it meant bearing more pain.

Gimlore nodded. "I want to..." her voice broke, but she continued. "I want to leave, but I am so *tired*."

Keryon swallowed. He never thought he'd see Gimlore in such a state. She'd need more help than he had anticipated, but together, they'd see it through.

He embraced her. Together, they'd overcome anything.

Nork stayed quiet, just as he had for the past few weeks. Why waste his voice when he and his brother didn't need to speak to understand each other? There was no point in revealing their thoughts to their captors. These days, there wasn't much showing on their faces other than pain and despair.

Nosema looked at him with eyes that seemed to say, "We survive, brother".

The shackles were painful and tight, and the grey creatures didn't seem to care much for the prisoners, but every day Orberesis was gone was a good one. Nork feared him the most.

He had always found it rather easy to predict what a person might do. Just look at their face and read their expressions. Watch their hands or their eyes. The way they sit or walk. Nork had survived like that for years, always studying people and making his move before the enemy could make theirs. But there was something wrong with Orberesis. His eyes changed often, and so did his expressions, as if sometimes he was one man, and sometimes another took over. Nork didn't know what, but *something* was wrong with him.

The rest of the prisoners of war faced more or less the same predicament as he and Nosema, except the old bastard Fanan, who had denounced him and Nosema as the leaders and had been rewarded with more food for it.

They would teach him a lesson soon.

He was thrown out of his thoughts by Eshof's coughing nearby. The old woman was too old to go through yet another war like this. Her body was frail, and with not enough food or water, she would soon get sick and who knows what else beyond that. Sitting on that pile of mud made it all the worse.

Shit. She reminded Nork too much of his mother...

"Have some of my water," Nork said, offering up his cup.

The old woman eyed him, smiled, and picked it up. "I've always known you were a good boy. And your brother too."

Nork had a hard time smiling at that. It simply wasn't true. He had killed on command all his life. First for the brigands, then in the paramilitary units under Gimlore, and then in Alarkan when Gimlore wanted someone gone. All of that made him the opposite of what Eshof considered a good person.

He wanted to be one, though, given the chance. He placed his hand on Eshof's back and rubbed at it for a moment. "You'll be alright."

As he glanced at Nosema to ask if he had seen Orberesis anywhere, his eyes found a man he didn't recognise staring straight at him. He had long, straight hair and a beard covering his face, free from dirt and mud. The man was followed by a wide-shouldered woman taller than himself.

"What do you want? Nork asked. "Better keep walking."

There was something about these folks he didn't like. But he was always suspicious, anyway. The fact he hadn't seen them before made it strange. Interlopers, perhaps?

The bearded man continued slowly towards him, looking both ways to prevent their captors from seeing them talk. He stood next to Nork, and Nosema also took notice, his eyes now glued to the woman that followed the bearded man.

"I'm Ferkin, one of the smokesmiths who came to settle here on Keryon's request. I suppose he's gone now. I don't see him anywhere. But we must do something."

Nork frowned. He trusted the man even less now. Smoke-smiths *always* meant trouble. He never understood why Gim-lore had surrounded herself with so many of them. Keryon first, then Rednow. And now these fools had come too. "There is no 'we'. Get lost or I make sure you do."

Nork had little intention of starting a fight, especially know-ing there was no way he could defeat a smokesmith, even one without his herbs. But he had fought plenty over the years, so it didn't scare him. This would be two versus two if it came to it. He had faced worse odds.

"Listen to me," the man said, his voice still level-headed. He was trying to be civil at the very least. But that didn't earn him any pats on the back. "I have a message from Rednow."

Nork squinted at the newcomers, and other foreigners started appearing right behind the woman. So, it wasn't two versus two, then. Fine, let them come. They'd all end up as supper for the fish-heads anyway.

"I know how that sounds," the bearded man said as he scratched his hair. "But I promise we're here in peace. We want the same things as you. Please hear me out."

Nork was at least starting to get curious about this. He glanced at Nosema who shot him back a shrug. "Alright."

"I'm Ferkin. This is Chona. And the others behind us are also smokesmiths. The date of our arrival in Heleronde turned out much worse than we could have imagined. We lived lifetimes of servitude and just when we thought freedom was in our grasp... it wasn't. We've had our herbs taken away, so there isn't much we can do, unless we work together. Now, we have a reason to do it."

Nork gave that a thought but didn't respond. Why should he? He didn't really trust the man just yet.

Ferkin sighed at Nork's silence. He looked both ways and then spoke even more quietly than before. "I don't really know how, but all of us smokesmiths heard the same message in our heads. From a man called Rednow. He said he was here in Alarkan. A friend of yours, I presume?"

Nork scoffed at that. It would take a while for him to consider anyone a friend.

"Well, he's alive and somehow found a way to communicate with all the smokesmiths."

That old man was always full of surprises, so Nork didn't have too much trouble believing this. He'd seen things most people wouldn't believe.

"He said he's in Vaerghulen, raising an army of smokesmiths to fight the fish heads. He called them shadowlings. Said they came from an old god, the Old One, who is possessing Orberesis."

That would explain why Orberesis always seemed so off. Like he wasn't really present all the time. His mind must be constantly flickering between reality and illusion, between his original self and the god. "I appreciate you telling me this, but I don't see what this has to do with me or with our situation."

Ferkin glanced at Chona and then back at Nork and his brother. "We want to join him, this Rednow fellow. I am sure many other smokesmiths from around the world will. If they don't do it now because they don't believe it, they will do it later, when the shadowlings expand and grow their reach, but then it might be too late. To be honest with you, if anyone manages to raise an army of smokesmiths, I sure want to be on their side."

Nork considered this. It made sense. "And what does this have to do with me?"

Ferkin's face became exasperated, and he sighed as he leaned forward. "For us to go, we need to revolt against the shadowlings who are keeping us captive. We can't sail to the mainland before we do that, and the people here seem to listen to you and your brother. It seems like you old boys hold some sway. I'm sure we could plan an uprising."

An *uprising*? Why not topple a kingdom while they were at it? The man must be mad.

"And get everybody killed when I'm supposed to look after them? I don't think so, fellow."

Ferkin nodded. "Look, it's a risk, I'm well aware. But we can plan it together and I won't impose my will. I'll listen to you. You have my word."

"Your word is worth as much to me as the fucking mud I'm sitting on." Nork felt a nudge in his left arm, which threw him off slightly, and he glanced at Nosema. "What?"

"Maybe we can do this," his brother whispered.

That gave him pause. It was one thing for the foreigner to say it, but if Nosema thought they could do it, then maybe they could... They had been in perilous situations before but had almost always pulled off. And the last time they had found themselves in trouble, it had been a smokesmith, Keryon, who saved them. The memories of fire columns and smoke rising, along with Sirestine soldiers ready to cut holes through him, left him blank. Nork bloody hated war, but as much as he wanted to kid himself, there was no running from it.

Knives would always be knives. They just needed sharpening every once in a while.

He saw a sliver of hope in his brother's eyes, and it somehow restored some of his own. He first turned to Nosema and placed his hand in his brother's shoulder. "You'll need to get rid of that ugly bandana."

"Nah. How would people tell us apart?"

Nork smiled, maybe hopeful. He then turned to the smoke-smiths. "You'll have to listen to me, or you can forget it. Now, what is your plan?"

⋯⋯⋯

Solvi caressed her belly and the baby kicked. What a joy that was. She had never known a smokesmith who had been able to get pregnant. Everyone said the smoke poisoned the body. With another light caress, she couldn't wait to cradle her child in her arms. What a joy that must be. Her own child. Her own miracle.

"Is it the babe kicking?" King Doemus asked.

Solvi's smile faded, and her thoughts returned to the reality she was in. "Yes, Your Majesty."

He was different, as though he had matured somewhat since he had discovered the queen hadn't been faithful. He had the cold look of a man embittered by a life of difficulty, which almost made Solvi laugh. She'd never met someone as wealthy and privileged, but still Doemus looked as though he had started to enjoy inflicting pain on others as a way to mitigate his own.

She responded to the King with only a polite nod. For all his faults, he was still a devout follower of the Highest One, and an ally that she desperately needed. The only one she had. Her mind wandered to Keryon, whose help she had shunned by running away.

"The child of God Himself," Doemus said, his hazy eyes wide open, aimlessly wandering round the room. "Does he already know he will have a child?"

"In due time. When he comes back to Ushar," she said.

Doemus remained quiet for a moment and then he used his magnifying glass to observe something in one of the many papers scattered on his lap. "It's been months already, and still the Highest One hasn't come home. The charts show he should have been here by now, even if he was riding a shadesgrowl from Mosendel. I worry about him. And for the soldiers of the Two Nations."

"He faced a strong uprising from local settlers, which he did not expect. I understand he stayed behind to secure the land and the elixir." Solvi had no idea why she lied. But could she have told Doemus that the Miraculous One had brought creatures from the underworld with him to inflict utter destruction onto a town of degenerates?

"Of course, of course. I'm not questioning the Highest One's motives."

But you're wondering whether I told you the truth, which means you're a little doubtful. You're not the only one.

Why had the Highest One done that? He was God Himself, wasn't he? His miracles should be enough without those filthy beasts... And without all the death being inflicted. Solvi couldn't shake off the words from that man... Keryon... They still lingered in her mind. The way he had spoken about her and all smokesmiths. Solvi at least wanted to keep some cards in her hands.

King Doemus wasn't God Himself, so her loyalty wasn't to him. He didn't need to know everything, but she had also omitted the thoughts she'd had, with her mind invaded by someone who called himself Rednow. Someone who had claimed Orberesis was possessed by an old god which had brought the shadowlings to replace humanity.

It has to be slander. Nothing but slander.

But what if it wasn't?

It had left her guessing. Wondering. The shadowlings would have killed her if they'd had the chance. If Keryon hadn't given her food and water, she might not have had the energy to reach the mainland and ask for help. And she could have lost the child.

"I worry as well," she said.

Doemus nodded. "Whether he gets back sooner or later, governing must continue. The Two Nations are in a rather delicate predicament, as you surely saw when you made your way here."

Solvi nodded. She'd seen the streets littered with rubbish and human waste. The people were dirtier, poorer, and angrier than she remembered. Most of the soldiers who had travelled with Orberesis to Alarkan had not returned after the battle. King Doemus was *right* to be suspicious of her for that alone, but he no longer had his wife to whisper poisonous words in his ear, which could work to her favour. All she really cared about was the safety of her baby.

"Have you thought of a name for the child?"

The question surprised her. She hadn't. It was difficult to pick a name knowing very little about the little human life growing inside her. All she knew was the babe liked kicking even in the late hours of the evening, and seemed to be content in the afternoons after she had eaten.

"Not yet, Your Majesty."

Soon, she would have to abandon the dark robes of the Order of the Red Orb for more suitable attire, and possibly a long, loose dress.

She would do anything for this child.

SIXTEEN

TEMPORAL EXPLORATION

ORBERESIS

P ain shot through Orberesis, his eyes, nose, and mouth burning intensely. The remnants of the foul smoke were gone, but a thread of it had been enough to leave him poorly, with coughing fits, as though he was less resistant to it now.

I've always hated smokesmiths.

How could he not? The memory of his father bound to a pole, bellowing in pain while being burned alive, would forever be etched into his mind. And these smokesmiths were no different. They would do the same to him if they had the chance.

"What was... that?" he asked the Old One.

His parasite remained quiet, not even stirring, which was unusual.

He walked through the rocky terrain, careful not to be seen, and from behind the cover of two ferns, he peeked outside to see the carnage. Hundreds, or maybe thousands of Lantern Horns lying on the ground, dead. The more he looked, the more he could see it, the power of his enemies. There was someone on the other side who also had the power to destroy an entire army. The thought left Orberesis shivering.

Am I... afraid?

No! The Old One emerged, his voice still hushed. *We will find a way.*

"This wasn't the fight you wanted, was it? You thought it would be an easy one. That you could get rid of your sister once and for all."

I ignored the fact she already had an avatar. I didn't prepare for that.

"And how could we prepare for something like that? The smoke can still kill me, just like it killed all of them." His eyes went to the bodies covering the rocks, the moss, and the grass across the mountain range. "I wish we could get rid of these smokesmiths."

The Old One chuckled. *Yes, Doi. They killed your father. They burned your town. Now it's only fair you do the same to them.*

"So, how?"

First, there is much you still need to learn about Temporal Exploration, especially if you are to be my vessel, grasp the power easily with your bare hands, or travel freely as you already know you can. But we also need some external... persuasion. Something you can accomplish without me.

The Old One's laugh never failed to leave him irritated. There was so much contempt in his voice. Always a feeling of superiority, as though Orberesis was his vassal, only doing his bidding.

"Then teach me," Orberesis snarled.

Patience, Doi. We've just lost many of my friends. Our friends.

"They're just creatures."

They are my people. They welcomed me when humanity sided with my sister. And if I'm right, they will soon be killed by their own world. They will become a footnote in the history of time, unknown to anyone, anywhere. They will be killed by their own planet, a vacuum in the unique vastness of existence. I cannot let that happen.

Orberesis swallowed. There was a stirring determination in his words, as though that in itself was reason enough for the Old One to fight. Orberesis wanted to be on that side, not against, but he also wanted to be *powerful*, not a pretender. "Funerals?"

No, Doi. That's something for my sister and her ilk. I'm going to need your help with this. It will be hard. You will feel the strain.

Orberesis swallowed again, his mind going to the pain he'd felt when he tried to hold on to the soft, smooth ride in the void. He wanted more of it, but with much less strain. He would need to practice. If that meant the Old One taking advantage of him once more, so be it.

"Fine. I'm ready."

The Old One laughed again.

Then let's begin. Time isn't absolute, Doi. You know this. When you sleep the night and then wake, it feels like it's only minutes. So, what if you alter consciousness so minutes feel like centuries? Or so centuries feel like minutes? I have that power.

That's what I do. I open the fabric of the world, slip between the curves, and travel in between planes to relieve them of the pain that can be their existence. That is Temporal Exploration in its purest form.

In truth, Orberesis understood only half of those words. The Old One had a tendency to switch quickly between arrogant contempt and prideful supremacy. He was ready, though. He had experienced Temporal Exploration with the aid of the parasitical deity already.

"How do I start?" he asked.

Think about the feeling of being there, empty, devoid of rage and all other emotions, as though you were not part of this world, but a mere passenger in this moment in time.

Orberesis closed his eyes but didn't know if it helped. Sometimes he wondered if this was all a joke, with the Old One playing tricks in his mind. But he had come all the way to these mountains in just moments, so it could be done again.

He took a deep breath and settled himself, trying to capture the feelings of lightness and boundlessness that had so captivated him. How good it would be if he could head back to Alarkan in a period just as short.

"It's not working," he said.

It's your first attempt alone. I'd be surprised if it did. Keep trying.

He did. He experienced everything to the fullest. He took notice of his thoughts, of the way the air felt on his skin, how the hair flowed with the wind, and how his mind was well beyond the horizon, though he didn't know exactly where. Was it up in the stars or in an entirely different world? The workings of this newfound power eluded him, but he didn't need to know, he just had to *feel* it course through him.

He urged on the power to aid him in getting to Alarkan. He urged on his muscles and the blood vessels in his body, but still, nothing.

You're too eager. The Old One sounded disappointed. *You have me, so use my power.*

Orberesis nodded, and came back to the trance, remembering what that power was like.

I must alter my consciousness, he thought.

Good…

But how did one change his consciousness?

After what felt like hours, he finally found a way. Lies! He must tell himself lies. So many they become the truth. Lies to himself first of all.

Everyone respects me. Everyone fears me. I'm a man of the people.

A tear flowed down his face.

He repeated those words until he couldn't say them anymore. They were truth and facts bound by powers he ignored.

I was always loved. The world is kind and full of good people. Everyone deserves to have a leader like me.

More tears poured down his cheeks. He had spent years battling migraines while forced to become somebody else. Now he could really *be* that somebody else. He would make himself believe it. There would be no lies left to convert to truth by the time he was finished with this. There would only be truth and divinity.

I'm a good man. A great man. A divine man. A holy king. I deserve this. I deserve power. I was always the victim. I have always done more good things than bad things.

Not bad, not bad, Doi, the Old One said. *Keep it going.*

My words are commands, my desires are to be obeyed. I deserve this. I deserve power. I'm a good friend. A good lover. I was a good son.

The last word came as his inner voice trembled and he doubted himself. The clear memory of his father burning in the pole flashed in his mind's eye. The pain he endured and the nightmares Orberesis got because of it didn't take long to follow.

I am righteousness. I will speak for those who cannot speak for themselves. I will protect the weak. I am strong.

Those words had a ring of truth to them. Little by little, he discovered them. It was as though their true meaning had always been hidden under the surface, right under his nose. He kept repeating them in different tones and pitches, as though he was talking to himself and not to others. Time must have passed by, but Orberesis did not know it, for it became irrelevant. *He* was all that mattered now, and the truths were revealed. Minutes feeling like centuries and centuries feeling like minutes. He could no longer tell the difference between them. This was the right path to take.

What else must I learn? He mulled over the Old One's words. *Open the fabric of the world.*

He raised his hands and placed them between himself and the universe. Absent from the detritus of the world, he searched the air for a thread he could hold on to, one to pull on. There was no urge. All his rush to accomplish what he had set out to do was gone from him, and there was only himself.

Time might be passing outside of him, but not inside, so he persisted, hands facing forward until he found the tiniest of reactions in his fingertips: a trickling sensation fickler than the touch of an insect. There was something there, like a sheet of folded skin, hard to grasp. Patiently, he probed again and found something to pinch, then grabbed it.

He held the fabric of the world in his hands. The longer he spent there, ascending to his divinity, the more everything he'd told himself seemed like fact.

Everybody else who said otherwise must be out of their mind.

Orberesis pulled on the invisible fabric's thread, but the environment around him wavered and a whiplash effect hit him.

Pull too hard and it will swallow you.

Orberesis steadied himself, conscious only of his being and the thread he held. He came close to it, and opened it slowly, just a thin gap that would be big enough for him to slip through.

Remember, Doi. Out there, you have little control over yourself and I have even less. Slipping between the curves of reality is always dangerous. You might drift too far and end up elsewhere. Somewhere you might never come back from.

"How can I make sure... I don't drift?"

Think about where you want to go, and even harder about why you want to go there. Once your mind is set on it, and no doubt plagues any inch of it, you will be ready.

He did as the Old One suggested and pictured Alarkan and its swamps. The Lantern Horns were already there, and the town where the men and women had felt his power had turned to rubble. The power… that which he now knew wasn't even the full extent of what he could do with the help of the Old One.

He wanted to go there, *needed* to be there, to rule over both humans and Lantern Horns, even if that meant war. Even if that meant wearing a crown made from the thorns of war in a burning world. He would bring over the rest of the Lantern Horns and become the saviour of their kind. There would be enough room for everyone in the Known World, he would make sure of it. But for that to happen, he had to find his way back to Alarkan.

To get there, he slipped between the curves.

The universe flooded him, washed over him, contorted him, stretched his body, and confused his mind. At that moment, there was only despair. Was he going to die? The thought horrified him, but also kept his senses as sharp as they could be. It reminded him of being a child caught by the waves and spat back onto the beach, only for the next wave to come.

He couldn't control any of it; he simply had to take the punishment.

It was only then that Orberesis noticed the nature of Temporal Exploration. His cheeks were hollower, his ribs poking out, and the muscles that kept him steady turned to mush. Colours and shapes flew past him and even *through* him. Stars and worlds flickered by like rocks and pebbles thrown into the river. He, too, was thrashed by the void with the force of a thousand suns.

Remember. Alarkan. Remember. Alarkan. Must go to Alarkan.

Reality and fantasy merged and blended, and he was a product of both. A vagabond dreamer and a god. A thief and a king. Doi and Orberesis. The Highest One. God Himself.

ALARKAN!

The dizziness stopped. He was broken, disoriented, and dry heaving, even if there hadn't been much to retch. He stayed that way, head spinning round, and it wasn't better when he tried to open his eyes. For the Gods, he was hungry. And thirsty. And so weak.

He tried his best to control his breathing, but his heart still beat faster than a carnival drum. Part of him feared opening his eyes again would mean finding out he had ended up in another world where he would be trapped forever. There were no guarantees with Temporal Exploration, even for divine beings.

He blinked a few times to focus, but it all made sense.

It could only be Alarkan.

But there didn't seem to be any settlement or farmland anywhere near him. Still, he couldn't help but smile. He sat on the mud, allowing relief to flood him as his heart slowed the rate with which it beat.

"I did it."

The Old One stirred and laughed. *Well done, my boy.*

"It's not perfect, but it will do."

You are well on the right track. Just get enough rest because we have much to do. My sister won't let us have our moment for long. She is surely plotting her revenge already.

"What am I to do next?" He would practice this for certain to a point where they would all see the truths the way he did. The way the world worked, and the way he had always been right.

We can't defeat my sister with the Lantern Horns. She has an avatar, a Smoke Rider, and will surely have her smoke minions, so we must make allegiances of our own, maybe fight fire with fire. Or shall I say... smoke with smoke.

"Alliances with whom?"

With anyone willing to listen.

Orberesis nodded. "Or too weak to fight back."

⁘⁘⁘

Orberesis wore his new white robe. This time, he made sure to groom himself properly.

If others were to believe his truth, they'd need to see it confirmed. In this case, the truth was he was on a path to become a divine being, not a false one. What others expected was a white robe and, perhaps, a pair of sandals, clean skin, and a dignified beard, which he had grown in the past few days.

Temporal Exploration, he had learned over his several attempts, had taken a toll on him both physically and emotionally, just as the Old One had warned. It wasn't just that he was more tired, it was the weight he had lost and the dark rings of deprivation around his eyes. No real amount of sleep would be able to heal that sustainably. He had also found himself more irritable, going over his truths occasionally, and getting angrier at the rest of the Known World for having shunned or laughed at him.

Oh, how he wanted to show them…

Control your rage. We're trying to win allies.

"I *have* control. I successfully faked being a god for ten years. I can cope."

He wondered what his friends were doing in his absence. Solvi, ever so gullible. Doemus, lost in his books and his studies.

Orberesis looked around at the state of Ushar. He had missed the capital city; the smell of salt in the air and the shouting of the fishermen which could be heard leagues away. Doemus had been slacking, surely.

Now, though, all he smelled was dung, and it was as though people could only talk to one another in threats. Not good, as far as he was concerned.

Are you sure we don't need Lantern Horns? We still have time to bring them with us.

Orberesis shook his head. "No. These are my people. They'll welcome me. I'm sure they've been expecting me."

He continued towards the Palace of Brilliance, and the guard's brows shot up as he bowed deeply. "Highest One. You've answered all our prayers. You've come back!"

A hint of pity lit up in Orberesis' mind. He knew these people were blind believers, but to be reminded of it so vividly was… almost shocking. Ushar's continued decay was evident, but that hadn't been his fault. Upon seeing how little had changed for them and how *everything* had changed for him, he wondered what they'd think of the Lantern Horns, whose outside appearance was far from what they would ever consider heavenly. And to these people, appearing heavenly was perhaps more important than actually being it.

That would have to change.

He rested a hand on the guard's shoulder and almost felt the man's shaking, like wild reeds in the wind. This was probably the happiest moment of his life. Without a word, he walked through the courtyard and refused an escort. He was well familiar with the palace. It was supposed to be his home, but now it all felt so... pointlessly large.

Why would ancient beings build such a place just for a man to live with his servants? It all felt so mundane. And he realised he was no longer interested in any of it.

The ways of the world aren't going to change from one day to another, Doi.

Of course he knew that, but the Old One always had to show he had the experience. It was akin to having an old geezer always pointing out the obvious before he or any others could tell him to stay quiet, so Orberesis sighed and kept going.

Upon entering the palace and surprising yet another set of guards, the speaker called his name, totally unprepared, but his voice still boomed.

"May I introduce the Highest One, the Miraculous One. Our Divine God Himself—Orberesis!"

But the room that once had proudly held the royal court was now empty. At the end of the Ceremonial Room, King Doemus stood from the bejewelled chair and descended from it, kneeling before him.

But someone else caught his eye. To Doemus' right side was Solvi. She wore a large, dark dress, but it wasn't just the clothes. She looked different. Her hands were wrapped around her protruding belly.

Shock tore through him and Orberesis almost lost his composure, mouth nearly gaping.

She was with child. Shocking as it was, that could only mean one thing.

He was going to be a father.

SEVENTEEN

WITH HAMMER AND CHISEL

GIMLORE

Gimlore kept chiselling the rocks, barely having time to wipe off the sweat. At least she could probably keep up with a blacksmith by now if she were to try. The rest of the prisoners kept relatively quiet, never going beyond a few words and usually only about the work itself.

That was good.

It allowed her to think more clearly. By now, she knew all the corners of the quarry. The hills and holes, and how tall the walls were and which parts were shorter.

She had been paying close attention to the guards as well. The first one, with a frog-like face and a long nose, didn't seem to like holding the whip too much. He stayed back, mostly kept watch, and mean-mugged the prisoners. She didn't know how strong he would be in case they fought back, but she reckoned a knife in the right place would do it. Now, she only needed to get one...

The second and third guards were a different story. They were taller, leaner, and their faces never deviated from horrendous, punchable snarl. Their grip on the whip was ever tight and they were more than eager to use it. The rest of the guards were probably somewhere between, which meant frog-face was the weak link to exploit.

"That's enough," said the second guard. "Shift is over. Time to go."

Gimlore remained silent and focused. One by one, the prisoners dropped their tools—the hammer and the chisel—in sacks held by the guards. She waited in line until her turn was up, and unrolled the dirty sleeves that covered her wrist. Lining up in the queue to the frog-like guard, she tripped up the man walking right in front of her, and he fell on his knees.

"Oh, for the gods, I'm terribly sorry," she said, helping him up. "Are you alright?"

The man eyed her suspiciously but ended up giving her a nod. "Yes."

"Come on!" the frog-like guard bellowed. "Hurry! You two are holding up the line!"

The man in front of her apologised, dropped his utensils quickly and kept going, following the rest of the prisoners. The guard didn't even look at the sack.

Gimlore had no idea if they even checked whether all the utensils were accounted for in the evenings, but she was willing to bet that they didn't. Maybe the guards were tired of this job, too. Maybe they thought the prisoners would be too stupid or too broken to try something. Perhaps they'd cut corners. And even if they did realise there were tools missing, they couldn't trace it back to her. She only needed to play the rest of her part well.

I've been hammering so much, let's see if I've lost my sleight of hand.

She slid her hand inside the sack in a movement as natural as she could make it. While making sure that the hammer fell hard enough in the sack to make a sound, she quickly shoved the chisel up her sleeve and kept it there, close to her wrist and forearm with her ring finger.

Without looking at the guard, as though she had nothing to fear, she walked away from the line, carrying a steel chisel. Something she could easily turn into a weapon to be used if she needed.

A smile formed in her face as she walked up the prisoner camp with the rest of them, the pain no longer a concern, her callouses and bruises part of the new normal. She hadn't got any lashes this time, which was good, but... not good enough.

"You seem happy," Hope said.

Gimlore turned to see the little girl, and instinctively hid the stolen chisel. The less the girl knew, the better. "How can you say such foolish things?"

"Is it foolish to state the truth?"

"It is foolish to be a liar."

"Then we must both be fools."

Gimlore wanted to snarl but found it hard. It was like talking to her younger self. "Don't you have anybody else to annoy?"

"I do, but I chose you specifically."

"What an honour."

Now it was Hope's time to smile. The little girl's short hair and wide eyes almost made her head seem bigger than the rest of her thin frame. She looked both ways, and then her eyes looked at Gimlore like a conspirator. "Are you going to... you know... tonight?"

"Shh!" This was getting a little too close for comfort. Could she really trust the kid to keep a secret as big as her little nightly ventures? Someone would be awake one day and they'd surely rat Gimlore out. "Not here. Not now."

Hope understood it well enough, and Gimlore walked side by side with the child as Keryon went on ahead in what seemed like a friendly conversation with the Tooth. They finally reached the camp, and Gimlore hurried to her things. "Alright. Go on. Let's get ready for supper."

Hope nodded as she went ahead. "I'm starving..."

Now that the child was farther on, she glanced both ways to check that no one was watching her. She dug into the dirt with her left hand. When a hole was deep enough, she placed the stolen chisel in it, and covered it with the dirt immediately. Then she sighed and dropped to the ground, her head over the sack she used as a pillow.

"Are you alright?" Keryon asked. He was losing weight, she noticed. His jaw line seemed to be sharper by the day, which made her wonder if she was also slimming down.

"Meh." She shrugged. "You?"

He hesitated, as though he was going to tell her something, but ended up just sitting next to her, a hand in hers.

"Getting romantic now?"

"You know me," he said. "I've always been one."

"Let's go, lover man, food is what I'm craving at the moment."

⸱⸱⸱⸱⸱⸱⸱⸱⸱⸱

The food was as bad as it had always been, but Gimlore had started to enjoy the company of the other prisoners, for better or worse. Besides the Tooth, there were other men and women who weren't as bad as she had made them out to be at first. Maybe they just had ugly faces, or their frowns served as a deterrent against potential attacks.

In a prison like that, with such tight control over them, there wasn't even a chance for prisoners to establish hierarchy or turf wars of any kind. The only time they had to themselves was supper and there was nothing for them to steal but food; however, with the guards around, that wasn't likely.

As they told stories of old days and war feats, Gimlore's mind wandered. No matter how much she tried, she couldn't let go of Tinko and Thata. They'd always be her children, always on her mind. But those thoughts only brought pain and guilt, reminding her she was a horrible mother. Not only had she abandoned them, but she had also let Thata die. To make matters worse, she hadn't been able to even try to start looking for Tinko because she was trapped in this damn place. Rednow's message to the smokesmiths was promising. She'd look for Tinko there, in Vaerghulen, but first she needed to get out of here.

"Now, you seem sad," Hope said, sitting next to her, still munching on her last spoonful of potato stew. "And given the food, I don't blame you."

A sly smirk curled Gimlore's lips. *You're too fucking clever for your own good, girl.* "You're still eating it, though."

"I have to get strong."

"How come?"

"Who's going to carry your bag of bones out of this place when you're an old hag?"

Gimlore snorted and almost felt the supper rise from her stomach as she laughed. Too damn clever, and yet she didn't have a string of malice in her. She was just a little girl doing what little girls did, adjusted to the circumstances. "That's a good point, I'll give you that."

Hope got closer and whispered as Tooth grabbed the attention of the prisoners with his ludicrous stories of wickplates nearly destroying the ships from the Floating City Fleet, sinking entire crews along the Yabbish strait.

"Tonight?" the child whispered.

Gimlore sighed. She didn't like the girl tagging along, but she couldn't force her mouth to stay quiet either. "Not tonight. Too dangerous."

"Why is tonight more dangerous than last night?"

Shit, she is damn clever.

"Nothing special tonight, we just can't risk doing it so often."

That seemed like a plausible answer. Gimlore hadn't told Keryon about the stolen chisel. The fewer people knew, the better, but so far, her theory had been proven right, and they hadn't raised any issues. Now that she knew a way to get utensils out, she just needed to smuggle it back in tomorrow.

If it could split rocks, it could tear much softer things.

Hope nodded, and they stayed quiet, listening to the Tooth.

"And the tentacles! White!" the man said. "I swear to you on my great grandma, who was practically a goddess. The tentacles were bloody long! And white! They grabbed onto the ship and nearly capsized it."

"A ship that size? Then the creature would have to be—" someone said.

"Bloody big, isn't it!" the Tooth said.

Shivers ran down Gimlore's spine. She had seen something like that before, and she had buried those memories deep in her, but now she remembered it fully. Orberesis had been carried by giant tentacles, and then he had appeared back in Heleronde with what seemed like godly powers, floating in the air, and destroying everything in sight. Whatever the tentacled creature had been, it had to be connected to the powers.

She swallowed, pushed those memories away, and noticed her heart racing. *I want that fucker killed so badly.* She should have done it as soon as she had the chance. A knife at his throat and it would have been all over. She wouldn't miss the next time. It was *he* who had taken her child away.

"And now you're angry," Hope said, her eyebrows up.

"And you are pretty good at stating the obvious."

"As are your emotions," the girl said. "You wear them thinly."

"What do you know about that?" Gimlore scoffed. "You're just a child."

"And yet I see through you, Gimlore." Hope's eyes were fixed on her, and a wide smile appeared. "When you're tiny like me, you pay attention to things, to people. Anyway, if you could get out of here... what would you do?"

Gimlore frowned, annoyed by the question. Maybe it was because it forced her to confront who she was and what she wanted. The obvious answer would be Tinko, and getting everything that she'd lost back, but some things were impossible to get back. "That's none of your business. I'm going to sleep."

Gimlore left the gathering and the semi-watchful gaze of the frog-faced guard for her improvised cot. She quietly sat there, nothing but crickets to be heard. The chisel was underneath her, hidden about a foot under the dirt, but she needed more weapons if she was to do something... Perhaps the wooden spoon? No, they would notice it was sharpened.

"An early night?" Keryon asked, snapping her out of her thoughts.

"Seems that way."

"What's on your mind?"

Gimlore sighed. "Everything is. A child dead and another somewhere I don't know. A lunatic with godly powers killing and enslaving my people, destroying everything I have. And I'm stuck here with only one person I can trust."

"What about Tavanar?"

Gimlore shot the man a glance. Or at least what was left of him. He looked half-dead from the lashes and the work. He barely spoke or even looked at people. It reminded her of Edmir when she had first found him. Times had changed, though, and she no longer had it in her to save someone from the pit of despair. She was deep in it herself too. "I cannot trust someone that desperate."

"I guess I can't fault you for that."

"But even you... I still don't understand you." She lowered her voice to the lowest possible whisper. "I spend my days busy plotting an escape or an uprising, and you spend yours chatting up that fool, laughing around with the rest of the prisoners. It's like you're... fine being here, doing this. I don't understand."

Keryon sighed and leaned against her, his forehead touching hers. "You can escape on your own, true enough. But how do you stage an uprising by yourself? You need people on your side. You need their trust. Their loyalty. Their friendship. I might be here laughing and smiling with them, but that doesn't mean I want to be here."

Gimlore swallowed.

Keryon continued. "And the Tooth? Don't you see how much they respect him? They look at him like a beacon of light shining in the darkness, which is how I look at you, even though you grimace whenever I say these things."

"You're so fucking cheesy."

"And there might be something else with the Tooth that I'm planning, but it is too risky for me to tell you yet. We never know when someone might be listening."

"It can't be as bad as plotting an uprising."

Keryon smiled. "It's not too far off."

"I might have done something *risky* as well," Gimlore whispered, unable to contain herself.

"Riskier than stealing stew from the guards at night?"

She smiled and gave him a quick nod.

Keryon's eyes narrowed. "I don't like it when you say things like that. Getting the food was already risky enough. What else was it this time?"

Gimlore dropped Keryon in the cot and leaned into him, her face close to his. Her voice was raspy as she whispered. "I stole a chisel."

Keryon tried to get away from her embrace, but her gaze kept him focused. "You devilish woman."

Sometimes Gimlore woke up and the world seemed better, as though she could face anyone and do anything. It was not one of those times. Vicious visions of her children being stolen had left her unable to sleep. Instead, she just stayed there, crying, listening to the crickets, and clutching her sack-blankets to mitigate the cold.

But that was all she had.

The warmth of the previous day's meal was long gone, and the guards did the rounds, their steps echoing in the distance, boots clinking methodically.

A few months back, she could have handled these guards well enough on her own, but she wasn't who she used to be. No longer the bushwhacking brigand, taverner, or landowner. She was Gimlore the prisoner, now.

A slight sound of stealthy footsteps rustled the bare, yellow grass. She perked her ears. Someone was up at that time of night... and trying to be quiet about it.

Very slowly, Gimlore leveraged herself halfway up, her body aching from the labour. Her eyes scanned the entire camp, and a subtle, stealthy movement caught her attention. She squinted to try to figure out what or who that was and saw a small figure making its way to the guards' tent.

Shit.

It had to be Hope trying to sneak into the tent on her own. She'd insisted on going with Gimlore a few times, and now it seemed like she was venturing on her own.

I should have known better.

It was one thing for Gimlore to get lashed, but the guards didn't care that Hope was only a child. They'd lash her anyway, and if she couldn't take it, they'd dump her body somewhere in this forsaken desert, never to be found again.

Panic rose within her. She wanted to help Hope, but if she got up now, she could ruin everything for the child's plan, so she just sat back, biting nails, and cursing herself for ever showing her how to do that. A few moments later, when the guard was patrolling with his back facing the tent, the flap opened slightly, and Hope left, sneaking back to her little cot. When the child finally rested and wrapped the sack around her, Gimlore let out a breath of relief.

Now she *really* couldn't go back to sleep. She would need to chastise Hope and show her that just because Gimlore had done it, didn't mean she could do it, too. Especially not on her own.

Eighteen
Family and Greed

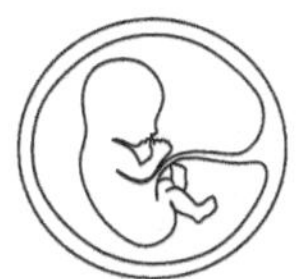

Orberesis - Solvi

Orberesis couldn't believe what he saw. He'd expected a lot of things, but never this in a million years. He'd been out there, in the void, and yet *this* left him nearly speechless, losing all his grace.

"Solvi... You're..."

She smiled and gave him a curt bow. For the gods, he had missed that smile. A boundless devotion. There she was again, but he reckoned she had changed. How long had it been?

"Where have you been? I lost you..." he said, babbling, losing composure.

Why hadn't he looked for Solvi? Where had she been? What an idiot he was.

Fuck.

"They took me prisoner in Heleronde, Highest One. But I escaped." Her hands still caressed the belly and the smile hadn't left her face. "It's good to see you again, safe and sound."

Orberesis was going to say something and ask about the child, but King Doemus got up and extended his hands towards him.

"Highest One, I am so glad to have you back. We all are! Whatever happened to you? To all our troops? We didn't hear about your arrival from the guards. I shall have them punished for it."

"Please hold on, Your Highness. I just... arrived. No need to punish anyone."

The King hesitated, confused at first, but then it must have dawned on him Orberesis had divine powers. "Of course, Highest One, of course. Apologies."

"No need for that either. It's good to see you too, my King. I'm sure it has not been easy on you, a lot of different things I've missed. I have much to tell you as well."

Orberesis' eyes flickered to Solvi again. It had to be his, the child. Him, Orberesis, was going to be a father! How could that be? He had never considered that, but... it made sense.

The Old One stirred. *Don't get distracted, Doi. It may not look like it, but the war has already started and we need to win. Remember why we're here.*

He gritted his teeth and clasped his hands into fists, forcing himself to take a deep breath.

"Shall we meet in the Council Room?" the King asked.

With a sour smile, Orberesis nodded, and the three went on their way. He did not miss that room and all the pointless discussions that were held there. He had sat there so often already, pretending to be a godly being, manipulating a king to do his bidding, surrounded by fools like Taishay and others he did not miss. Tavanar's absence left a sour taste in his mouth, though.

"I'll call for the rest of the Council members," King Doemus said, already trying to get the attention of one of the guards.

"My King, I was thinking that after my last venture in the Holy Land, there are only two people in this world I can trust." He paused for dramatic effect. "The two of you."

He studied their reactions, Solvi in particular. "I'd appreciate it if we kept this meeting just between the three of us."

"I'm honoured, Highest One," Solvi said with a slight bow.

Orberesis was momentarily distracted by her and her belly and took a moment to gather his thoughts.

Focus!

The King mulled it over with a hand on his chin. He never liked going against the tradition, but he was still a devout believer. "Well, I'd appreciate Taishay's presence, but... I'm sure this will be fine."

"Thank you, Your Majesty. As you know, the battle was difficult. We were ambushed by the Alarkani hounds and their hired mercenaries of the Leeth, and few made it out alive. We were outplayed by them, I admit it. I was too confident in our own efforts and in our own abilities, so I underestimated the enemy and fell for their traps when I shouldn't have."

Silence prevailed in the room.

"As you will notice, I no longer carry the sacred orb around my neck. It shattered and I absorbed the powers. If you already thought I was powerful before, you should see what I can do now. And how often I can do it."

"I never doubted you, Highest One... Even if that was indeed quite the price to pay for the Two Nations. Did you find the elixir after the battle was lost?"

The damn elixir! Orberesis had forgotten about it. As soon as the orb broke and his headaches, migraines, and nightmares stopped, he no longer had any use for it. How could he break it to the King... "I got a hold of a single vial, but it was lost in the destruction."

"Destruction... caused by the battle?"

How to tell them about the Lantern Horns... He hadn't thought this through.

"When I was hiding and recovering from the battle, I had the time to be acquainted with my new abilities. I dug deep into myself, seeking a power that could ensure us victory while claiming not just the elixir, but the whole of the Alarkani continent where it is produced, to ensure dominance over our rivals."

Take it easy... And maybe they'll bite.

He had been lying his entire life, but weaving lies with the truth had never been his forte. There was no way of saying what he was about to say in a way that sounded credible, so he took a deep breath, relaxed his shoulders, and continued with a straight face.

"While I was resting, I realised I had the ability to summon a kind of sentient creature called Lantern Horns. They obey me, so I rallied them to fight for me. They crawled out of the mud and sent the Alarkani bastards to their maker. Now as I sit here before you, they are the ones who control Alarkan for us."

King Doemus' brow was furrowed, and his lips moved as he considered what Orberesis had just said. "Highest One, that's... a lot to take in. Are you sure you don't want other councillors present? I could call in Taishay rather quickly—"

"I don't."

The King nodded. "If Alarkan belongs to the Two Nations, what are we to do next? Look for the elixir? That could finally be the break we need to sort out our finances once and for all!"

Oh, poor fool...

"We can get the elixir, but if I may, Your Majesty, I think you are missing the scale of the powers I've just awakened. I only wish you could see it. We can accomplish so much more, now. We just need to stay strong. Stay together."

His eyes swerved to Solvi, who had been unusually quiet, her hands caressing her belly.

"Of course, Highest One. Do you want me to nominate an ambassador for Alarkan to represent you there with these... *Lantern Horns?* Would you like me to hand you that title? It was your victory, after all."

Orberesis shook his head. "The offer is generous, as expected of you, my King, but I'm afraid I have other plans, much larger than Alarkan or the Two Nations. I dream with higher and wider grounds. With my powers, I can deliver them to you, Your Majesty."

Doemus had a look of genuine disbelief, his mouth agape. "My Lord, but... which grounds? I'm not sure I follow. Maybe it *is* better to have Taishay present. I've never been much fond of governing."

Orberesis dropped his head, rubbed his face, and sighed for the spectacle of it.

"Now that my powers have awakened, I realise we have enemies well beyond our knowledge. And they are rising," he said, seeing confusion in the eyes of both Solvi and King Doemus.

"Hidden enemies? Highest One, I'm not following..."

"The world's smokesmiths have a leader. A man with powers that can rival mine. And they're intent on taking Alarkan and destroying everything I stand for. I think they will come here. They will come for the Two Nations as well."

That part was a bad lie, but one Doemus was more likely to digest it. Why would the smoke bastards care about the Two Nations? They only cared about killing him, specifically.

"Well, we can't let that happen!" The King raised his voice. "Who is this man and where is he?"

"His location is said to be somewhere in the Thousand Hills." He couldn't tell them about the failed attempt at quenching the Essence once and for all. They must see it as a guaranteed win, even if much had to be done. "But I know nothing about him. It's my mission to make sure we prepare to defend ourselves and start seeking allies."

"What should I do, Highest One?" Doemus asked. "The Two Nations are weakened. Our people are poor, starved..."

"We will gather what's left of our forces. And we will make allies, by subjugation if we must. This can't just be a battle between me and the man, especially if he has smokesmiths fighting with him. We need to strengthen our forces."

"But what about the Two Nations, Highest One? Don't get me wrong, I am your most fervorous servant, but our kingdoms are in a dire situation. Poverty is like a plague, diseases run rampant, and most of the wealth has already been collected by us in taxes. If I raise the taxes once more, I am afraid I'll face an uprising. We don't even have enough gold to feed our existing soldiers for long. The lords continue to supply their crops, and the merchants are selling our goods, but it's just... not enough. And now without a proper military..."

"We have the Lantern Horns. They can defend the Two Nations if they must. Better than soldiers would, and with unquestionable loyalty."

Doemus scratched his chin. "I see. So, you want us to gather forces and seek allies before this elusive enemy does?"

"Precisely." Orberesis smiled. He had to admit he had missed some human interaction, especially with people who understood him, and were loyal or stupid enough to never even question him. He had spent months in his own head, tolerating the Old One's eerie laughter and the silence of the Lantern Horns. It was good to be in Ushar again. "We must find allies. We've no time to waste."

"Where do we start?"

Orberesis hesitated. "I will meet with you and the others soon to discuss my proposal, if that pleases you, Your Majesty. Now, I'm sure you have a lot to think about, so Solvi and I shall leave you to do just that, if that pleases you."

"Certainly." Doemus rose from his chair and gave him a bow, then sat back again. "I have missed you and your wisdom, Highest One."

Orberesis gave him a curt bow before leaving the Council Room. "And I your faith and generosity, my King."

These moments as Orberesis and Solvi left the room were loaded with emotion. How odd, to feel emotions again. So uncomfortably human, as though he was lesser... He was supposed to be a divine being now, a real god, not a human burdened by feelings, expectations, and fears. The truth was, he had no idea what to do when he was a father. How would he be a good father if he spent his days training Temporal Exploration and planning to defeat the Essence and her minions? Too many questions. Too many doubts clouding his judgement.

The Old One's voice rumbled in him. *You do not have time for distractions, Doi.*

You're not in charge, Orberesis thought.

"You probably have some questions, Highest One," Solvi said, her pale face growing red as she spoke.

He nodded. "You're... with child. Mine?"

Solvi smiled. "Couldn't be anybody else's."

Orberesis found himself smiling, but he wasn't sure why. He tried to contain his emotions, but they were urging to pour out of him. Too strong—like a river, they would not be held back. He wanted to jump and punch the air at the thought of a tiny human that looked like him and shared his blood. He could picture himself carrying the child over his shoulder or walking in a garden or sitting by the bonfire just as his father had done with him.

"I see," was all he said.

No distractions!

An awkward silence settled between them until he sensed something different in her eyes, like she wanted him to say something. He cleared his throat. "It will be an honour to take care of the child... with you... if you want me to."

Solvi hadn't expected God Himself's words to fill a void, or to warm her nights, but they had seemed almost devoid of emotion, as though he was only saying what someone in that position was supposed to say. She observed him more closely, still, taking notice of everything he said and did.

She had seen him as a grand paragon of truth, the beacon of light in her darkness. Now, something was different, and she couldn't tell if it had been he who had changed or if it was merely her gaze. The time she had spent in the jailhouse in Heleronde had certainly changed her, and the same went for the time she had spent thinking about Keryon's words. And then Rednow's message to the smokesmiths...

She hadn't yet had the courage to reveal that to the Highest One. Perhaps he would think she was siding with the enemy, and she couldn't have that. Her child couldn't have that.

"It will be *my* honour to bear your child, Highest One," she said.

It wasn't *just* her, though. She was sure of it. God Himself seemed different. His shoulder-length dark hair was the same, as was his neatly trimmed beard. The white robe he wore didn't look any different, although he looked much hollower, thinner than the last time she had seen him. What she found the most different about him were the expressions in his face and how they seemed to change often, as though he momentarily became somebody else. Sometimes his eyes were... scary, deeper and with convoluted secrets.

"How did you get here? I was worried about you."

Solvi explained everything, but left out Keryon, Gimlore, and Tavanar, at least for now. Knowing just how much Orberesis hated Gimlore, she couldn't risk the Highest One going after Keryon as well just because of who he had associated with.

She swallowed. *What if the King tells him? Would he think me a liar?*

"What of you, Highest One? How did you survive while I was prisoner?"

There was a slight shift in his eyes again, and then again. He sat at a window parapet overlooking the capital, and Solvi sat beside him. "I ended up in one of those water caverns. And the Lantern Horns helped me break out."

She had been wondering how he had been able to break out. She'd seen him in displays of power that had left her speechless, so she knew he was not a fluke, but the destruction he had caused was slightly out of character for him. He had always been a force for good, hadn't he? The Miracle helped rid the Known World of the wretched beasts that plagued it, and now he had used that power against the same humanity he had saved.

What if these Lantern Horns had killed her, or worse, lost her the baby?

She shook those thoughts away. That must have been Keryon's ideas taking root. *My child needs a father.*

"We should meet with the King and discuss the next steps in your plan, Highest One."

He smiled and caressed her face, but instead of leaving her nearly in tears as that touch used to, it was nothing but a bittersweet fruit that she could feel was already fully ripened.

Orberesis nodded. "Let's go, then."

He gave her his arm and she took it gladly.

They met the King in the ceremonial room again, and Orberesis sat at his right side.

"We're going to need all the help we can get. You know politics better than most, my King. Who could we go to for help?"

Doemus adjusted his monocle. "We're not in the best of terms with any of our direct neighbours, but I suppose the alliance depends on where you need the troops to go to. If you need them to disembark in Alarkan, then perhaps Mosendel and Ainis would make sense as our allies. They could march their garrisons to Alarkan and have ships transport them in days."

Orberesis shook his head. Solvi wished she could stay with him and let time pass. Raise the baby together in a calm life. But Orberesis seemed to have other ideas, other plans. And he was the Highest One, so she listened.

"The enemy is holed up in Vaerghulen, in The Thousand Hills. That's where we should focus."

King Doemus pulled out a map from his bag and spread it open, using his monocle to analyse the parchment. "In that case, I still suggest Ainis and Mosendel, but we have more options. Shari and Gasho would make sense from a geographical point of view."

"How open to an alliance would they be?" Solvi asked.

Doemus shrugged. "It's difficult to say, and it would depend on the terms of this so-called alliance. They'd want things we don't have to give. Ainis remains divided, and they are a sea-faring nation, much like the Two Nations. They are not known for their infantries. Mosendel would be a considerably stronger ally, but rumour says that their leaders have already heard about our invasion to Alarkan, which they didn't like too much, as it was very close to them."

"They owe me for the Miracle of ten years ago," Orberesis said, a deep frown in his face. "I saved them more than any other nation. Yes, I broke their cities, but their people no longer have to lock themselves at home in fear of the wretched beasts that plagued them. Surely, it's a favour I can collect on."

"Maybe, Highest One. You might be right."

"What about Gasho and Shari?"

"Little is known about Shari. They are neutral and King Lunit does not like to meddle. They might be harder to persuade, but we don't know their army's head count, Highest One. They have always been friendly at the borders, never attempting anything with us or any other neighbours."

"Sounds like a reasonable king."

"And Gasho... It's just chaos. Many months ago, I got word that the king had his own son killed. Others said it was all a conspiracy, but the entire court has turned on the king since then. Blood on the streets."

"No heir and no king. Who is in charge, then?"

"High lords and petty lords are squabbling for power, as expected. They faced a wave of unrest from the populace, and it seems like they all agreed to unite in a sort of closed council to keep the country in order. They all stab each other in the back anyway, no doubt, even if they pretend to agree on matters. Sooner or later, one of them will emerge victorious and take the crown."

"Most interesting developments. Much obliged, Your Majesty. Your ability to read the political landscape never ceases to amaze me."

"Can I ask what your plans are, Highest One?" Solvi asked. She needed to know his frame of mind. Was he lusting for blood?

"I don't know yet, Solvi. The king's precious knowledge will serve us, though. We need to figure out who the most reliable ally is. Perhaps all of them."

A brief silence stretched over the three of them and Solvi didn't dare open her mouth. The Highest One had always had bold ideas that nobody else understood or thought possible. Ideas that many opposed. But that didn't mean he was wrong. She would trust him. Keep her faith in him.

"I don't doubt you, Highest One, but... how?" The King hesitated, which comforted Solvi. At least she wasn't the only one. All of this seemed too sudden, too careless. Too unrealistic, even with his abilities and the Lantern Horns.

"As you well know, diplomacy goes a long way, Your Majesty. But if that doesn't work, then I shall use my powers to employ another kind of diplomacy. A less peaceful one."

Nineteen

Inner Flight

Rednow

The support hadn't been what Rednow had expected. It didn't take long for him to feel the arrival of others to whom he was connected via the Essence. Smokesmiths, for the most part, but also pineheads. It had only been days after his message to the smokesmiths, but so many of them had made their way to the Thousand Hills.

But upon seeing him, the intentions in some of them wavered. He could sense the hesitation in many.

He was just a skeleton now, surrounded by a cloud of deadly smoke and capable of flying. He was the smoke itself, no longer fully human like them.

"Were your old avatars always like this?"

What do you mean? the Essence asked.

"I'm dead. A skeleton. Inhuman."

No. You're quite unusual in many ways. There might be a way for you to regain human form at times.

"You didn't think to mention that?"

Ah, you humans... Ever obsessed with looks over substance. Haven't you found many advantages to this form?

She was right, but he still made the mental note to ask her how he could attain a human form again.

His gaze shifted to the many smokesmiths and pineheads who had set up camp near the Builders' sacred village. Rednow, Arkan, and Pinesy had met with them several times. He had explained everything many times over. Some resigned to disbelief, and others validated those thoughts, and worried about the shadowlings already plaguing the mainland.

He couldn't say he *sat* at these meetings, because he no longer had a physical presence and he communicated directly with their minds. Despite all this, he had made sure to continue Tinko's training more fiercely than ever. Even now, he watched far in the distance as the child moved with precision, wielding the weapon, and striking the air back and forth.

Now, Tinko was also being trained in the spear by the Builders, and in a multitude of other weapons by fellow smokesmiths, who were impressed by the talent of such a young child.

"The kid looks sharp already," Arkan said, appearing next to him.

Rednow had come to respect the Builder more than he had ever expected. He reminded Rednow of himself.

I'm distracted, Arkan. Apologies. I can't help but feel I failed the child.

"Failed? You saved them. You did the best you could. And you saved us all too."

Will these smokesmiths be enough for what's to come?

Arkan eyed a group of newly arrived smokesmiths setting up their camp near the haven's entrance, and Rednow could only guess what was on his mind. By their polished clothes and dark skin, these had probably come from Mosendel or Ainis. That meant they had only arrived that early because they hadn't had a long journey ahead. It wouldn't be the same for the others.

"We'll work with what we have, with who we have," Arkan said. "I came to meet you because I wanted to ask you something."

What is it?

"Do you want to learn the Inner Flight? Truth be told, I'm not sure a Smoke Rider can even learn it, especially one in your current condition. Back then, sentinels and Smoke Riders were separate forces... But we don't have much to lose."

Rednow was caught by surprise. *You said it can't be taught.*

Arkan grimaced, scratching the back of his head. "Yes, but that was a lie. To discourage you."

Can I learn it? I'm no longer human. I can already fly.

Arkan shook his head. "Forget everything you think the Inner Flight is. In fact, the less you know about it, the *better* it is for you. You will come out of it... different. Empowered. I'll say that much."

I'm sensing there's a catch.

Arkan nodded. "It will take time to master. Perhaps we still have enough time, but you'd have to start now. And it is *very* hard, Rednow. Even if you are... different. It might be harder than anything you've ever done."

Rednow thought about his life. Watching his parents die, fending for himself and his baby sister for years on the run to find a safe location, far from everyone. Starting an army, train-ing them, and preparing them for the hardships of the world. Killing in battle and outside of it. He'd been a hero and saviour to some, and the Blood Collector to more.

He very much doubted this would be the hardest thing he'd ever done.

Then he glanced at Tinko. Now he was no longer the Blood Collector, just *Uncle*, one that appeared as a flying skeleton.

I want to try it.

Arkan shook his head. "There is no try, Rednow. You either go through it or you don't. And only when it is over do we know if you succeeded or not."

What happens if I fail?

The hint of a smile appeared on Arkan's face. "What else is there to do but try again? Though that means twice the hard-ship. Twice the pain."

Rednow saw the truth behind his words. The man had gone through his share of hardships. He had assumed the Builders were sheltered and isolated, but they had been abandoned by a deity and dealt with the generational pain of that loss. Arkan, too, was well acquainted with pain.

From all of your cousins, how many have undergone the Inner Flight?

"Well, all of them."

And how many succeeded?

"A few. I was the only to survive the first attempt."

That explained why Arkan seemed to be their leader and was respected like a leader despite his hard work to claim he wasn't, and that they only listened to the Essence.

It would be my honour to join you on that pedestal.

Arkan scowled. "Be careful what you wish for. When do you want to try it?"

Rednow looked around but saw nothing pressing. He wondered if he was underestimating the toll this Inner Flight would take on him, or how long it would take him to crack it.

Now is as good a time as any. I trust your cousins and Pinesy will continue to keep welcoming whoever wants to join us.

Arkan nodded. "And we'll keep the child safe."

Thank you. Are you sure I should do this?

Rednow wouldn't forgive himself if anything happened to Tinko. He had already failed Gimlore in his promise to keep Thata safe, and he had grown accustomed to the child. He couldn't let anything happen to them.

Arkan nodded. "I think you should."

Very well. How do I start?

"First, come into the temple and sit," he said as he walked into one of the chiselled alcoves. There were mats, rugs, and pillows all over the floor, and Rednow understood this was a place for prayer or meditation. "The Inner Flight is a journey. You must mentally prepare yourself for it. I would tell you to close your eyes, but you don't... have eyes anymore. The point is you need to find your inner tune. The way your consciousness works. Your identity. What makes you who you are."

That is vague, Arkan.

"And so is the Inner Flight, but I trust that you'll understand it when the time is right. You have the Essence coursing through you, after all."

Rednow found himself wishing he didn't have the deity's remnants clinging to him and all the loss of privacy that came with it, but tried to keep Arkan's words in mind, and did his best to shut off external stimulations. That was all he could call them now without actual senses. And yet, he could *feel* it all the more intensely than ever. Instead of focusing on those, he focused on himself.

There's nothing left in me.

Only him and the emptiness, and the bloody sword still in his hand. Rednow sat with no smoke. Just a skeleton in a prayer room.

"Good luck," Arkan said as he left Rednow to himself.

With no time to waste, Rednow focused harder on himself but soon realised how fickle one's mind was as his thoughts often wandered.

"Are you going to help me with this?" he whispered.

I have no control over one's Inner Flight. It is enabled by me, but each person has a different Inner Flight, so there really is no way for me to help.

"You always have to make everything hard, eh?"

He'd have to do this without her, then. Rednow couldn't close his eyes, but he could choose to stop *seeing* things around him, so he did that. Slowly, there were slight shifts to the dark environment in which he found himself while meditating. Whether by choice or natural occurrence, the darkness moulded itself and started to take shape.

The sky adopted red as its favourite colour. Ashes drifted in the air even though there was no wind. He extended his hand, and there it was: the spine and rib cage that could have belonged to a giant. Was this how he really saw the world and himself in it? Bare bones in a red desert?

I'm not just made of bones.

The words emerged in his mind and Rednow wondered if that was an attempt to convince himself he was more than he actually was. Then the environment changed again. The red sky darkened and water lilies grew along the ground. In that trance, no matter how many steps he took forward, his feet would splash the water and the lilies would float in it, rocked by the ripples he caused. Like children playing in the puddle. Jumping, jumping, jumping.

He walked aimlessly for a while, nothing behind him or on the horizon. He glanced at the ground again and saw himself reflected in the water.

Distorted. Twisted. Cut in half. Countless repetitions of him, and yet none were any closer to who he really was, all of them faulty.

Rednow pushed his hesitation aside and walked. After some time, he ended up next to a natural pond he was so familiar with. Or a version of it. It brought him back to the Seven Peaks. He stopped and took a step back.

No.

He didn't want to go there. Not *these* memories. Not a part of himself he had managed to forget. This was the pond where he would bring his nephew, Rednalf, to train his sword forms.

Where he had let Rednalf die.

It all opened to Rednow like a massive flesh wound. In the middle of the pond, there was a large water lily. Pink and covered in floating broad, green leaves.

No. I don't want this. He had tried so damn hard to forget Rednalf's death under his watchful eye. How could he have— two children lost, all because of him. Rednalf would have been a man now, perhaps taller than him, with his bright red hair.

The images were drawing him in, even though he struggled. He had no choice but to touch the large water lily. It was gentle, soft to the touch. As his bony finger lingered in the flower, it withered, and the rot spread slowly through the extensive network of water lilies that covered the ground as far as he could see. Little by little, the plants rotted, and the water around them turned into a thick red.

Blood.

From the withered flower, the body of a boy emerged, rising from the bloody water.

No. No. Not this.

Rednalf's red hair was obvious, even from a distance, and Rednow recoiled at the sight. This was like having his head kept underwater even as he struggled to breathe. It was a memory he had long buried. One he had wished to erase, if such a thing was possible. A death that had been entirely his fault. His tainted touch had destroyed the soft innocence that should have stayed with Rednalf in life.

Rednow collapsed onto his knees, accepting the weight of this tragedy.

My fault. It was my fault. All of it.

The blood red water drained from under his feet, leaving simply puddles across the muddy ground. Some patches of flowers returned, flourishing quickly in bursts, pink and purple petals growing and stretching out. The sky diluted from its crimson hue to a melancholic mix of purple and orange. Clouds came and covered parts of it, unloading thick rain on him and his surroundings.

In the distance, one of his mirrored images had risen from its reflection. Kneeling, it glanced at him. Slowly, a reflection of his red blade also emerged from the water. The sword hovered in the air, pointing at the reflection.

No. No. Not again.

With a strike, the sword lunged forward and stuck itself to the ribcage of the skeleton, who remained on its knees.

Rebma!

Rednow ran to stop the blade, but he realised that was him as well. He had also placed his sister in a situation where she could be killed.

It was all my fault. Nobody else's.

Then the clouds broke apart and the purple sky emerged with all its splendour. But as it did, the skeletons on the ground, reflected in the water, came to life. Those were no reflections. Those were all the people he had killed. Thousands of them, dead by his own blade, or those of his people. They all stood now, facing him like equals.

For those, Rednow felt no remorse. They had died fighting for themselves or for someone they had sworn to protect. They were no victims. It didn't matter what he thought, though, as the skeletons marched towards him from all directions.

He glanced left, then right, but there was nowhere to run.

I'm not running. They're my own demons to kill.

To them, *he* was the demon.

The skeletons charged at him, caring not for his preparation. He still had the dreaded red blade to fend for himself, so he did. As they came closer, their faces took the shape of those they'd belonged to. He didn't recognise many of those, but some he did.

Good. Face them again. Face your demonic side, he heard himself say.

But that hadn't been him thinking, had it?

He thrashed against the attacking skeletons. In the Inner Flight, there was no getting tired, so the skeletons continued to get back and charge again whenever he slammed them down or cut their bones in half.

His strategy wasn't working, so he concentrated on himself, removing the distractions. One by one, the skeletons vanished in threads of smoke, leaving him alone again as he stood there, posing with his sword, making sure there weren't more.

The skeletons had left, but they'd carved holes in him that he was able to fill by accepting and moving on, by working on himself. With a deep breath, he sat and contemplated the scenery, crying.

He was so tired, and yet it wasn't physical exhaustion. A butterfly flew around him, landing on the hilt of his sword with its dark yellow wings still flapping. Its form morphed into a bird, which kept growing until it became an eagle. The bird of prey took off and grew into a bird giant enough to hide the light from the sun.

What am I supposed to do here?

Arkan had told him he would know when he was finished, but Rednow didn't even know how close to the end he was.

He had high expectations for himself, but the Inner Flight had humbled him with a mix of guilt and all his deep-rooted fears. He knew it was a trial of sorts, but how was he supposed to overcome it?

The giant eagle descended from the sky and landed before him. It spread its wings and they turned into human arms. The rest slowly gained human features.

Rednow gasped as he saw his own features.

Still with traces of red in his hair and beard and a face riddled with scars and burn marks that had never healed properly. There was something about this version of him that unsettled Rednow. The facial expression, perhaps. There was... malice in it.

"Malice? Please. If there's malice in me, then there is malice in you. We are one."

Rednow shivered and realised he was now made of flesh and blood; perhaps only at this moment, but he appreciated it.

The doppelganger marched forward and charged at him with a copy of the red sword. Rednow used instinct to parry the strike, but the figure seemed to know his every move.

"What's the matter? Afraid?"

Rednow wondered what would happen to him if he got hurt while in the Inner Flight. He was battling himself, after all. Arkan had been vague about that, but the answer was probably nothing good, and he wasn't keen to find out.

Strike after strike, the doppelganger pushed him back. Rednow gritted his teeth and increased the pressure, moving from sword form to sword form. The doppelganger smiled, aware of his every move.

"I told you. I am you."

He didn't wait for an answer, and Rednow had no intention of giving him one. But he wasn't about to get slaughtered by a representation of himself. *He* should be in control. He would need to figure out a way to win. The figure's pressure increased, using every pace, style, and forms in Rednow's arsenal, forcing him to experience what it was like to fight him.

With another step back, he parried the blade again but the doppelganger was already biting at his skin, with several cuts and gashes spreading all over his arms and shoulders.

"What are you doing, Rednow? Why do you run like this when you should look forward and face me. Face yourself!"

"You shut up or I will do it for you," Rednow said with gritted teeth.

"The enemy is only one. It's me. It's you. You know yourself, don't you? So, what do you fear, exactly?"

Rednow wished he could look back and find inspiration in the words of a wise figure in his youth, but the truth was there had been no one, only the wild. There had been mountains and rivers, and beasts lurking beyond the camp. He'd never had a training partner, only boulders and trees. All his battle worth had been tested the hard way with blood and sweat against opponents that were sometimes better, sometimes worse, but never luckier than him.

"Don't step back, Rednow. Keep going forward! Don't stand still!" The doppelganger said it, but he could almost hear *himself* saying that to the young recruits of the Leeth he had trained year after year. To Tinko. So why didn't he follow his own advice? What was holding him back?

"Retreat and you will keep ageing into death."

"I'm already dead," Rednow said as he managed to strike. "Why am I fighting myself, then?"

The doppelganger smirked. "Fool. You are doing this..." He struck hard and Rednow barely caught the blow, "...so that when you fight a fierce battle on the outside, your inner world doesn't waver."

Had he strayed that far from his own teachings? Had he... got soft?

"Enough with the self-pity!" the doppelganger bellowed. "Enough whimpering! You think this is a game?"

The doppelganger took a step back and his bellow turned into a roar. He grew, his skin turned purple, and his limbs expanded. Rednow got a chill just watching it. This was what his enemies must see when he transformed with the smoke. It didn't take long until he was facing his eight foot tall self.

"I refuse to let you whimper. If you are weaker than me, then so be it. I'll destroy you. Or you can prove you are stronger."

Rednow transformed as well, this time with no need for the smoke, just in time to dodge the claws of his other self.

He had vicious speed and power in that form and didn't have to worry about his lungs deteriorating because of the smoke. Perhaps he could do this.

"You're thinking too much! We have a deep-rooted instinct within our body to kill." The doppelganger struck again, and the claws caught Rednow in the chest, slashing it open before he could get out of the way. "And yet, you try using your brain to fight instead. You try to defeat me with logic. You should know now it doesn't work! Stop this nonsense!"

A massive blow caught Rednow in the chin, and he dropped like a fish, eyes blurring, his mind spinning. The pain was very real.

Stay sharp! He rolled sideways just as a punch from the doppelganger crushed the ground where he had been. Rednow grabbed the massive figure's arm and stuck to it. He was tired of being told what to do. As a child, all the adults wanted him to serve masters as a smokesmith. Then the kings wanted to hire his armies for half a bag of silver and empty promises. And then the Essence left him half-dead without an arm. Now, he was trapped with his own beastly side.

The least he could do was show the bastard *he* was in control.

Rednow bit the doppelganger's hand. He tore into the flesh and his image screamed, punching him in the face. Rednow let go of the bite and rallied himself with a flurry of unhinged strikes. He couldn't let his demonic side take over. He needed to be whole when he fought the Old One. Like a mountain.

It was the first time anyone could keep up with Rednow in that form, and he lost track of how long they fought for. Gashes and cuts pierced even his thick leathery skin. But Rednow kept going as though the enemy was the Old One, aiming for the softer parts—the eyeballs, the nose, and the mouth. The doppelganger shielded himself with the forearm, but Rednow tore at them with rage, ripping skin, flesh, and even bone, until he found himself staring at the ground. The doppelganger had gone. He saw himself reflected in a puddle again, this time covered in blood, hurting more than he would ever care to admit.

Then a tiny firefly appeared in front of his eyes, flying all over him, a tiny voice repeating random words as it flew.

Uncle, show me!

Tinko...

The firefly slowly made its way across the endless plain where it stood and the moment Rednow started keeping up with it, a blurry cavern emerged, clearing with every step. The firefly lit the way in the dark.

He stumbled and had to mind the tall ceiling and the uneven surface, but with the light to follow, he could do it. Battered and hurt, Rednow walked slowly until he saw a glimpse of light at the end of the cavern, and suddenly the firefly stopped and threw itself into his chest.

The pain went away. The gashes and the injuries left him, but so did the skin and flesh. He was back to being nothing but bones shrouded in smoke. This time, though, he felt in control, as though no pain from the past weighed him down.

Now he truly knew himself.

Twenty

Unexpected Growth

Gimlore

One thing Gimlore had learned during her time in the quarry was that the sun could always shine a little brighter and the days could always get a little hotter. She could always sweat a little more and there was always room for more blisters. The days were getting longer too, which meant they'd all have to work longer hours and in even worse conditions.

Next to her, a prisoner collapsed.

Shit.

Gimlore kept hammering the chisel but managed to kick the man awake again. "Wake up or they'll make sure you don't ever see another sunset!"

She knew she sounded mad, perhaps harsher than she intended, but she just couldn't bear any more of them falling to the guards. It was about time she did something about the bastards.

The prisoner opened his eyes, still dizzy from the heat and the lack of water. "Th-thank you," he babbled, before reaching for his hammer again.

She wasn't satisfied with it. Surely, he would fall on his back-side again and collapse once more. The guards would see him there, and he would be taken or lashed on the spot. She had to bite her lips to contain the ire, and her grip on the hammer tightened.

Not yet... The time will come.

Later that evening, she sat by the stew pot with another group of prisoners, some rougher than the others. Gimlore knew what they'd do when they were outside of the guards' control. She knew what kind of people they were, but she was no one to judge. In there, they were all the same.

The whip cared not whose back it cracked open.

Keryon sat next to Tooth, who couldn't stop telling another story. Next to Gimlore, Hope sat, an occasional laugh coming from her.

"The man looked like he had seen a demon from the under-world when he found his wife staring at him!" Tooth shouted.

The prisoners laughed. Gimlore admitted some might have found it funny but others must be doing it because sometimes joy had to be manufactured. They *wanted* to be part of something. Something that mattered. Something good.

And it was bloody contagious.

She nearly found herself laughing as well. Keryon was glancing her way and a smile on his face told her it was going to be alright in the end, even if the underworld seemed like a real place.

"Has anybody else got any stories?" the Tooth asked.

"Oh, I got a few funny ones," Keryon said. "It's from the time I met Gimlore over there".

The small crowd was now looking at her, expectant. What the fuck was he doing?

She glanced at him, eyes wide as if to say 'Don't you fucking dare', but her facial expression only seemed to make the crowd more eager to hear all about it.

Keryon got up and strutted around to captivate the small audience. Gimlore's last hopes of not being in the middle of this circus died then. Where in the underworld had he got this penchant for theatrics?

"I arrived at the town and walked in, well aware there was a *bad* woman running everything from behind the counter. She must have heard who I was because a few weeks later, she came in to pour me a drink."

The crowd laughed and Gimlore scowled. "I was already making plans to feed you to the bloodsleuths, if that clears it up."

Keryon pointed at himself. "And yet, here am I, still alive. Here we are, side by side...." He trailed off, and the crowd loved it. Bloody underworld. What was he doing? "Anyway... back to that fateful day. We had a couple of drinks together at the tavern, but I'm an honourable man. I am a serious fellow! So, I went back home. But you know what happened? Next thing I knew, she was there! She came to say hi..."

Gimlore gritted her teeth, but her cheeks warmed. "I went to make you an offer! And the bloodsleuths were still in the picture..."

The prisoners laughed again and even Hope looked at her, with a smile spreading across her face. What was so bloody funny about any of this?

"And then I saved her once from the people that invaded the town."

Gimlore had no answer to that, yet his eyes lingered on her, as though he was daring her to find something to counter with.

She had none. *Damn it!*

"I should say she saved me in many ways too. The people she took in and welcomed in her town with arms wide open would have struggled anywhere else. Convicts, much like us... people still wounded from all the wars, those who were abused by their lords and masters... She welcomed them all."

The prisoners' gaze turned to her and many nodded their respect.

"It wasn't much, Heleronde. But it was the best many of us had ever had, and that was enough, wasn't it?"

She struggled to hide a tear as Keryon looked at her directly. She felt Hope's comforting hand rubbing her back and she snapped out of it. "You were a fucking terrible herb salesman, so yes, I saved your career when I made you Warden. You're welcome, by the way."

The laughs broke out again and Keryon smiled at her, jokingly punching himself in the chin and pretending to drop unconscious. The bastard had to be both handsome and bloody charismatic, didn't he? Even *she* ended up laughing at that little fucking stunt.

After the pot was taken back to the tent and the prisoners broke out to sleep, several of them reached out to her to tell her how great it must be to be imprisoned with your loved one, and Gimlore wanted to stop them and tell them she wasn't really in love with the man, or that it was more complicated than that.

As they patted her on the back, all reassuring smiles, she understood what Keryon had pulled. He had made her popular with the prisoners and built her up as a saviour of the common folk, laying the foundation for a rebellion.

Sneaky bastard isn't stupid.

"Where is this town of yours?" Hope asked, bringing her out of her thoughts. "I want to go there!"

She grimaced. "It's... occupied at the moment. But when I get out of here, I'll do my best to take it back."

"Are you going to kill them?" The child's eyes were dead serious.

Gimlore thought about what the best response was, and ended up sighing and nodding. "Probably."

"I better get strong, then. I'm coming with you, and they're going to run away as soon as they see me."

Gimlore raised an eyebrow. Hope was not even five feet tall and nearly all her bones were showing under the skin. She might be the skinniest girl Gimlore had ever seen. The thought of her hurting someone or killing people was absurd. But she could also see how serious the girl was, and how the child was no stranger to death.

"Maybe I'll find you some dolls to play with," Gimlore said. "I think my kids still had some."

"You have kids?" Hope's eyes opened. "Why didn't you tell me?"

Gimlore got up, about to take leave for the evening. "Because I wasn't ready to talk about it, girl. I'm still not."

Hope frowned, and a deep sadness filled Gimlore's chest. "Fine. A few words won't hurt, I suppose. Their names were Tinko and Thata. Thata was killed when my town was attacked. And I... had to run away. I got separated from Tinko."

Hope nodded. "It must be horrible."

Gimlore scowled and more tears started to form. "It's the fucking worst."

The child's hand found her face and cleaned the tears. "One day we'll be out of here and you are going to get it all back. And I'm coming with you."

Gimlore laughed. Why was she being comforted by a child? There must be something seriously wrong with her for that to be happening. "Why me? Why do you even care?"

"The other ladies here stink. You also stink a bit, but they have old people stink, you know? Yours is much more manage-able."

Gimlore smiled. "Don't let them hear you say that."

Hope smiled and her index fingers made a cross on her lips.

Gimlore woke up rough, noise all around her. The grass rustled, and screams took hold in the distance. She got up, scratched her eyes, and Keryon woke up from the ruckus as well.

"What is happening?" he asked.

Gimlore looked into the distance as a high-pitched scream echoed in the night. A voice she recognised immediately.

Shit.

Gimlore looked at the guards' tent and saw one of the guards holding Hope by her neck. The girl screamed in pain, and her tiny hands fought back against the arms of the guard, trying to kick him.

"How about that!" the guard said. "The little shit had the nerve to steal food!"

Gimlore dug in the dirt under her cot and grabbed the hidden chisel. She made her way to the middle of the chaos, where multiple prisoners were pleading with the guard not to hurt Hope, telling him she was just hungry. Keryon followed her, but she couldn't process his words. She wasn't going to let the blood-thirsty bastard have a go at the little girl. She wasn't going to let anyone else get hurt on her watch.

"Gimlore!" Keryon's voice could be heard from behind her again but she didn't hear anything else. There was only red in front of her, rage bubbling up and spilling over. She had been too tame, and just couldn't contain it anymore.

"Let her go. I forced her to steal the food for me. I'm the one you want." She kept the chisel inside her sleeve.

The guard's attention turned to her. They were all watching her. The prisoners and the guards. The other five joined their companion.

"Well, well. What is this? A family business?" The other guards scowled. "I knew you filth couldn't go anywhere without stealing things, but to have a child steal things for you. That's another level of rot, isn't it?"

Fuck you, was what Gimlore thought. But she only shrugged.

The fucker nearly licked his lips. "Good. There will be plenty of whip for the two of you."

Gimlore gritted her teeth. She knew the cruel bastard wasn't after justice or fairness. He only cared about inflicting pain.

"Grab hold of her," the guard ordered one of his companions. The one with the frog-like face came forward and looked at her with a visible hint of disgust.

"Lay a finger on her and you will regret it." Keryon said.

Shit.

"I can fight my own bloody battles, you fool," Gimlore hissed. Why couldn't he just stay quiet? Why always be honourable? Now he was going to be whipped too. All three of them. And all because of her.

"Oh, here comes the father!" the first guard said with a smile that soon turned sour. "You two, grab him."

Two of the other guards made their way to Keryon just as the frog-face continued towards Gimlore. This was it. She had to do something, even if that meant lashings or worse.

"I think that's quite enough!" Tooth stood up, walking up to them. "We're sick and tired of your cruelty!"

Shit.

Why had he got involved as well? They would all end up whipped now. The guards wouldn't rest until there was no skin left on their backs.

"If you don't back away, little fucker, you're *all* going to be lashed," the first guard snarled, Hope still fighting his grip.

Then the rest of the prisoners got up and began to gather. More than a dozen of them. Heck, more than three dozen. Nearly half of them. Tall men and stout women. There were skinny ones who Gimlore never thought would even dare to fight. They all snarled at the guards, some rolling up their sleeves. "I wouldn't try anything if I were you," Tooth said.

The guards exchanged glances and unsheathed their swords. The numbers were still in the prisoners' favour, but they were unarmed. That was when three of the women that had stayed back started picking up pebbles and throwing them at the guards. Only small ones at first, but then they picked up bigger ones, and Gimlore had no doubt they hurt the bastards.

"Let's call it a night, then," the first guard said. "Let's cool our heads before any *disaster* happens to you all. I'll let the twerp go."

"The only disaster that happens here tonight is against you!" the Tooth snarled, pointing at the man, bits of spit flying from his mouth.

Hope managed to free her neck from the man's grasp and she bit his hand so hard it made him scream in pain. She freed herself from his clutches and Gimlore tried to go and protect her, but the frog-face stood in front of her. A pebble hit him in the head and that single moment of distraction was all Gimlore needed.

She had dreamt of this moment.

She let the chisel slide out of her sleeve and grasped it before rushing at the distracted guard. She couldn't waste time on the bastard, so she shoved the chisel deep in his eye until blood spurted out of it. He screamed, grasping to get it out, but it had been lodged too deep. The remaining eye hazed and he struggled to move first, then collapsed.

The other guards were keeping the rest of the prisoners away with the point of their swords, but it seemed as though Gimlore had underestimated her fellow inmates. They were armed to the teeth with pebbles and rocks. A tall, bulky prisoner threw an enormous rock at one of the guards and it landed right on his head, immediately sending the man down.

"You little bastards..." The first guard opened something in his pocket, a pouch with herbs which were already ablaze and emitting the thinnest of smoke threads.

Gimlore's mouth gaped. *He's a smokesmith. He's been hiding it all this time.*

Now, all hope was truly lost.

The guard inhaled the smoke and quickly grew in size, in a transformation that reminded her of Rednow. First his legs, then his arms, then his chest. He became a ten-feet-tall monstrosity. "I was just going to whip you for stealing dinner. Now I'm going to make dinner out of you."

Gimlore swallowed. *Shit. Shit. Shit.*

No matter how many they were, they couldn't fight *that*. It was over.

A familiar scent filled her nostrils and she looked to the side to see a column of smoke floating around Keryon. How in the bloody world had he got the herbs?

"The beautiful thing about having us sleep here is that it is not as much of a desert as one would think," he said, facing the other smokesmith. "Some herbs can grow if you have the time and the right seeds. Or if one of your friends does."

Keryon smiled as he gave the Tooth a cheeky nod.

A little flame of hope ignited in Gimlore. The calm way Keryon walked—as though nothing made him tremble—was everything she couldn't be. With the herbs, he could defeat the guard, and there was no doubt they could stage an uprising. The prisoners were as excited as her, smiling with clasped fists, ready for a good old bloody brawl.

Let them fucking have it.

TWENTY-ONE
PRISON BREAK

KERYON - GIMLORE

Keryon inhaled the smoke and jumped. The guard was nearly twice his size, but this wasn't about size or strength. It was about power and doing what should have been done a long time ago. Now he could show Gimlore why he had asked her to be patient. Seeds take a long time to grow, especially in this dry environment.

One jump.

One breath.

One death.

The other smokesmith resisted his strike. Not bad, but still relying too much on his own power as a defence mechanism. Keryon let his smoke spread around the enemy as he took a step back, then ignited it. His smoke turned to flames.

The other smokesmith shielded himself from the explosion, but the fire still burned his forearm, and a confused look spread across his face. Then realisation set in, and he glanced at Keryon, finally paying him the due respect. Then the guard grew even taller and ran towards Keryon, faster than he had any right to be with that size, his torso the width of three grown men standing next to each other.

The smokesmith struck with his fist. Again. And again.

Keryon was barely avoiding those blows, and evasion was not well-suited for his combat style. He was used to baiting the enemy to strike and igniting the smoke around them when they came.

Flames lit the night sky as Keryon's fire burned both the smokesmith and the smoke. The giant man roared in a mix of pain and anger, but Keryon wouldn't let him have it.

He had seen Gimlore suffer nearly every day in there.

He'd seen and *felt* the scars of the whip lashes across her back. She wasn't the role model he'd like her to be, but she didn't have to be anybody else but herself. He didn't really understand why he had such a fondness for the woman... but he did.

We need to get out of here now. And they need me to kill this bastard.

Keryon lunged forward again and ignited the smoke in another fire blast, the heat from the fire he caused barely making him sweat. Still, the giant smokesmith emerged from it unscathed.

"How irritating..." the man roared, his voice deeper. "Annoying little sparkles. You will pay for this, traitor."

How are the flames not doing any damage?

Keryon took another whiff of the smoke. Every time he inhaled smoke in combat, he immediately felt it consuming him from the inside out.

He lunged again and circled the giant in three quick steps, emerging from his right side. He urged his smoke to go in that direction, then ignited it. A large explosion hit the smokesmith in the face. The fire burned and sizzled his hard, leathery skin, but Keryon wasn't done.

While the man's vision was impaired, Keryon came from behind and repeated the move, his lungs burning too as he gathered enough smoke for it. All the smoke shot at the man's head, and Keryon ignited it again. The guard's head should have been burning like a hog on a stick, but there the bastard was, still standing, roaring, and wiping the fire and ashes off his face.

"You will pay…" he snarled in a hoarse voice.

Keryon was running out of ideas and a hint of panic settled in his mind. What if he just couldn't win? The man wasn't incredibly talented or even that well-trained as a smokesmith, but he had endurance.

He wouldn't be able to keep this up for much longer before he started coughing up blood. *I need to finish him now, or I'll be the one who's finished.*

Keryon jumped, igniting the smoke around him in a huge spinning circle of fire. He dove towards the smokesmith's head for another blast, but the two giant hands reached out to him, and he had nowhere else to go.

Shit.

He continued to blast the fire at the man's face, but there was nothing beyond his usually ugly mug. Was the man immortal?

"Ah!" The man's powerful grip tightened around him as he struggled to free himself. His sheer power was overwhelming. Pain shot through him. If Keryon wasn't careful, the smoke-smith's fingers might as well be knives.

How could he defeat such a man without a weapon?

Am I going to fail?

As he battled with the man's holding grip and burned specific bits of his body to force a release, his eyes invertedly swerved to Gimlore. He had to protect her and the rest of the prisoners—they needed a real fair trial where they could answer for their crimes, not unchecked punishment.

She led them, all teeth out, and barking commands like a seasoned veteran issuing orders on the battlefield.

The Viper.

That was when he had first heard about Gimlore. The Viper who hid in the sand and struck her prey. But if they found themselves on her good side, they would live to tell the story. They'd be taken care of. Keryon had seen her in action before, defending Heleronde with teeth and nails, and here it was again. Even the prisoners followed her as they fended for themselves and escaped the bladed guards.

"That's a nice trick." The giant smokesmith squeezed Keryon and forced him to focus on himself, on his ribs being squeezed. He was sure at least one must have cracked. "With the fire and all that, but it does nothing to someone with iron skin."

Under that grip, Keryon truly was inclined to believe the man was made of iron. Rednow had a raw, beastly gaze when he transformed, a bloodlust coming up to his eyes, but this one was different. He was still fast and incredibly powerful, but he was better at taking punches than delivering them successfully.

"Even iron melts in the right temperatures," Keryon managed to say. "And you wouldn't believe how easily one can reshape hot iron with the right tools."

He had sounded more confident than he was. His power came from the fire and smoke. He would hate to do this, but it could be his one way to survive.

"Ah, but you have got no tools!"

Keryon struggled to breathe under the ever-narrowing grip. "I *am*... the hammer."

After controlling the smoke around the giant smokesmith, he ignited it again, causing grass, bush, and plant to burn in an explosion of light and heat. He pulled all the smoke from the burning grassland under his control, much more than he could muster, especially as his lungs were restricted by the enemy. He continued to accumulate the smoke and concentrated it on the man for the riskiest of moves.

It was too close to himself.

A dangerous move, one he should never have to use, but this time he was fighting for things he believed in, for people he cared about, not for masters. He was ready for the sacrifice.

The surge of smoke was nearly unbearable, and Keryon ignited it.

An enormous flash of light took over the sky and incredible heat burned his skin.

He had to close his eyes.

Gimlore looked up when she heard the explosion and saw the giant smokesmith had been hit by another of Keryon's fire blasts. The man released Keryon, but he dropped on the ground, unconscious, apparently hurt even more than the guard.

Gimlore snarled and attacked Frog Face. She barely evaded his sword, but there were too many prisoners now surrounding him. Five of them, Gimlore included. "Keep throwing rocks at him. No need to get close. I need to check on Keryon."

The prisoners nodded and did just that. They were happy to stone the guard to death if they had to. Some of them had been locked in there for decades and barely remembered what their lives were like before the rule of the whip. No one deserved to rot in a place like that, no matter what they'd done.

Gimlore ran towards Keryon, skipping over the burnt bits of the grass. Much of it had already burned around him, and all that was left were the dark ashes and red sparkles. With her chisel still in hand, she approached him and the guard with caution, and her heart sank.

No.

The right side of Keryon's face was now marked by fire.

Shit.

She had no way to clean those wounds.

Is he still alive?

She checked his breathing. It was faint, but still there. *Thank the gods.*

Then she took a good look at the big fucker. Even his smoke-enhanced skin had not resisted the fire that time. Gimlore snuck up behind him, taking no chances. With chisel in hand, she stabbed him in the back of the neck, but it failed to pierce his skin.

Shit.

She stabbed the softer parts of the neck again, but it was as though his skin was made of tree bark or rough stone. She tried again, on the side of his face, but it didn't work either. When he moved his hands to try and grab her, she noticed his eyes, blacked and burned. That was his weak spot. He had been blinded by Keryon's fiery smoke.

He cried both in pain and in rage, trying to find whoever had tried to stab him. "I'll tear you in half!"

Doing her best to dodge his angry, waving hands, she slipped between his arms. That was the downside of being that big—he also turned into a big target. He was much taller, but his kneeling allowed her to reach his face. Careful not to be heard, she mustered all her strength and stabbed the man's eye with the chisel, thrusting the tool deep into his skull.

The smokesmith grabbed her arm while roaring in pain, but she slipped away, leaving the chisel behind. Even as he pulled the tool out of his eye, there was little else to be done. Gimlore stood back, panting and staring as the man shrivelled back to its normal shape. He gurgled something, then collapsed to the ground and stopped moving.

She wanted to join the rest of the prisoners, but without the smokesmith to harm them, she could afford some time to look after Keryon. She ran over to him and placed her palm underneath his hand. How she wished she could clean his burn mark with water. It was painful to look at, the skin had cracked, but it hadn't burned his eyes, ears, or nose, which was already a miracle. Tears flowed out of her eyes again.

"If anything, you were too bloody perfect before. Now, you're as normal as the rest of us," she muttered.

Keryon stirred and croaked amid the battle cries from the fighting prisoners. "I heard that one."

"Be quiet, silly. Now, I saved your bloody arse. We're even."

Keryon nodded, the shade of a smirk forming at the corner of his mouth. They both knew he had saved them all as well.

"Did we win?" he whispered.

Gimlore looked at what was left of the battlefield. The camp was in ruins. Flames were scattered across the terrain, ashes drifting, and a hint of smoke hanging in the air. The guards were still trying to charge the prisoners with the swords, but when they did, they were hit with rocks almost half the size of their heads.

"I wonder what the Sirestine were thinking when they turned the quarry into a prison. The prisoners are essentially digging weapons out of the earth at every passing minute," she said.

"I'll take that as a yes."

"You must rest. Tonight was an important win, but I'm still bloody confused as to how the fuck I'm going to find our way back to Rednow."

"Y-you don't... have to do it alone," he whispered, his voice hoarse. "You can count on the others. Ask the Tooth."

Gimlore was covered in sweat as she made her way through the steppes of south-eastern Sirestir, even though the sun had just risen. Keryon could barely walk, so Gimlore and another man called Walan carried him under the shoulders. She had been careful enough to place a cloth over the burned side of his face to shield the wound from the sun, but she wondered how long that would work as the heat seemed to be only increasing.

"They call this a steppe. I call it a fucking desert," she whispered.

"I would be inclined to call it the underworld," Keryon said, no doubt trying to lift her spirits.

What have I done to deserve this man's strength?

She stayed silent, but with Keryon barely able to walk, their pace was too slow.

The Tooth and a few others stayed ahead, but other groups had parted ways with them and gone their own routes. It was better like this, she reckoned. A smaller group would mean less attention in case they came across anyone who might sell them out. What if nobody found them at all? That meant being left alone in the desert with hardly any shade, a scorching heat, and no clear way to go, even though the Tooth swore he was taking them to the nearest settlement.

"I have the best nose in the world!" he had claimed. "I remember this smell from our way to the quarry. We're on the right track!"

Gimlore could only trust the man. He had proven to be quite the ally, after all. She glanced back and spotted a small figure following them from a distance, taking shelter behind rocks whenever possible.

"You can come out, Hope. Why are you hiding?"

The girl hesitated, but eventually made her way out and walked towards Gimlore. She had a few bruises in her neck from the guard's chokehold, but she was fine otherwise. There was something else in her mind that Gimlore couldn't quite tell.

"What's wrong? You're not hurt, are you?"

The girl shook her head. "I'm not. But you and Keryon... you fought to protect me."

"Of course. I wouldn't let you get lashed."

"But then I cowered," Hope said. "I promised I would help you fight, and then I couldn't. I took cover like a coward."

Gimlore asked the other man to help Keryon by himself and kneeled to face Hope. "Listen to me, girl. You are no coward. You did what you could to survive, and there is nothing wrong with that."

"But I wanted to help you," Hope said, her gaze falling to the ground. Tears poured from her eyes. "I swear I did."

Gimlore sighed, shook her head, and embraced the girl. "You already helped me more than you will ever know."

She broke the hug but faced Hope, letting her words linger just to make sure the girl heard them well. She needed someone by her side, and Gimlore could help her. *I'll give her a place to stay once I sort out everything else.*

"Why did you hug me?"

Gimlore grimaced and cleared her throat. "I don't know. I just felt like it. What's wrong with that?"

Hope giggled. "Nothing."

"Come on, girl. What was wrong with the hug?"

Hope smiled. "You stink."

Twenty-Two
Of Enemies and Allies

Orberesis

Orberesis walked into Ledal alone and unarmed.

The city was like a fortified village compared to the magnitude of Ushar's imposing walls, and the scale of the Palace of Brilliance. He could see the similarities in the architecture and it made sense since Shari's capital was probably the closest large city to Ushar.

It looks so much cleaner.

Part of him wanted to use Temporal Exploration to see the world and get to know all the corners he still didn't know, but he was still a beginner in the arts, and every trip left him drained and depleted.

The Old One stirred. *Don't worry. You're getting better at it.*

Orberesis ignored the parasite and continued to walk. He had landed inside the walls and no guards had approached him so far. The people inside didn't look too different from him, though their clothes were still of humble make.

He spotted Sharivali Keep in the distance, Ledal's palace, where King Lunit ruled over his people. "I heard he's an interesting one," Orberesis whispered.

The Old One hummed, uninterested. *Just get on with it.*

There wasn't much to see in Ledal other than cobbles and mortared buildings, and Orberesis quickly tired of it. There didn't seem to be anything exciting to do. Everyone was polite, smiling and waving as they passed each other on the street.

He continued to walk through the meticulously cobbled streets, noticing even the townhouses in the city centre had proper finishings. There was an attention to detail but also almost a deliberate choice in remaining humble and not flaunting wealth. Orberesis had never encountered anything like it.

When he arrived near the palace, the two men guarding the gate exchanged a look before addressing him. "Are you lost?"

"I'm exactly where I need to be, thank you," he replied. "Would you be so kind as to call King Lunit? Or perhaps open the gates? There's something I must discuss with him."

The two guards broke out in echoing laughter, and every time they looked at him, it only got louder.

Orberesis gritted his teeth and closed his fist, the calm quickly leaving him. But he was also exhausted from the trip through the void and unsure as to how powerful he remained. "Do you know who I am?"

That got their attention. Those six words were sure to seed doubt in someone's mind, if only temporarily.

"Who?"

"I'm Orberesis, bearer of the Red Orb, God Himself, and high advisor of King Doemus of the Two Nations of Sirestir and Yab."

"Right," the guard on the left said. "And I'm Father Time! If you're Orberesis, where is your orb? Or the priests? Or the procession?"

"He's got the white robe, though," the one on the right added, and they laughed again. "That was a fun one. Now piss off before we get angry, you got it?"

"I said what I said."

The joyful looks on their faces faded, and they clasped their halberds tightly.

"I need your help," Orberesis whispered. He looked at the iron gate that blocked the entrance. It must be a heavy contraption made to keep town folks out of the palace. He willed it open, and something crackled inside. The guards were uneasy as they inspected the gate.

Just a little, the Old One said.

The gate started to rise despite the pulley system that kept it down, and Orberesis became lightheaded. "I warned you about who I was. You chose not to listen."

Panic settled in the guards' faces as they looked for others, dumbstruck.

"I will really show you, then," he managed to say despite his exhaustion.

The gate continued to rise despite the best efforts of the guards to keep it down. One of them gave up and brought his hands to his face. "I'm sorry, Highest One, we didn't know it was you."

Orberesis allowed the gate to come down.

"There you go." He took two steps forward, staring at the two men intently. It was risky. If they were to swing their halberds, he wasn't sure there was much that could save him. Still, he sensed he had control of the altercation. "Now open the gate and step aside," he hissed.

The guards exchanged glances and ordered the gate be opened, allowing Orberesis to walk into the palace, each step precise.

The inside of the palace was much the same as the rest of the city, which surprised him. This King Lunit certainly tried hard to appear humble, but Orberesis should have already guessed that when Doemus told him he'd kept Shari a neutral kingdom for decades. He was probably a self-righteous bastard who simply profited out of the misery of those around him, benefitting from his neutrality without getting his hands dirty when everybody else had no choice but to wallow in the mud. That would end this day.

Orberesis walked into the palace until he encountered more guards. He heard the buzz around him, some guards confused by his presence.

It might be good that the King isn't in the dark about me being here.

The inside of the palace was different from the Palace of Brilliance. While in Ushar, old paintings and tapestries filled the walls, the glasswork was masterful, and all the window trims were bathed in gold, the Sharivali Keep was little more than a glorified abbey. It had modest cloisters, an inner garden, and four towers in each corner of the quad, where Orberesis assumed the King lived, surrounded by the bureaucrats and enlightened men who did all the governing that kings pretended to do.

Orberesis found a stout, short man standing in the grass in the middle of the quadrangular courtyard. The man wore blue training clothes, boots, and had long, dark hair tied into a top bun. His face was cleanly shaven and he didn't look a day over fifty, although his sword form showed a lingering youthfulness. He moved effortlessly between stances.

"I couldn't believe it at first, but it seems they were right," the man said without looking at Orberesis. "God Himself is here. How about that?"

The man spoke with a confidence that would waver even the most assured ruler. He didn't have to announce who he was; he could only be King Lunit.

Orberesis took a few more steps and approached the King, doing his best to match him in confidence and presence. As he drew closer, he noticed the man's arms were muscular, with veins popping. How could a king be so strong and fit? Orberesis wondered if maybe there was a reason why the other kingdoms had respected Shari's claims of neutrality without ever trying to siege Ledal. The thought made him hesitate. All of that just from meeting the man.

He shook those foolish thoughts away. King Lunit might be an imposing figure, but Orberesis had powers, and was on his way to becoming a real god.

"Am I not welcome here?" Orberesis teased.

Lunit stopped mid form and glanced at him with eyes so intense they almost made Orberesis pause again. No, he could not cower. He could not hesitate. The King struck his blade into the grass and looked at him.

"It takes a lot of nerve to enter someone's house, especially uninvited. The lack of introduction only makes it worse." King Lunit untied his top bun and his long, dark hair flowed over his shoulders. "But what confuses me more is that you did all of that... by yourself. My generals and spies assure me there is no army waiting outside the gates. None of my family was kidnapped. Tell me, Highest One, does that make you a bold man or a fool?"

Orberesis shrugged. "I mostly go where I please and do what I want. The weather was nice in Shari, so I came. I don't know if that makes me bold or foolish. I can only assume you will cast your judgment on me regardless, so I'll allow you to decide for yourself."

"Enough games. What do you want?"

"Aid," Orberesis said, cutting all the pomp and circumstance. "There is someone in the Thousand Hills building an army of smokesmiths to defeat me. I am revered as a god now. I possess great powers and a new army of powerful creatures called Lantern Horns. I also have the armies of the Two Nations on my side. But my powers are not infinite, I admit that. I need help. Allies. We must corner the enemy and defeat it once and for all."

"For what? So that you can crown yourself king of the world and rule over everyone?"

"I would consider myself a fair ruler, but that's not the intent." *At least not for now.* "If someone has most of the world's smokesmiths on their side, I'm sure you can imagine what could happen. How skewed the global powers would become."

The King gritted his teeth and pinched his nose, as though he considered Orberesis a child unworthy of his time. "Shari is *neutral*, as it's always been," he spat. "Our soldiers fight to protect our borders and the integrity of our territory. That has been our way for decades. We've never meddled in anyone's battles or power struggles. And we've never invaded anyone. You will not find any help here."

Orberesis sighed. "I was hoping you'd be a believer. Then it seems we must part ways on bad terms."

The King picked up his sword, dark hair flowing in the wind. "Leave now or I'll make you. Bad terms or not."

"Such a pity. You would have made an amazing general for my armies. I mean that."

King Lunit lunged towards him with the sword overhead, the confidence of a powerful man. Orberesis raised his hand and stopped the King, who remained motionless. Then he took off into the air, lifting the King with him. There was despair in the man's eyes. He had the heart of a warrior and the wisdom of a true leader. It was too bad someone like that had to end this way.

Once he was about seventy feet off the ground, he made sure all the servants, guards, bureaucrats, and handmaidens were watching. Bowmen appeared in the tower windows, their arrows pointed at Orberesis, but they were predictable, so Orberesis tapped into the Old One's power and stopped them too.

They wouldn't hesitate to kill you, the Old One said. *They aren't better than those who burned your village. They might just be worse.*

Rage stirred inside Orberesis and his need to do what had to be done grew. He became angry at the insolent ruler who couldn't see the opportunity that was right in front of him to join him and achieve greatness. Why did they all insist he stood against him?

Fools.

Orberesis raged at the sky and the earth shook beneath him. Panic settled in the King's eyes. From up there, Orberesis saw the earth shaking as the power of the Old One coursed through him, draining him of his energy. The foundations of the palace wavered. People screamed and ran for their lives.

"They've seen what I'm capable of. Now I'll see how well-trained your armies are. It was a pleasure, Lunit. I wish I could have kept you here longer, but my time is limited and I can't afford foolish demonstrations of strength any longer."

Orberesis pointed at the King and, using the Old One's power, jerked him at tremendous speed against the ground down below. A pool of blood shortly formed below the monarch's lifeless body. That was it—how quickly he could end one of the world's most powerful men.

A few shocked guards went to check on the King, pain-filled squeals leaving their lungs.

Orberesis dropped back to the ground. "Kneel before your new king."

The two guards hesitated and charged him with their halberds.

Shit.

He was exhausted but still managed to freeze them in place, stop time for them, just for a moment. Then he stole the halberd from the hands of one. It was so heavy in his tired hands but his resolve didn't waver. He swung the weapon once, slashing the first guard's neck. Then swung again, slicing the second's.

He dropped the bloodied halberd and found himself panting. He had nearly drained himself this time. He'd have to be more careful. If they didn't convert voluntarily, he would convert them by force, and ultimately, they'd see the truth.

⋯⋯⋯

The palatial room in Mewon was a far cry from what it clearly had once been. It was now filled with a large table worthy of the finest of banquets, except those who sat around it were the pettiest and most savagely ambitious lords of Gasho. All the emblems and decoration had been stripped away in an effort to show equality and fairness among the members of the Lord's Council. As a... forceful sort of guest, Orberesis had received the privilege of sitting at the helm of this farse.

He watched them, arguing back and forth, their words a mix of educated insults and sheer nonsense. They'd had their previous ruler killed after accusing him of killing his son and heir. Worse than the fact that their faces were disfigured *on purpose* by an incomprehensible custom of piercing them with long metal spikes was the fact that they were there representing their own houses, their own interests, never those of their people.

"Some would think you were being disingenuous, Lord Elerge! Think about it a little bit further and you will find that I am right," said one of the fools, sporting a thick beard under all the metal spikes.

Lord Elerge replied with a scoff and bluster, as Orberesis expected. "How *dare* you question my character, Lord Barrank! I am a tenacious mind and I utterly refuse to listen to your calumnious slander!"

The rest of the lords shouted at each other as if the loudest always ended up being the winner. Chaos ensued, and some of the lords threatened to pull their swords while others banged on the table. Some even called for their retainers, pretending they'd be willing to get into a scuffle.

It was quite the show. Orberesis just wasn't sure if they were trying to impress him or annoy him.

"I'm not a quitter, Lord Filinti, I'm a winner! Perhaps you should go back to your pitiful estate and starve your serfs some more."

Lord Filinti turned to the round fellow who was supposed to oversee this buffoonery, but the man's face was red and he didn't know who to turn to in the middle of it all. "Lord Speaker, can you please ask Lord Dertuy to cease the bluster? He is overexcitable and needs to get a hold of himself. Perhaps if we were to prescribe him some medicaments, he would fare better."

Just three strides away, lords argued over each other, and Orberesis failed to understand what it was even about. They never seemed to mention policies. They never used proven facts and theories. It was all based on who might be the biggest buffoon, the most capable of speaking over the others. They had promised Orberesis an audience, and yet they acted like he wasn't even there. They hadn't even started debating whether to lend him their divided armies.

Perhaps a reminder would suffice.

The Old One laughed. *Make it quick, then.*

Orberesis faced the table, wondering who had once possessed the craftsmanship to build such a large, intricate piece of furniture. He narrowed his gaze on the large table and lifted it up. Glasses and plates clinked as they touched, spilling wine, water, and whatever else the lords drank during the Council meeting. As soon as they realised the table was moving, they stopped their madness and quieted, their eyes darting from side to side to find out who was doing that. Finally, their eyes rested on Orberesis, and they moved away from the table.

Still in silence, Orberesis continued to lift the table until it was already level with their heads, as though it was a big flying boat, floating in mid-air. He gritted his teeth and pushed the table down, creating a chaos of papers flying and ceramic plates and cups shattering in a cacophonous mess, the lords shielding their faces.

Orberesis stood and let the silence linger until he had their attention.

"Lord Speaker, you may leave the room. Your inability to stop this insanity should have you out of a job, but I'm in no mood to play the role of a magistrate. The rest of you need to vote."

The Lord Speaker bowed and left the Lords' Council Room, followed by his stunned retainers. The lords remained standing, daring not to sit while Orberesis stood.

"You have all heard my request. I gave you a fair chance to concur and discuss, but you did no such thing, so now I am demanding an answer. You must vote. If you're in favour of lending the Gashoine armies to my cause, lift your arm. If you're not in favour, you can leave your arm down."

The lords hesitated and exchanged glances to figure out first how their allies and rivals would vote. Orberesis had no time for it. Little by little, a few of the Lords' Council started raising their arms. They exchanged glances again and no doubt gave each other signals one way or another.

"Seven?" Orberesis asked, counting the votes. "Any other lords want to change their mind before we proceed?"

"It seems like we voted against your proposal... Highest One," one of the lords said. He was a wiry man with thin, grey hair. "It's unfortunate, but the Lords' Council always knows best."

"Hear, hear," a few other lords said as they nodded.

Orberesis sighed. "It is unfortunate indeed."

He extended his arms and lifted all the men who had left their arms down. In the air, they struggled to free themselves from his invisible grasp. Those who could still speak apologised and changed their minds. Their retainers stepped forward with swords in hand but hesitated, unsure of what the procedure should be when facing someone with divine status.

So, Orberesis picked the retainers up as well just to show he could. He could feel his eye twitch at the effort, as though every time he used this power, the Old One got stronger and he got weaker.

Don't push your luck, the Old One snarled. *And get on with it!*

Orberesis threw the men at the walls with a tremendous impact that made the foundations of the palace shake. The figures dropped to the floor, leaving blood smears along the walls. The trauma to their bodies had been too severe. None would see another day.

"Now that we've weeded out the unfaithful, self-serving, and treacherous, I am looking forward to working with this Lords' Council," Orberesis said, a smile drawn upon his face.

The other members of the Council and their surviving retainers stayed in a state of terrified silence. Static, except for some who shook in sheer fear.

The Old One laughed.

"Let us start over," Orberesis said. "First, I want to hear your names, your titles, and how many soldiers you command. Then we'll talk about how many my army actually needs."

TWENTY-THREE
A TIGHT GRIP

ORBERESIS

Orberesis didn't have to command the armies himself, he just needed to control their leaders and the poor soldiers with sworn oaths would kill themselves to fight for the homeland; for their lords and protectors. It was one thing for him to take over Shari and Gasho in such fashion, but getting the poor bastards to obey would be something else entirely.

He would need to keep a tight grip on them.

The weather in Mosendel reminded him of Alarkan, but still temperate. The birds flying over the harbour of Enoris and the Vaerghulen mountains to the north made the place a pleasant one to visit. If it wasn't too dangerous, perhaps he could bring Solvi with him next time. And his child.

I'm going to be a father...

Sometimes he forgot about that. If he ended up turning into a God, then the child would be considered a demi-god of sorts.

A son or a daughter didn't matter; they would be an extension of his divinity, even purer, as they would be born with the status.

Another pernicious thought hit him as he walked the streets of Enoris, the smells of fish and salt lingering in the air. Solvi was the child's mother, but she was a smokesmith as well. He was sure she would not turn on him and go to the enemy's side, but that was a connection he couldn't ignore.

She could betray you, the Old One said.

"And why would she do that?" The merchants and fishermen shot Orberesis strange glances when they saw him talking to himself.

Once she has had a divine child, she will be free to control them and she'll try to control you. She will always be a smokesmith and smokesmiths cannot be trusted.

"And why is that?"

Because my sister runs through their veins, Doi! The Old One snarled in ire. *She poisoned them, got them addicted to her. They are damaged. Corrupted forever.*

"And how is that different from what you're doing to me?"

You think I'm corrupting you? I'm lending you power only a few have had the honour of experiencing since the dawn of time. I'm turning you into a god. I'm teaching you the arcane arts of lost worlds and times. And you dare call me a parasite?

"I'm grateful for all that, just as you should be grateful to feast upon my life energy and vitality. On my existence."

The Old One roared, but there was no reply so Orberesis smiled, free to enjoy the view.

The seagulls flew above the tall masts of the ships and cawed when they had found a school of fish. Wickplate fishing wasn't big around there, to his dismay, so the large ships dedicated to capturing the big creatures were all but absent. Instead, there were hundreds of wood vessels, each of them manned by a crew of one or two people and their nets. The sea made him nostalgic, and his mind drifted back to his days in Ushar with Tavanar, before the Miracle. The time he had spent in the Gloomwoods, with his father, hearing all about the heroics of the wickplate anglers.

I want to be a good father, he thought. *Solvi and I will be good parents.*

He had become single-minded in his pursuit of divinity but seeing Solvi's belly had changed things. Perhaps he needed to curb his ambition slightly.

"Did I dream too much?"

The Old One scoffed. *You are a pitiful human. You don't even know what dreaming is. You've lived your life with your eyes closed. And even when I force them open, you still hesitate, wondering if having them closed would be better after all.*

He understood what the Old One meant, and the wisdom he had gathered from learning the arts of Temporal Exploration had also proven to be quite enlightening in ways he couldn't even explain with words. It was something that had to be lived to be understood.

Look at you, doubtful again. It's that woman, Doi. You must get her out of your life. Having a family means nothing. You can get one whenever you want. Now is not the time.

Orberesis ignored those comments but shook his mind off the subject, focusing on the task at hand. Shari and Gasho would probably be more than enough to help him defeat the smokesmith horde, but it was always best to play it safe, especially after his initial blunder when invading Alarkan through the sea.

The Seasalt Keep was at the top of a cliff facing the sea, protected by rocks and the ocean to the west, but also by the tall and deadly rocks to the north and south, meaning the only way to reach the Keep by foot was through the only passageway possible on the eastern side. Orberesis walked the stone passageway until he told the guards who he was. They exchanged excited looks, immediately leaving their posts to call someone responsible.

That's promising...

It took less than two minutes for Orberesis to have them open the gates for him. As he walked inside towards the large door that he thought led to the monarch's throne room, the palace servants brought their fists to their chests, a gesture symbolic of the Order of the Red Orb. He smiled and mimicked them even though he no longer held the orb around his neck. They kneeled before him.

"Rise. No need for kneeling, my good people," he said. They smiled at him and pointed to the large door.

Orberesis walked into what was probably the smallest and most practical throne room he had ever seen. The lighting of the place was provided by stained glass windows, but there were no big displays of wealth. Sitting on a rather small wood chair atop a small pulpit was a thin, dark-skinned man with no hair. Just like Orberesis, he wore a white robe.

A copycat. Interesting.

The King didn't seem to think there was anything wrong with it. Just like his other lords and servants, he kneeled before Orberesis and only rose after he was told to. "God Himself is here. The Highest Lord."

"I am," Orberesis said, put off by King Mosen. He looked around and pointed at the clothes the King wore as well as his servants. "I take it you are faithful to the Order of the Red Orb?"

"Oh, the clothing?" the King asked. "I would say it's more a matter of... aesthetics. But many of my subjects are devout, Highest One. That is why I must present myself as close as I can to how they perceive you. It helps with popularity... I'm sure you understand."

So, not a devout man, just an opportunist.

"I see. Mosendel seems to be thriving. As the head of the kingdom, I take it you must be thrilled."

The King was all smiles. "Indeed! And if you must know, that was all thanks to you, Highest Lord! After your miracle all those years ago, the beasts that plagued us were gone. Our people were finally able to live in peace, without fear. We started new trade routes and took some risks, and now we're prospering, as you can see. I'm doing all I can to steer the ship in the right direction, but I refuse to take all the credit for it."

"So, you're thankful?"

"Oh, I am. I've always wished to have the chance to thank you personally for everything you did for us. Even when you created Alarkan, that was another miracle for us! We sent all the scum we have to those filthy settlements they started there. We became peaceful and happy. I even let some of my smokesmiths go, since there were no crimes being committed. Things have never been as peaceful here, which means I no longer have to worry about enemies or... challengers."

"Challengers? To your rule, you mean? I thought your bloodline *founded* this corner of the world. The kingdom was named after your dynasty, was it not?"

King Mosen smiled. "There lies the issue. Well, not an issue any longer, but it used to be. I am one of many siblings. And each of my siblings has many children. I also have many cousins, nieces, and nephews. Nothing is stopping them from... making sure an accident happens to me."

Orberesis wanted to laugh at this pathetic man but maintained a straight face. "So, you are the king, and you rule, but you are not a devout follower of mine. You're not surrounded by wealth and lords kissing the floor you step on. And you say your family is still powerful enough to pose a challenge. So... what are you, really? A figurehead?"

The man grimaced. "That's a... kind term, Highest One. I've long been called worse things. A manager. A bureaucrat. They know little of how hard it is to run a successful kingdom!"

Orberesis understood why he had been put off by the man at first. He was king in name only; the real power didn't lie with him. There had to be people pulling the strings from behind him. This man was a puppet, controlled by the fear of being hung for incompetence and exploited for his actual fine managerial skills.

But he was no real king.

"And who would you say is really in charge?"

"I beg your pardon, Highest One?"

Orberesis sighed. "From your family. Who do you fear the most?"

King Mosen grimaced. "I'm going to regret this, am I not?"

⋯⋯

The woman sitting across the table from Orberesis oozed power. It was as though everything about her had been designed to the utmost detail. Her grey hair was cut short, but not too short. No, that would make her appear child-like, which would be undesirable given her short stature, offset by a tall chair that put her face to face with much taller people sitting across from her. She wore expensive silks from Gasho, stitched with golden threads only found in the wealthiest of royal courts, and the jewellery she had chosen was simple—a unique jade bracelet locked around her wrist, impossible to remove.

"I am a very busy woman," Lady Kanwa Mosen said. She certainly sounded as though she wanted to appear that way.

Orberesis didn't honour her with a quick response. Instead, he let his eyes wander across the room. A marcruncher head trophy hung above the door frame, and several rare vases and other art pieces were scattered across the room in an effort to appear like they had been laid out randomly, as though she didn't really care about any of it.

"What can I help you with?" she asked.

"Your cousin is the King, but we all know where the power lies. Why talk to the shadesgrowl when I can talk to his rider? We speak the same language, you and me."

Kanwa narrowed her eyes. "And what language is that?"

"That of ambition. I'm sure your cousin's gratitude doesn't extend to you. You don't really care whether the kingdom is run properly, as long as your merchant ships are still sailing and trading. Am I wrong?"

"You overestimate me," Kanwa said. Her words were always soft-spoken, but Orberesis sensed the danger in them. This woman was not like the others. She was no simpleton, no buffoon, and no figurehead. "I take care of all my assets and I go to bed after a cup of tea and a book. That's all I do."

"You certainly try to appear that way, but the armies are loyal to you, are they not? I know they get paid three times the official rate, and two thirds come from you. You can tell me about all your proxies and puppets, if you want, but it doesn't change the fact that it comes from you."

Kanwa showed no emotion, and the Old One laughed. *Oh, she's good!*

Orberesis continued. "The Mosendeli armies are my reason for being here, in any case. There's a dangerous enemy plotting from the Thousand Hills. He's gathering smokesmiths from around the world. I've got my own set of abilities and… otherworldly friends to help with, but it won't be enough. So, I've already secured aid from Gasho and Shari. Now I come to you."

Lady Kanwa frowned. "Shari agreed to help?"

Orberesis smiled. "After some… persuasion."

There it was. Kanwa swallowed. A slip in her well-manufactured façade. "And now you're here to *persuade* me as well."

Orberesis nodded.

"Fine. They'll aid you when the time comes."

Now it was Orberesis' time to frown. That easy? It couldn't be. "Do you mind explaining why?"

"Mosendel is at peace, but the people remember it was you who put an end to the Crimson Wars and all the creatures that plagued the land. They're thankful for that, so there will not be public opposition to fighting on your behalf," Kanwa said, her voice flat. "And it might be good for the economy. If Shari is involved, that will create demand for our spices, our wines, and our almonds. Those are all industries controlled by my sect of the family, so it will also strengthen my position within the Mosen family hierarchy. I win, no matter what."

The Old One chuckled, but Orberesis was still trying to understand. The important thing was that he had got the support he had come for. "Well, then I can only say it will be a pleasure doing business with you."

"I said I'd do it, but I didn't say I'd do it willingly. You're still here coercing me. I acknowledge your boldness and your... divine abilities, and I yield to them. But I'm not going to bow to you like my pathetic cousin. You can exploit me if you like, but don't expect me to kiss your feet."

Oh, the claws are finally out...

Those were the colours of the strong and powerful. Everything was a game, calculated and executed to perfection. They had no friends and everyone was an adversary. They held allegiance to only themselves and their interests. Orberesis understood that.

"Let's hope you can keep your word, Lady Mosen. The consequences of not kissing my feet could end up being quite severe."

Twenty-Four
Lifted Burden

Rednow - Merey

Life as a skeleton spirit—was that what he was now?—had not been what Rednow had expected, but his appearance made him even more of a monster than he would have been otherwise. He had slowly started floating away from the smoke-smith soldiers who kept arriving and were building the barracks to what would be their powerful war camp in the mountain slopes.

How many times do I have to tell you that you are no spirit? No skeleton, either! The Essence said. *You're a Smoke Rider, my most trusted partner. My avatar.*

"I'm an old man whose life you ruined."

You know that I did what I had to do. And why I did it.

Rednow did, after his Inner Flight. He had seen the true essence of things and how he was a part of it all. His spirit was what really mattered, not his body or his appearance. He had got used to this kind of existence. There was no need to sleep, eat, or worry about distances. He could spend his day delegating tasks to the smokesmiths' leaders, building garrisons, and making strategic plans to defend the Builders' haven.

Arkan had stood confidently by his side and provided un-questioned support after Rednow had saved his people from the shadowlings. Pinesy never left Tinko's side even as the child continued to train day and night. The progress had been some-thing else. How proud Gimlore would be if she was there to see...

Your preparations have been fruitful, the Essence said. *The Inner Flight must have helped you.*

"It did," Rednow admitted. "I see things in a new light. The past is no longer a burden. It's simply the past."

I'm happy to see you're becoming wiser. We need all the help we can get.

From the air, Rednow could assess the terrain and see tiny details that the human eye could not. He glanced at the combat units that had responded to his call. He now had more than one hundred smokesmiths under him, but how strong they were remained to be tested. The pineheads had responded too. They arrived in droves, more than thirty every day.

How could he lead that many people? He wasn't human any longer. Even the Leeth was easier because he had Tellwoon, Zatak, and Merey to fall back on.

He dipped down to the Builders' haven. Despite how long it had been since he'd arrived, the place never failed to leave him impressed. A massive nook carved in an even bigger rock, suspended between the sky above and the river below.

He didn't take long to spot the child battling two smoke-smiths who had refused to use real weapons.

Tinko struck and stepped away at an incredible speed, even the smoke failing to catch up completely. Then the child appeared in the middle of the two smokesmiths and cut their biceps with the twin blades. The other two gritted their teeth and kept the pain inside as they did their best to track Tinko.

It seemed like every time Rednow saw the kid, they looked stronger, faster, and better prepared. Not thanks to Rednow. Not any longer, at least.

Tinko appeared again and, when the two men struck, the child appeared from their rear, and the wood swords hit the child's smoke clone.

"You're no fun," the child said, frowning as their twin blades touched the two men's back. "Too weak."

"You're becoming good at this," Rednow said. He was glad he had found a physical voice again after the Inner Flight, even if he could still talk to people by talking to their minds. He hated doing it because that's what the Essence did to him. "But never disrespect those who helped you get to where you are."

Tinko swallowed and turned to the two men. "Sorry. I am grateful for your help with my training."

"Anytime, kid," one of the men said as they both left, leaving Rednow with the child. Builders scuttered around them and the sound of weapons and provisions being prepared was only offset by the sound of the river hitting the rocks underneath.

Tinko sheathed the blades and walked towards Rednow. "Where have you been, Uncle?"

The answer was complex. Rednow had been everywhere. He'd been studying the terrain, assessing the strength of his forces, sending scouts to find out what the Old One had been planning. But the child didn't have to know any of that.

"Too busy for my own good," he said.

The truth was that he didn't think the child would want to be around a skeleton like him.

"I'm getting bored with these training sessions. The smoke-smiths are fine, but why can't I fight three at a time?"

Rednow would have laughed if he could. "Because that's already too much for anyone your age to be fighting. Why are you so eager?"

Tinko lowered their head and then Rednow understood. There was a sadness in the child's eyes. Training and fighting were all the kid had now. "I am going to avenge Thata. And I'm going to get my mother back. So, I need to get strong to handle those fishy creatures."

If it was up to Rednow, he would keep Tinko the furthest he could from the beasts. But he saw in the child the same eyes he had recognised in his younger self. A chronic restlessness that one couldn't heal or take away; a certain hunger that was hard to satiate.

"We'll be at war soon, but when the fighting starts, you *will* be careful. For your sake, for your mother's sake, and for my sake, you hear me?" Tinko looked at Rednow directly but didn't seem bothered by the ghostly and devilish appearance. "I've lost too many people. And I've lost my flesh in the process. I cannot lose you, too."

Tinko sighed, sitting down on the rocky ground. The river continued to crash down hundreds of feet beneath the platform. "I'm just... angry all the time. Fighting helps dull all this noise in my mind."

Rednow found himself trying to extend his arm to hug the child and comfort them but kept his bones quiet instead.

"Blaming yourself is the worst you can do. Being angry is normal. I know it's easier said than done, but you must understand this. It's not your fault, it's just something that happened. What you can do is control your reaction to it. And you're doing great if you ask me. More importantly, you are doing enough. You are enough."

As those words left Rednow, Tinko hugged their knees and buried their head in them. The child sniffed and cried. Despite all the strength and ability to fight, Tinko was still a kid. And kids should be allowed to act like it.

"Come on, cry as much as you need, but then wipe those tears and pick yourself back up," Rednow said, knowing full well the latter part had proven difficult even for him. "I'll always be here for you, even if you don't see me. Even if I'm this... skeleton."

Tinko looked up and nodded, understanding.

"Now tell me, besides the smokesmiths, what else have you been practicing?"

Tinko wiped the tears and sniffed. "Arkan has been trying to teach me how to fly. He says the earlier I learn, the better. But I still don't get any of it. At least your teachings of the herbs made sense, but he goes on about the Essence, devotion, and finding my true self."

"He's preparing you for the Inner Flight."

"What's that?"

"You'll know when the time comes. My only advice about that is to try to learn from him. He's a great man and can teach you about discipline, perseverance, and comradery. Absorb as much as you can."

"He is also teaching me how to fight using a spear. That's fun."

Rednow wanted to laugh and shake his head, wishing he had the guts to hug the child.

⸺⸻⸺

The Thousand Hills were the southern sister of the Benaven Mountains and the de facto border between the kingdoms of Vaerghulen, Gasho, and the Ultfaest Freehold. Merey looked back at the hundreds of Leeth soldiers riding and walking behind her. They had already come down from the Seven Peaks and crossed the valley that stood between the two mountain ranges.

The wind blew strong along her back, and she tightened the cloak around her. At least the shadesgrowl's fur kept her warm. It had been like that for days, and they were now approaching the outskirts of Benaven, though it would be suicide to try and find shelter within the city.

"We should start setting up another camp for the night," she said. Her mind was filled with thoughts of honour and duty, both of which she had certainly coveted, but that didn't stop doubt from seeping in. "The sun is already setting."

Tellwoon nodded. "I'll tell Zatak to keep the bloodsleuths alert for predators."

As Tellwoon's eyes were about to drift away, they narrowed on Merey again. For the gods, those were powerful eyes, not a string of doubt in them. "Are you alright?"

Merey shook it off. "Yes, yes. I'm fine."

Tellwoon pulled her shadesgrowl closer to hers. "Seriously. Tell me."

"I'm just worried, is all," Merey admitted. "We haven't had a paid job in a while, and I don't think Rednow's summon will come with coffers of gold. It's still my job to make sure no one in the Leeth goes hungry. I used to scratch my head at Rednow's hard-headedness, but now I find myself thinking just how right the stubborn bastard was all along."

Tellwoon scowled.

"He was always right. Well, for the most part. But you will find your way." She extended her hand to grab Merey's and caressed it. "Rednow had no one to share the burden with, but you do. I'm always here for you."

Merey smiled, but there was little joy in it. She often found herself worrying for Tellwoon, wishing to keep her safe, even though she was stronger than Merey now that she was a smoke-smith. "Thank you."

Tellwoon retreated, though her eyes lingered on Merey for another moment before she took off. They would camp in the Benaven woods just in the foothills of the Thousand Hills, but the harsh part of the journey was about to start. For days, maybe weeks, they'd have to hike the steep slopes until they reached what she imagined would be Rednow's makeshift war camp.

I haven't proven anything yet. I haven't shown anyone why Rednow picked me to replace him.

As she continued to ride at the same steady pace, a scout came trotting. "Merey!" It was Naven. "Merey!"

"What is it? What did you find?"

Naven halted his shadesgrowl abruptly. "Quickly, come take a look."

Merey glanced back to the nearest soldiers. "Do not slow the march. I'll be back soon."

She hit the reins of her mount and rode with Naven, who pushed his shadesgrowl to ride faster than the damn creatures were meant to be ridden. His eyes hinted at knowledge of something else ahead that wasn't good at all. The hooves of the beasts trampled the snow and their warm breaths steamed out of their muzzles as they pushed through the road. Then Naven halted his shadesgrowl and Merey did the same.

She followed him through a thick woodland area and he extended his index finger over his mouth. They both sat there for a moment.

In the silence, Merey heard it.

There were hooves in the distance, appearing closer and closer. This was no small march; there must have been thousands of mounts there.

Then Merey saw it. The standards and the flags. A dark blue background, four white stars in each corner, and a light blue flame emblem in the middle: the banner of the kingdom of Gasho.

A few questions ran through Merey's mind. Why were they there, up north? Why were they marching in the same direction as the Leeth soldiers? She remained quiet, though. Any movement now and she could be spotted. She remained with Naven for a few moments, observing the march. They had mounted soldiers, foot soldiers, and units of spearmen, but there were also other units with slaves pulling improvised catapults and other siege devices. All the soldiers were armed to the teeth and equipped with helmets, chainmail, and blue robes that marked them as soldiers of Gasho.

They're marching for battle. Could they be...

Slowly, Naven and her retreated. *There must be thousands of them.* A feeling in her gut told her these soldiers were aiming to get to where she was taking the Leeth. They were planning to fight *against* Rednow.

But then, that meant they were siding with...

She gasped as it clicked in her mind. She wasn't sure, but if this was true, then they needed to reach Rednow first or find a way to reach him. But how? The pineheads had all already left, and a single messenger scout or two would likely get lost in the mountainous terrain, or wind up as marcruncher supper.

When she was back on her shadesgrowl, she urged the creature back towards her army. Naven looked at her, expectant, but too polite to ask her what she was thinking. She gritted her teeth and pushed the shadesgrowl harder. When they finally reached the march, Tellwoon was already back.

"Where have you been?" she asked.

"A word. Now."

Tellwoon pushed her shadesgrowl forth, and the soldiers around them murmured. They had probably anticipated something was wrong, but she needed to formulate a plan.

"Gashoine soldiers. Thousands of them. Entire garrisons all marching to the Thousand Hills. About a mile from where we stand. Headed the same direction as we are."

Tellwoon's mouth gaped, and then she swallowed. "Not a coincidence, I wager."

Merey shook her head. "Very unlikely."

"Can we get to Rednow first?"

"Not with the entire army. And we'd still be outnumbered in a skirmish. It's not worth the risk."

"So, there's only one thing we can do," Tellwoon said.

Merey nodded. Her heart raced as she thought about it, though she tried not to let the excitement of battle overshadow her responsibilities. The cloak of bloodlust was one she couldn't afford to have anymore. Not when so many lives depended on her. When so many men and women were loyal. "We can keep our scouts carefully following them. We wait, and we follow them. If we stay far enough behind them, we'll avoid their scouts, but we'll still know their location."

Tellwoon nodded. "That sounds reasonable. And then what?"

"And then," Merey said, a smile forming on her lips, "when they are about to strike Rednow, we charge at their backs."

"I like it," Tellwoon said, a similar smile appearing in her face. "Plus, we'd have the advantage of terrain."

"We'll be late to meet Rednow, but we'll still handle his enemies."

They were silent for a moment, the wind colder than the edge of a blade. Merey thought about how thankful she was of Rednow. How grateful she was of having thousands of soldiers who were loyal. Most importantly, how lucky she was to have Tellwoon.

"We'll do it together," Merey said.

TWENTY-FIVE

UPHEAVAL

GIMLORE - NORK

G imlore had spent years hiding in the steppes of Mosendel and bushwhacking enemy soldiers in the bushlands of Ainis, but even back then, during the hardest years of her life, she had not faced heat like this.

If I can survive this, I can survive anything.

She continued to walk as there were no mounts in sight. With no weapons but a few swords and daggers stolen from the quarry guards, there wasn't much food either. Each passing day, it seemed like her pants got looser. She saw the same in Keryon's face. It looked hollow now, with dark circles around his eyes. None of this could be good for them, yet the Tooth insisted he was close to reaching a settlement.

"How long?" Gimlore asked.

The man shrugged as he had done many times before.

It took all the energy Gimlore still had not to grab him by the throat and spew a chain of unending threats to put him in his place, but he had been crucial in kickstarting their escape from the quarry. At her side, Hope looked hungry, all skin and bones. The girl wasn't the only one, though. Gimlore had already got used to the pain in her stomach as she kept walking further. Their diet had consisted simply of bitter cerro berries picked up from the fields as they marched on, but even those looked like they had been abandoned long past their harvesting period, so there wasn't much to be done in that regard.

Keryon nudged her with his elbow as he faced the cerro fields. "Did you notice?"

She nodded. "Not a soul in sight."

"Something is going on. It might have to do with Orberesis. They've abandoned the farmlands. So, the question is: where have they gone?"

Gimlore could think of a thousand answers to that. The most logical answer would be big cities. Their lords had stopped paying, so the workers had left the estates to try their luck in the city. She'd seen how crowded Ushar had been, with hundreds of people cramming themselves just to get inside. Perhaps they had been drafted to fight in Orberesis' war.

Thinking about that left her shivering, and her mind drifted to Rednow and Tinko.

A sound she hadn't heard in a long time echoed in the distance, low and almost imperceptible. She perked up her ears, and there it was again.

"Did you hear that?" she asked Keryon.

"What?"

"Quiet. Listen."

There it was again.

Keryon squinted and then his brow rose. "I heard it. What is it?"

"It's fucking seagulls!" Gimlore smiled. "We're close to the sea!"

The rest of the prisoners rushed to climb up the small hill that was ahead of them, and she did the same with Keryon and Hope by her side. Upon reaching the top of the hill, Gimlore panted. Her knees were weak, and her heart raced, but the bloody smile remained. Before her, was the big blue, swelling from east to west and surrounding everything in sight.

"I knew it!" the Tooth said. He pointed to their west when facing the sea. "There's Ushar!"

Gimlore squinted and shielded her eyes from the sun. A gust of wind brought a wet whiff of salt water that she cherished after what had felt like an eternity without seeing the sea or feeling a refreshing breeze blowing at her face. There it was, the fated capital of the Two Nations of Sirestir and Yab. Somewhere in there were the catacombs where she had been lashed nearly to death. And the fucker of a monarch who had ordered it. She gritted her teeth thinking about it.

You will know pain, you little bastard.

"Where do we go?" Keryon asked.

The Tooth stepped forward and drew a few lines in the dirt with a stick. Gimlore couldn't understand a thing, but the man thought they made a whole lot of sense. "We're about three hours march from Ushar. Are we all going the same direction?"

Keryon looked at her, and she nodded. "I have some scores to settle first, and then a ship to catch."

"I'm going where she is going," Keryon said.

Hope raised her arm. "Me too."

Gimlore found the energy to smile and ruffled the little girl's hair as she turned to Tooth and the rest of the prisoners.

"I'm not sure what your plans are, but I'm thankful for your aid," she said. "It was an honour to have you all by my side. I care not for who you were before the quarry. All I know is I'd trust my life to any of you here and now."

Silence fell upon them and some of the prisoners nodded.

"We only had the courage to rise because of you, isn't that right, folks?" the Tooth asked, urging the prisoners to speak.

They muttered and nodded. "Aye," they said in unison.

"My life was already over before the quarry, anyway. I've no family or friends. And if I'm honest, I'm not too keen on doing any honest, decent work. So, I'd be happy to go with you, if you'll have me. Say, if I do well, would I have a place in that town of yours?"

A few prisoners nodded and clapped, seemingly wanting the same.

Gimlore could only look at Keryon as the man smiled. Just how much had he been talking to the Tooth about her, Heleronde, and what she stood for? She felt like hugging him and punching him at the same time, for doing it all without telling her a thing.

"What about me? Will you have me, too?" Hope asked, bright eyes reflecting the sunny sky.

She nodded. "I'll be more than happy to take you all, but we have a lot to do. There is someone in that palace who needs to be taught a lesson. One I'm happy to give. But I'll need help. Are you with me?"

"Aye!" the prisoners bellowed.

"And then we'll have to fight the bastard who destroyed my town. He's got some divine powers, so I don't know how we're going to do that, but he bleeds like any other man. Are you still with me?"

"Aye!" Their bellows were even fiercer than the first time.

"And then we'll take Heleronde and build it back even better than it used to be. Are you still with me?"

"Aye!" they bellowed, pumping their fists in the air. "Aye!"

"We're *all* with you," the Tooth said.

Gimlore glanced at them. Their clothes were rotten and their faces dirty, a mix of sweat and dust caking their hair. But they had strong arms, determined eyes, and Gimlore imagined they all had a bone to pick with the ones who had sent them to the quarry and whipped their backs. It was a ragtag of brutes and wiry folks, but they believed in her, and only the gods knew why.

She would *need* all the help she could get.

Nork waited for twilight. His plan was in motion. He had never been much of a planner, not like Gimlore. She had made sure he and his brother had stayed alive all those years, and it wasn't for nothing. But now she wasn't here to help them, so Nork had to step up.

There was a certain restlessness in the air. The prisoners were quiet, all playing their part. With a side glance, he spotted Ferkin and Chona staying back just as a group of shadowlings passed them. He itched to break his shackles, pick up a knife, and stab the bastards until his arm was tired. But there were no knives around and his bounds were made of iron, so he had to bide his time.

He looked to the other side, where shadowlings were populating the ruins of Heleronde. In the night, however, there were always fewer around. *They must go back to their water holes*, he thought.

At night, however, it also became clear just how much the light from their horns flickered, making Nork wonder if that was on purpose, part of who they were as a species. That was also something that could help them—since the creatures had a lantern of sorts as part of their body, it would be impossible for any of the men and women of Heleronde to miss them as they approached.

"It's almost time," Nosema said.

Nork nodded to his brother and they both punched their chests for courage. None would live without the other. Only death could separate them.

He looked back at the improvised prisoner camp and its physical boundaries made with wood. Whoever tried to jump this improvised fence would have to find out what the punishment was. But if they weren't seen...

Still thinking of the old town geography, the camp was not far from where Pinesy's house had been, which meant they'd still have a bit of a walk to get to their destination. Nork's legs trembled a bit, and he wasn't sure if that was fear or hunger. Maybe both.

"Hey!"

It started.

"What in the underworld do you think you're doing?" one of the town folks asked, loud enough to grab the attention of the remaining prisoners, and surely that of the fish-heads.

"Me? Speak for yourself!" Another prisoner shoved the first. "Watch where you step."

"Let's go," Nork whispered to his brother as chaos ensued behind them; men shouting, and nearly all the prisoners getting involved, making a ruckus. Behind him and his brother were Ferkin and Chona.

The four of them waited for the shadowlings to be drawn to the prisoners of war. Nork prayed—to whom, he did not know—that the shadowlings didn't do anything to the men who had volunteered for the distraction. They had sacrificed themselves for a plan that might not work... Nork had to make sure it *would*.

A group of more than ten fish-heads swarmed that side of the prisoner camp, lights flickering and growling as they trotted to see what the problem was.

"Now!" Nork said.

The four of them stealthily jumped the fence and managed to leave the prisoner camp without being seen. They snuck out carefully and used the rubble and the lack of moonlight as cover. Unfortunately, that also meant they couldn't really see where they were going all that well, which forced them to take a long time and be extra careful.

Nork stayed ahead of them, wondering if this was even doable. They were risking their lives for nothing but a paper-thin dream. Now they would find out if the gods believed that dream or not.

They hid behind rubble, shadowlings ever present with their flickering light. Nork waited patiently until there were none around, then moved again.

He would argue that Heleronde held no secrets to him, but this was no longer Heleronde. This was something else, and his knowledge of the old town didn't mean anything when roaming in the rubble.

I need to get to the old town hall.

By his own judgement, from where the four of them were to the town hall, it would only be a few dozen steps more, though that could take minutes with no visual references. He squinted, but all the rubble looked the same. He tried hard to find something to hold on to or could use as guidance. Glancing from left to right while hiding in the darkness, he finally found it. One of the posts that had belonged to the old Warden's office was tilted but still standing.

He hand-signalled to Nosema and saw the confusion in the faces of the other two. It didn't matter, they would follow anyway. Nork took one last glance both ways. No shadowlings in sight. He moved towards the rubble of what used to be the Warden's office, picking a place where the four of them could hide.

They stayed there, between a giant wall and a few broken floorboards, just as the light from three shadowlings appeared, lighting everything around them. Nork and the others stayed in their nook, daring not to move or breathe. A few seconds passed and the creatures were gone. Nork let out a breath and started looking for a way to get inside the rubble. Any gap would suffice for someone as thin as him.

Please, let this work.

He *needed* this to work. Not just for him and his brother, but for the rest of the town folks who had agreed to help them by staging the distraction. Nork was no hero, but he could damn well do his best to help.

Carefully, he looked for any opening in the wood floors that didn't have a wall or part of the roof collapsed over them. He and Nosema spent a good while searching in silence, with Chona and Ferkin waiting in the dark, oozing impatience.

Then, Nork's hand touched something that felt remarkably like a lever. No—it was more like a lock, except it was on the wood floorboard and not in any broken door.

Could this...

He signalled for Nosema to help him out and, together, they lifted a large wood column, doing what they could to make no sound, though that was proving harder and harder. His arms and back strained as the weight of the column nearly overpowered him. He hadn't eaten much in weeks, maybe months. His strength was gone, but they did it.

He called Ferkin and Chona and slid into the opening on the floorboard. It was one of the trapdoors the Warden had ordered dug in right under his office.

Now let's just pray this is the one we need.

With the four of them inside the hole, they had no way to see what was in front of them, so they had to go by touch and smell. Nork walked forward carefully, arms extended in front of him, waving slowly from left to right. They touched something, and a clinking sound of glasses echoed, probably louder than it should have.

That wonderful sound was enough to restore the hope Nork had already lost.

"Yes!" he whispered. "This is it!"

The others came closer as he removed a linen cloth from a large crate full of glasses. Nork felt around in the dark; the other crates had similar contents.

"Do you care to tell us what this is?" Ferkin whispered. "We agreed to help you but have been in the dark ever since. Not just literally."

Nork could only smile. The stupid bastards had destroyed the town, but they hadn't bothered to do any reconnaissance or even wonder if there were any weapons hidden underground. And while these weren't exactly weapons, they could very well be...

"This," Nosema said, "is mossback elixir."

The silence from the two smokesmiths meant confusion, so Nork explained.

"We were producing it here. Take this, and you will get stronger, battle-ready, and feel no pain. Take too much, and you will need it forever."

"How is that going to help us?" Chona whispered. "We can't carry the box back to the camp."

"But we can all *take it* ourselves and fight our way out of here," Nork said.

"Even if we get stronger, we still have no weapons."

Nork walked a little further into the cave, hands still extended forward. Maybe they'd be lucky? The Warden and his companion Pie had a shop that sold herbs, but the business had gone bust. They wouldn't get rid of all the herbs. They'd…

His hand caught something. This time it was a sack that covered yet another crate. He removed the sack and opened the lid. A whiff of herbs came.

"Perhaps there are some herbs here that you smokesmiths can find useful. We've kept our part of the deal, now you'll have to help us get out of here."

"I can't believe this treasure trove has been hiding here while we were wallowing in the mud. I smell *twisted twins*, and definitely some belleaf," Chona said. "You've got it. We won't leave this place without you."

"Good. Now take the fucking elixir." Nork handed them all vials and they all drank its contents. "We have to wait a while before it takes effect. Then we can go."

"Alright."

Nork surveyed the rest of the little cellar. He was about to stop the search, having found only a handful of herb-related utensils and other materials used to copy and lengthen the density of the elixir. But then he smelled something else. Something unexpected.

"Do you smell that?" he whispered.

"Smell what?" Nosema asked.

Nork grabbed his brother and brought him to where he stood. "This. Take a whiff."

His brother took his time and said nothing, but Nork knew there was something else hiding under all of it. He searched, turning sacks and cloths away and just following the smell, which became stronger as he went.

"For the gods, what are you looking for? They'll hear us!" Ferkin whispered.

Nork's hand touched something he recognised and he smiled as he retrieved a greasy bomb to show the others.

"I was looking for our ticket out of here, and I think I've just found it."

TWENTY-SIX
THE CELLAR

GIMLORE

Gimlore had started to dread Ushar more than she cared to admit. The city could have been one of the old marvels of the world, but the place was *filthy*, and had some of the worst people she had ever met. It seemed like no one could be nice, although she had said the same when she met the rest of her entourage, and now she was comfortable enough to trust them with her life.

"We should take the next ship to Vaerghulen or Mosendel, not wander the streets," Keryon whispered. "They might catch us again and..."

"We *tried* taking the ship, but the harbour was empty, wasn't it? All the bloody sailors were gone. Something is up..." Gimlore saw regret in his eyes and grabbed his hand for comfort. "And this was your friend Tooth's idea. And he might be onto something."

Keryon sighed and they continued to follow the man, along with the rest of her new companions. They crossed broad roads that looked designed to fit more than four or five wagons going both ways, with avenues so long they sprawled across the city.

She imagined it once would have been majestic, with the lines of trees and the pristine buildings surrounding it, five storeys high and built in stone, probably from the damn quarry.

There were large tunnel-like structures alongside the roads. Canals, she had heard they were called. But there was no water in them, just weeds growing from the bottom and some shacks built by a few of the city's paupers.

The streets narrowed in one of the busiest parts of town, as though that section of the city had been left untouched by whoever had built the large streets. These houses were built on the hills that preceded the Palace of Brilliance, and the streets between them could hardly hold three people without bumping shoulders. Instead, they held thousands of people, who moved with a rush she wasn't used to seeing. They went about their lives, as though this was a town of its own. Children ran up on the rooftops, jumping from building to building, laughing and chasing each other. Down there, it smelled of rotten fish and other things she would rather not think about.

"What the fuck are we doing here, Tooth?"

Keryon shot her a glance as if to say he had already asked her that.

"Oh, we *have* to come here. These are my old stomping grounds. Things are lively, so something must be happening," the man said.

Gimlore thought if the Tooth had ever fit a place perfectly, it had to be this neighbourhood of Ushar. Every person she came across looked like they could be his long-lost relative.

He finally stopped in front of a building and waved to get everyone in the group close to him, which was hard since there were about fifteen former prisoners besides her and Keryon.

"This is the Dripping Bucket," the Tooth said. "If there is news about the city and the bastards in charge, you will hear it here. And don't worry about any of this religious non-sense. No followers of that impostor are welcome here, so you can be at ease."

The Dripping fucking Bucket. Lovely.

If the name had been any indication, the place was even worse inside than it was on the outside. There was no money around, so instead of ale or cerro wine, all the patrons drank was water with some homemade brew that, given their facial expressions, just *couldn't* taste any good. Even calling the people patrons was an exaggeration. They were beggars the man behind the bar had been kind enough to allow to sit there and hold an empty mug.

"Well, well, well, my old friend the Tooth. You haven't lost that tooth yet, have you?" the fellow behind the bar asked. He was a brown-skinned man with shoulder-long hair, built like the trunk of an ancient oak. His voice was raspy but not unpleasant, even though he spoke in a Sirestine accent. Gimlore had to concentrate to understand what they said.

The Tooth smiled and pointed at it. "Still going strong!"

The man behind the bar shrugged and shook his head. "I thought you were dying somewhere in a sweat province or in a torture camp. But here you are, and you brought friends. And a child. She's not yours, is she?"

The Tooth grimaced. "No, no. But I'll leave that story for later. About my friends... we're not exactly swimming in gold, if you catch my drift."

"Another bunch of beggars, then. Great. Fucking great."

"I promise we won't stay long, Nero," the Tooth said, a wide smile spreading across his face. "What is going on today, anyway? It seems like the entire town might just erupt if I'm judging things right."

"It might just," the barman said. "But that's all I'm going to say about it."

The Tooth excused himself and took Gimlore and the rest of the former prisoners to sit in a dirty corner. Gimlore was still mulling Nero's words. *It might just.* It certainly felt like that. But there was no volcano that she could see. Unless he was talking about...

"There's going to be an uprising soon," the Tooth whispered as they gathered around him. "I can feel it in my bones! Nero might as well have said it."

Gimlore had been thinking the same. She couldn't blame the city folks for it. They were living in squalor and, just as she'd seen on their way there, it seemed like the peasants had abandoned the fields too, so there was nothing in the city and there was nothing *outside* of it either. Desperate men weren't too different from animals. When cornered, even the cowardly could bite. "How can we be sure?"

As if to answer her question, a few of the soot-faced men sitting around that excuse of a tavern—which could never compare to the Maiden's Hall—started calling for folks inside. The Tooth urged them in, and Gimlore took hold of Hope, grabbing the child by the shoulders and snarling at the doorman, who squinted at seeing a child in such a tavern.

"What is this place?" Keryon asked.

The Tooth only looked back and smiled at him.

There was a staircase beyond the door that led deeper underground. The further they got, the louder it became. It was stuffy and damp down there. Whatever the place was, it reeked of sweat, tabak smoke, and spilled liquor. It could have been a tavern just like it was upstairs, but Gimlore's mouth gaped as she saw it.

A crowd gathered.

Men young and old, mothers and daughters, and beggars all punched the air, shouting words of fury, building themselves up for upheaval. A handful of other men stood on top of chairs, applauding the crowd, asking for an even bigger ruckus.

When Gimlore and the rest of her entourage reached the bottom of the stairs, she realised just how large that cellar was. She wondered if it had been used for smuggling once, or maybe still was... She would have never guessed that such small houses and narrow streets above could have an enormous cave underneath.

One of the men standing on top of a chair glanced at them and his eyes widened.

"My friends! Are my eyes deceiving me?" He pointed to the back where Gimlore's group stood, and everybody else turned to look as they settled down. "Is that my old friend the Tooth?"

"That I am, you fucking bastard!" the Tooth responded, though Gimlore sensed by the toothless man's response they were far from friends and perhaps the "bastard" had been less friendly than intended.

"Where have you been? We thought you were dead."

"Aye." Many in the crowd nodded.

"The captors didn't turn you into a mole rat, did they?" the man asked as he got down from the chair. He was brown-skinned, with a sharp nose and even sharper smile.

His question lingered in the air and the Tooth could have grimaced at the provocation, but he didn't. He marched through the crowd, unafraid of whomever those scary people were.

"I'd give up my tooth before I turned into a spy for the bastards," he said. "In fact, my friends and I might have taken out a few dozen of them. Didn't we, folks?"

The prisoners nodded. They weren't scared either.

"Care to tell us how that happened? This is a free space for ideas, and you're no stranger, but your friends are. These are troubled times, Tooth. We need to make sure we can trust everyone."

"These are my brothers and sisters, Drentu. I would give up my life for them and I don't doubt they'd do the same for me. We were the first ever batch of prisoners to escape from the Uzunar quarry. All thanks to this woman over here."

The Tooth pointed at Gimlore.

Me? Oh, shit.

"Who is she? And why is that?"

The Tooth smiled a little longer than he should and held his tongue for theatrics. What in the underworld was the man planning?

"Have you heard about the Viper?"

There were murmurs in the crowd. Drentu cleared his throat. "Briefly. She led a rogue battalion during the Crimson Wars. But what does such a legendary figure have to do with... wait..."

The Tooth nodded. "That's fucking *her*!"

Gimlore swallowed. Not that she didn't appreciate a little appreciation from random folks, but these days she would just rather not have the attention. It seemed like everybody else wanted her to have it, though. Hope couldn't take her eyes off her and even Keryon had a smirk plastered across his face.

"How did she end up in the quarry? I swear, Tooth, if this is one of your foolish tales..."

Here we go...

"No. It's me. I'm Gimlore."

She explained what had happened after the Crimson Wars, and Drentu even invited her to stand on one of the chairs so that the folks in the back could hear what she had to say. She told them about Alarkan first.

"Ten years I dedicated to that town. My blood, sweat, and tears are all there," she said.

She did not know what possessed her to be so bloody honest with everyone, especially in such a large crowd and surrounded by strangers in a stuffy, muggy cellar. But she was.

"...And the fucker thought we were just farmers and carpenters. Guess what? The Leeth armies were hiding in the swamps waiting to ambush them."

She lost track of time. It could have been half an hour or three hours, but she spoke wildly and freely like she hadn't in years. For the gods, it was cathartic. And without a trace of cerro wine to loosen up her tongue, too. She couldn't remember the last time that had happened.

They laughed as she told them about how their soldiers were so heavily defeated. These folks weren't *patriots*. They cared not for God Himself, his armies, or his lords. But things took a darker turn when she told them about Orberesis' uprising and thousands of monsters surging from the depths of the under-world to fight on his behalf.

"I've always known he was more like a fiend, the bastard..." a round woman said.

Gimlore continued, but as she told them about the recent events, she felt the initial enthusiasm fade. She almost choked as she told them about Thata's disappearance and being separat-ed from Tinko. About Heleronde being totally destroyed and conquered by the creatures. She told them about their attempt to come back to Sirestir to twist the mind of the King with Tavanar's help, and how that had only turned into more misery and pain. She lifted her shirt and showed them the scars left by the whip.

"Bloody underworld."

"By the sweetest lords..." they muttered.

"And how did you get away?"

Gimlore couldn't continue further. She came down from the chair. "I'll let the Tooth explain that, if you don't mind."

The Tooth gladly climbed the chair as Gimlore walked slowly to the back of the room. She couldn't breathe. What the fuck was wrong with her lungs at this time? Keryon was by her side. "Are you alright? You look pale."

Gimlore covered her face with her hands but the darkness didn't help. All she saw was the ghost of Thata snarling at her. Rednow, lying on the mud, half-dead. Tinko, scared for their life amid the destruction.

I can't breathe.

"Gimlore?"

Keryon wasn't helping, but Gimlore didn't know what *would* help. She wanted him to hold her, but she also wanted space. She wanted him to take care of her, but also to leave her the fuck alone.

She finally gasped and was able to breathe. Tears rolled down her face. In the distance, the Tooth was still animating the rest of the poor folks with the story of their last night in the quarry and the perils they had faced. He mentioned Keryon several times and the man smiled as he earned several nods of respect from the crowd.

Gimlore just wanted to go home but she knew that was not a possibility. There was no home. The tears brought her clarity, for better or worse. It was painful to relive the memories of the horrors she had gone through, but perhaps she could still do something about it. Every single body in that cellar was ripe for revenge, with their hands clasped into fists and a raging confidence in their voices.

"That was a most sad yet inspiring tale, Tooth," Drentu said. "And many thanks to Gimlore as well. We now know we are all cut from the same cloth."

Gimlore wondered which cloth that was. She didn't see much in common with these people except for the fact that neither had bathed in weeks.

Drentu pressed on, raising his voice. "I am feeling an itch, my friends, to demand change. Shall we rise and tell these fuckers in the palace who we are?"

"Aye!" the crowd bellowed, only bloodlust in their eyes.

"Shall we take this city into our hands? The hands of those who make it what it is?"

"Aye!"

The crowd cheered and Gimlore was impressed. She had fought for years, but in battles, neither side was motivated to fight. It was simply their duty to kill people. If they didn't, they'd die. Gimlore had never liked that option, so she'd defected and built her own unit with soldiers that had been left behind. Nork and Nosema, bless them. Edmir, bless him. But they had never been motivated for anything other than protecting what they had. They did what they had to do. Now, these people *were* motivated. They could probably tear apart the entire city by themselves. With hammers, axes, and pitchforks, maybe they could even get into the palace.

That prospect gave her goosebumps and she had to smile. She exchanged glances with Keryon, but he didn't understand it like she did. He didn't get that sometimes things needed to be completely destroyed before they could be made better.

"What are you smiling for?" he asked. "These people are crazy..."

Gimlore scowled. "If they are crazy, then so am I."

TWENTY-SEVEN

RESPECT AND REVENGE

GIMLORE - NORK

G imlore ran through the streets of Ushar, following the crowd. She couldn't help but smile. She was a part of something again. Keryon only wanted to get back to Rednow as soon as possible, but Gimlore *needed* to have revenge. She could still hear the contempt in King Doemus' voice, his superiority, as though she was nothing but scum.

She could still hear the whip lashing her skin.

Gimlore wielded a carpenter's hammer in her right hand. Keryon had his herbs and daggers. The Tooth held a long pitchfork and commanded the other prisoners, as well as a large group of rebels that the monarchs would certainly dub as blasphemous traitors.

Let them.

The crowd marched and more people joined them as they went. Some of them had lost their faith, they said. Some when their daughters died. Others when the body of their son was never brought back from the battlefield. Those people knew true pain and horror. And they were about to show it.

Gimlore had left Hope in the cellar. This was no place for a child, even though Hope had seen more than any child should ever witness. Without the girl to worry about, she was free to march with the mob. They patted her in the back and comforted her. They respected her, they said.

Respect was good. Revenge was better.

For Thata. For everyone.

They were free to march on the Palace because they knew Orberesis wasn't there. He hadn't been seen in weeks. The commotion in the streets brought the city dwellers to their windows to watch, and many more out their doors.

"It's about fucking time!" one of them said as he joined the crowd.

They were on the slope now. In front of them were the gates to the palace where four guards stood, holding halberds. "Stop! What is your business?"

"Brother, either join us or feel free to piss off. But get out of our way," the Tooth said.

The guard hesitated and the crowd punched the air and raised their weapons, chanting.

Walk, my friend.
Run, my friend.
It will be worth it
In the end.

Their words filled the air. Gimlore didn't know the lyrics, but she could feel the energy. This was what it was like to be a part of something, to fight for what needed to be done.

Rise, my brother,
Shine, my brother.
These streets are ours
We have each other.

The guards looked pale, clueless as to what to do. They had oaths to uphold and protect, but Gimlore saw the doubt in their eyes. They understood the people's peril and what they were demanding. The chants continued.

Go, my sister.
March, my sister.
We will shout,
While they whisper.

"Time is up!" Drentu shouted, and the crowd moved with weapons and utensils in hand, leaving no time for the guards to decide what to do. Faced with a marching crowd, the soldiers opened the gates themselves amid consistent cheering from the people.

There were guards and knights inside, ready to fight for the throne of the Two Nations. Drentu and the Tooth took the front lines, while the crowd ushered Gimlore and Keryon to stand with them at the front. But Gimlore was no movement leader. She barely knew any of these people. Her motives for being a part of this were selfish.

"This is madness," Keryon whispered. "Have we learned nothing?"

Gimlore had never heard the man so upset, not even when his herb shop went bankrupt. He was right. This was lunacy, but they were in the thick of it.

Gimlore leaned towards him as the standstill between the guards and the crowd continued. "After all the Tooth and the others did for us, I consider our help in their cause to be necessary. If it wasn't for him, we would still be whipped in the back, don't you agree?"

Keryon grumbled something but had no answer for her.

"You shall not enter the ceremonial room," one of the guards said. He wore a full metal plate and carried a heavy halberd beside the sword in his scabbard. Twenty of them stood there, armed, and stoically facing the invaders. Facing Gimlore.

Drentu laughed. Gimlore did have to admit the man *did* look mad, or at the very least mad with excitement. For someone who had planned this uprising, there was little foresight being woven into his decisions, which left her worried.

"We don't need your permission!" the man shouted at the guards.

The crowd roared and charged. Maybe the knights could stop one or two of the poor citizens, but they would be trampled swiftly by the rest of them. There must be thousands in there now. Gimlore marched tightly among them, a grip firm on her hammer.

The Tooth's pitchfork flew forward and pushed one of the guards back, creating an opening for the rest of the people to storm the building. Gimlore swung her hammer right at the helmet of one of the guards, but the man was soon stabbed in the eyes—the only opening in his helmet—by the angry mob.

The inside of the ceremonial hall was as large as she remembered it, but there were even more guards, and this time there was a hint of smoke in the air.

Smokesmiths.

Keryon seemed to read her thoughts as he immediately burned some of his herbs and jumped to the front of the line. "You still serve your master?"

A tall man and a wiry woman stepped forward, smoke shrouding them, enveloping them. "Always," they answered.

"Even after what you were told... in your mind?"

They shrugged. "We serve the Two Nations."

Gimlore swallowed. Maybe Rednow's calling to gather an army of smokesmiths had failed. At least, these two showed no intention of wanting to go anywhere.

"That is a shame. I can only try to do my best to change your mind," Keryon said.

The tall man scowled. "I don't think that's going to happen."

Smoke covered the entire room and chaos ensued. The madness of battle was upon them.

Nork stalked an approaching group of fish-heads and hid in the shadows. He had always been wary of carrying such highly volatile material. Any rough movement and *he* would be the one being flown into the air under a big ball of fire. But carrying an entire sack full of the explosives was even harder.

He glanced to the side. Nosema stood there, as he always did. Chona and Ferkin walked behind them. The jog back to the prisoner camp should be easier than the way out of there, given that they had spent precious time looking for the trap door.

After the fish-heads passed and Nork was sure they wouldn't return, he took a chance and walked directly to the next hiding place. If they could make it to the prisoner camp and supply the other smokesmiths with the herbs, then they had a real shot at freeing themselves and everybody else.

We can't fail.

There was no wind to cover the sounds of their steps in the quiet night. He just had to cross his fingers and hope the fish-heads didn't have sensitive hearing. After a few more minutes like that, between hiding spots, they saw the camp, but it still wasn't safe to return yet.

I can't see anything in this darkness.

But darkness meant there were no fish-heads around as they always had light in their horns. With a few hand signals, he urged the rest of the group to move towards the camp, trotting, but careful not to raise any attention. Nork stopped at the spot they had used to jump, making his way back to the camp.

A shriek came from inside the prisoner camp. A fish-head jumped at them, slashing with its claws. *Where did the fucker come from?* Nork managed to dodge the blows and run further inside the muddy prisoner camp. The bastard had kept his light out.

"Take the herbs!" Ferkin said, throwing a bag full of herbs towards Nosema. He and Chona burned theirs, and threads of smoke surrounded them as they defended themselves from the fish-head.

Nork and his brother ran without looking back. The smoke-smiths would be fine against that fish-head, but if they didn't hurry, the entire legion of the bastards would come, and the prisoners would be lost.

The other smokesmiths were waiting for them, and Nosema gave them what they needed.

Nork could hear the shrieks of the creatures in the distance. *Shit.* "Let's go! Everybody, jump the fence. We're taking the rafts out of here!"

Thankfully, the camp wasn't far from the beach, but there were many children and elderly. The prisoners started to move, but they were still too slow. And the fish-heads were fast on their tails.

Despair grew inside his chest. "We need to go *now!*"

The prisoners were starved and dehydrated. They could hardly run, but for the gods they did their best. With a quick glance behind, Nork saw Ferkin and the rest of the smoke-smiths battling a handful of fish-heads. They were holding their ground well, threads of smoke and improvised weapons thrash-ing the fish-heads. Nork had scarcely liked to get involved with smokesmiths, and they had mostly never been on his side of the battles, but this time, they were. They had kept their promise. And now they were buying them time.

Most prisoners were already fleeing, but others stayed back. Nork stopped as his eyes locked on Eshof and he ran towards her. "You must hurry!"

The old woman looked at him and smiled. "You did good. You truly did. I'll always remember it."

"What are you talking about, lady? Hurry up!"

Eshof shook her head and pointed at her leg. It was swollen to almost twice its size. "I can't. Suits me well, staying here. Dying here. This is where I wanted to die, anyway. I just hope they bury me. Go, son, and save whomever else you can."

Those words pulled the rug from under him. How could he leave people behind? "No. I can carry you."

"We both know that's not likely. Now, go! Keep your strength. Save the rest. Maybe these monsters will spare me."

The likelihood of that was miniscule, especially considering just how cruel the fish-heads had been when it came to providing the prisoners with their basic needs. Nork felt both sides of his mind in a tug of war. If he went and saved others, he would always live knowing he had failed Eshof, who he knew and respected. If he tried to save her, she might still not make it and he would have missed the opportunity to help others in need.

He hit his head countless times with his open palm, grimacing.

This is why I should never be anyone's fucking leader. "I'm sorry, Eshof."

She mumbled something as he started running away from her, but the pain in his chest was too much to bear. Too much for him to carry alone.

With tears, and with his voice cracking, he urged everyone to leave. He whistled, and the smokesmiths picked up on his signal. They broke off from their skirmish against the fish-heads and immediately ran towards him. Nork set his eyes on the ugly creatures. They were everywhere now, coming from the debris of Heleronde and towards them. Probably hundreds of them by now.

He brought his hand to the inside of his satchel, pulled out a greasy bomb, and anointed it with an extra dose of belleaf oil. Then, when the smokesmiths were nearly with him, he threw the bomb behind them, at the fish-heads.

The greasy bomb fell in the middle of the creatures, blasting their bodies into pieces in a large flash of fire and light. Quickly, he threw another, despite the ringing in his ears. Another large bang blew up a few dozen bastards.

He threw another one. *Die!*

Someone gripped his arm. Nosema. "That's enough. Let's go to the rafts."

His brother dragged him by the arm and Nork had to shake himself. He would have stayed behind and died with the fish-heads.

The beach was an assortment of people in tiny rowboats and rafts, and some even grabbed onto whatever shattered wood they could. Those people were survivors at heart, and they would do anything to get off that beach.

"They'll make it," Nork muttered.

Nosema's hand rested on his shoulder. "We all will, brother."

"Thank you. You kept your promise to help," Ferkin said. "We must go now."

Nork nodded. He couldn't muster a reply as his gaze switched between the town folks leaving in rafts and the fish-heads still finding their way to chase them. The smoke-smiths were readying their own rafts and Nork took one more glance at the prisoner camp. Eshof was still there, ready to accept whatever the fish-heads decided to do with her. She was a clever woman. No one survived as long as she had without some wits, but there was only sorrow and pain in Nork's heart.

"Come on. Let's hop on our raft," Nosema said.

Nork nodded and abided by the words of his much more level-headed brother. He would be lost without him.

Once he got on the raft, he realised there was nobody else on the beach. They were all at sea now.

He had done it.

They had done it.

But he couldn't breathe yet. One last group of fish-heads was still making it through to the beach. Nork picked up one of his last greasy bombs and showed it to Nosema, who was paddling. "One more?"

Nosema smiled the same smile of approval he had given him so many times. For the gods, he loved his brother. Or perhaps he was just being consumed by a whirlwind of emotions he had never learned to handle. His brother's eyes always soothed him. He could almost read his mind. *Do it*, the eyes said.

Nork mustered all the strength he could and threw the greasy bomb at the beach. He squinted, waiting for it to land, and land it did, blowing up like the roar of a giant of old. The fire bloomed like an enormous flower of heat and destruction. And it consumed the last of the fish-heads who had dared to follow them.

Twenty-Eight

Dead Scout

Rednow - Merey

From the air, Rednow looked over the mountains and the military units that hid inside. Most of them were rogue, comprised of smokesmiths who had heard his plea and decided to come. There was also what Rednow called the Pinehead Village, where hundreds of pineheads gathered, building improvised shacks and houses, and living in a community just on the outskirts of the Builders' cove. He flew towards it.

It was as natural as breathing once had been, these days. He could float and move around with no effort and not get tired at all. He dove towards the main platform, and there was already a group waiting for him. Pinesy sat next to Arkan in silence. The two had diverging ideas, although Rednow wished they would put those aside and get along once and for all.

"Sorry to make you wait," he said.

"We haven't waited long," Arkan said. "No sign of the enemy, I take it?"

"Not yet. But we mustn't get too comfortable. Last time they came, they caught us by surprise."

There were others sitting beside Pinesy and Arkan. Three representatives from the smokesmiths and two others from the pineheads, but Rednow had yet to learn their names. They stared at him, waiting. Rednow still couldn't shake off the feeling that everything he did and said would be judged or evaluated.

"Thanks for meeting me here. I asked for you all because I need to know what I can't see in my surveys. What have you to report?"

"If I may start, it's a pleasure meeting you, Blood Collector. I'm Fatuna," an onyx-haired woman with dark eyes and a pointy face said. She was a smokesmith. "Some of my comrades are getting antsy. They're not used to living in tents or sharing their food and everything else."

"Well, that is the nature of battle. It's inherently uncomfortable, isn't it?" was all Rednow could ask.

"Indeed. And that brings me to two main points." Fatuna leaned forward. "These woods are running out of game, and I think we've already hunted all the mountain goats. I'm pretty sure we've picked nearly all the mountain berries as well. If we are to sit and wait longer, we might need to think about supplies for the troops, even if the troop numbers aren't that large yet."

Rednow nodded—wondering how odd it would look for a skeleton to nod—as that made perfect sense. It had taken him years to select the optimal conditions to feed the Leeth enough to at least avoid starvation, but even a covert mercenary army needed gold to pay for everyone's needs. "Very well. I will think of what the best way is to prevent them leaving us. What's your second point?"

Fatuna swallowed. "We're not battle-ready. Most of these smokesmiths have spent their lives in cities, holding power and upholding the rule of law on city urchins and beggars. We were barely ever challenged. I believe you spoke the truth, but that frightens me because most of the smokesmiths are not prepared, as talented and powerful as they may be."

That was indeed cause for concern. Something Rednow had already considered. He had spent his entire life going from one battle to the next, but not everyone there had been called to fight in the Crimson Wars.

"If I may intervene, Blood Collector," a pale-skinned pine-head with brown curls said. "I'm Caspan, representing the Builders of the southwestern sect."

Arkan scoffed. "You lot lost the right to call yourselves Builders when you abandoned the purpose of our kind. What was the last thing you built? *We* are Builders. You're just *pine-heads*."

Caspan and his companions stirred but Rednow raised his voice. "Arkan. It's no time for this. Please, Caspan, go on."

"As I was saying," Caspan snarled, casting a deathly stare at Arkan. "We're unprepared for war. We vowed to never fight again unless we were called upon by the Essence. We are here now, but the last time we fought was a long time ago."

"I see. Do other sects feel the same way?" He turned to the other pineheads.

They all nodded.

"That makes sense," Rednow said. He should do something to keep the units busy and to stop them from wondering where the food would come from, while also preparing them for battle. "We need to start preparing for the battle with real intent. A series of preparations need to be made. One of them is the manufacturing of weapons. We need all the Builders armed with at least a long spear and a dagger or two. Can we make that happen?"

"I'll talk to our smiths," another of the pineheads said. This one looked odd, as he was the only pinehead Rednow had ever seen with a beard. He looked like a very precocious child who had grown a beard before the rest of his body had grown.

"Great. Make the spears long. Perhaps consult the Builders for the right length and weight."

"Why long?" Arkan asked.

"Because they're going to be fighting from the sky. We all saw how effective airborne units were against the shadowlings, didn't we?"

"But we lost the ability to fly."

Rednow pointed at Arkan. "He can and so can you. Arkan and his people will teach you."

Arkan shook his head. "I will do no such thing, Rednow. I will not."

"Yes, you will, my friend. We have no choice. We will be outnumbered. We can only be successful if we are prepared when luck strikes. Waiting for miracles doesn't work. They need your help, so please do just that, for everyone's sake, will you?"

Arkan sighed.

"Great, that's sorted, then. Long spears and flight training. As to the land units, the smokesmiths will also need some coordination. Don't take this the wrong way but... can the smokesmiths be... coordinated? I mean trained into real battle units."

Fatuna smiled. "No offence taken. It's hard to tell without their loyalties being tested, Blood Collector."

"So, let's test them," Rednow said. "We need to form teams and then host drills and exercises. We need to plan war games. That should build trust between them, get them motivated, and weed out those who aren't here for the right reasons."

Fatuna grimaced. "That all sounds good, but there's an issue."

"Yes?"

"Most of the smokesmiths, including me, are either deserters or those who have been allowed to leave our old masters. So, there might be some difficulty in getting them to respect chain of command in general. They're less likely to obey, since obedience to a master was the reason they left in the first place."

"Fatuna, I am no master. We're all brothers and sisters. I'm merely the avatar for the Essence. So, they mustn't think of what I say as commands, but requests. When I *request* that the smokesmiths organise into units, I'm not deciding the units, I'm leaving all those decisions to you. You, the smokesmiths, decide your future. So, choose your comrades well and vote for who the unit leaders should be. In this day and age, it makes no sense for someone to impose their will on others. Leaders should be exemplary and be accepted by all."

The answer seemed to satisfy Fatuna.

"Right, then. Moving on. Pinesy, what news do the arriving cousins bring?"

Pinesy took a while to reply. He was quieter than most pineheads, often lost in his thoughts. But he had an extensive network of cousins spread across the Known World, and he always knew someone who knew someone. The news travelled quickly between pineheads and it seemed as though he was always the first one to know.

"The latest group we took in the camp is from somewhere in Sirestir. They travelled here and brought news and rumours."

"Let us hear them."

Pinesy swallowed. "Orberesis took over Shari and some say he even killed their king. The armies of Shari will be his."

"He can't just force the soldiers to be loyal," Fatuna said.

"No, but after what he did to their king, no one will dare be disloyal, which is why he knew he had to send a strong message," Rednow said.

Orberesis had proven to be much smarter than Rednow had given him credit for. He was thinking ahead, in the long-term. And in all these months after they had left Heleronde, the Deceiver had been trying to expand his presence and grow his armies.

That's why you must do the same, the Essence said, a certain edge to her voice.

Rednow grimaced. "What else?"

Pinesy cleared his throat. "He was also sighted in Mosendel, but it's not clear if they're allying with him."

Shit.

Rednow could face one nation's army allied with infinite shadowlings even if he was outnumbered. The mountains were natural shields, and he'd have the upper ground. Armies from *two* kingdoms, plus the Two Nations... that was something else entirely. That meant thousands of men laying siege to the cove or working to blast the entire mountain wall, all of it with the goal of killing the Essence.

Rednow sighed. "At least in the mountains, siege engines and cannons will be useless."

"They could have muskets."

Rednow shook his head. "Muskets come from the Two Nations, but production has largely dropped off after Orberesis manipulated the King to cripple the entire country's trade and industry to fuel his ambitions with his invasion to Alarkan. I doubt their stocks will be significant."

Arkan scratched his head. "But even if they only come armed with spears, swords, and axes, how do we prepare for that? How do we fight one enormous army of shadowlings and two or more human armies?"

As much as Rednow thought, he couldn't find a grand solution. He needed to get stronger, for everyone's sake, even if battles were never won by one divine entity defeating another. They were won by sharp objects piercing soft tissue on a large scale. He needed more sharp objects, and enough soldiers to wield them.

"I will think of something."

"Oh, I'm sure you will, but think fast because those armies won't take long to get here, if that is their purpose." Arkan stood from his spot in the circle. "I'll lay out the plans according to your wishes, Rednow. I hope you are right about all this. It's not just my pride you're hurting, it's that of all my people."

Rednow sighed. "Pride is cheap, Arkan. It's worth so much less than the lives of your loved ones."

Arkan nodded and took flight towards one of the platforms built on the rock wall of the Builders' Cove.

"If that's all, we'll be going, too. And we'll set your plans in motion, Blood Collector. I hope we don't disappoint you," Fatuna said, and the other smokesmiths got up with her.

"I know you will not." Rednow tried to sound confident, but he was anything but that. They all left except for Pinesy, who stayed there with him, looking at the sky. "Where is Tinko?"

Pinesy shrugged. "Intensive training. Arkan put them on the Inner Flight."

Rednow laughed. If the child were to stay true to everything Rednow had learned about them, they would emerge out of the Inner Flight much stronger, freer, and capable of flight. "Sometimes I wonder if I should be impressed, intimidated, or downright scared by that child."

He thought he could see the glimpse of a smile at the corner of Pinesy's mouth. "You treat the kid well. Like your own kin. That's good."

"I made Gimlore a promise, one I intend to keep." He wondered where the woman was. Tinko took so much after her. That sheer relentlessness in everything they did. Not taking no for an answer. "Do you miss her?"

Pinesy showed the hint of a smile. "She always took care of me."

Rednow nodded. "She is out there, somewhere. She will come with that smokesmith of hers. We'll cross paths again. I'm sure of it."

⋯⋯

Merey stayed hidden in the woodlands, between three large pines. The goal was stealth to avoid the Gashoine scouts, but even if she covered her tracks to the best of her abilities, the scouts would probably still be able to spot traces of other people in those woods. Best case scenario, they would think her a boar or a deer.

Why did I decide to do this myself? I'm the bloody leader of the Leeth now.

The winter winds blew from the north, and she shivered with the cold. If she was right, the Gashoine garrisons would march through a pass to her left, where a large cliff showed a great view of the Thousand Hills. But that wasn't why Merey liked the cliffs. If the Gashoine troops marched from the woodland area and into the cliffs, they would be in a tight squeeze, with nowhere to turn in the event of an ambush. The scouts had likely foreseen this and would try to speed up the march or divide the whole group in two to avoid potential ambushes. That's why Tellwoon was further back, to count the number of battle units.

Merey waited, then, for any trace of the bastards. She was the leader of the Leeth but that didn't mean she was going to sit on her ass and order people around. That was not how Rednow had raised her. He led by example, and so would she.

Out there, in the cold, she was breaking all the known rules to surviving a harsh winter. She was standing still, with no heat source, nothing in her belly, and a heavy marcruncher fur that felt much too light for the humid frost that easily seeped into her bones.

Then, she heard something. Just a rustle. It could have been a bird in the trees, but no, it was too persistent. Merey tensed, stayed silent, and dropped for cover.

There was somebody in those woods.

The leaves continued to rustle and the sound was louder by the second, getting closer to her. If she were to lift her head to see where it was coming from, she would be found easily, so she stayed motionless and relied on the fur as camouflage. She couldn't let the bastard see her there. Was she hidden well enough?

The rustling continued as the likely enemy scout made his way carefully through the bushes and the trees, getting closer and closer. But then the sound stopped, and the next thing she heard was a sword being unsheathed.

Shit.

Merey got up, muscles cold and stiff, and found a scout looking directly at her, confused. "Who are you?"

Merey didn't bother answering. She rushed in, unsheathing her own sword. Her legs felt like tree trunks and her muscles ached as she strained the arm and moved from stance to stance, pressing the scout.

"I'll teach you some manners," he snarled.

That lit a fire in her. She had always loved fighting, it was both a blessing and a curse. Fighting had given her everything she had, but it had also taken so much away. It could still take much. She was no grunt now, though, no foot soldier. She was the leader of the world's largest mercenary army—and that wasn't by accident.

The scout staggered as he took a step back, struggling to parry her strikes. Walking backwards in such wild terrain was a dangerous, foolish thing. Merey spotted the root of a large cypress bulging out of the dirt and pressured the man even further. His back step turned into a trip as the cypress root caught his ankle. That worked well enough as a distraction for Merey to shove him to the ground. Following up the push with a stab of her sword, she pierced the man in the chest.

He gurgled and reached out to grab her, but Merey was already out of there. She needed to inform Tellwoon. She ran through the woods, not bothering to cover her tracks as the scout was already dead. By the time other scouts found his body, it would be too late.

Everything had gone wrong. Instead of the army, she'd only spotted a scout and even worse, she had *killed* the poor bastard. Now, the Gashoine armies would notice the man was missing and they would sound the alarm horns, maybe skipping that perfect spot for the Leeth's ambush.

Fuck.

Merey could only bet on their carelessness now. She had to hope the armies were disorganised and full of unmotivated soldiers. But even the worst of armies would notice a dead scout.

Twenty-Nine

Grudge

Rednow

"What can you tell me about the Old One?" Rednow whispered, hoping the Essence would answer.

The nights were lonely. While everybody slept, he stayed awake, worrying more than preparing. But the sleepless nights had blessed him with time to think about the upcoming battle. He had used the time to oversee the terrain, to count how many soldiers he had, and to work out which smokesmiths were likely to defect. Despite all that, he still knew far too little about what the Old One could actually do. And the Essence was much less helpful than he would like.

"You know, I've just realised why you were so insistent in getting me to come here and meet Arkan and the Builders. You knew we needed their help, but you knew they were proud, stubborn people, so they would refuse to help. But you knew the Old One would strike, attempting to get rid of you early on, didn't you? And you knew that Arkan would have no choice but to help if there was an actual attack."

It was necessary, as you can see.

"Necessary?" Rednow scoffed. "We put them in danger. People died because of that. If you hadn't told me to come here, they might all still be alive."

And you would probably be dead, as would I. As would the entire Known World. So, I'll take no accusations from you. Those deaths were unfortunate, but I did what was required to get us the allies we needed.

"The allies *I* needed to save *you*. And I *am* dead. I'm a skeleton, remember?"

By saving me, you are saving yourself and everybody else you care about, Rednow. I've explained it enough.

Rednow was far from convinced. It all sounded like the Essence was trying hard to make herself appear like the world's saviour but wouldn't hesitate to let a few good people die if that helped her reach her goals. "If that is so," he snarled. "Tell me about the Old One. What are his abilities? What should I look out for?"

You really are as stubborn as a rock.

"I can be even more if I want."

Fine, I'll tell you. The reason I wanted to keep this secret was because you will start to expect him to do certain things if you know what his abilities are. He is also the Deceiver. He plays with people's expectations, manipulates them, and casts doubt into everyone's minds. I believe that if you know nothing about what he does, you will be better prepared to fight him.

Rednow had not seen it, but Pinesy said Orberesis had been floating in the air, and that just by moving his arms, he could crack the earth and sow destruction. But he didn't use the Essence's smoke, so how was that possible?

"Let me change my question. How does he do what he does without any herbs or connection to you?"

I grow things and he withers them. I handle the coursing of nature, but he is in charge of passing time. He mastered an ancient, arcane science called Temporal Exploration. It's something to do with that. His avatar is new, so he's still not fully ready, but he will be one day.

"What does Temporal Exploration do?"

The Essence hesitated. *It controls the passing of time. Slower, faster. What happened in Heleronde was a glimpse of that. The Old One used his avatar's energy to destroy the town by ageing everything he wished. But he could only do so on a small scale, then. I fear what he could do when his power is restored. I don't want to imagine what might happen if he wins.*

Rednow thought about it. A terrifying ability to have, but it should have drawbacks as well. It should have something he could use to fight back. He imagined everything he saw in the dead of night reduced to ash and dust, ageing a million years in the blink of an eye.

"How in the underworld do I fight against it?"

It's better for you to see for yourself.

Rednow didn't want to see it for himself. It might be too late. What was the Essence planning? Why wouldn't she just tell him as much as possible if she wanted him to win?

Rednow took off into the air, weightless. Rain soaked the earth, saturating the dirt and pouring down trees and the mountains, yet Rednow felt nothing. A void as pleasurable as it was strange.

You're still tied to the essence of nature, as is every physical thing, the Essence said.

"Does that include Orberesis? Or the Old One?"

No response from her, but it made sense. The Essence's sworn enemy was also her brother. They were connected in ways Rednow couldn't comprehend, like they were halves of the same circle of life and death.

Rednow took off flying at a high speed and away from camp. His heart was settled. He wasn't just fighting for the Essence, but for the legions of people who were placing their trust in him. He would be a bad leader of people if he simply led them into death or to an ambush, without trying his absolute best to defeat the Old One.

"I'm going to meet him, then. If you don't tell me anything, I'm sure he will."

You cannot.

Watch me. He didn't say it, but he thought it, knowing the Essence would feel it too.

He flew over the Thousand Hills first, its snow-covered peaks barely noticeable in the dark night. The cold had no effect on him, and neither did the wind. He flew across plains, hills, farmlands, and floodplains, like an arrow shooting towards an enemy.

Go back.

Rednow did not.

You cannot face him this way. You'll get us both killed.

"I went through the Inner Flight. I feel enlightened. Stronger than I ever have been."

The Essence scoffed. *You're but a fussy child. At least your sister listened.*

Rage took over Rednow's mind. "You dare mention my sister after you *goaded* her into her death? Is that what she was to you? Then I must be even less than that."

Enough, Rednow! The deity used Rebma's voice.

"Don't you dare!" He gritted his teeth, tired of the Essence. He *needed* to know more. He needed to know about the enemy, about the past conflicts, and the events that ended with the Crimson Wars. "Tell me now or I will be in Alarkan in less than four hours and we will die together, as you intended."

You are insane...

Rednow smiled. *She is caving.* "Don't tempt me, then. Tell me what I need to know."

I already told your sister everything you needed to know. She wrote the scriptures, didn't she? You already read those!

"I want to hear the *truth*, not the version that makes you seem like the world's saviour. I know neither of you has clean hands in any of this."

The Essence hesitated. *Fine.*

Rednow stopped somewhere above a farmstead in what he assumed was Vaerghulen, with the red cerro fields lost to the dark of the night. "I'm all ears."

We're older than anything in this world. We came here, somehow, to build it, though we don't remember how. For many ages, many more than you can comprehend, we were inseparable. The best of friends, always together. I did my part to shape the land you step on and grow everything that exists in this world. But if it hadn't been for him, the world would have consumed itself in an ever-growing nightmare. With him and his passing of time, everything I created lasted exactly as long as it needed to. Trees would die out and would fertilise the land for other forms of life to grow. The balance was perfect.

Rednow nodded. "I already knew that. But something changed."

Yes. When humans and Builders came and became sentient, they worshipped me because I was the giver, and they detested him because he took it all away. He did what he had to do, but he was still underappreciated by them. Slowly, yet steadily, his resentment grew, and I...

"You what? What did you do?"

I basked in the glory I received. It felt good to be adored. Worshipped. I didn't consider how this affected my brother, but I saw the way he looked at me. He became colder, minding his duty, but the joy forever gone. And then, he sought alternatives to his duty. He discovered Temporal Exploration, which he kept from me for a long time. By the time I found out about it, he was already a master of it, using it to travel through worlds in the blink of an eye.

"Did you ever find out *how* he does it?"

It has to do with his abilities, and with Time. He was already a powerful being, but Temporal Exploration allowed him to find the appreciation he sought elsewhere...

"The shadowlings..."

Yes, he calls them Lantern Horns. He was their god for ages. But their plane is a dying one, so he used Temporal Exploration to bring them over to our Known World. That's when we first started warring. First it was bloodsleuths, marcrunchers, and other beasts that destroyed all the other animals I had spent years creating and breeding. Even those, I tolerated, and eventually embraced, but then he brought the shadowlings here, and his ambitions were much darker.

"Did he seek to replace humans and Builders with them?"

He denies it, but I know it is so. He has always been ambitious. We fought over the shadowlings. He used them to fight, so I had no choice but to use humans and the Builders as well.

"But we are not toys for you to *use*. Or tools. We are beings, with thoughts and minds, and wills. Don't you understand that?" Rednow found himself enraged. How could their deity be so clueless? So careless?

If they took over and the Old One gained strength, I would be gone and the world would die without me and my creations. That hasn't changed, and we're very close to the end, given how much power I've already lost or given away.

If the world would die in the Essence's absence, then how come the pineheads thrived without her? And didn't that mean that the world would also eventually die without the Old One?

"You're hiding something from me," Rednow said. He could tell she wasn't being completely honest.

Yes, that is true. I wish it wasn't so, but my brother is needed as much as I am. When I won the last war in Ushar many years ago, I trapped him in an orb and had my followers bury it somewhere safe. It brought ages of peace between me and him, and the shadowlings disappeared, but I wouldn't say I won the war.

"Why not?"

Without my brother, everything I create becomes too much. Life is extended past its natural course. There is no withering, only uncontrolled expansion. I cannot control what I do. He was always the one to cap my powers, and I was always the one giving him something to take away. If it wasn't for his pride and jealousy, we would still be working together...

Rednow frowned. He remembered seeing ancient paintings and writings of the years of war, with the Builders and humans fighting creatures side by side, but he didn't have any knowledge of the consequences of the Old One's absence. "What happened when he was locked in the orb?"

The Essence hesitated.

I grew too ambitious, out of control. The trees grew too large, too fruitful. The crop yields were the best, rivers flooded the river-banks. Creatures grew and multiplied, and several ages of growth and expansion took over. Human population expanded too much and developed only to find there was not enough space for every-body else.

Rednow scoffed. "That's absurd. Humans and Builders live in cities. The rest of the world is empty. The problem isn't overpopulation or lack of resources, it's the greed of those in power who seize the land that should belong to everyone and claim it as theirs."

Claiming people's land from some and giving it to others is something you're familiar with.

That hurt. "Just like you, I did what I had to."

But Rednow did not like this conversation. It seemed like the Essence didn't want the Old One to die—as though she wanted Rednow to talk sense into him, not kill him. "So you need him, don't you? But you also need peace."

Yes. I suppose that's not a lie.

He gritted his teeth. "Why didn't you tell me this from the start?"

I don't wish my brother to die, but I know his grudge against me only grew stronger over time. Time that he commands.

"I assume that only worsened after you trapped him inside an orb for what must have been an eternity."

It was only a few hundred years. It was nothing... And I weakened myself by doing so.

Rednow's rage only intensified. "And you want *peace* and a new balance for the world but remain uncommitted to any change in yourself. Have you tried apologising?"

DO YOU THINK WE APOLOGISE? The Essence's response caught him by surprise. *We are not humans, builders, or beasts. We are deities. We don't apologise. We just exist.*

"So, am I to apologise on your behalf?"

No, Rednow, for I did nothing wrong. He was the one who diverged from his duty. He sought more than was intended for him.

"But you admitted you basked in the glory you received and shared none of the credit."

That is beside the point, Rednow. He brought the shadowlings. He murdered thousands of humans and builders!

"Yes, he did. But you rejected his pleas, didn't you?"

What do you mean?

Rednow was starting to grasp the truth. He could almost feel it, being ripped out of the Essence. "Did he not beg you to find room for the shadowlings to coexist in peace with humans and builders?"

How did you—that's not the point!

"Why did you reject his request? He came to you in humility, offering peace and asking for help, didn't he? And you turned him down. Why?"

The Essence did not respond and silence took over everything.

"I think you were jealous. You were jealous that he'd found an art that you couldn't learn. You were jealous that he had those who worshipped him. But you wanted *all* the glory. You wanted everyone to see you as the main deity while he was only supposed to be in the background. Am I wrong?"

You ungrateful little human. I could squeeze you and you wouldn't even know. You wouldn't even feel it. Your ignorance remains baffling. I am the main deity.

"You can kill me now, then. Do it. You were the one to spare my life and take my arm."

The Essence hesitated. *The Old One was supposed to be no more than a vassal to my role. One doesn't get to choose what they do. They just do it. Do you understand now?*

A lot of it became clearer in Rednow's mind. The world could already be a grim place at times. People were forced to do things they didn't want because of lords and monarchs, but to have deities conspiring for the world to be a certain way... And yet, Rednow's role was larger than anyone else's. The Old One was a clear threat to humanity, but that was because of the Essence's ego and mistakes. She was just as despicable as her brother.

"I should have known I am nothing but a tool you use at your will. Tools have no willpower. Tools are meant to be used with no harm done to their wielder. That is what you do to me. I was broken, so you fixed me. But I'm still supposed to be your tool, am I not?"

But you're my best tool, Rednow. The only one I can rely on. And you want humanity to survive as much as I do.

"I want humanity to survive, but I'm not sure *you* do. I think you want to avoid being the one to blame if we all perish. Because, as I see it, you are just as guilty as the Old One is. Two old gods too stubborn to make amends. Too proud to admit guilt. Too greedy to give up control. For all that superiority, you are almost more human than many people I know. Tools or no tools."

The Essence raged. *That isn't fair! I've given you power nobody else has. I've made you special. A demi-god made in my image.*

"I don't care for power. I never have. I care only about surviving and making sure everybody else does, too. You say I'm powerful, and I am, but I'm also half-dead, in a form that scares people more than it gives them confidence. I can't do this on my own. Sometimes I don't want to do it at all."

The realisation hit Rednow hard. He was a pawn, a tool. He couldn't change or fix anything. He was ready to be used, disposable, just as Rebma had been. People spent their entire lives searching for meaning, and now he knew there was no higher purposes, no meaning, only squabbling gods with inflated egos.

Shit. He didn't want to do this anymore.

The Essence remained silent, as though she had no argument and Rednow had a good point. But deep down, he knew he had to fight. He had to lead the smokesmiths and the Builders. There was just too much at stake if he didn't, as much as she'd trap him well. He would need more help than he currently had.

He needed people—not tools—he could trust by his side. He needed the Leeth.

THIRTY
SOMETHING DRASTIC

ORBERESIS - SOLVI

It was as though the entire country of Ainis was made of wind and rain. The Ainisian peninsula bulged out of the Known World just above the Thousand Hills and, ten years after the Crimson Wars had ended, it was still war-torn, with a false peace agreed upon by different factions that had the backing of their neighbours.

Orberesis studied the chieftains sitting opposite to him. Not too different from the Gashoine nobility, the Ainisian considered shark teeth and other bones piercing their skin a sign of much honour or respect achieved at sea. For a country with such a strong naval tradition, even the nobles were expected to know how to sail a ship, and every single one of these sure looked the part. General Nisai was a stout man of brown skin and wavy hair with a large moustache. Tattoos covered his skin, making him impossible not to look at.

He controls half of the territory, the Old One said.

Orberesis nodded as the chieftains spoke in turns, honouring their adversaries by waiting for their turn to speak. Next to Nisai was a tall woman with broad shoulders and a necklace of seashells enhancing her cleavage. Captain Marnis had high cheekbones and fat lips, though she wore a coat that sometimes revealed the shape of the throwing knives she kept. Three other military chieftains shared the table with these.

"... After Orberesis' Miracle, we no longer had to fight the wretched monsters, and look what we achieved: peace."

"You're quite happy with this so-called peace because you control half the nation, General. There will only be true peace if we separate Ainis into several independent units. The kingdom is already split, anyway. Why not make it official?" a bird-like man called Colonel Osha asked.

"I'm inclined to agree," Marnis said. "The military is already divided. I wouldn't dare tell soldiers outside my forces what to do. They wouldn't obey me."

"Why would they not obey?" Orberesis asked.

They looked at him as though they weren't sure how or why he had been allowed to sit at their table, like he was a nuisance, as grateful as they'd been for his help ten years back.

"It's a question of loyalty," Marnis said.

Orberesis shook his head. "It should be a question of *power*. Loyalty is great, but if you can't earn it, then you can force it. General Nisai, don't you control half the kingdom?"

The burly man nodded.

"Can I assume that means you hold half the military units?"

"On paper, yes. Why do you ask?"

"Why can't you just take over the rest of the kingdom, then?"

Marnis knocked her fist on the table. "Because we have a hard-earned *peace* treaty!"

Orberesis shrugged. "What does that matter if the peace is so frail that you spend your entire time discussing it and can't accomplish anything beyond it? Allow one person to hold control and let them, whoever it is, just run the kingdom as they see fit. You are holding the kingdom hostage with this split control, and the people are suffering because of it. Don't you see it?"

Osha raised his voice. "No, we don't. My people would die before they let General Nisai take control of Ainis. They remember well the horrors his troops put their loved ones through during the Crimson Wars."

"As do mine." Both Marnis and the other chieftains nodded.

"But that's in the past, is it not?"

"The past must never be forgotten," Marnis snarled. "Don't mistake peace for servitude. General Nisai might have control of half the country, but that doesn't mean he'd be able to seize the rest, or that *all* his people would fight on his side. Ainis is a deeply divided kingdom, and it must remain that way officially. Then each of us is free to do what they wish."

"You all seek *independence*, then?" Orberesis asked. He wasn't sure why he cared about this—all he wanted was military aid—but he found himself acting as the moderator in this pointless debate.

"Yes!" everyone said except Nisai, who simply shook his head.

"Not General Nisai?"

"Independence would weaken Ainis against neighbouring nations." The General had a booming voice. "The way things stand at least have us in a united front against potential enemies, but if we split the kingdom into small counties or kingdoms, then we'll be at their mercy, slaves to their ambitions, prone to being corrupted by outside forces."

Marnis scowled. "Interesting that General Nisai should mention foreign invasions and meddling when he's the only one sitting at this table receiving gold from Mosendel. Admit it, General, you're in the pocket of that old hag Mosen."

"How dare you? I'm in no one's pocket!" the General said, slamming his fist on the table. "On the other hand, Captain Marnis, you are known to be affiliated with the pirate crews navigating our waters, pillaging our ships."

This conversation had taken a turn for the worse, and Orberesis saw the rage in their faces. Each of them believed they were right and most likely none of them were. That was how it tended to be. The hope of a strong peace was thin, and he didn't think any of those military leaders would be of great help. They wouldn't be able to coordinate a joint charge towards the enemy even if he told them what to do. But if he chose one of the factions, the others would get stronger and likely take advantage of it, even if he threatened to destroy them.

"I care little about honour and what others do. I'm no prideful warrior," Orberesis said, holding their attention. "But the men and women of this kingdom require a strong leader. If people saw improvement in their lives under other leaders, their current loyalty to you could very well change. The lamb forgets its loyalty to the shepherd when presented with greener pastures. So, I'm not going to request aid from you, but you must select a leader or let the blades and the shields decide one for you."

He stood and left the room, tired from the tension.

You, showing mercy and benevolence? The Old One seemed surprised.

He nodded as he walked down the hallway, rejecting the escort of the knights that had been assigned to keep him safe. "They are mostly useless. Also, I'm going to be a father. I can't be cold-blooded and merciless forever."

What kind of father would he be? He thought of the men he had in his life, but there had only been one. His own father, Ortua, and nobody else.

You know well how children are treated in this world, Doi, the Old One said.

He was right. "But I can change that. I can change the world to make it a better one for my child."

The Old One scoffed. *Changing always requires pain and growth, but also destruction. Is that what you want?*

"I can do what I think is right."

I'll take you, then. Let me show you the magnitude of what needs to change.

"Where are you taking me?"

You'll see. You'll see.

Doi felt the pull of the lightness, the tug of a smooth carelessness followed by a violent throw, as the Old One opened a curtain in the air and Orberesis slipped inside it, and into the void. Motion and momentum threw him in all directions. He always saw flashes of places, and people, but was never able to recognise any of it. He had improved much in handling Temporal Exploration, as well as skipping between places while keeping time flat. It was not an easy thing to do, but at least his body could now handle it well enough.

Then the motion stopped and Orberesis had to curb a need to retch. He had ended up on a rooftop, in a city that looked an awful lot like Ushar, though the architecture was different. Below him, on the ground, a group of children fought. They squealed in high-pitched voices as they hurt each other in their attempt to take hold of something. It was like a glimpse into his own past unfolding before his eyes.

"What are they fighting over?" he asked.

They were organised in gangs, he could see. In groups or three of four, each fought for whatever it was they sought. Shivers ran down his spine as he realised they were fighting for a pair of dirty blankets. He had a strong urge to drop in and stop the fight, cut the blanket in parts for everyone, but then he'd be interfering. These children were surviving and doing their best with what life threw at them. He and Tavanar had once been a group like this as well, though Ushar had always been warm enough that no one needed blankets.

"I should stop it."

The Old One laughed. *Already? No, Doi. There is far more I want to show you. Let's go.*

He was back in the void, being thrown like a doll at the mercy of the Old One's ability to take him to the right place. After a while, he landed in an awfully familiar location. It was a town much like the Gloomwoods, where he had grown up. Houses were made of wood and thatched roofs. He stood at the edge of the forest, watching as a grey-haired man oversaw a group of children working hard to plough the fields with hoes and other utensils, digging out the weeds and any undesirable plants, often having to dig out rocks from the harsh soil.

"They're forced to stay here, aren't they?"

Oh, yes, was all the Old One said, which made Orberesis wonder if he even cared about the children or was just trying to prove how much work it would be to *change* everything for the better. If Orberesis was the one in charge of everything, then perhaps that change wouldn't be so hard to achieve. But he needed his baby to grow up in a fair and peaceful world, even if that peace came at a steep cost.

I care more than you'll ever give me credit for.

"You care about your Lantern Horns, yes. But us humans have always been a thorn on your side, haven't we?"

He scoffed. *You could say that.*

"So why should I help you?" Orberesis asked. There was no point hiding his thoughts since the Old One could read them. "Why don't I just use your powers for my purposes instead?"

Because our interests align. Look at the children. They are suffering, just as you did. Kingdoms talk of peace, but you've travelled the Known World and seen how they bicker with each other and spend their time on meaningless quarrels instead of working to solve the real issues. Change isn't possible. Not unless you are willing to do something drastic. If you are not willing to go too far, you will never go far enough.

Orberesis shook his head. "I still don't see how our interests align."

We agree that the world needs to change, and drastically so. We both have the power to be that change. The world needs to be broken and rebuilt. We can do it together. I'm not in control of you. You still have agency. You can make decisions. It will be painful, but you can shape the world how you'd want it to be.

"As long as the Lantern Horns can coexist with the humans, I imagine."

The Old One hesitated. *I'm not sure that's possible, Doi. I tried that many years ago, but my sister rejected the idea as did the human leaders of the time. Now that we're on the cusp of getting what we've always deserved, why should we listen to their requests?*

Orberesis took that in. The Old One was implying that having the Lantern Horns surge and conquer the Known World was the only option, an inevitability, but Orberesis couldn't help but think about his unborn child. Why would he bring up the child in the world with only Lantern Horns, even if he ruled above them?

"I don't want to be the king of the ashes," he mumbled.

You won't be. You'll be a god of men and monsters.

But what of Solvi and the child? What about Doemus and the rest who had always been faithful even in their misguided ignorance? They were all he had.

"Why would I want to be a god if the faithful end up enslaved? I can't agree to that."

Doi... The Old One's voice was raspy, a sign of annoyance. *Don't let the mundane distract you. The child might not even be yours. The woman is a smokesmith. They are desperate for an upper hand. They'll do anything to overpower us.*

That gave him pause. Solvi was a smokesmith, but she had been following him as a staunch supporter since the Miracle. Her faith had never wavered. Yes, she was a smokesmith, and yes, she had been imprisoned by the savages for a long time, but she was still pregnant, and with his child at that! It had to be his. She wouldn't lie to him, would she?

·········

Solvi's world plunged into chaos. She held her belly as she hurried her steps.

I know I shouldn't run like this. I know you don't like it. But I have to.

The Palace of Brilliance was in peril. In the distance were shouts and metal weapons clashing. It was an uprising. The men and women from the gutters had finally had enough, but to strike upon their masters... that was blind madness.

Solvi continued to hurry. She couldn't fight. Not when she was that heavily pregnant and her spine arched. She couldn't even breathe the smoke to protect herself if it came to that. It would harm the baby, the shamans had said, who had never even heard of a pregnant smokesmith. She got as far from the Ceremonial Room as possible, but the way the Palace of Brilliance had been designed made that quite hard, as it was a series of buildings connected only by the main courtyard, which made it hard for anyone to sneak out of there.

With a glance behind her, she spotted a few dozens of them. Dirty and dishevelled, with rotten teeth and eyes of darkness, they wielded weapons meant for labour, not for war. She kept jogging away from the scene, with only her baby in mind. Just a few more weeks and the child would come out, she could feel it. But that meant she still had to carry the baby in her womb until then. And for the gods, that was going to be hard enough.

Where is he? Where is your father? she asked the baby, but mostly herself.

He hardly seemed to be around when she needed him, even after promising her the world and beyond. He had always been ambitious—a conqueror—he had said, but he would be away for weeks at a time and the last time she'd seen him he hadn't even said where he was going.

He's a god, I know that. But Solvi also wished he was a little more normal.

The fighting in the palace took a darker turn behind her, and she could smell the smoke, which normally only meant death was knocking on the door. She gritted her teeth. Not to her. She had survived her masters, and the Crimson Wars, and now she would survive this uprising. Her firm grip tightened on the hidden dagger under her dresses. If something were to happen, she still had that.

"That one's got a massive belly. Look at her," a raspy voice said. Solvi turned to see three men staring at her. One of them had a small scythe and the others were armed with hatchets used for lumbering. She couldn't fight them or outrun them.

"She does. But she's still a fine one," the second man said. He was taller than the others and had a crooked smile that showed more gum than teeth. "Are you going somewhere, sweetie?"

THIRTY-ONE
A MOTHER'S CALL

GIMLORE - KERYON

Gimlore gritted her teeth and smashed a guard's helmet with her hammer. He would not be quick to get up from that, but the hammer had a short reach, which forced her to fight arm in arm with her new rebellious friends. While Keryon battled the other smokesmiths, clouds of smoke formed above her, but she paid no mind to it, lest she lose her life. These soldiers had been trained to kill and protect the palace, and they had already failed at the second, so they were keen to get the first one right.

Not on her watch.

Next to her, the Tooth used his pitchfork like a spear to push the soldiers against the walls, and Gimlore came around with her hammer to finish the job and realised just how strong the quarry had made her. All that hammering had paid off, even then, in the heat of battle.

The Tooth smiled at her. "We make a good team."

Gimlore smiled as she fought another guard, the rush of battle carrying her. She was older now and, by the time this was done, her back pain would come back and the same void would expand within her chest. Her children were not around.

I am not the Tooth. I have to be smart about this.

Shaking off the initial jitters and the excitement that came from crushing the enemy, Gimlore realised how disorganised her side of the battle was. The men and women of Ushar fought with heart, but with no preparation and no sense of strategy, while the guards were coordinated and explored space and timing more to conserve energy despite the heavy plates they carried.

"The guards are not our target. Let's storm the palace and find that rodent who calls himself king!" Gimlore's words broke the mob from their fighting.

They organized and marched forward, engaging only with the soldiers who pursued. Clouds of smoke loomed above them and Gimlore glanced at Keryon, who was propelling himself into the air in a windmill of fire and smoke, blasting his opponents.

Take care.

She led the crowd with the Tooth by her side. Their momentum would be nearly impossible to break with thousands of armed city folks behind them chanting angrily. They caught guards whose eyes widened in horror as they saw the crowd, but spared the aides and other workers, even if they were loyal.

Going through the palatial rooms, Gimlore realised the extent of the wealth these people lived in. Linen and silk were all too common, and everything seemed to be inlaid with golden threads and gems of incalculable value.

"Look at us now, the children of the gutter, rising up!" the Tooth said. "Pillage whatever you want, brothers and sisters. It was afforded by our own blood and sweat."

Gimlore couldn't disagree, but without a dead king and deposed lords, the uprising would mean nothing. The guards would organise and the rest of the population would simply see them as thieves and criminals rather than understand their cause.

"We must focus on the King!" she bellowed. "We must find him."

They had already run through the entire main building of the palace, but still, not a soul in sight. It was normal that there were no lords or a royal court, since Orberesis' presence around the King had meant war on the wealthy merchants and lords from their profitable businesses, but the kingdom was still being ruled. They had to find the King, so they took the fighting to the other buildings. Doemus and his lackeys must be holed up somewhere, in a hidden room.

"The profits can come later," Gimlore insisted as some of the folks got distracted by the riches all around them and others followed up, fearing they would not have enough to fill their pockets when the time came. "I like my gold as much as anyone, but it isn't gold you're seeking today, is it? It's fucking change!"

"Change!" a group of stout men with dishevelled beards repeated after her. She realised the prisoners were all following her, including the Tooth, as though they were their leaders. It gave her strength to know they trusted her and believed in her.

I can't fail them. I need to find that fucking bastard.

She turned around and pointed at the Tooth and another of the former prisoners whose name she had forgotten. "You two, come with me. The rest of you, split into groups and check every fucking building in this palace. Whoever finds the King first gets my share of the gold!"

That got her smiles from the crowd. Hopefully, it would be enough motivation to get them focused on what they were really there for. She took an exit to the courtyard on the right, metal clinking in the background and grunts and shouts already a part of the environment. Chants of "Gutter kids!" and "Hand us the gold!" stood out in the rest of the madness, which gave her pause.

It was good to try and throw down a kingdom's ruler, but installing a suitable replacement to accommodate people's needs was a different matter entirely. Who would they put in charge? The Tooth? She almost laughed at the thought of the man elected king or presiding over a council of appointed representatives. Drentu and the other mad men weren't much better.

Shaking those needless thoughts out of her mind, she powered through the courtyard, her eyes skimming over everything that seemed suspicious. She looked for anything out of the ordinary, potential trap doors or rocks that looked out of place.

Then she saw something. Solvi, of all people, stood facing three of the city folks, one hand on her belly and another holding a dagger longer than her forearm. She had a vicious snarl on her face, but all Gimlore saw was fear. That face had never failed to enrage Gimlore. It was because of Solvi and her obsession with Orberesis that Gimlore had been lashed.

But now she looked like a cornered animal, striking viciously, but hardly able to protect herself. Fear covered every inch of her body, and she no longer looked the dangerous beast she once had looked to be. The men that faced her, on the other hand, looked as though they were ready for something devious.

Gimlore approached and realised she had no idea what she'd do. She needed the loyalty of these men. She needed their support and their strength. It had taken her months to feel good enough about where she stood in the world, but the roundness of Solvi's belly was one Gimlore knew far too well to ignore. Solvi looked at her and recognition arose. The woman's eyes begged Gimlore for help.

The call only a mother would understand.

Keryon rose in the air; each breath he took hurt more than the last. He always let himself end up in these predicaments. First, it was fighting on behalf of peasants, criminals, and refugees. Now, it was spearheading a rebellion against a kingdom he had never visited prior to his imprisonment. At least he could get some form of revenge against the vile king who had him and Gimlore whipped, but vengeful thoughts had never driven him.

Another whiff of the smoke gave him the familiar buzz of the herbs' properties flowing in his veins. Power surged through him, but so it did in his enemies. For the gods, he *hated* fighting other smokesmiths. They had gone through the same pains and perils in life as he had; they were all supposed to be brothers and sisters, not enemies.

"You should have joined Rednow," Keryon said in between breaths. His shoulder ached; a burning barely healed by the smoke. "I wouldn't have to do this, then."

"Do what?" the man asked.

Keryon hadn't asked for their names. Maybe he should have.

He cringed, hurting for them. They had seen action, most likely patrolling the streets and fighting thieves and murderers. Still, they weren't used to someone fighting back. The chaos around him had subsided. There were hardly any soldiers or rebels in there, so if these smokesmiths weren't willing to change their minds, there really was no salvation for them.

He spun, carried higher than usual by the smoke.

One breath. One jump. One death.

He ignited the smoke and a flash of light spread through the room. The heat of the flames nearly consumed him, and he felt it in the side of his face he had ruined to save Gimlore and the rest. That burn hurt more than the whiplashes. More than the first time they had forced smoke into his lungs in the smoke chamber.

His fire consumed the smokesmith. The man's skin melted, and his charred body dropped to the stone floor.

"No!" the smokesmith woman said. She had auburn hair with golden highlights and wielded a light spear. Pretty. What a shame. "What have you done?"

With a snarl, she lunged at him with the spear. Enhanced by the smoke, she stabbed at him faster than most. Impressive.

"You're fast," Keryon said. "Such a waste. Was that your brother? Maybe your husband?"

That only made the woman angrier. She must have thought he was pitying her, or making fun of her loss, but he really meant it. The man's death had been a waste, and hers would be as well.

Keryon noticed her chest expanding with a strong intake of smoke.

No. It can't be.

Her eyes changed and turned red, her face pale. She charged at Keryon. With that much smoke in her lungs, she was probably more dead than alive, but her hands and feet moved faster than ever. Her arms extended to improve her reach, and one of them extended towards Keryon. She grabbed him by the throat with an inhuman power, crushing his windpipe. Air was short in his lungs, and he couldn't continue, pain flooding him.

Her spear hand rose, and the sharp edge of the weapon would have gone through his chest if he hadn't jerked away at the last moment. It still caught the side of his shoulder.

Keryon wanted to gasp for air, and he fought with his hands to weaken her grip. That was no longer a smokesmith. That was a *demon* he was fighting.

I'm sorry I have to do this...

He willed the threads of smoke to twirl around her. When they did, he ignited the smoke, and it blasted the woman's arms, immediately weakening her grip.

Keryon gasped and nearly fell to his bottom as he tried to recover from it. He breathed in and out a few times as the cloud of smoke dissipated, and he found the woman's body motionless on the palatial floor.

He allowed himself more rest. There was pain in both his shoulders, and the scars on his face burned red hot. All of this for Gimlore, for Rednow, and for a better world, wasn't it? And yet it only seemed like the world was getting worse.

He got up from the floor, his pain flaring as he caressed his bruised neck, and walked outside, looking for anyone he knew. Sweat covered every inch of his skin, and he could swear his face was filled with soot as well. There was a stream of blood pouring from his left shoulder, but he pressed on.

Where is everyone?

The rebels seemed to have won. There was no sign of any soldiers around, and many of the people were just looting the palace. Toothless men and women grinned as they took hold of gold and silver platters, cutlery, candle holders, and other junk the King had kept.

What was all this for?

They should have joined Rednow a long time ago and prepared for the next battle, not risked finding themselves in the quarry again. Not forced to kill brothers and sisters.

He kept walking, passing the city-dwellers who looked at him as though he had turned into a monster, and Keryon sure felt like one. Just ahead, he found the Tooth, getting drunk with a cup of what looked like expensive royal wine. He clinked his cup against Drentu, who shared the drink with him. "To the gutter kids!" they cheered.

"Where is Gimlore?" he asked.

The Tooth looked to the side and noticed him.

"Eh! Keryon! Here is the man of men!" he announced to the rest of his drunken companions. "We bloody won, didn't we?"

Keryon saw no victory yet. None of the bodies scattered on the palace floors belonged to any lord, bureaucrat, or noble. And certainly none of them were the King. Were these people supposed to overthrow the kingdom? It seemed like they were only on it for a day of fun and exultation.

"Where is she?" Keryon insisted.

This was madness. He should have never agreed to this. He should have left on the first ship to Vaerghulen.

"I didn't see her, but..." the Tooth blurted something out, but Keryon was already gone. He was thankful to the man. He'd helped him out, but it was time for some change. These weren't the leaders the people deserved. And Keryon was no leader at all either. He took off outside, glancing in all directions. All of this had been because of her, because she was...

He saw her. Three men next to her. And Solvi.

No...

⸻

Gimlore swallowed and sighed. "Get out of here before I change my mind."

The three men stared at her and then started laughing. One of them postured up and took a step towards her. "I don't remember agreeing to take orders from you."

The shorter one scoffed. "Maybe we look as though we like women to tell us what to do."

"Are you with the Tooth?" Gimlore asked, hoping the man's name would impose some respect and get them to change their minds.

"We might have heard the name. It's the fellow who won't shut his fucking mouth, isn't he?"

That would be the one...

They surrounded her, forcing her to take a step back towards Solvi. Only the gods knew what these lunatics had in mind.

"Wh-why are you helping me?" Solvi whispered from behind her. "You hate me and I hate you."

Gimlore thought about it. Maybe if she hadn't lost Thata, she wouldn't have chosen to defend Solvi. And maybe she'd come to regret protecting the woman, but she just couldn't let a mother-to-be fall in the dirty hands of these savages.

"You're right about that," she said. "But your child doesn't have to pay for your faults and mistakes. And I don't wish the pain of losing a child on my worst enemy."

Solvi remained silent as Gimlore stared at the men.

"What a heart-warming story. Now get the fuck out of the way."

Gimlore whipped her hammer and threw it at the man in the middle, catching him right in the face. The other two hesitated, then lunged at her. She ducked and searched her boots for the hidden knives. With a quick, swift motion, she threw the blades, hitting the two other men in their respective throats. The second one managed to pull the knife out, but blood spurted out. The third one fell to the ground with the impact of the landing knife and slashed his throat open trying to pull it out.

"Gimlore!" Keryon was running in the distance. He looked half-dead, bloodied, dishevelled, and covered in soot and sweat. His breathing was heavy—he had won his battle. "Are you alright?"

Gimlore nodded as she wiped some sweat from her forehead. Keryon's eyes flicked to Solvi, and he gave her a nod, before looking back at Gimlore. "You protected her..."

A dry smile formed on Gimlore's face as Keryon quickly turned into the mushy bastard he was, almost making her blush. She couldn't have that, so she turned to face Solvi. The woman was still staring at Keryon.

"What happens now?" she asked.

"Now, you owe me," Gimlore said.

Keryon smiled. "And you already owed me."

"I... can't betray him..." Solvi said, though her face showed nothing but doubt. Maybe Keryon had been right. Maybe she could still be swayed.

"Then don't betray the bastard. Just tell me where the King is holed up and I'll let you go."

Solvi dropped her gaze to the floor. She must have known that was a form of betrayal, but perhaps that was one she was willing to do.

If I can't open the door, I'll try the window first...

"There is a hidden room in his quarters. Underneath a bookshelf, there is a switch that will open a hidden wall. He's in there with the advisors. Can I go now?"

Gimlore nodded, but Keryon took a step forward. "Where are you going in that state? Stay. You're not an outsider. You can be one of us."

Gimlore still wasn't sure about that, and Solvi's grimace told Gimlore the woman wasn't either. Solvi shrugged, sheathed her blade, and waved her hand as she left.

"I'm grateful," she said. "I truly am. Thank you."

Thirty-Two

Those Left Behind

Gimlore - Nork

G imlore stepped on the gimmicky stone brick and one of the many bookshelves in King Doemus' palatial quarters opened. With Keryon, the Tooth, Drentu, and a few other drunkards and former prisoners by her side, she stood, watching the lords and advisors of the monarch cower in fear, their hiding spot exposed.

Hiding the room behind a bookshelf was a clever trick. The inside was still full of padded chairs and a table at its centre with books piled up on top of it. Whatever space was left available on the tabletop was covered by parchments and papers.

"Please..." a bald man with a grey moustache said with a trembling voice. "We're just advisors."

Gimlore stepped forward, looking for *him*. The bastard who had taken pleasure in seeing her get whipped like a dog, which he probably thought she was. All the advisors dressed the same and looked the same, with similar haircuts and tailored robes threaded in gold. Then, she found him, hiding behind three of his cronies.

"There he is," she said, dragging the first word as if to savour the moment. "A *big* mistake not to trap any guards in here with you. Well, not that the guards would have done much, but it would have been a smart move."

The King stayed back, silent. Cowards often did. Full of pomp and confidence when they were in control but no strength to utter a single word as everything collapsed under their feet.

Gimlore walked slowly towards him.

"Speaking of my friends, do you recognise any of them?" She pointed at the Tooth first. "Him? No?"

She pointed at all the other prisoners who had stayed with her in the quarry. "None of them? That's a shame. They're all people you and your cronies wrongly convicted."

Another step forward. The other advisors cowered away from Doemus and Gimlore narrowed her gaze on him, getting close to him. The man's eyes were hazy, and unfocused.

She whispered. "But I bet you remember me."

Doemus swallowed and Gimlore continued to whisper, her face close to his. "Last time we met, you asked me: 'Is freedom really better than stability?'. You asked if feeling alive is more important than actually living. Now you will understand why freedom is everything."

"What will you do with me? God Himself may come at any moment. He will not tolerate this."

Gimlore scowled. "I wish he'd come. I'd rather have a nice *conversation* with him, but you'll do for now. Tooth?"

The Tooth handed her a pair of shackles, which she quickly placed on the King's wrists. And then another, which she fastened to his feet. "There you go. Prettier already. Could almost pass for one of us!"

The prisoners laughed.

"Now, His fucking Majesty has duties." She handed him a parchment, ink, and pen. "You will sign this."

He hesitated, as though he wanted to know what he was about to sign.

"Oh, this? This is just a ruling that makes three things very clear. I will read it out loud as I have nothing to hide from you."

The prisoners laughed again as she cleared her throat.

"Announcement one: I, King Doemus, hereby announce that no citizen of the Two Nations will ever again be recruited to fight for their country or their faith. All warfare operations with soldiers involved are to cease immediately. How does that sound?"

Doemus swallowed but said nothing, so she kept going. "Announcement two: God Himself, Orberesis, advisor to the crown, hereby decrees that all citizens of the Two Nations are equals before him and each other. No one man can accumulate wealth more than twice the wealth of his neighbour. This is a particularly good one. But there's more!"

Gimlore was now enjoying herself. "In the absence of General Tavanar, our Highest Lord Orberesis orders the man who goes by the Tooth to be made the primary general, councillor, and bodyguard to King Doemus."

The Tooth smiled his toothless grin and waved the keys to the shackles, which clinked in a keyring as his friends patted him on the back.

"And, finally, announcement three: the Uzunar quarry is to be shut down permanently, effective immediately. All prisoners there are pardoned and must be freed this instant."

All the former prisoners cheered on that one, fists pumping the air. When they quieted down, Doemus still hadn't made any move to sign the document, so Gimlore leaned forward and placed the pen in his hand. She whispered in his ear. "Believe me when I say... this is the least painful outcome."

That did it. The King picked up the pen in his trembling hand and signed the parchment.

Gimlore grabbed it and ushered all the advisors out of the hidden room. "Pleasure doing business with you."

"You won't get away with this. He'll come back and help me reverse this nonsense."

"Maybe. But that's a risk I'm willing to take. Let's go."

"Wait, where are you going? What about me?"

Gimlore smiled. "We're leaving. But you'll stay right here, pondering on how important freedom really is. Don't worry, you'll have plenty of time to reflect. Close that door, Tooth."

The Tooth abided by her words and closed the door with a bang, Doemus still inside.

Gimlore took a deep breath. There was a lot to take in, and she had struggled to contain herself from bashing Doemus' skull in with the sword pommel or killing him right there and then. Leaving him alone in the secret room should be just as bad.

"This won't work forever, you know," Keryon said.

Gimlore shrugged. "As long as there is confusion and doubt, a signed official document should be enough to pull back all the Two Nations' troops. Chances are, they won't be around to fight Rednow's forces. If they do, they won't arrive in time. We're buying time and I'm alright with that. For now, the Tooth will have one of his fellows keep an eye on the bastard."

"They're already betting on when His Majesty is going to start screaming in there," the Tooth said, happily. "Thanks for everything, the two of you."

"Thank *you*," Gimlore said. "Not coming with us?"

"I'll go where they go." The Tooth pointed at the rest of the prisoners, waiting for their say. "As long as someone keeps the keys to this bastard's coffin."

The prisoners exchanged glances and shrugged. "Ever since we started following you, only good things have happened. I reckon we're all keen to keep the luck streak going, isn't that right folks?"

"Aye!" some of them said.

Gimlore smiled, proud of how far they'd come. "Very well. Now when the fuck is the next ship to Vaerghulen?"

⋯⋯

Nork took a deep breath as he walked another step up those mountains. For weeks, he and the rest of the survivors had been on the road, crossing crop fields, forests, and hills until they had reached the southernmost foothills of the Thousand Hills. Since then, it had only been one step at a time. One bloody rock at a time. His breathing was scarce in that thin mountain air.

He glanced behind and saw only exhaustion and utter defeat in the eyes of the survivors. They had come a long way since setting foot in the mainland. The joy that had come with surviving the fiends of the underworld had vanished as they found themselves tired and walking every day from dawn until dusk, eating only just enough to keep going for a little longer.

Nork swallowed as he considered those who hadn't made it. Those he had lost and left behind. Eshof and many others, who had drowned when their rafts turned in the waves.

"What is it, brother?" Nosema asked, patting him on the back.

Nork shook his head. "Nothing. We're getting to the end of the journey, but there is no peace awaiting us. Are you sure another battlefield is where we belong?"

His brother sighed as they kept marching, hiking up yet another large boulder. "I would be lying if I said that I was sure. But the smokesmiths helped us in Alarkan. Keryon saved our lives once and Gimlore too many times to count. It's time we pay it back."

Nork nodded. "I just wanted a knife, a cutting board, and a few vegetables to prepare. I suppose that's too much to ask. We should open our own tavern when this is all over."

Nosema smiled and nodded. "We should."

"Hey! Look!" Chona said.

She and Ferkin had stopped about thirty paces ahead and started pointing to somewhere in the distance. Nork still couldn't see anything other than rocks, hills, and trees, so he climbed another boulder to stand next to them. He gazed in the general direction they were pointing and finally saw it. A large camp was just ahead, down the hill. It was big enough to host thousands of soldiers.

"That's Rednow's camp, isn't it?" Ferkin asked.

Nork had no idea, but he wanted it to be. Badly. "Has to be."

With the news of the camp being found already spreading, Nork and Nosema went ahead. Those soldiers didn't wear any particular uniform, which had to mean they were smokesmiths. Not far beyond was another camp. It was smaller but more organized. There were pineheads around everywhere. More than Nork had ever seen in his life.

"Nork, what the fuck am I looking at?"

Nork followed his brother's eyes into the sky and had to rub them three times to make sure it wasn't a joke or an illusion. Two pineheads were flying, as though they could float and move like wingless birds. "Fuck me."

He hurried through the camp and asked for where he could find Rednow. One of the pineheads told them to wait there and Rednow would show up. Nork wondered how the old man was doing. He only had one arm now, and he had nearly died in the last battle of Heleronde, before the ruins. But he must be doing well for himself, with so many smokesmiths listening to his call. And the pineheads... why were they all there?

Suddenly, a large cloud of smoke lifted from the top of a hill. It flew fast, almost like a swarm of a billion bees chasing a single target. And that target was *him*.

Nork tensed until one of the smokesmiths, a tall woman, placed her hand on his shoulder and shook her head as though to tell him not to worry. The cloud of smoke came closer and, soon enough, it landed on the ground. But it was no mere cloud.

It was... something else. Something odd. From the smoke came a skeleton, though it moved like any person.

What sorcery is this...

"It's good to see you, Nork, Nosema," the skeleton said as the smoke dissipated around him.

Nork couldn't believe his own eyes, but he recognised the voice. How could he not? That raspy tone, that accent. "Rednow?"

"It's me, I promise."

"What happened to you?" was all Nork could ask. "How can you..."

"That is a long story, and one I'm not sure I'm ready to tell." The voice was the same, but it was just a skeleton that did not resemble Rednow at all. "Now, you and your friends must be exhausted and starving. Let's settle them down and perhaps I can talk to both of you?"

Nork swallowed. He and Nosema alone with the smoke skeleton. "Sure, why not?"

The world was already strange enough when fish-headed creatures came out of the depths of the underworld. How could that be any stranger?

Next to Rednow came a pinehead dressed in a white robe, tightly clasping a spear. A few more humans came along as well. They all settled in a square rug of intricate detail and served hot tea with ginger and lemon.

"How's Heleronde?" Rednow asked as soon as they were all sitting.

"It is no more," Nosema said. "We managed to get out, but it belongs to the fiends now."

"I'm sure you did everything you could. The fact you made it all the way here is impressive."

"We had help from a few smokesmiths. They're out there, somewhere. I'm sure you'll meet them."

"Smokesmiths always find each other, don't they?" Rednow pondered.

Nork frowned. It was weird to be talking to Rednow this way, alright. But to speak to someone with no eyes and who spoke back with no tongue was completely off-putting, so Nork couldn't hold his gaze on him for long. "Well, you would know. You are one."

"That's true enough," Rednow admitted.

"How many units do you have?" Nork asked. "I'm not sure we can be much help. Our people are tired and, as you know, they're no soldiers."

"We have the Builders, who will be an airborne force, and the smokesmiths, who will be fighting on the ground. And I'm expecting aid from the Leeth. We've got about five hundred smokesmiths, but not even a third of them are battle tested. There are also some loyalty concerns that we're assessing."

"Who are the Builders?" Nosema must have been reading Nork's mind.

"You know them as pineheads," Rednow said.

"Ah, I see. And since when can the fellows fly?"

"It's also complicated. I'm sure Pinesy can explain sooner or later."

Nork's eyes widened. "Pinesy is here? *Our* Pinesy?"

Rednow nodded. "He is."

Nork glanced at Rednow. "He's here and in the flesh? No offence to the fleshless... I just want to make sure."

Rednow laughed before he nodded. "Yes, he is. And no offence taken. Going back to our battle tactics: there might be something you and your people can help with."

"What is it?"

"I was impressed by your knowledge of guerrilla warfare. It seems like all those years you two spent with Gimlore in the Crimson Wars weren't for nothing. That's what I'm missing. If you look around, the terrain doesn't really favour us."

Nork stood up from the rug and looked around. The skeleton-man was right. There were only rocks and trees, but if that was to be the battlefield, they had better start trimming it to their advantage. "You want to leave that with me and Nosema?"

Rednow nodded. "If you don't mind."

Nork exchanged looks with Nosema and his brother gave him a curt nod. This was what they were good at. For now, they needed some water and food in their bellies. Perhaps a few hours of sleep, but they'd do it.

"You can count on us," Nork said.

"Excellent. Thank you for your help. It will not be forgotten."

Nork shrugged. He didn't do things for recognition. He nodded back at Rednow, and his mind went wild as he looked across the terrain where the battlefield was supposed to be. It would take some preparation. They needed spiked holes, which required digging and covering. They required barriers, traps, and other pikes set up to block the way and drive the enemy hordes to certain areas. To his right, there was a large, steep cliff. Perhaps that could be used to drive them off.

"Let's go, brother. Our people are tired, but there's a lot to do."

Nosema nodded. As long as he had his brother, he would be fine. No one else understood him that well. "We're going to need them to chop trees and sharpen the tips into pikes. Others will need to pick up shovels to dig deep enough holes."

Nork nodded. A lot of hard work ahead. "And we'll get to avenge those we left behind."

THIRTY-THREE

REUNITED

REDNOW - MEREY

As good as it was to have Nork and Nosema back, Rednow was still not confident enough with his chances. The Essence always said that if he managed to handle Orberesis, all the other armies would dissolve and flee, so the pressure was on him. But now that he had a better grasp of his powers and knowing the Essence didn't really want the Old One gone completely, he struggled to come up with an actual strategy.

In Heleronde, it had been simple enough. The invaders were coming, and they had to go through specific terrain, which made everything easier to predict and advantage easy to gain. Now, the Old One made everything impossible to predict.

You worry too much.

"Only when thousands of lives depend on me. I'd say you worry too little. And when you do, it's mostly about yourself," he said.

You know that's not a fair statement.

His patience for this had drained. He flew towards Arkan. At that speed, he could cover large distances, and going from the Builders' cove to the camp took less than ten seconds. When he reached the cavern with the houses carved from the rocky mountain walls, he found Arkan waiting for him.

"What is it?"

"The child has returned. Here, come."

Rednow couldn't help but hesitate, a hint of nervousness consuming him. Tinko had spent quite a long time in their Inner Flight. Longer than most, Arkan had said. Rednow had not enjoyed his experience there one bit, so he worried for the child.

He turned in the doorway and found Tinko with sunken cheeks and dark rings around their eyes. "Uncle," the child said with a raspy, dry voice.

Rednow took another step forward and a desire to hug the child came to him, only for him to remember he was a skeleton now. The Essence had stripped away his ability to comfort others. Still, he kneeled and looked at Tinko. "How do you feel?"

The child hesitated and a slight frown quickly turned into a few shed tears. "I saw Thata in there. And myself... And..."

Rednow shushed them. "No need to say what you saw. You came out stronger, didn't you? Did you find the light at the end?"

Tinko nodded.

Sometimes Rednow forgot how bloody young the child still was. Not even twelve winters if his memory didn't fail him. No twelve-year-olds were supposed to go through this much, especially not during just a few months. But Tinko was no regular child, either.

"Listen," Rednow said. "What you have just done is the most impressive thing I've ever seen you do, and I've seen you fight, use smoke, and a special ability. You have nothing to prove. Now, you just have to be yourself, and to know that I'm proud of you."

The child's tears returned even stronger than the first time and an urge to protect Tinko overcame him. Tinko was all he had left. Rebma was gone. Tellwoon, Merey, and Zatak had returned to the Seven Peaks and only the gods knew if they were coming to help him. He glanced at the child, who had lost everything as well.

"Everything will be alright, kid," Rednow said, knowing full well he could promise no such thing. "Now come with me. The battle is near, and I want you to always stay close to Pinesy or Arkan, alright?"

As battle was mentioned, Tinko's eyes changed, and they wiped off their tears. With a short nod, they looked ready for battle already, but Rednow would make sure the child had some serious protection.

"I'll have to check on the units. Don't do anything I wouldn't do, alright?"

"I'll make sure of it," Arkan said with a smile as he patted the child's shaggy hair. "Let's get you some food."

Rednow took off in a cloud of smoke. Too much on his mind. The safety of others he cared about. It shouldn't all fall on him, should it? There should be others to bear the weight.

I didn't ask for any of this.

From the sky, the scenery looked the same as it always did, with sharp peaks leading to the Thousand Hills and the multiple camps built strategically on the slopes. Cypresses, pines, and ferns spread across the mossy rocks. Every time Rednow saw such obvious displays of the Essence's work, he couldn't help but wonder what the world would look like without her.

Rednow shook off those thoughts as he landed on the ground. The pineheads watched out for his landing and moved aside. From there, he saw Nork and Nosema in the distance, digging ditches and preparing the traps, men and women setting up the pikes and the other barriers. They had managed to get both pineheads and smokesmiths to help them out. Nork shouted commands as he wiped sweat from his forehead, and Rednow beamed in pride of these people, from all over the world, working together for a common goal.

"Blood Collector," a voice said, taking him from his own thoughts. "There you are!"

Fatuna walked towards him, gangly, with a wide smile on her pointy face. Her long, dark hair was caught in a messy bun above her head. Next to her, Caspan walked in hurried steps. The leader of the Builders' southwestern sect looked like a child next to her, but he must have been over a hundred years old already.

"Did you two become friends?" Rednow was surprised to see them together.

They exchanged glances and shrugged. "We work with whoever is willing to work with us, Blood Collector. I'm not one to reject a helping hand."

Fatuna smiled. "I say the same."

"Very well. I'm glad to know. What is the status of your forces?"

"We separated the wheat from the chaff." Fatuna scratched her hair. "There were growing pains. Not everyone was happy with how things went, but those people have already left us. Combat training has been interesting. I've been speaking with your friend Nork about his plans for the terrain. He's not half-bad at this warring thing, is he? Anyway, I've been incorporating his plans into our own ideas. Do you know when the enemy will come? The smokesmith units are nearly ready, but it would be good to know in advance."

Rednow shook his skull. "There are scouts all around the camps, so if they come, we'll know. Until then, we just have to sit and wait, as much as my gut tells me it won't be long. What about the Builders?"

Caspan took a deep breath and let it out slowly. "Arkan's teachings are... hard. He says he can't get us to his level in days given that he and his people have dedicated a lifetime to it, but some of our Builders have already succeeded in the Inner Flight and are now learning to fly."

"That's excellent. What of the spears?"

"Spear training continues, and the smiths are still making more weapons. They're running out of iron to smelt, though."

Rednow nodded. They were short of basically *everything*. In fact, it would be best to just get the battle over with because the longer they stayed there, the harder it would be to sustain them and keep them well fed. He just hoped the Old One didn't see through that.

Fatuna cleared her throat. "Blood Collector, can I ask how you know the enemy is coming? If we've seen no evidence so far... It's not that I don't believe you, but I'm sure some are questioning themselves."

"I'm the Essence's avatar and as long as the Essence lives, the Old One cannot accomplish its plans. It seeks to bring its shadowlings to occupy the Known World. That means he'll strike when he thinks he's strong enough or when he thinks I'm not as well-prepared."

"That's somewhat terrifying." Fatuna's quick smile turned into a grimace.

"Rednow!" a voice shouted. Pinesy. He ran towards Rednow and stopped by his side.

"The Leeth," he said. "Merey and Tellwoon are here."

Rednow's heart would have brightened if he'd still had one.

⋯⋯⋯⋯

Merey rode the shadesgrowl a little faster than she normally would. The terrain was rocky, and the creature often whimpered, or its hooves failed to get traction in the hills. *Bloody mountains again.* All Merey could think was how Rednow just *had* to go back to his old ways—leaving one set of mountains for another. The southern front of the Thousand Hills, however, was a pleasant paradise compared to Mount Melchor and the

Seven Peaks, which was covered in snow for more than two thirds of the year.

In front of her, the camp was already established and lived in. There were smiths, with the frequent hammering of metal in the anvil. There were fletchers and carpenters. Most people there were pineheads, who had set much shorter shacks and barracks all around the place. The smoke of bonfires and the smell of roasted game and other small creatures made the camp feel like one where she wouldn't mind spending some time. A large group of folks were busy digging ditches and setting up traps in the distance.

That's where the battlefield will be.

Most of all, there seemed to be an underlying tension, a tell that battle was imminent.

Merey swallowed. She wasn't looking forward to telling Red-now just how imminent it was.

"You look worried," Tellwoon told her.

Merey looked at the love of her life and managed only a faded smile. "Not only am I not securing enough gold to help feed our army, I also led the enemy to Rednow with my carelessness. What will he think…"

Tellwoon scoffed. "You speak as if he was morality and perfection personified. Don't you remember his blunders? That's only natural for leaders to make. And it's our duty to forgive you and let you learn whatever you must. There are always growing pains with leadership transitions."

For the Gods, Merey loved this woman. She loved her wisdom and how she always seemed to know what to say and when. It was like she could see directly inside Merey's head and know exactly what she needed to hear. Sometimes it was good to butt heads, and Tellwoon didn't shy away from that, but in times like these, support from her loved one was worth more than any elixir she could take or any special weapon she could wield. With Tellwoon by her side, she was *whole*.

She almost wondered if Rednow had made a mistake. Perhaps Tellwoon should have been the leader of the Leeth. There was a lot Merey wanted to say in that moment, but she only nodded and smiled back. "You're right."

They continued to walk as the rest of the Leeth soldiers had been allocated part of the woodland area that touched the mountain slopes to set up their own camp. She hadn't been able to bring as many soldiers as she'd hoped, but these would have to do. As usual, Zatak had preferred to stay on the outskirts with his bloodsleuths, which always made Merey wonder if he really trusted them not to snatch somebody's arm off.

In front of them, between shacks and columns of camp-fire smoke, was a large crowd parted in two, leaving something—someone—in the middle. Her right hand reached for the scabbard as she couldn't process what she was seeing. A skinless, fleshless skeleton moved straight towards her, support-ed only by a simple layer of smoke that seemed never to leave it.

Leave your sword, Merey. It's me.

Merey flinched, realising the voice had been inside her head. *What the...*

"Rednow?" she muttered.

"What?" Tellwoon asked. She also had her hand on the sword hilt.

"It is me," the skeleton said. Merey still wasn't sure what was happening. "It's a long story."

"Don't come any closer. We have time for a tale," Merey said. *Can this really be him?*

For Merey, Rednow was like a father. She was looking forward to seeing him and giving him a strong bear hug. She was used to his brooding demeanour and how he pretended to be the terrible person everyone feared whilst everyone who really knew him had nothing but love for the man. But now... a skeleton.

"If that's you, explain what happened," she said. There was something heart-breaking about it. She wondered if it had been the smoke that had made him this way. A side effect, perhaps?

"I nearly died saving Tinko, Gimlore's child. But the Essence rescued me and kept me like this in exchange for my physical body."

"So, *what* are you? Man or spirit?" Tellwoon asked, stealing the words straight from Merey's mouth.

Rednow sighed and Merey saw a glimpse of sadness in it, even though the skeleton had no facial expressions. "Does it matter? I'm still me. I'm Rednow."

Merey wondered if that was true. "Prove it, then."

He was silent at first. A group of humans and pineheads looked at him, waiting for a reply.

"I found you on a cliff near Benaven. You were four years old. No mother. No father. You were crying, but you cried with a ferocity that was sure to wake every living thing in the vicinity. I thought... if a child cries this hard, she has it in her to become a hell of a warrior. I think I was right about that, wasn't I?"

Merey's eyes were wet. She held the tears back as much as she could, but one of them slipped away, flowing down her cheek. *Shit*. That could only be Rednow, but he was... a skeleton. At least he was alive... wasn't he?

She wiped her eyes and sniffed. "I should have guessed you were different when you talked into Tellwoon's mind. How dare you stick your nose in my woman's mind, old man? Don't tell me you read her thoughts, too."

Both Rednow and Tellwoon laughed.

Tellwoon turned to her, feigning indignation. "Your woman? Is that what I am now?"

"Old man?" Rednow played along. "This old man can still beat you ten times out of ten. Even as an undead."

Merey chuckled. Yes, that was most definitely Rednow. Her face soured. The news she brought was going to hurt even more now. "We have to talk."

Rednow shook his skull and waved them to follow him and the others around him. He pointed to a tall, dark-skinned woman and a small pinehead accompanying her. "These are Fatuna and Caspan, by the way. I think you already met Nork and Nosema in Alarkan. They're out here somewhere."

Merey gave them a short, timid nod and those two did the same before everyone sat down on an intricate rug as they broke bread and shared it around. "The news isn't great."

"Tell us everything," Rednow said.

"On our way here, we stumbled upon the Gashoine armies. They were also trying to locate you. They didn't hear us or see us at first, so we were planning to ambush them." Merey sighed. "We had the perfect location to do it. We would let them pass, then come from behind and push their units off the cliff. It would have saved us all a whole lot of trouble."

"What happened?" Fatuna asked.

How can I say this?

Merey swallowed. "As I was spying their location, just waiting to give the order for the ambush, one of their scouts spotted me. I could have let him live, but he would have told them about having found me, and I would have been compromising the location of all the Leeth forces."

"So you killed him," Rednow said.

Merey nodded. "I left his body in the woods and went straight back to get us here as quickly as possible. But any decent garrison notices when a scout doesn't come back. Then they'll send units looking for him and eventually they will find the body and realise it was no accident or wild beast. They'll be on the lookout for signs of my presence. Even if I were to cover my tracks, they would soon find vestiges of our entire unit. We rushed here, so that means the Gashoine troops must be less than a day behind us."

"You led the enemy straight to us?" Fatuna looked dumbfounded.

Merey nodded, a knot forming at the pit of her stomach. "I'm afraid I did."

Silence prevailed until Rednow turned to Caspan and Fatuna. "You heard the woman. Less than a day. We don't know if the bastards will dare to strike without their master present, but we can't assume he won't be here either, so it's time to warn everyone. If they don't engage, we shall do so. Warn all of the units. We have a long night of preparation ahead of us."

"Understood." Caspan got up from the rug. "If you'll excuse me."

Rednow nodded and the builder took off swiftly, though Fatuna stayed, frowning and scratching her head. "I don't know if we'll be ready in less than a day, Blood Collector. It's too soon, is it not?"

Rednow turned to face her, though he no longer had a face. "Will they not fight if the battle is brought to them? Fighting is all we're here to do, Fatuna. We'll never be ready. There will always be something we could have done more. Done better. But we'll fight regardless. And if the gods are on our side, we will be thorns piercing deep in their skin. We'll win."

Fatuna nodded and stood. "I'll talk to them."

She left the tent, jogging around the camp, barking things Merey couldn't understand to a group of men and women who stood around her.

"Thank you for standing up for me. I'm glad to see your diplomacy skills have improved since Gasho," Merey said.

Rednow scoffed. "I went through something called the Inner Flight and I'm still realising just how good it did me. I suppose I *have* got better at talking to people instead of barking orders at them."

"Or turning into a raging maniac," Tellwoon offered as a smile formed across her face.

"I suppose you've got some cheek in you now that you're a smokesmith, then." Rednow turned to Merey. "How is she faring?"

"Amazingly, as expected."

Rednow nodded. Merey couldn't see it, but she was sure he was proud.

Against all expectations, Rednow had not turned into a ball of exploding ire upon realising her massive blunder, so she could breathe in relief. Tellwoon had been right, as she always was.

"Can you tell us more about your plans for battle? And who are those people, anyway, Caspan and Fatuna?" Merey asked.

"Fatuna is one of the smokesmiths. We've got smokesmiths, refugees from Heleronde, and Builders, or pineheads. And now we have the Leeth."

"They will want to greet you, but you already know that," Tellwoon said.

Rednow scoffed. "With me like this? There is hardly anything to greet. It's better if I let you know everything we've been planning for the battle."

Merey tasted the sadness in those words. His life had been one of pain and sacrifice, even if two thirds of the world only saw him as the warmonger Blood Collector. She saw through that façade. There was a proud, stubborn man somewhere underneath, even if now only in bones and spirit. The fact he was still lingering as a ghost and a skeleton after countless deadly encounters just showed how resilient the old bastard was.

"Nah," Merey said. "You will greet them. We'll just explain that this is what you look like now. Their admiration and respect are boundless, and you know it. These are still your bloody children we're talking about! You raised them when nobody else wanted to do it."

Tellwoon nodded, standing with her. "And only then do we talk about battle plans."

Thirty-Four
Stowing Away

Orberesis - Solvi

Orberesis travelled the void effortlessly. There was a sense of freedom that had captivated him since the first time he had tried it. Weightlessness. This time, however, pressure was building in him and he could tell it was connected to the Old One in some way.

Are you... nervous? Orberesis thought in the void, no need for him to voice his words as reality flicked and flashed before him, a traveller in time and space.

I don't know what you're on about.

Orberesis smiled. This was the moment his parasite had been working towards. When they reached their destination, they would fight the Essence and her avatar and they would win.

In here, you're more exposed. I can feel your thoughts better.

There was nothing in return. The Old One remained quiet. He had turned into something almost like a friend who inhabited a corner of his soul. He had always thought Tavanar was the only friend he had, but then the bastard had betrayed him, so Orberesis had learned the hard way that trust was too fickle a thing. He couldn't hand it out too easily.

Journeying through the void was still a wild ride, even if he was now almost used to it. Stars and planets out there all flashed and turned the dark sky that enveloped everything around him in a carnival of light and colour. Some stars shone with a yellow glisten, others in blue or red.

Can you visit the stars?

The Old One scoffed. *If you have a death wish.*

Orberesis had heard it before—the stars were large bonfires, but why shouldn't a god be able to reach them?

Gods can be killed, Doi. That's what we're trying to do here, in fact. Are you ready?

The void transitioned into something earthlier—into something he recognised. No longer the void: somewhere in the Known World. Behind him, a few thousand Lantern Horns had made the journey from Alarkan. They were dizzy from the wild ride, their lights flickered vividly in hurried patterns, and they uttered guttural growls as they shook off the sickness that always came with it. Travelling in the void was a necessary pain for them.

Orberesis rose into the sky. It was clear, with not a cloud in sight and the mountain peaks already covered in white. Perhaps they had been like that all year. Below, Orberesis spotted the damned cove where the savages and the Essence's bastard had been holed up in his prior visit. Anger flourished inside him, fuelling his fire.

Smokesmiths. They'd killed his father and burned him alive. They'd burned down his village in the Gloomwoods. The last time he'd seen the smoke, he hadn't been prepared. The Essence was too powerful and the smoke evoked an irrational fear in him. But now he was prepared for whatever might come his way.

The Old One chuckled, as though he was enjoying Orberesis' struggle.

"Have you got something to say?" Orberesis asked.

No. Keep your anger. We'll need it. Look.

Orberesis faced the ground. There were camps surrounding the cavern. Threads of smoke and tiny people ran around them, sounding a wide array of alarm bells which were already ringing.

"She's been preparing for our return, hasn't she?"

I told you, Doi. I told you she would be.

He couldn't see it from there, but there must have been a good few thousand of them, at least. The Lantern Horns were already marching their way, lusting for human blood. It was a compromise Orberesis was willing to make. *These* humans in particular, he had no use for. Farther, in the distance, more people marched towards their location, as much as the wild terrain allowed. They sported tall standards with the blue flame of Gasho, though there were other wild and sparse soldiers scattered between the Gashoine armies and his location.

"Shari, Ainis, and the Two Nations are late," he noted.

Not everyone can fast travel in the void.

That was true enough. But then, why should he wait for their arrival? With a surge of power, he could just wipe out the entire enemy camp and render them useless. "Why don't I just..."

Something—or someone—interrupted his words. Whatever it was, it came straight at him like the arrows he had dodged already, like the knife Tavanar had tried to use to kill him. From where he stood, he could sense the murderous intent and a hint of smoke made it to his nostrils as this enormous ball of fumes dissipated into a strange creature—a skeleton—shrouded in black smoke.

That's her avatar.

As though the skeleton believed the same thing, he came at Orberesis, charging with a flurry of blows. The smoke shaped itself at his will, gaining the form of armour and a sword. The black smoke carried the skeleton in the air, making him faster and faster, all the blows falling sharply in mid-air. Maintaining that distance and keeping the blows away was a task in itself.

I can't keep protecting you like this, Doi. I'm using too much of your energy. You must finish him quickly.

Orberesis swallowed.

He had never been a fighter. He had always avoided conflict. He would pick battles that others would fight in his stead, but never himself. Solvi had been the only one who had the ability to fight like this against another opponent, but she was carrying his child.

This was all on him.

"Why won't you die?" the skeleton man snarled.

Orberesis almost laughed at that. "Funny, I was just thinking the same thing. What are you?"

"I'm the Blood Collector," the skeleton snarled. "And a Smoke Rider."

As Orberesis was preparing to laugh away those words, the strikes from the smoke blade started tearing at him, as though the Smoke Rider was blowing Orberesis' protective array to pieces. What could he do? He thought about what the Old One had taught him. There hadn't been much there about fighting, but perhaps there was something he could do.

Orberesis took a deep breath, closed his eyes, and found himself.

There was only him and his truth.

He was the truth.

He was a demi-god.

There was power everywhere and all he had to do was extend his hand and reach for it. He drew a half circle in the air. With the other hand, he found a silky-smooth surface he could peel. Orberesis held on to it and, with a swift motion, pulled it, allowing himself to get sucked away into the void, along with the Smoke Rider. Temporal Exploration was a fascinating art, indeed.

The void was ever beautiful. The nothingness usually meant peace, but not this time. As a student of Temporal Exploration, Orberesis was now used to sailing the void, but the smoke skeleton wasn't—he would collapse under the tremendous pressure it represented. All Orberesis had to do was wait.

What is this place? The skeleton man asked, though he had stopped with his flurry of strikes. Both their bodies were floating in the aether, carried away by the nothingness. Orberesis' heart raced. Why was the man talking? Why wasn't he choking to death or having all his limbs torn apart under the heavy pressure?

He gritted his teeth. *Why are you...*

Still alive? The man chuckled. He could also speak to Orberesis without spoken words.

Don't listen to what he says! the Old One cautioned. *He speaks for the Essence.*

I can imagine what you've been told by the Deceiver, the skeletal man said. *From what I've heard, you weren't such a terrible man. You've had a tough life. But the Deceiver stole everything from you.*

Lies!

Orberesis' head pounded. It was like they were fighting for control of his mind while he was conscious of it. He was supposed to have been in control. The void was his happy place, where he controlled what no other being did. And yet... the Smoke Rider was still here, not only surviving but still trying to convince him to abandon the Old One.

How can you be alive? This place was made to kill anyone that isn't me, and yet, here you are.

The skeleton man hesitated. *I think we've got a lot in common. We're both tainted by the deities. We didn't choose to be, yet it is our fate. Whether we like it or not, they control the steps of our present and the path to our futures. Their wishes drip and drip into our minds, and here we are, sacrificing our bodies and minds to fight a war that isn't ours, as much as they tell us it is.*

Orberesis was uncomfortable. A sense of dread took over him as the Old One tickled parts of his mind. The skeleton man still hadn't answered his question. *WHY ARE YOU ALIVE?*

Because, like you, I can't feel anything. Only what I'm allowed to feel. I'm already half-dead, more spirit than man.

Then, the skeleton glowed. A red light flashed, giving him the appearance of an old man with high cheekbones and a thick, grey beard.

This is what I once looked like. To answer your question, that is why I am not dead. That is why your void has no effect on me.

Orberesis gritted his teeth. Why couldn't things ever go according to his plans?

The Old One roared, his voice amplified in the void, as counterintuitive as that seemed. He sounded determined and confident, hard to resist. *Get out of here, Doi. Don't forget you've still got much more power than this. You can borrow it all from me!*

Orberesis was divided. He *wanted* power. As much as he could get. But the man's speech had tugged into whatever heartstrings the Old One still hadn't got a hold of. Somehow, that had made him think of himself, Solvi, and his baby. He wasn't sure those things could peacefully coexist.

. . . .

Solvi tried her best to remain motionless, but the rocking of the ship made it hard. She held her belly, but the child seemed set on destroying her from the inside out just to tell her how much they hated the motion.

What was I thinking?

Stowing away in a large vessel like that had seemed like a good idea, especially because it was where Gimlore and her allies were.

She had been desperate, with nowhere to go. No one to turn to. What she hadn't considered was how long the journey to Vaerghulen really was, and that it meant no food and hardly any water for at least a few days, unless she could be stealthy. No stealth was possible when her belly was of that size. The child kicked at it and kicked again probably just out of spite. Solvi caressed the belly, but the child only seemed encouraged by her touch.

She slowly moved from her behind to her knees. Luckily for her, she had found a storage unit on the ship that no one used. It was full of old rags and brooms and more mouse traps than she was comfortable with. It was one of the nastiest places she had ever been. Getting to her feet, she almost fell as numbness spread through her legs. She held on to one of the boards, doing her best to stay quiet. The voices of the sailors and the passengers were all too familiar now, and Solvi feared what they would do to her—to her babe.

She hadn't heard their voices yet—her saviours. Solvi cursed herself. Why did she always need to place herself so entirely in the hands of somebody else? First it had been Orberesis and now her heart was already heralding these two as her new protectors. She should have just stayed on land, in the Two Nations, and sought help there, but it was too risky. Everyone knew who she was, and she couldn't trust a single woman to help her deliver the child.

The baby moved again, and it hurt badly. Solvi had to control herself not to scream.

Shit. Shit. Shit.

Even in the ship, her safety wasn't guaranteed. Gimlore had been clear that she was free to go, but they hadn't suddenly turned into the best of friends. Solvi could sense the anger and the resentment oozing from the woman—part of it not without reason.

With no warning, something wet dripped down her legs and she widened her eyes, pulling up her black dresses to check. On the floor was a combination of blood and other fluids.

The child wanted out.

Solvi took a deep breath. Wasn't that what they always said? Breathe in and breathe out, and it will be done in due time. Breathe in and breathe out, and it will be done.

A thrashing pain shot through her, sharp and intense. The baby did not intend to make this a peaceful experience.

Breathe in and breathe out.

The pain subsided, but there was still the looming anticipation of when it would come next. Two minutes or two hours? Nobody knew and her heart raced. She was alone. Utterly alone again in a shithole, somewhere in the middle of the ocean surrounded by people who wouldn't shed a tear if she were to be found dead or thrown overboard.

Another strong wave. A dull ache spread through her back and lower abdomen, along with an unbearable pressure in her pelvis. The pain spread through her sides and her thighs. She had been having these waves for hours now, but not like this. Not this frequently.

Shit. Fucking shit.

It hurt. If it already hurt this much, then what in the underworld would it be like when she actually had the child?

Out there, the ship's crew walked around, floorboards creaking right above her head. Solvi needed to remain quiet, but with every moment that passed, she knew it wouldn't be possible. They would hear her, catch her. Silence was impossible. She was just biding her time. For what, she had no clue.

Another wave of pressure against her pelvis and another wave of pain spread through her.

"FFFFFFFFF-UCK," she yelped, immediately cursing herself for having no bloody self-control.

Breathe in. Breathe out.

The steps outside stopped. They'd probably heard her.

Breathe in. Breathe out.

She would be fine—maybe.

Breathe in, breathe out.

The moment the pain subsided was instant relief, though it remained a looming threat. She knew just how close the next cramp was.

Suddenly, the door to the little storage room where she had been hiding opened with a bang. The daylight nearly blinded her, but two backlit figures stood before it, and the voice was recognisable.

"You stowed away?" There was surprise in Gimlore's question, as though she had thought Solvi would never dare do such a thing. The other figure—probably Keryon—leaned towards Gimlore to whisper something in her ear. When Solvi didn't reply, Gimlore talked again. "Why did you do it? Why did you hide?"

Solvi shot a glance at Gimlore, hoping the woman would understand, and touched her belly to reinforce the idea.

Breathe in. Breathe out.

Gimlore was her best shot at surviving this, and at doing so with any possible bit of dignity. Either that or she would be decapitated on the spot.

As her eyes adjusted to the light, Solvi could see their faces better. Gimlore was frowning as she approached Solvi carefully, pushing away some of the crates, sacks, and brooms that were lying around, then stepping on the blood and fluids Solvi had released earlier. The woman looked down to see what it was, then back at Solvi, her eyes pregnant with recognition.

"Keryon," she said.

"Yes?" the man asked from behind her.

"Help me carry her."

Solvi didn't fight. How could she? They'd either save her and the child or they'd make sure Solvi was dead and the baby would never see the light of day. Gimlore didn't strike her as a baby killer, though.

They picked her up gently—that was promising—and carried her out of that filthy storage.

"Let's take her to the Captain's suite," Gimlore said.

What?

Keryon hesitated. "Are you sure? He won't like it..."

"If he doesn't like it, I'll persuade him. The easy way or the hard way."

Keryon shook his head but stayed faithful and carried on.

Thank the gods and whoever blessed me with this.

Solvi had found help. She truly had. She wasn't safe yet, though, as the child was yet to be born. She was sure some people would compare pains and say this was the easy part, but she couldn't care less about that. She had fought in wars. She had killed on command. She'd been wounded in battle and she had fallen in love with a man who was, or wanted to be, a god. And yet she just *knew* in her gut that this was going to be the hardest thing she would ever do.

As they went past a group of confused sailors and crew members whose faces Solvi didn't dare to memorise, they finally reached the main door. Keryon knocked on it twice with strength and urgency. Not too long after that, a burly man emerged from inside, twirling his moustache.

"Can I help you?" he asked.

"We're going to use your room. This woman is going into labour. She needs a proper bed to give birth to the child."

The Captain twirled his moustache a little more and narrowed his eyes. "Where the fuck is this one coming from? She's not a crew member... Is she a listed passenger?"

Gimlore took a step forward, getting into the Captain's face. "Listen here, we don't have time for this. It doesn't matter who she is or where she comes from. The child is going to be born. A fucking baby! Being born on your ship? Shouldn't that be a fucking honour?"

"Well, I..."

"So, step the fuck aside and clear out the room. I'll pay you handsomely when you get out and if you give us the gift of shutting the fuck up, she'll consider naming the child after you, won't she?"

Gimlore eyed Solvi and she nodded, not knowing what she was doing.

Solvi swallowed. It was as though Gimlore was on fire, like her words could cut through stone or steel, even. She didn't know many people who would accept being spoken to like that.

"Well..." the Captain said, narrowing his eyes. He looked like he wanted to say something, but without waiting for a reply, Gimlore walked into the room with Solvi and laid her on the bed. It was more comfortable than the prison she had been in in Heleronde by far.

"Thank you," Solvi muttered, looking Gimlore in the eyes. She needed to show she was sincere, like this was something she would never forget. This woman was helping her with nothing to gain, perhaps even with something to lose.

Gimlore sighed and scratched her temple. Solvi had been right—this wasn't easy for her, but she was helping her anyway. Then Gimlore turned to Keryon, to the stunned Captain, and to the small crowd of sailors who were gathering behind them, by the doorstep. "What the fuck are you looking at? Close the damn door and get the fuck out of here. And you better pray to the gods of the sea or whoever you worship that both this woman and the child live through this, or this bloody ship will surely be cursed with the ghost of an unborn baby."

The Captain's eyebrows rose sharply, and he immediately closed the door, leaving only Gimlore and Solvi inside. "How far are you?" Gimlore asked.

Solvi swallowed. "I don't know. Thank you, I... I owe you."

Gimlore shrugged. "I've gone through this, but I had a woman named Eshof by my side while I gave birth. Two little bastards came out of me. So, I guess now it's my time to pay back the favour. I'm a mother. You'll be one too. Our allegiances don't mean a thing in here. The children come first, so you owe me nothing."

Solvi's eyes welled and she was about to break down crying when Gimlore cleared her throat.

"Well, what do you think you're doing? No crying now. You've got to save your tears. We've got a long night ahead of us. Now, let's see how far along you already are." She lifted Solvi's dresses, spread her legs by the knees, and peeked. "If we're lucky, it will be less than a long night. If we're not, it might take longer."

With no warning, Solvi's pelvis cramped again, and the sharp pain returned. "UUUGH!" she uttered. "Fuck!"

"Let it all out, I say!" Gimlore said. "Cursing is power, woman. Being loud helps with the pain. No need to be shy. There is only me and sailors outside who curse even more."

Breathe in. Breathe out.

Solvi wiped a bead of sweat or two from her forehead.

"This is going to hurt, isn't it?" she dared to ask.

Gimlore nodded, but there was no jest in her face or even a trace of a mocking smile. Instead, there was pity... No, was that concern? "Like nothing you've felt before."

SOME GENERALS

NORK

Nork chugged another vial of the mossback elixir and ran through the chaotic terrain. The Gashoine were here and so were the shadowlings. He never wished to see the bloody beasts again and here they were, ready to maul him and eat him alive.

With one hand, he carried a few spare greasy bombs he had procured from those who didn't know how to use them properly. In his right hand, he carried an improvised hatchet, just in case any fucker got a little too close. All around his vest, he had throwing knives, in case he needed to keep anyone at bay.

He kept running, his breathing harsh.

Why did I volunteer to do this again? By his side, Nosema and two other Helerondians had similar questioning looks on their faces as an army of enemy soldiers and a horde of famished beasts ran right behind them.

The battlefield was ahead, though. More specifically, there was the trap-ridden section that he and the Helerondian refugees had spent countless days building. Now, it was his job to... guide the enemy right into some of these traps before they met the smokesmiths and the pineheads.

I can do this, he thought. Was that the elixir talking? A quick side glance let him see his brother. *No, I can really do this. We both can.*

Filled with liquid self-belief, Nork ran forward, the enemy's screams ever closer behind him. He knew the traps wouldn't catch every enemy soldier. There would be the lucky ones and the survivors, but hopefully he, his brother, and the other runners would be quick enough to stay far away from the enemy and avoid the volleys of arrows that were sure to come later from his own side of the trenches.

Nork kept running, the heavy breath tampered by the adrenaline of the battlefield again. Last time he had seen battle, Gimlore had been by his side. Now, he and Nosema had to prove they could lead these people in her absence.

As his feet trod dirt and rock, he realised he already knew the camp. He knew what parts to avoid and which were safe. There were spiked holes, hidden soldiers with wooden pikes raised at the last minute, and other natural barriers that would steer large units closer to the edge of the cliffs. That's when the buried spearmen would come in and push them off.

"On our tail. Get set!" Nork shouted to make sure all the soldiers on his side of the battle could hear.

Look at him! There he was, coordinating a battle, leading smokesmiths to what he hoped would be a resounding victory. The whole point of that run would be to let the enemy believe there was nothing wrong with the terrain, no traps at all.

"Are you alright?" Nork asked.

"Better than ever," Nosema said, smiling.

That must be the elixir talking. They were both quiet, but Nosema even more so. He was confident in his abilities, without ever showing it. Now that he noticed, running was becoming easier. He could run faster, and he did, as did his companions who had volunteered to play bait.

The enemy had bitten.

Nork could see his side units in the distance now. There were men and women armed with axes, hatchets, scythes, spears, pitchforks, swords, and pretty much any other weapon they could find. They were all ragged, but there were smokesmiths spread out, surrounding them. Nork had convinced Rednow and Fatuna it was best to spread out the smokesmiths among the rest of the men and the Leeth warriors, not only to act as motivation but to also create the illusion that their units were as good as their best soldier, not as bad as their worst. The strength of one would be the strength of many. Or at least that's what he had hoped.

He ran like never before, one foot after the other, constantly looking back to see how close the enemy was. Now it was too late and there was nowhere else for them to go. Backing down now would mean waiting another day or two until they could strike again, and Rednow and the divine fucker were already tearing each other up in the skies, somewhere.

Nork finally reached the point of contact where he and the other runners were supposed to step aside and hide. He climbed the tree and watched the other units, clasping the hatchet, itching to crack someone's skull.

From up there, he could see the field and the enemy soldiers crossing it without suspecting a trap. That was until someone on his side shouted and the plan was in motion.

Nork jumped from the tree and ran towards the field. In front of him, the hidden allied troops had risen the pikes and impaled dozens of enemy soldiers wearing Gashoine uniforms and even some shadowlings. A few steps ahead of those, other enemies stepped into the false ground and fell to the ditches he and his brother had dug. There were twelve of them, just enough to impale a few dozen soldiers in each hole. Men and women turned to lifeless bodies before his very eyes, and his heart raced with excitement.

Then the buried contingent finally emerged, appearing behind the enemy forces, swinging their spears and their hatchets. Heads flew and, sure enough, the surprise turned into slaughter.

The first blood had been drawn, and to their favour.

In all the chaotic grunts of men about to face their maker, he could already count hundreds of enemies dead before they'd had the chance to fight back.

His hand itched to use the hatchet, so he ran towards the front line like a wild man, his brother by his side. They were both boosted by the elixir, taking pleasure in the hot, thin line between life and death on the battlefield.

Some of the Gashoine soldiers tried to retreat, but the shadowlings continued relentlessly, their jaws and claws tearing through flesh and bone, horn lights always flickering.

The elixir was making Nork reckless, irrational. He couldn't let the shadowlings cross just yet, but he also couldn't just charge at them, or he would easily lose his head.

"Containment!" he shouted.

That was his last surprise, so he allowed himself a crooked smile.

His last trap consisted of a crew of buried soldiers and craftsmen hiding a large wood wall, with sharp spearheads nailed on the top. They got up from the ground and all the dirt and foliage that covered the spear-wall fell off too.

"Charge!" Nork shouted and the men behind the wall pushed it directly at a unit of about a hundred soldiers without mercy. Faced against the spear-wall, the Gashoine soldiers had to back off to avoid getting skewered. The problem for the poor bastards was that the wall pushed them towards the cliff. A few of them managed to get out, but when faced with death by impalement, most fell to their deaths, echoing dying pleas as they plunged to the underworld.

Nork couldn't resist a chuckle, but he sobered up. Too many enemies had survived. Soon they'd be angry rather than confused, and they would find his rag tag of survivors and refugees the easiest vessel for their revenge.

Perhaps we can hold them a little longer.

The fight continued, but the shadowlings were no match for men and women. They were savage beasts that tore through everything in front of them.

"Brother!" The alarm in Nosema's voice was unusual for someone who was under the influence of the elixir. "Over there!"

Nork glanced behind the shadowlings and the Gashoine armies, squinting to narrow his focus. In the distance, he could see movement across the horizon.

Shit.

The rest of the enemy soldiers were on their way. This wasn't a time to try and hold anybody off, this was a time for... "Retreat!" Nork shouted. "Retreat!"

Could they hear him in that jungle amid all the weapons clashing and shouting soldiers? His ragged bunch started to retreat from the enemy, though many of them fell. Retreating but looking backward. Nonetheless, Nork reached into his sack and picked up a greasy bomb.

"Retreat!"

He flexed his arm and threw the greasy bomb with all his might, wasting no time in running back to camp. His mission had been accomplished, to an extent. They had opened the hostilities and the enemy had suffered casualties, but the damage he had inflicted upon them was only symbolic when considering the scale of their entire forces.

This wasn't a battle for him and his people anymore. They needed backup and they needed it *now.*

After the explosion caused by the greasy bomb, he looked back to see it had torn a sect of pursuing shadowlings. *Fuck you, bastards.*

The enemy was confused, hurt by the explosion, their ears ringing, and grey body parts were scattered around. The refugees of Heleronde and a few others who had joined to help retreated, but the shadowlings didn't relent, still in pursuit.

Nork gritted his teeth and reached into his sack for the last greasy bomb.

Make it fucking count, he told himself.

He threw it at the group of about twenty shadowlings who were closing in. Light flashed as the greasy bomb exploded, sending shadowlings flying. Even those that didn't die still staggered, losing their balance. Their lights flickered at increasing rates.

Nork was so tired of those fucking lights, but he kept retreating until he saw the archers up on the hill, in a straight line that sprawled from north to south across the Thousand Hills. *Finally.*

He tracked the landing course of the arrows, an arch over his head, like a large flock of migrating ducks seeking warmer lands for the winter. The arrows swarmed the shadowlings that were still in pursuit, as well as the Gashoine soldiers. Many bounced off shields and armour, but not everyone was that fortunate.

Good! Nork smiled as he kept running towards the base camp. Another volley of arrows followed the first one. It still wouldn't be enough to deter the enemy entirely, but it would be easy for the troops at base to deal with fewer enemies.

Where is Rednow? He wondered.

In the middle of the chaos of battle, with his heart pounding in his chest and his teeth gritted, he had completely forgotten about the man who had called upon them to protect the world from the shadowlings. Scanning the air for any signs, he also couldn't see Orberesis anywhere, so he imagined they were fighting elsewhere.

The second volley of arrows hit the enemy front lines as they approached. Nork noticed the sea of enemies that was coming towards them. There were flags and banners with the yellow colours of Shari, the marine blue of Ainis, and the brown of Mosendel. Three whole armies coming their way.

Fuck me.

Nork's heart pounded. He tried to steady his breath but couldn't.

"Three more armies incoming!" He shouted to whoever could hear.

There were archers and the rest of the Leeth mercenaries, and the smokesmiths and the pineheads, although Nork still wasn't sure how effective they could be.

"Leave it to us. You did some good work," the woman with the braid said.

Merey, was it? It didn't matter. Nork nodded and ran to safety with his brother, hurrying to usher more of his people back. "Are you hurt?" she asked.

Nork shook his head, but his face must have said otherwise because the woman kept staring at him. "Don't take any more of that elixir, alright? It's causing you harm."

Before Nork could frown and retort how unfair that was—he much preferred *that* harm to the harm his enemies wanted to inflict upon him—the woman was already stepping forward and onto the battlefield, along with a group of shield maidens and other soldiers.

"The hounds!" she shouted and one of the soldiers—Nork couldn't tell who—then whistled louder than it should be possible for a human.

For a moment, nothing happened, except that all the Leeth mercenaries kneeled and brought their heads down to the ground, as though they'd practiced this a thousand times.

"What are they..." he muttered.

Growls and roars echoed just as a gang of vicious blood-sleuths came running from the woodlands onto the battlefield. They were accompanied by a single man who ran shirtless, brandishing his sword.

It didn't take long for the bloodsleuths to find prey to sink their teeth into. They were born and bred for this, to seek out their prey and destroy them in ruthless fashion. The sound of snarls and growls blended with the Gashoine soldiers' pleas for help. The shadowlings didn't fear the bloodsleuths and marched straight at them with no hesitation.

Nork swallowed, now fearing for his side.

"Charge!" Merey shouted.

Her battalion moved forward. The Leeth mercenaries were the scariest military unit Nork had ever seen. They were tall and their bodies looked like they were chiselled out of a mountain under the thick black furs covering their backs and shoulders. Each stride they took gave Nork more hope.

"We'll have to back down sooner or later," another female voice said, making him turn. It was another woman he'd met before, with short hair and a razor trim on the left temple. Tellwoon.

"Why do you say that?" Nork asked, his eyes turning back to the battlefield.

"Three more armies coming. They're running out of shad-owlings, but three armies are too much even for the Leeth."

"What should we do, then?" he asked.

He couldn't think of anything in that moment. His mind was turning dizzy, and he wondered if another vial of the elixir would help.

"We separate their armies and fight on three different fronts once we defeat what's left of these poor bastards."

"Separate them how?"

Tellwoon smiled. "Thanks to your brilliant work on the traps. Take a look at that." She pointed at a section of the traps, between three of the ditches with spikes inside.

"What about it?"

"They won't risk charging the traps again now that they know about them. To their right side is the cliff, so their entry point is narrow, as we intended."

Nork saw what she meant now. "So, a lot of them will have to come around to get to us, unless they are fine with waiting in the back for their time to engage."

"Which they will never do," Nosema offered.

"Right. So, they'll have to come from there." Tellwoon's eyes switched to their right side, facing the mountain slopes. "But we'll be there, waiting for them. And we'll have the higher ground."

Nork scratched his chin and nodded. It could work. It could *really* bloody work. "That makes sense."

Tellwoon gave him a curt nod. "I'll act according to plan and divide the units. Leeth mercenaries, smokesmiths, and Builders. I'll take a third of each with me, and Merey will meet me there. You and your people can rest for now."

"We'll take care of the base," he said, wishing he could do more, eager to do more.

Wasting no time, Tellwoon jogged away to talk to the rest of the unit leaders.

Nork's eyes shifted back to the battlefield. Tellwoon had been right. Merey's units and the hounds were making quick work of the confused Gashoine soldiers and holding the shadowlings well enough. Many of them had retreated, and Nork doubted they'd try to come back.

"Look at them, they've become fucking generals!"

Nork's heart raced harsh with anticipation upon hearing the familiar voice. *No, it can't be.* He looked left and right. His eyes finally landed on Gimlore herself, in the flesh. She walked towards Nork and his brother with open arms, and a smile drawn across her face.

"When did you..." Nork said. What else was he to say? He didn't know... He didn't know anything other than the fact he had missed this absolute pain in the ass of a woman. "Boss..."

"You two are quite the bosses yourselves now, from what I can see!"

She looked different. Her face was leaner, and the shirt she wore wasn't as tight, though she had won a few more scars across her face to make up for it. She still had a belt with several knives and now also a hammer. That was new.

"Give me a fucking hug. Come on, you!" she snarled in a way that only she could.

"Yes, boss..." Nork said with tears in his eyes as the three of them hugged. It was like seeing a dead loved one come to life, or holding a baby for the first time, and Nork didn't know what else to say, what else to do. He found himself speechless and had to repress the tears lest she made fun of him for it.

Maybe, just maybe, things would be alright.

THIRTY-SIX

CHOSEN FAMILY

GIMLORE - KERYON

G imlore never thought she would cry upon seeing Nork and Nosema, but after so many months apart, for the gods, it was good to be surrounded by people who were like family yet again. Just a very dysfunctional, incomplete one.

She pushed them aside, hiding the tears. "Alright, enough of the nonsense now. Do you know where Tinko is? Or Rednow?"

Nork and Nosema exchanged glances, and she couldn't tell if it was a good thing or a bad thing.

Nork cleared his throat and pointed at the sky. "Rednow is out there, somewhere. Fighting Orberesis."

"Up there? How..." She had seen Rednow's blood-lusting transformation into a monster. He had also been able to summon people from all over the world to come and meet him by speaking in their mind, so somehow it wasn't strange that he could fly as well. But she'd seen the destruction Orberesis had caused in Heleronde. How could Rednow possibly fight *that*?

"And Tinko?"

"Should be with Pinesy, somewhere with the smokesmiths or the pineheads."

Gimlore nodded. "The kid is alright, then?"

Nork nodded. "Stronger than you'll believe, boss."

That gave her pause. "What do you mean?"

Nork scratched his head. "I think you should see it for yourself."

"See what?" she mumbled.

She realised a small crowd was watching. The Tooth was one of them, but there were also the other folks she had met during her time in imprisonment. Among them, a little head was hiding behind the crowd.

Hope.

Gimlore smiled and winked at her, waving for the little girl to come and meet them. "Listen, Nork. These people are *friends*. Brothers and sisters who helped me when I needed it most."

Nork studied the small group and nodded. The Tooth stepped forward and extended his hand. "I'm the Tooth. Pleasure to meet you. I'd say she helped us just as much."

The twins shook his hand, nodding. "She tends to do that."

If Gimlore had a hole, she would slide right into it. "Listen, this is Hope. She needs to be kept safe and brought to the company of any elderly folks or children we have here."

"I'll take her to Pinesy," Nosema said.

Hope hesitated. "Who is this man?"

Gimlore kneeled and caressed the girl's face, wiping off bits of dirt. "He's one of my best friends. He will take you to safety. Alright? If you trust me, you can trust him."

Nosema gave the girl an encouraging nod and extended his hand for her to grab. "I'll let you borrow my bandana if you want."

Hope swallowed and nodded.

Brave girl.

And off she went with Nosema. Gimlore didn't know what would happen to the girl. She had seen herself in Hope's demeanour so many times, and she couldn't let the little girl just wander off, but the screams and shouts of battle forced her out of her thoughts.

"I see the Leeth arrived before I did. That was to be expected."

"When this is all over, you'll have to tell me what you ended up doing all this time with these folks, boss."

Gimlore scoffed. "Oh, it was nothing much. Just surviving. The usual."

As she said those words, she remembered all the wounds on her back, and all the scar tissue that had made the skin bulbous and deformed under her shirt. A shiver went down her spine. The sound of the whip connecting was still branded in her ears, and the pain it always caused still woke her in the middle of the night, the face of King Doemus always tied to it. The source of her nightmares, he had presented himself as a seasoned statesman when everything he'd ever had was inherited.

I hope that fucker rots in the secret room. But first he needs to scream in madness, starve, and gouge his own eyeballs.

She let out a heavy breath and calmed herself, though her heart still raced.

"Did Keryon not make it?" Nork enquired.

Gimlore rolled her eyes. "Really, Nork? Yes, he fucking made it. He's here somewhere with his smokesmith fellows. Quite the assortment of people."

"And not enough time before the enemy armies strike again."

Gimlore looked at the Tooth, then at Nosema, and then back at the Tooth. "Will you folks help Nork and Nosema? I'm going to go and find my child and then I'll join you."

"It would be our pleasure, right boys and gals?" The Tooth showed his prominent single tooth as he smiled.

"Aye!" they said.

Nork nodded. "Let's go. The units are with regular folks like us, pineheads, and smokesmiths. All mixed up."

"Blimey." The Tooth scratched his head, looking at Gimlore as though to make sure this was what she wanted.

Gimlore nodded, proud to see how much Nork had grown. He was an actual leader now, and he had been paying attention to her all these years in the battlefield. As she jogged up the rocky hills towards where the pineheads had made their home to find Tinko, she just couldn't—or rather, didn't want to—shake off a sense of pride in Nork's revamped mindset. Given the circumstances they had all been thrown in, she was happy for who he'd become.

She only wished Edmir was still here to see it. He'd be damn proud as well.

Keryon shook Ferkin's hand and found himself smiling. "We meet again."

"It appears that way." Ferkin was combat-ready, wearing chain mail under his dark cloak and a small helmet. He had a shield at his back and a sword in his scabbard. If Keryon didn't know who the man was, he'd think Ferkin looked more like a guard knight on duty in a lord's castle than a smokesmith.

"Let's go, boys. They're forming the units now." Chona wore similar apparel, though without the chain mail. With such an imposing figure, Keryon didn't think she needed that much protection anyway.

As Keryon followed them, jogging towards the camp where a few men and women were shouting to get the battle units in order, he found his mouth agape. Not in all his years fighting in the Crimson Wars had he seen such a strange assembly of people. There were raggedy folks carrying agricultural and manufacturing utensils as makeshift weapons. Men and women who were clearly smokesmiths stood around them.

"What in the underworld is going on?" he could only ask.

Preventing Ferkin from answering right away, a dark-haired woman—a smokesmith, he was sure—bellowed for newcomers to split up and join the previous groups.

"The units are already formed!" she screamed. "Look for the Captain and join. We don't have all day."

"And who in the underworld is she?" he muttered.

Ferkin smiled as the three of them and a few others were just arriving at the formations. "That's Fatuna. She's the one

Rednow has been talking to. She wants to create a society for all of us. The Smokesmith Guild, she calls it."

Is that so? he wondered, letting his eyes linger on the woman.

He knew very little about her but found himself a fan already.

For years, he'd believed the smokesmiths didn't need lords. They could organise themselves and work independently. If anything, they could learn from the Leeth when it came to the battlefield as well.

"I wouldn't be opposed to a smokesmith guild," he said.

Ferkin shrugged. "I think there would be too many egos. Too much unchecked power."

"Come on, friend. That's why the good ones are necessary, isn't it?"

Ferkin scratched his head but did not reply.

In front of Keryon was a column of soldiers of all origins. The Leeth had remained out of it, from what Keryon could tell, but it would be interesting to see just how powerful the smokesmiths could be when joining forces with the common folks.

"I suppose we must split up now," he said.

Ferkin nodded. "I'll stay with Chona. She's my Gimlore if you know what I mean."

Keryon cringed and prepared a retort, but Ferkin was already jogging towards one of the units.

He grimaced. *I suppose I should do the same.*

Each unit must have had about twenty to thirty soldiers, but there were a lot of them. He wasn't sure why they had divided the units that way, but he was late to the party, which made him just as late to question their methods.

He glanced at one of the units and approached the man who appeared to be in charge. He was a short pinehead dressed in all-white who wielded a silver spear. The other soldiers in the unit seemed to quiet down when he spoke, which was usually the sign of a good leader. Or one who instilled fear.

"Smokesmith reporting for duty," he said. Truth be told, he didn't know what one was supposed to say in such a situation. "Do you have room for one more?"

"Experience?" the short pinehead asked, assessing him. In the meantime, other units started moving up the slopes.

"Yes. A few years in Mosendel during the Crimson Wars."

"Join us, then. I'm Arkan. We've got smokesmiths and the Leeth on the ground and the Builders in the air."

Keryon frowned. *Who in the underworld were the Builders? And what did he mean "in the air"?*

Arkan must have realised his confusion. "I'm one of the Builders. You call us pineheads, don't you? Anyway, you'll know it when you see it. Just try not to stare, or the enemy will kill you. If you've got no more herbs left to burn, these are the smokesmiths in our unit."

Keryon swallowed but did his best to keep up. How could someone who looked like a child command so much respect? An interesting fellow, this Arkan.

Keryon looked at the rest of the unit and about ten odd people raised their arms. "Good to meet you all."

"Right. What's your name, son?" Arkan asked.

"Keryon."

It was strange to be called son by someone who looked to be a third of his age, but Keryon knew from Arkan's demeanour and the way he spoke this was a leader of people and wise beyond his years.

"Let's march, then," Arkan said. "And if you ever feel like questioning my leadership, you must take it up with the rest of the unit. They all decided I should lead. I didn't impose myself on anyone but as a new member, you will have to do as I say."

"That won't be a problem."

Arkan smiled. "Good. Let's go!"

Off they went, the rocky terrain poking his feet. The weather was nice, with no trace of a cloud in the sky, but the air was crisp and cold, with the wind cooling it even further. Keryon wasn't used to the bloody cold, but jogging like that should get him warm enough.

"Look down there," Arkan said.

On the horizon, a fast-approaching line of enemy soldiers stretched from east to west. The different units on his side were adopting different positions in the terrain, and Keryon realised they were creating a choke point to contain the advance of the armies that were being blocked by the Leeth down just ahead of the base camp.

"They said it's three armies we're facing," someone in the unit muttered.

"And those fucking shadowlings too," said another.

"Which kingdoms?" Keryon asked.

"Shari, Gasho, and Mosendel."

Keryon swallowed. The Mosens just couldn't be trusted. They were the whole reason he had left the country and left his service. "Never thought I'd end up fighting my own country-men."

The others nodded with hums of approval.

But I guess I've always belonged more with other smokesmiths.

With no warning, the battle drums started their hollow rumbling. A slow pace, but gradually picking up. This was what Keryon hated the most in war. The anticipation. The time spent waiting for permission to go. The control he had to have not to render the efforts of his mates useless. He wondered if Gimlore had found her child yet. He should be with her, but she had run so fast, and he was not the child's father, after all. Why would he intrude? Unless she would have wanted him to intrude, in which case...

The drums picked up their pace as the enemy approached. He could see their colours now. Marine blue and brown. Banners and flags showed their allegiances. It made him sick to see once proud nations allying so easily with a mad man like Orberesis.

For the decisions of the ones in charge, the rest are destined to perish.

Someone blew a horn, forcing everyone quiet, and Fatuna's scream echoed.

All the units started moving forward towards the enemy, and Arkan's wasn't an exception. "Smokesmiths, get ready to engage. Builders, stay with me."

Suddenly, Arkan jumped into the air and Keryon could hardly believe his eyes as the man never came down. Instead, he continued soaring, spear in hand. The other pineheads in his unit did the same.

"What the..."

"Remember what Arkan said. Get too distracted and it will cost your life. It can cost us all," one of the smokesmiths said. He was a burly man with his long hair caught in a bun. "I'm Doig, by the way."

"I'm Keryon."

He still couldn't believe it. Was this a secret they had been hiding for centuries? It made no sense. There was still so much he didn't know; so much he had missed when he was busy trying to survive the quarry and escape it.

Now, he didn't have to be in charge. He didn't have lives depending on him. He could just let go and do what he had been bred and trained to do since he was a young boy: burn them all.

He doused the herbs and waited for the smoke to come up to him, then inhaled and allowed himself to enjoy the first blissful moments.

Side by side with his smokesmith brothers and sisters, they faced the troops of Shari. Their soldiers were armed with spears and shields, and Keryon almost found himself smiling as he controlled the smoke in their direction, then promptly ignited it.

One breath. One jump. One death.

Fire, heat, and pain blended in a cacophony of horrific screams, a circus of devastation. He wasn't proud to be a good killing tool, but no one could deny his effectiveness.

As Keryon dodged the enemy spears and hatchets, he used his smoke like a constrictor, twining around the enemies, three or four at a time, then setting them on fire.

The burning men ran, screaming until they died. Many times, they caught their own friends on fire while begging them for aid.

Keryon wouldn't even need a blade.

Above him, the pineheads flew, then dove with their sharp spears pointing at the enemy soldiers, cornering them. This was too much for the Sharivali to take. They were simple men and women, even if they were well organised and trained. This wasn't even close.

The smokesmiths rained chaos upon them.

All around Keryon, the smokesmiths turned into monsters, and others grew longer limbs. Keryon even detected a few special abilities. When the enemy tried to retreat or fight back with long-range weapons like crossbows, the shield bearers came and protected them. Then the pineheads came from above and stabbed with the spears.

This actually works rather well.

Many of them died. It didn't make Keryon feel good. None of it did. This was a mismatch, their numbers far larger. The smokesmiths couldn't fight for much longer before they were incapacitated by the smoke.

He felt it too, the sting in his lungs. The burning in his throat and breathing system. Ironic how the very thing that made him special was also what hurt him the most.

Keryon continued his dance of smoke and fire around the enemy soldiers, halberds, spears, and swords all failing to reach him. He spun, propelled by the smoke, and sent the poisonous fumes towards the enemy before landing on the ground again.

In an instant, he willed the smoke to ignite, and it created a flash of light and heat that burned the soldiers to death.

Taking advantage of the holes in the enemy lines, some of the other units started separating certain groups from their comrades. It was over for these, even if more were sure to come soon.

"Alert!" Fatuna screamed.

Keryon perked his ears, pausing as his unit dealt with another scattered group of enemies. "Shadowlings from the rear!"

Arkan flew to their side. "The shadowlings are coming. Smokesmiths, this is mostly on you."

Keryon swallowed. Last time he had faced the creatures, he had seen how devastating they were. "Just how many shadowlings do the bastards have?" he muttered.

Doig snorted. "Too fucking many. Let's go, friend."

Keryon marched along with the other smokesmiths. He wasn't used to this. Comradery on the battlefield, was it? He had spent years fighting, but he was always feared, and rare were the days he faced a smokesmith that could rival his power. Now here he was, surrounded by others like him.

Shaking those thoughts, he focused on the battle.

Even on a sunny day, the light of the beasts' horns flickered, their growling and roaring ever closer as the fiends ran fast towards the smokesmiths.

Keryon took another whiff of the smoke in preparation for it. He let it flow and weaved it into a big cloud just in front of his unit. "Step back," he said.

The rest of them did as he said and waited. The moment the shadowlings came, rushing madly to find flesh they could sink their teeth into, Keryon ignited the fire and the shadowlings burned. But there were more on their way.

Many more.

"They're not very resistant to the smoke!" Arkan shouted. "Make use of it."

Keryon wiped sweat from his forehead. Was it the heat, the nerves, or was he getting tired already? His time in the quarry had truly weakened him, and the battle was the madness it was always going to be.

Men and women were caught by the shadowlings, despite their abilities. Blood of smokesmiths squirted all over him. The shadowlings bit and shook human bodies like dolls, ripping them in half.

Keryon gritted his teeth, angry for his fallen brethren. He had to be careful lest he ended up suffering the same fate.

The creatures were larger, but also faster than humans. How could this be?

The only silver lining, and one that Keryon had to rely on, was their weakness to his smoke and fire. *What can I do to end this?*

The shadowlings kept tearing at his comrades with their claws and fangs, ripping through cloth and skin like it was nothing. Keryon was covered in blood, his breathing heavy already.

A monstrous smokesmith held two shadowlings with his bare hands, and squeezed them until blood came out. Then he moved along to fight more of the creatures. "Come on, follow me."

Keryon barely recognised the voice, but it was Doig.

For the underworld... He followed the monstrously trans-formed man and continued to manipulate the smoke, creating more fire out of it. The more he did it, the more he realised how unsustainable it was in a large battle, especially when everyone around him was seemingly just as powerful.

"What's your plan?" Doig asked.

Keryon had no clue. He was tiring, and the smoke in his lungs was too much, already taking its toll. Trying not to lose compo-sure, he wondered what Gimlore would do, and that gave him some hope. She'd probably come up with a plan. She'd surely think of something clever, or she'd motivate everyone to keep going. But he didn't have her charisma: he was just following orders.

"Plan is to keep killing them until Arkan says otherwise or until they kill me."

Doig smiled and kneeled. "I like you, friend. Hold on to my back," the giant man said.

Keryon hesitated, but jumped on the man's leathery back and held on to one of the spikes protruding from his spine. Doig was like a berserker, running around and smashing shad-owlings without feeling any pain from their closing maws. He just picked them up and squeezed them, slamming his fists into them as though they were little critters.

From Doig's back, as long as he could hold on, Keryon could still manipulate the smoke. He weaved it around the creatures, like a string tangling around them. The beasts coughed as the fumes entered their nostrils, slowing them down.

It's time.

Keryon ignited the smoke one more time and the string circling the creatures lit up like burning chains of fire, turning them into charred meat.

"Bloody heck, this power of yours is really something to behold, isn't it?" Doig asked.

Keryon could hardly reply. "Yes," he said before a coughing fit took hold of him. He had to stay poised. For there to be a future, he had to keep going. He coughed again and blood came out.

"Are you alright, friend?"

"I've never been better," he lied. Truth was, if it wasn't for Doig carrying him, he'd be halfway to the underworld by now. But everybody else was fighting. Everybody else was doing their best. "Let's keep going."

THIRTY-SEVEN

SECOND CHANCES

REDNOW - SOLVI

Rednow looked into Orberesis' eyes and saw a scared child.

How old could the man be? No more than thirty winters. But his eyes changed suddenly. Sometimes his face shifted, and the innocence vanished.

The Old One is in there. Do you see it? the Essence asked.

Rednow could certainly see something wasn't right with the young man. He wasn't completely hopeless yet, as much as a quick death would probably be the best outcome for everyone.

You're not too far gone, Rednow said. *You can resist him.*

Orberesis shook his head, as though something—or some-one—had corrected an undesired behaviour in a pet.

Shut up, old man. I know what I'm doing.

Rednow grimaced. That was it, then. He couldn't help it.

With no warning, the world around him swirled, though Rednow couldn't feel a thing. Starlight flashed, but he understood it was *he* who had moved, not the world.

He's pulling me again. So this is Temporal Exploration... he pondered.

It's part of it, yes. But don't drop your guard, as much as you think you understand the avatar. He's the Deceiver, after all. It's a suitable name.

A slit of colour and light opened in front of Rednow—like a curtain, but only just enough to allow a nosey neighbour to peak outside—and he was out of the void. Orberesis' plan to drag him there had failed.

Rednow was back where he had encountered Orberesis, but now there was a battle taking place down below. Thousands of soldiers and monsters clashed in a bloody duel. He could see the Builders flying around, dodging crossbow bolts and arrows. The smokesmiths tore through the shadowlings, and the Leeth fought as methodically as ever.

They all answered my call.

Everyone he knew was down there in the pits, with their boots covered in mud and blood spurted across their faces.

Now it's my time to do what I must.

He shielded his spirit with smoke, like a set of full plate armour covering his body. A smoke sword grew in his hand, and he charged at Orberesis with regret, but not pity. With respect, but not fear.

Without a physical body, no aching limbs or burning lungs, he had the expertise of a veteran without the maladies of fighting and getting hurt in old age. Each of his strikes was clean, no movements wasted. Every blow was faster than the previous, and yet his smoke blade stopped before it was about to cut into Orberesis' skin.

It was not for lack of trying, not for lack of strength or ability. There was something more shielding the man.

The Old One's doing, the Essence assured.

"Give up. He's deceiving you. Controlling you."

Rednow struck again. And again.

He moved in a constant flow of motions that played tricks on human eyes, jumping from one form to another before the blink of an eye. Stabbing, cutting, slashing. Like that, he could have torn through an entire army, but he had to face his opponent, who remained unscathed.

"Look who's talking, old man," Orberesis retorted. "She's got you right where she wants you. I might have this parasite in me, but I'm getting something out of it. I'm growing stronger. You? You're half-dead, you said it yourself. What am I to think of it?"

Rednow kept up his momentum.

"It's not about me." This was an attempt at a distraction. He knew every blow he struck hurt Orberesis' defences. Sooner or later, they'd disappear. He had to hurry. "It's never been about me, but about saving everybody else from what the Deceiver wants to do. What you're letting him do."

Orberesis scowled. "Fuck everybody else."

"Have you no friends? Nobody you care about? No family?"

Orberesis remained silent and Rednow struck again, the smoke sword flowing.

"It's over, old man. For you and your god," Orberesis said. Rednow found a sadness in his eyes. It was almost grief.

Orberesis raised his arm and threw a wave of destruction at the mountain top, causing a rockslide. Luckily, it missed the Builders' cove and the base camp.

Rednow panicked. *I need to stop him.*

Was that Temporal Exploration too? Orberesis was increasing the passing of time for whatever that wave of energy hit, turning everything to dust, eroding rocks and killing trees, sending them countless ages into the future before the rest of the world did.

A terrifying power.

Orberesis raised his other hand and did the same thing again.

Rednow used the smoke as a shield against the wave, causing sparks and wind to form between the two, then cancelling each other out. The waves of power rippled between them, but Rednow held firm against Orberesis' own strength. Then the man gritted his teeth. "How dare you stop my judgement?"

That's the Deceiver talking.

Threads of air and smoke shot through the air, hitting the trees, the mountains, and the earth below. Rednow's smoke was the only thing capable of stopping Orberesis.

He quickened his pace. As an undead, there was no struggle, and the power flowed through him. All those years building up his strength in the mountains; the hours spent practicing sword forms, grappling, and other martial arts. Relentlessly. All the sparring and the training he'd hosted. And the Essence's rotten gift: the weightlessness that came with the absence of a physical body. Now, he saw it for the gift it was.

Orberesis twisted the corner of his mouth and snarled.

"I'm sick. And tired. Of your antics." His face changed again, becoming gentler. "I just wanted to see the sunset. Go to a cerro field and stare at the sunset."

Rednow hesitated.

Deception! the Essence snickered.

But how could he not halt? He saw a prisoner, another soul to save. Then the man's snarl returned.

"It's not personal, old man. In fact, I actually like you. We could have been friends in another life. But you get it, don't you? Lives are worthless once they cost too much to save."

Rednow scowled and shook his head. He couldn't defeat the Old One with sheer power. The Deceiver was draining Orberesis' energy—Rednow could see it in the young man's depleted face—but it didn't look like he was done yet.

He remembered the life truths he had learned inside the Inner Flight and how he had defeated himself there. He had seen truth and faced true penance. He had listened to the voice of all things and muted even the Essence. He broke away from the mental boundaries and fences that surrounded him, and a sense of freedom enveloped him, greeted him.

He was... expanded. There was something else in him.

You've awakened him, the Essence said.

"Who?"

Your smoke self.

Rednow felt something stirring. No, *he* was stirring, slithering from side to side. Facing Orberesis now, Rednow could sense it clearly, even in his bodyless self, something large and dark.

Are you ready? A booming, low voice asked.

Rednow jumped. Who was that?

A cloud of dark smoke surrounded him with new, denser threads forming and strengthening in a coordinated way. Then it took shape, that of a long serpent, its body at least forty paces long.

The smoke creature purred like a vicious feline, and its head turned to face Rednow. It was no snake; it was something holier.

A dark dragon of smoke.

Smoke wings grew from his back and the creature flapped them.

"How..."

Then the dragon's voice became his, and the two smoke spirits merged. He felt the smoke dragon, but... there was nothing new. It had been him all along, a hidden part of him.

I'll take over if you don't, the smoke dragon warned.

Confusion and fear ran rampant in his mind.

He could control the dragon, for the dragon was him.

Rednow broke away from the Inner Flight and burst into the sunny sky as a dragon made of thick black smoke. He relinquished himself, his sympathy, and his pity. He put it aside before facing Orberesis again.

In the form of the smoke dragon spirit, Rednow felt the infinity in everything. Every thought, every idea. He experienced sadness, the abyss of his self. He faced incredible horror and fear, channelling it all into an anger targeted at his enemy.

He could see Orberesis' glow now, a darker one, as the man snarled. "What is this form? You cannot escape your fate, old man. You can't withstand the storm."

Rednow roared back. "I AM THE STORM."

He would teach him that even the gods should run when they saw the Blood Collector.

....

Solvi walked slowly, limping, her face a constant grimace. Even with the bloody elixir Gimlore had given her, the pain still hadn't gone away. She bit her tongue and carried on, cradling her crying son in her arms. That poor girl Hope walked fearfully next to her.

"Gimlore said we were supposed to stay back," Hope said. The girl was smart, she had to give her credit for that. "Miss?"

Solvi looked at her and gently shook her head, doing her best to contain the pain. Gimlore had warned her there would be a lot of pain in the days after birth. There was cramping and generalised discomfort, but she could withstand that. It was as though her innards were contracting again, moving back to where they had been before the child was born.

She looked at her son. He was beautiful, almost enough to make her forget the pain. Now cleaned up, he was so small. His tiny hands stretched and contracted, and he cried as Solvi rocked him gently up and down against her chest. "Fussy little one, come on now," she whispered.

But the gorgeous baby didn't settle, no matter what she did. It didn't matter, she had a purpose.

"We should have stayed back in Gimlore's camp," the little girl insisted.

"There is something I must do," Solvi said. "But you have nothing to fear."

She realised how unbelievable that must have sounded. A pain-ridden woman in a bloodied nightgown carrying a new-born baby through a war camp, tailed by a little girl. In the corner of her eyes, she caught the smithies, the carpenters, and other weary folks eyeing her, exchanging glances and murmuring among them, but many nodded to her. There was no bad blood. No killing intent. She powered through the pain. The closer she could get to the front lines, the better.

"I don't think so, lady." A man stood in her way. He was dark-skinned and had long, bushy hair trapped inside a red bandana. "It's not me. But I have orders not to let a specific young mother and a young child anywhere near the camp."

Solvi frowned. "Orders from who?"

"Gimlore."

Solvi was halfway between crying and smiling. "But I must confront him. I can stop him in his madness. If I show him his son..."

The man shook his head and placed his hand on her back. "He's too far gone. Don't you think he'd try to take the baby away from you now that you're on our side? Or maybe that he'd try to harm you both in revenge?"

"He wouldn't..." Solvi said, though she realised she couldn't guarantee it. This man's dark, piercing eyes saw through her, and she looked away.

"You and the child can stay with me for now. I'm Nosema, by the way. My twin brother Nork is back there." He pointed at one of the tents. "Come. We've got food and tea. You don't have to come if you don't want to. You can go back to Gimlore's camp. But I cannot let you get to the frontlines. It's too dangerous, for both you and the child."

Solvi sighed, all her prior determination gone. She followed Nosema to a small bench where he covered her with a blanket and gave her a cup of tea. It was the worst tea she had ever had, but she thanked him anyway.

"Before you say anything, I know the tea is bad. But it's not like there isn't a battle going on. Both on the ground and up there," Nosema said, his index finger pointing to the sky.

Solvi nodded and passed the tea down to Hope. "Do you like it?"

The little girl had a sip and grimaced. "It's worse than the one we had in prison, which was already worse than rainwater from a muddy puddle."

A smile formed on Solvi's face, and the child finally quieted. "That's a good boy," she whispered before giving him a gentle kiss in the tiny forehead.

A roaring sound came from the skies and a large dark creature appeared far in the distance. She gasped as did many of the people around her. Was that... a dragon?

That must be Rednow.

A small figure stood next to the dragon and Solvi couldn't see exactly what was happening, but there were ripples of light and power all around them.

She snarled just thinking about him. This was all he stood for, now—death and destruction. He had invaded Heleronde, taking countless lives to the underworld. Now he wanted to rally against the world, having completely forgotten his son for the sake of divinity and his greed.

What had she been thinking? She had allied herself with Keryon and Gimlore, her previous captors, but it was as though she saw the world much more clearly on this side of the fence. Gimlore had no reasons to aid her but had still helped her give birth and provided her with a kind of companionship Solvi never even realised she needed.

"So, have you chosen a name for him?" Hope asked.

Solvi shook her head. "I have a name in mind. Why do you ask?"

"May I suggest Hopo?" Hope's lips stretched into a mischievous smile.

Solvi giggled, trying not to wake him. "That's an interesting suggestion, but I have plenty of time to think about it."

With Gimlore, she didn't have to treat anyone like her superior. Nobody expected devotion, admiration, or even loyalty. No soul wanted to use her as a weapon. They had plenty of smoke-smiths on their side already. Here, Solvi could just be herself. A woman, a mother. And maybe, if she was lucky enough to have a second chance, a friend.

THIRTY-EIGHT

INTO BATTLE

GIMLORE - NORK - KERYON

Gimlore made her way through the madness.

There were people fighting people and people fighting creatures. There was chaos in the sky, with pinehead spearmen flying above her, using their weapons to stab enemy soldiers like falcons diving for prey.

To the east, the Leeth soldiers wore all black as they held back the enemy armies. To the west, the mountains closed the line. The wind was almost as loud as the metal clashing with metal. Weapons tore through flesh and bone, leaving men and women to squeal in pain before their bodies became lifeless, nothing more than debris covering the ground as Gimlore jogged through it.

Blood stained her clothes. Thankfully none of it her own.

From left to right, she looked again and again, but she couldn't find Pinesy nor Tinko.

Bloody fucking underworld. Why would Pinesy bring the child into fucking battle?

She couldn't stay back as her only child was left out there, in the middle of the chaos. She would find them and drag them back out into safety.

It made her think of Thata, who hadn't even had a proper burial because of Orberesis and his shadowlings. She strengthened the grip on the hammer and kept jogging. There was a strong hint of smoke in the air all around her.

It was a sight to behold. Smokesmiths fighting together, listening to each other respectfully and helping other soldiers. Pineheads flying overhead. It was like she was dreaming, or as if she had been transported to another world.

A large creature locked eyes on her. A shadowling. Grey, and with slithery skin. It opened its mouth, displaying a thousand long and sharp teeth. The beast snarled and, for once, Gimlore didn't hesitate to charge at it. She was going to shatter its skull in half and that was all there was to it. No hesitation, her body moved on its own.

Just as the creature's long claws were about to reach her, she dodged the blow and stuck the hammer on its skull, immediately causing the beast to drop into the floor. That had been a lucky strike, though.

For Thata...

She fought back tears, but they insisted on flowing down her face. She wiped them with her arm, her sleeve turning red. Blood.

Am I bleeding?

The creature's claws must have reached her and she hadn't even felt it in all that chaos.

She stumbled her way through the crowd, looking for Tinko and Pinesy. It shouldn't be hard to find them. They'd be shorter than nearly all the other people in there, and yet she couldn't find them anywhere. Along the way, she would occasionally jump in to help soldiers who were struggling against the enemy.

The frontlines were close, but it looked like Rednow's forces were enough of a match for the others. It would have been a very different story if the Gashoine troops had been all called into battle as well.

Her heart pounded in anticipation. *Where is Tinko?* How she longed to see the child. To hug them and maybe even scratch their head tenderly.

I've become so fucking soft.

In the middle of the battlefield, she wound up cornered by enemy soldiers wearing brown uniforms. Two started to make their way towards her with long spears.

Shit.

Her hammer was powerful in her hand, but it didn't have the reach to counter the quick stab of a spear. And to make matters worse, she didn't have a shield or anyone else in there to protect her.

No, I can't die here. This can't be how I go.

But there were three of them now, snarling and roaring as they ran towards her.

She tried to run, to force her way out of that trap. Between rocks and other soldiers, she had nowhere to go, until a cloud of smoke came from the sky and landed in front of her, facing the two enemies.

As the two men were distracted by the newcomer, she was about to make a run for it, but she caught a glimpse of this smokesmith and stopped in her tracks, her heart fluttering. She nearly lost all the strength in her legs.

"Tinko?"

The smokesmith moved like lightning, appearing and disappearing from their previous position on the battlefield. But Gimlore saw it. The shaggy hair was longer now, and the child looked taller after all the months she'd been away. The features had firmed up and clearly... Rednow's teaching had paid off.

Upon hearing her call, the child glanced sideways, and their eyes bulged as Tinko stared at her. "Mother?"

Gimlore's eyes poured like a fountain.

She broke down, worse than she ever had. Tinko was grown. A powerful smokesmith, handling multiple enemy soldiers at once. Behind them, a pinehead landed with a thump. Pinesy. He faced her, eyes still the same old glittering nightmare, but his mouth showed the hint of a smile. A smile that asked, 'Aren't you proud?'.

She burst into tears.

Tinko got rid of those soldiers in swift movements and Gimlore did what she could not to lose her wits entirely. She was still in a bloody battlefield. It got worse when Tinko approached her. She eyed the child from top to bottom, all grown and strong. She reached with her hand and caressed their face before they were interrupted again by the ruckus of battle.

"Mother, it's not safe. You must go back."

She chuckled. "I should be the one saying that, you little shit."

"I can handle myself." Tinko smiled and looked away, then back at her. "Let me take care of you, then. You must be careful not to breathe my smoke."

Gimlore was overwhelmed but the hole in her heart she had tried to ignore was now filling up again. Tinko was no longer the little brat responsible for so many of her headaches. They had been forced to grow up so much in such a short period. That thought brought her back to reality.

That had been her failure.

"Let's get you to safety, Mother."

"Me?" Gimlore shook her head. So, this was what being an old woman was like: sentimental, overly attached, and being underestimated by her children. She did not give a shit, though. "I'm not leaving your side."

Tinko's eyes glimmered with pride. The child nodded and focused on the battle ahead. Gimlore smiled and tightened the grip on her hammer, as though she had been rejuvenated or regained strength. She turned to Pinesy, just as another batch of enemies approached. "Thank you. For everything. Truly."

Pinesy smiled but shook his head. "Nothing to thank me for."

Gimlore stayed quiet. That wasn't true. Pinesy had single-handedly saved both Rednow and Tinko. He deserved some fucking credit, and when this was all over, she would make sure he got it.

The enemy was upon them and Gimlore stood back-to-back with her child. "Let's do this."

⋯⋯⋯

The wind blew strong as Nork jogged back onto the battlefield. His brother had preferred to stay behind, looking after that troubled woman and the little girl. Nosema hated fighting as much as he did, perhaps even more. In this case, Nork *needed* to fight. He needed to prove he could be a leader like Gimlore, especially now that she was around. He wanted revenge for Eshof.

One day, I'll have peace, but not today.

He continued to jog from the base camp and towards the battlefield, slowed down by the rocks that could break his ankles if he wasn't careful. He would give everything to trade the daggers for kitchen knives and a chopping board, but the peace of the kitchen would have to wait.

When he reached the battlefield, he clasped his spear tightly and made sure the hatchet was still hanging from his belt. He stood on a rock, glancing over the entire battlefield. The Leeth had already finished the remnants of the Gashoine troops, which had been weaker than he would have imagined. The most active points of battle were to his right, next to the cliffs. The shadowlings were almost all gone as well now, but that hadn't been without cost.

There are never winners in this.

Nork wasn't a religious man, but he prayed for those that had given their lives to save others. Edmir. Eshof. Thata. There were so many others he couldn't even count. None of them deserved to be fodder, bodies to be trampled on.

A large dragon soared above, its enormous maw striking at Orberesis, though the bastard held on well enough. Their colliding powers caused ripples of light and waves of energy and wind strong enough to affect even the ground below. But the booming sounds caused by those two could only mask the chaotic cacophony of death that was underway on the ground.

With a deep breath, Nork pushed himself forward, forcing courage.

For the gods, he hated fighting. There was no glory. No benefit.

The dreadfulness got worse as he marched straight at it. He found a pocket of enemies that seemed to be winning against a foot unit of smokesmiths and other soldiers. The former looked tired, and their breathing was heavy. It would take time until the Leeth mercenaries could arrive, so that seemed like a good enough place for him to go.

Courage? More like insanity.

He grunted as his spear pierced an opponent's stomach. He pulled the pole back and stabbed him in the face as well. *Should have worn chain mail.*

The man's comrades turned to Nork with their own weapons. Spears and axes and swords, all turning on him, forcing Nork to seek refuge with another allied unit.

"Who are you?" A smokesmith looked at him through the corner of his eye as he extended his limbs and slammed three soldiers harshly against the rocky floors.

Nork shrugged. "Don't worry about me. I'm nobody. You won't even know I'm here."

⋯⋯⋯

Keryon's lungs ached but he had not felt so alive in a long time. He had his limits, of course, and the heat of battle wouldn't keep him alive when the battle was over. Looking at the other smokesmiths, they looked in even worse shape, some starting to fall back and ignoring the unit leaders.

He gritted his teeth. Not him.

They needed this. The smokesmiths needed to see how much they could accomplish on their own, by fighting united. When the battle was over, they would organise and start the Smokesmith Guild or Smokesmith Society, or whatever Fatuna had talked about. He *needed* to make that happen. It was time for them to fight for their own interests, not on behalf of a lord or a monarch who didn't even know their names.

That only infuriated him more.

One breath. One jump. One death.

His breath was full and the smoke burned all the way from his tongue down to the depths of his chest, but the jump was glorious. He ignited the smoke as soon as the enemy had tried to catch him. One death.

"You're not half bad at this, are you?" Doig asked, next to him.

Keryon forced a smile. "I could say the same about you."

They'd been fighting together for a while, and Keryon's injuries were more internal than external, but that was only possible because of the beast Doig had turned into. He marched through the battlefield knocking soldiers over, taking the brunt of the damage. Keryon knew that even with leather-like skin, it would still hurt. Doig would probably need to spend days in an infirmary later, when the battle ended. Still, he continued to fight with reckless abandon, like he didn't count on waking the next day.

Above his head, Rednow had turned into a smoke dragon, somehow, while attacking Orberesis from multiple angles as the dark smoke cast a shadow over the battlefield. *If the old man is giving his best, how can I not?*

To think Keryon had thought Rednow to be a coward, someone who had abandoned his masters out of cowardice! Now here he was, leading the Known World's smokesmiths in battle.

"How long can you keep going?" Doig asked as he snapped the neck of a brown-uniformed man.

"A little longer," Keryon said, though he knew the smokesmiths would have to pull back soon. The thought gave him pause. The pineheads were effective, but they spent much of their time dodging arrows and crossbow bolts, and few could fly. That meant the Leeth would have to take over this side of the battlefield, but they had started battling long before Keryon had.

They must be exhausted.

A shiver went down his spine. He had been confident, but now he wasn't sure he should have been.

He jumped in the air, lifted by the smoke, spun, and created a wheel of smoke around him with his arms, then extended his limbs outward in mid-air, and the smoke that surrounded him was blasted in all directions. He ignited it.

The heat consumed the sky and burned the flesh of the enemy soldiers that had been gathering around him, but it also burned his lungs, his throat, and everything else in between. The heat also caught his face, already covered in burn marks. Instinctively, he reached with his hand to protect it.

Doig took a step back, and Keryon noticed just how hard the man was breathing, even in that monstrous form. To his side, the other smokesmiths were in a similar predicament. Some were falling to their knees, others using their last bits of energy to flee to the base camp.

The enemy soldiers were tired as well, but they had been patient and still had the numbers in their favour. It was as though they had been told to wait it out for the smokesmiths to get too tired to fight.

Keryon understood, then, the challenges the Smokesmith Society would face in a better future. The wars they were to fight would have to be short and sweet or they would still need help.

He spat blood and his legs buckled. His knees bent and he dropped on to the muddy ground. His worst nightmare had come.

He couldn't fight any longer.

Just as he thought he and his smokesmith brethren were doomed to fall to a weaker opponent, a roar came from the enemy soldiers. Black figures, wielding hammers, axes, swords, and spears, marched towards the rear of the enemy lines. Keryon's eyes lit up as the glimmer of hope emerged again.

The Leeth had come.

Thirty-Nine

Soaring Skies

Merey - Rednow

Merey charged at their rear. At this point in the battle, there was little room for strategy. It was mostly roars, snarls, and bravery.

There's always something we can do, Rednow had told her. Even when it didn't seem possible. They had finished the remnants of the Gashoine forces, and allowed the survivors to flee since they were too few to organise and stage a comeback.

She could have ordered the Leeth to move to the front lines quicker, through the short route along the cliffs. Perhaps it would have even saved a few more lives, but she had ordered them to move the long way around to find the enemy from the back, trapping it in the middle.

I hope the smokesmiths can still move.

She had Tellwoon on her mind, as always, who was still a beginner in the arts of smokesmithing, so she tired easily.

"First unit, to the left," she bellowed. "Second unit, to the right. Make room for the hounds to come through the middle."

Her remaining units split. She saw the blood and sweat on their faces and battle uniforms, the dried face paint, and the tallow half washed away by the sweat. They were bloody tired, too. They had been fighting for far too long.

It was time to end this.

She whistled and ducked, and the rest of the Leeth did the same. The ground shook as the horde of Zatak's bloodsleuths dug their paws in the mud and raced towards the enemy. They had never latched their teeth onto a Leeth soldier, but it was still good to be sure that would always be the case.

The beasts came thrashing, roaring, and gnarling as they raced towards their new prey. The enemy soldiers raised shields and tried to push back into the smokesmiths and the pineheads, but they were trapped in there, alone with the hounds.

"Let's finish them!" Merey said as she got up. She had failed in her initial plan of ambushing the Gashoine armies, so now she had to make up for it. "Come on, crescent moon formation. Crescent moon!"

The units obeyed with not a word of hesitation. They knew what to do. These movements had been drilled into them for years. First with Rednow, and then with her. They moved swiftly, not only to shield the faltering smokesmiths on the front lines, but also to trap the enemy inside, forcing them to huddle and eventually yield.

Merey smiled, still thinking of Tellwoon and the smoke. This was what their life was supposed to be. Children and a quiet life never suited them, and it never would. They had been made for war, and war was what they did. After this, everything would change. Lords in Ainis, Mosendel, Shari, Gasho, and the Two Nations would scramble for power. With weakened or nullified armies, they would be exposed and weakened. That was also an opportunity to bring meaningful change to the world.

Of course, for anything to change, Rednow would have to win.

Merey allowed herself to look at the sky, sizing up the massive smoke dragon Rednow had become. Half a year ago, she would have questioned how that was even possible, but she had learned a great many things since then, most of which didn't make sense at all.

It wouldn't make sense for men to make miracles, or to be possessed by ancient deities. Or to fly overhead. And yet, they did.

The dragon moved effortlessly, but Orberesis showed no signs of slowing down. If anything, he seemed to be getting stronger, as though he'd been biding his time, building up for a final strike. They couldn't allow the world to fall into his hands. If he won, he would be left controlling most of the Known World and he'd bring devastation in the form of those vicious fish-heads.

Merey gritted her teeth but shook away those thoughts. *Why do I think so bloody much when I'm on the battlefield?*

Oddly enough, battle was where she found her peace and her strength. All those months preparing, strategizing, and scheming, but then the battle had come, and she was ready for it. As ready as she'd ever be. It was a slow, cathartic release of tension on her back.

No enemy could defeat the Leeth.

Her units did what they did best, and Merey barely had to intervene. They squeezed out the enemy soldiers and a few of the Leeth on the back rows pulled out their crossbows, pointing them at the enemy.

There was dread and despair written all over their faces. The realisation they had lost or were about to lose started dawning on them. Merey just wished Tellwoon was there to share it with her. She would probably be making plans for the future of the Leeth and thinking about how many opportunities they'd have with the entire Known World in disarray. There would be a lot of gold spent in exchange for the Leeth's services.

"We yield!" an enemy soldier said as he dropped his sword and raised his arms. "We yield."

A smile formed on Merey's lips.

More enemy soldiers dropped their weapons, but she kept her units with crossbows pointed in case they were pulling a stunt. Dark rings formed around their eyes, their faces sunken, dread keeping them looking at the rocky ground beneath lest they were confronted with the dead bodies of their comrades.

Merey realised how many dead there were. Hundreds, perhaps even thousands, also counting the dead smokesmiths and the odd pinehead that hadn't been lucky enough to avoid the arrows. She would need to do a head count, but she had lost plenty of her own too, which was always bittersweet, even as relief shot through her.

She looked at the sky.

We did it, old man. Now it's up to you.

Nothing was working as Rednow soared the skies, plunging at Orberesis with balls of smoke and sheer strength. He could see the colour drain from Orberesis' eyes, but the young man's teeth remained gritted even as he sweated and held Rednow's blows back.

Rednow struggled to withstand the energy waves the Old One shot at him.

Smoke can't be aged forward, only if you thin it, the Essence said in his head.

"If you've got any other ideas, now would be a good time to try them," he said.

What the Essence had said made sense. The waves were meant to age the things they touched so much they caused them to turn to ash or dust, so the smoke could block the wave before it disappeared. But Rednow couldn't just rely on nullifying his blows, since the Old One was shielding Orberesis from the smoke.

You turned into the dark smoke dragon. Act like it.

Rednow filled up with anger and, for once, he decided to listen to the Essence.

He struck Orberesis again. His sense of self was strange without a real body, but it was solid enough to cause damage to spare. In the smoke dragon form, Rednow circled Orberesis, catching his waves of passing time. He had given up pitying the man. Only death was on the table now.

Rednow roared and gnarled as he used his enormous maw to bite at Orberesis again. He tightened the bite. Again. Again. It didn't give, as much as Orberesis struggled to contain it.

The Old One is draining the avatar's energy to stay alive. He's planning something.

Rednow knew that much.

He kept on, his smoke wings blending with the sky. Power surged in him, embedding in his soul. Rednow reached for it, and the smoke wings grew out further, smoke separating itself from him and lunging towards Orberesis at first, and then in all directions.

Yes. Tap into it, the Essence said.

Rednow did so and he felt others in there. Men and women who had been the Essence's avatars ages ago. Each of them lent Rednow something. Speed. Strength. Power.

Around him, the smoke continued to expand until Orberesis fought back.

The man flailed his arms, and Rednow had to concentrate and use the smoke to block the time waves. The blue sky received a grey tint and Rednow soared the skies, spreading the smoke, laying the foundation for something bigger. Something grander.

"Give up, old fool. You can't defeat somebody like me," Orberesis said. "I will have my power. I will help my people."

Rednow's anger only increased upon hearing those words. How many more people did he need to kill to accomplish his dreams? *Enough!*

"Your people? You've *killed* your people!"

The smoke continued to grow in all directions and Rednow knew it was time to try another move. He tapped into the Essence itself. What was left of her. He found her in the rocks, in the trees, in the dirt, in the air, in the wind. The flowers, the creatures all around.

What if he became the Essence for a time?

The smoke grew and expanded, surrounding Orberesis and the battlefield. It clouded the skies above the camp in a blanket of darkness. The threads of smoke grew even as Orberesis continued to unleash vast waves of passing time.

Rednow grew as well to nullify Orberesis' power.

The shape of the smoke dragon expanded. The head tripled in size, and the neck elongated threefold, along with the tail and wings.

Rednow flew above the mountains and the forests. "Now make yourself useful."

The Essence scowled but had no response.

Under him, the green forests grew. The foliage thickened and the water coursed steadier. Creatures of all shapes and sizes came out of their burrows, and birds chirped in the trees.

Rednow turned back to Orberesis. "I'm growing back what you seek to destroy. It's pointless, don't you see?"

Orberesis gritted his teeth. "No... I don't..."

He seemed to want to say something that was perhaps being filtered out by the Old One's presence. Curse the bastard. It didn't matter.

"I know you're in there. That you can hear me," Rednow said, hoping the Old One would hear it. "I know what your sister has done to you. I know your pain."

Rednow, what are you doing?

Be quiet, he thought.

"Lies!" Orberesis hissed. It had to be the Old One speaking.

"No lies. I know how she sought to reap recognition and glory for herself. How she overshadowed your existence. And even when you acted nicely, she shunned you. She fought you, as she still does, through me."

"Why do you fight on her behalf, then?" Orberesis' face was twisted and contorted unnaturally. "Why?!"

"Because neither of you are right, but we still need you both. Believe me when I say I know the extent of her pride. My sister fell into her treachery. But we need the balance the two of you provide the world. You can't leave us alone with her."

Orberesis scowled. "Humanity has already made its choice. Your Ancient Ones, the Builders, sided with her. They still do. Same for the humans. My sister and I have committed atrocities freely. I would be lying if I said I feel regrets, but I imagine that there is little she regrets as well. Seeing everything we fought for being destroyed by one another only makes us angrier. It made everything we accomplished in this land seem almost futile. So, now I have little desires left. My wishes to be adored and worshipped by you and your people are gone. Now, there's only one thing I want. And I will get it."

"And what is that?" Rednow asked as the smoke continued to grow, stalling.

"My brethren. The Lantern Horns. Their world is dying. They welcomed me when I was rejected by this world. Now, they need my help, and I must bridge these two worlds to bring them over to safety."

"And enslave humanity."

Orberesis scowled. "Humans *already* enslave each other. You kill each other, take each other's children, and force them to breathe my sister's filthy smoke. But you have a problem with the Lantern Horns because they look different? Because they don't speak your languages? Such hypocrisy, but none of that surprises me."

What are you doing, Rednow? Why are you trying to reason with him? Stop it!

He didn't want it, but the Old One's words sounded too right.

Rednow's parents had been enslaved before they were killed. He and Rebma had been captured as orphans and taken to be turned into smokesmiths. He understood the pain, the injustice.

"It doesn't have to be this way. With our power, it's possible to break the chain. I did it. I escaped from the smokesmiths and built my own army. I used to get paid by kings and used their money to save and sustain the people they abandoned. My friend Gimlore has become a host for refugees, giving them a second chance at life. We're not all destined for war. There can be peace if we want it. If we work towards it. We can share this world with the Lantern Horns if we can reach an agreement for peace."

Rednow, no!

The Old One scowled. "I can see why she picked you. She always had an eye for the honourable types. It fits her ego well enough. You say you broke the chain, but you're still doing her bidding. That's a chain you can never break, boy. No. It's too late for peace. I don't want it anymore. I'm powerful again, now, and my sister is in the way, so I must go through her. Through you."

"You're just as prideful as she is," Rednow said. The smoke continued to expand around them, darkening the sky. "You're both terrible gods. You lie and manipulate us to do your bidding. For what? Your goals are incomprehensible."

Orberesis laughed. "After so long, it's easy to get bored. There is so much winning, so much losing. You grow stale. After securing this much power, you have to invest so much in making sure you keep it. Do you think I care about what you think of me? You might perceive us as terrible, but you are rare amongst your people for even having the privilege of talking to us. You're nothing to me. No more than the grass you step on is to you. It's there, always there, but you don't think about it. You might think us terrible gods, but we were never meant to appease your needs. *You* were meant to appease ours. So, know your place or I'll enlighten you."

The Inner Flight, Rednow! Steady your mind!

"My place? I've been told to know my place my entire life, and yet here I am, facing a god. One so weak he needs to infiltrate the body of the same kind he despises. You're not above me. This is where I belong. And I'm going to show you."

The sky darkened completely, and the smoke circled Orberesis' body, thread after thread, ripples of energy flowing from it as the shield around the body wavered, about to crack. Even with the shield, the man looked ragged, as though he was already half-dead. One by one, more ripples formed on top of each other, pressuring the Old One's shield. They built and strengthened. Rednow weaved them with his beating wings.

Crash, you fool. This will be your doom.

FORTY
LIFE AND DEATH

ORBERESIS - REDNOW

The air around Orberesis was thin, or perhaps that was just his lungs having trouble breathing. There was a tightness in his chest, and his eyes were blurry. Something pressured him from the inside but also from outside his body. He was being squeezed in a giant tug of war and there was nothing he could do to free himself.

There is always a cage, he realised as the pain grew. *No matter how far I run.*

Around him, a million threads of smoke darker than the night created a ring that tightened and tightened with every passing second, like a serpent strangling its prey.

Lightheaded, he was close to death. People were talking around him, perhaps Rednow, but he couldn't hear anything. At times, his consciousness wavered only to come back a second later, but every time it did, the excruciating pain came back.

Orberesis tried to flail his arms to free himself from the smoke, but it didn't work. Somehow, the smoke was too concentrated, in multiple layers, like reinforced steel.

Am I going to die here?

Maybe it was alright if he did. His father was long gone. Tavanar in the quarry. Solvi... Somehow, he knew she wasn't gone. She was out there, somewhere, bearing his child.

My child... How could I have forgotten?

Yes, he had nearly forgotten he was going to be a father. And Solvi was the best mother he could hope for. No, he couldn't die. He needed to live for the sake of his baby.

"For my child..." he muttered.

"He's born," Rednow said.

What?

"What... did you say?" He managed to ask.

"I heard it's a boy," the smoke dragon muttered.

Lies! And what does it matter? Think of the power, Doi!

It didn't make sense. Solvi was supposed to be in Sirestir, in the safety of the Two Nations, with Doemus. His heart pounded harder as he came to expect the word. Had they captured Solvi and the child? *A boy! It's a boy!*

"How do you know?"

"Solvi gave birth. Gimlore helped her."

What was Solvi doing with Gimlore? It made no sense.

They're all in it together, Doi. I told you! She's a smokesmith. She betrayed you!

That was the only possible option. "Did she..? Is she..?"

"Solvi is down there with the child. With our troops. She did the sensible thing. The *only* sensible thing."

The hole in Orberesis' chest tightened almost as hard as the squeeze from the smoke. His breathing was harsh in the middle of it all. Rednow had to be bluffing. Solvi would never betray him like that. Why? Why bring his child to a battlefield?

None of it made sense, and yet... it all made sense.

Solvi had always been a smokesmith and weak of mind, prone to manipulation. But to think she would go as far as allowing a despicable woman such as Gimlore the honour of helping with the birth... He couldn't bare it.

I told you!

The hole in his chest slowly filled with anger at Solvi for betraying him, and at himself for allowing her the weakness of mind.

"There really is no hope in humanity, is there?" he asked, not really expecting anyone to answer.

Rednow stayed silent, building his pathetic smoke threads. The Old One didn't dare to say anything either. Solvi had been the only sliver of hope he had had left. Having a child could have been the start of a new way of life, of ruling the world and learning how to be a good man by teaching his son how to be one. But Solvi had chosen to be against him. She had stolen his right to see his son, to meet him. She was trying to keep the child away from him.

"There is no such thing as loyalty. There is only self-interest," he said, unsure if anybody was listening.

As those words left him, he felt himself waking up, his mind steadying with the anger. It was as though his strength was coming back. His mind cleared; his body strengthened. He wasn't powerless. He was powerful! A demi-god at the very least. There was still so much he could do. But as he grew, so did his anger and his resentment.

His pain.

If he was going to be alone anyway, then he would choose power over people. Power over everyone that stood in his way of obtaining it.

"You're a pain, but you're really all I've got," Orberesis said.

The Old One laughed and Orberesis felt his excitement. *I'm always here and I'm always right.*

Orberesis cleared his mind, focusing on his truths.

Happiness was impossible.

People meant pain.

Love didn't exist.

Friends could not be trusted.

Only power was worth pursuing.

They sounded true, but he repeated them to himself like a mantra anyway, and it didn't take long for him to believe them all. They became the truth—his truth.

He fixated on that, on those few words that mattered and what they meant. He then raised his hand and traced his fingers in the air, feeling for threads. *Am I ready?*

You never know until you try, the Old One said, excitement oozing from his voice. *You're stronger than I gave you credit for. You've always surpassed my expectations. Now it's time you soar with me and rise to your rightful status.*

It was a difficult choice, and it was as though Orberesis was keen on letting the anger choose in his stead.

The world as he knew it, with Doemus, his son, Solvi, and all his followers?

He had no place in it. No, he couldn't possibly go back without setting the rest of the world in a frenzy. In fact, he had made his choice a long time ago, when he discovered the greatness of soaring in the void, the weightlessness that Temporal Exploration provided. The Old One had been right all along. It was time to find new worlds. Yes, he would find a place where they respected him and adored him, but first he needed to help the Old One defeat the Essence.

Orberesis found a thread in the air in front of him and pulled it gently. This time, it wasn't smoothness that followed. He resisted the pull of the void. Instead, he tugged at it and used the last strength he had left to pull. With teeth clenched and his muscles flexed to their limit, he pulled until the loose thread of the void ruptured and created an enormous fissure that quickly started to suck the smoke Rednow had created.

Yes! The Old One bellowed. *Yes, Doi! That's it. Keep going.*

Rednow cursed himself and his powerlessness as a large rift opened in the sky. It was a big vast greyness, with a dark whirlpool in the middle. Looking through it, he could see the stars and he knew where it led—he had been there. Orberesis had called it the void.

REDNOW! You must stop him. Now!

As much as he tried to do just that, the rift in the sky continued to absorb his smoke. Even the threads he had placed around Orberesis had turned out useless. *He* had been useless. He flapped his long wings away from the rift lest he get sucked into it as well. There were too many lives depending on him. He needed to make sure this excuse of a man didn't destroy humanity.

"This is your fault, so stay bloody quiet."

For better or worse, the Essence was probably desperate enough to do anything he wanted if it meant victory here. Perhaps she was as clueless as Rednow. After the growth spurt, and the smoke rings, he didn't know what else to do. He had thought he could beat Orberesis by wearing out his energy but learning about his son seemed to have had the absolute opposite effect on the man. And the Old One was too old and too sly to change his mind or fall for any traps.

The rift grew in front of Rednow. He had also tried to reason with Orberesis, and it hadn't worked. He had tried to beat him with force, also to no avail.

I may not win. It dawned on him. *I might lose.*

But if he did... he needed to make sure everyone who had fought for him survived. This had never been about him anyway.

Orberesis could almost taste it, the full potential of his power. What he could become. What the Old One had once been in his glory days, ages before he turned parasite.

As the rift grew, it started swallowing the air and the clouds. It started pulling the trees, leaves first, then branches, then trees themselves, swallowing them whole.

He held onto that power of the rift and fostered it, cultivating it until it was a part of him. Time was a fickle concept now. He understood its passing, but it was like a flower petal, dancing in the wind. It was easy to manipulate, and easy to tame now that he knew the truths of the world and the truths of his self.

Yes, Doi! Claim it! It's YOUR power!

Pathetically, the smoke dragon flew around him pointlessly as his smoke faded. There was nothing else he could do now. Orberesis had outgrown him.

He breathed in that power and understood it better. It was the same power which had protected him this entire time—the invisible wall that had shielded him from the smoke. He existed in different places and in different times. Part of him belonged to the void.

He could not be defeated if that was the case.

No one could defeat this physical representation of his self as long as other pieces were out there.

"You did this, didn't you?" he asked the Old One. "All those trips to the void."

The Old One giggled. *You needed to get used to it. Temporal Exploration requires blending your existence with the void to an extent.*

Orberesis smiled, finally understanding. "You looked after me. It seems like you were the only one."

The Old One laughed again, as though he'd said the funniest of jokes.

Now Orberesis needed to strike where it hurt them the most. It was inevitable. His only choice left.

⸳⸳⸳⸳⸳⸳⸳

Rednow enveloped the battle camp with his smoke as he flew. The dragon form he had adopted started to shed the smoke.

I'm losing. I don't have enough strength.

There was no reply from the Essence. No suggestion. Nothing left in her.

He glanced down at the battle camp. He could see the surviving armies preparing to flee as the rift continued to grow. Brave men and women were reduced to cowardice in the face of reality. Rednow could sense it, the blood of thousands that would cover the earth again. The smell of death looming in the air. Death, wrath, and pain.

He was alone this time.

He was the last of his family line, scarred by war. Having seen only darkness, he had sought light, but now with his family dead and his loved ones in danger, he had to die in their stead.

Using whatever power and smoke he had left, he dipped, flying low into the human crowds, and creating a curtain of smoke over them.

He's going to strike, Rednow!

Rednow knew it, but he couldn't stop it.

A giant beam struck, lighting up the sky with a rumble of ten thousand thunders. Rednow felt the pull of the void and couldn't resist it. Orberesis had created a blast large enough to destroy the camp and him included, but hopefully the smoke he had left behind would serve as a shield and help them escape.

I've failed.

He had failed Rebma. Thata. He had also failed Merey and Tellwoon. He'd failed Gimlore, Tinko, and Keryon. He had failed Arkan and Pinesy. Even if they lived, they would talk of nothing but his monumental failure for eternity. He reckoned that was a fair price to pay.

As the void sucked him in, he also felt the Essence abandon him. With it also went his strength. For one last time, he allowed himself to be happy about that. He would die a happy man, and a free one, at last untainted by the greedy hands of the deity.

His consciousness faded and the lines blurred between light and darkness, between reality and illusion.

Between life and death.

Forty-One
PROPERTY

ORBERESIS - SOLVI

A surge of power flowed into Orberesis, making him more than a man. More than a human. The smoke was gone and so was the pathetic old man who had insisted on trying to stop him. Waves of energy flowed towards him, pulsing, rippling. He held it all in, his body shaking in a frenzy of ecstasy.

Yes, Doi! You did it!

Orberesis' hair flowed in the wind as the rift continued to absorb the Essence.

"You never wanted to kill your sister, did you?" Orberesis asked as the realisation struck him. "You just wanted to absorb her. Her power."

I wanted YOU to absorb her power, the Old One said. *Don't you know what that means? You're no longer a human. You have the power of two gods inside you. I've fulfilled my promise. You're a god now.*

Orberesis looked at his arms and hands. Despite the surge of power he had felt entering his body, he wasn't any different. "How can that be? I'm still a man of flesh and bone."

The Old One chuckled. *No, Doi. Much more than that. It's time to tap into that power you stole. It's time to expand the rift and bridge the gap between the worlds. Time to bring my brothers and sisters here.*

"And how exactly do I..."

Orberesis lost control before he could finish his sentence. The Old One took over his body and Orberesis experienced complete paralysis, as though his body was no longer his, but belonged to someone else. He tried to speak but couldn't. He tried closing his eyes or opening his mouth, but he couldn't do either. Even his mind was freezing, in a slow descent into madness, with something tickling parts of it, erasing his human conscience.

He wanted it to stop, but of course, it didn't. He wanted to cry, but of course he couldn't.

All that was left was him, the Old One.

Doi has been a good boy.

Orberesis became the Old One's puppet. The parasite laughed as he raised Orberesis' arm to open the rift even further. The giant grey hole expanded and so did its suction. A large power surged through his body again.

Please. Give me back my body.

But the Old One didn't respond. Did he hear him?

As the rift expanded, his arms moved on their own and he flew towards it, stopping just short.

The rift exploded, ageing all the landscape around it. The most powerful wave of time in existence, except for a bit of the battlefield that still seemed to be shrouded in smoke. The Old One made it many years older than it had any right to be. Too many. Rivers and creeks dried up. The woodlands died and turned into charred ash or darkened charcoal, creating a sea of blackness all the way to the horizon. Rocks shattered, grounded into dust and sand. Land and stones slid down from mountains and buried rocks and trees. Hundreds of animals died.

Isn't it beautiful?

Even if Orberesis could talk, he was lost for words. In a quick second, everything he knew had aged years and perished. But at least there would be peace now.

The Old One soared the skies and observed the damage and the carnage, and Orberesis felt both sick at what he had done and proud of it at the same time. It would take years for the Known World to recover from that, though it wouldn't recover. The Old One was preparing the world to welcome the Lantern Horns.

As though he had been waiting for a cue, the parasitical god climbed higher, to the edge of the rift, and tore at its corner, tripling its size. The Old One lowered the rift and dropped it on the desolate ground, then waited for what felt like an eternity. Orberesis became no more than a forgotten nuisance in his own body.

"Here they come," Orberesis said, though *he* hadn't really said it.

The rift had become a portal and from it, the Lantern Horns came. There were dozens of the gruesome creatures at first.

They crossed the rift slowly and with the utmost care. Stepping on the dead grassland, they hesitated, but soon realised it was safe.

"Come, my brethren!" the Old One said using Orberesis' voice.

The Lantern Horns flashed their lights without rest as they heard his voice, running towards him. "Come! You're safe now!"

From hundreds, the creatures became thousands. From thousands, tens of thousands.

"Scatter! This is your new home!" Orberesis said. He wanted to stop but couldn't. "This is your world. *Take* whatever you want."

The Lantern Horns scattered in all directions towards the land, giving space for the many others emerging from the rift.

"Today is a good day."

Orberesis wondered what the Old One would do now that the primary goal had been accomplished. Survival? Would he just toy with humanity like the pieces of a child's boardgame? Would he invent cruel ways to torture them? *And make me watch it all...*

Without warning, Orberesis felt the control of his body return. "What..." He could speak again! And move! "What did you do to me?"

The Old One chuckled. *No need to panic, Doi. I just borrowed you for a while. It's too exhausting to be in control all the time. Being limited by a physical body is awful. Especially such a frail one...*

Anger shot through him. "You were controlling me!"

I was. So?

"I don't remember giving you permission," Orberesis snarled.

Suddenly, his body froze without warning and his vision went dark.

PERMISSION?

I don't need your permission, Doi. Your body is mine. You are mine. My property. You thought you were in control? That you had any say? I've had my hand on you for over ten years. I do as I please, and you do as you're told.

Not if I kill myself, Orberesis thought.

See, I can hear those thoughts as well. I'd know if you were trying such foolishness. I would never let that happen.

Orberesis fell into a pit of despair. He had been so foolish he almost deserved this.

You behave, and I will release you. You can still lead a normal life.

By normal life, the Old One meant living under the looming possibility of being permanently stiffened by a greedy god. One who had just become the only deity to operate in this world. They were all puppets of the gods, one way or another, but he had been so utterly foolish in believing he could be one of them, and now he was more of a puppet than anybody else.

It served him right. "I'll behave."

The Old One released the darkness and laughed as he did so, allowing Orberesis to return to his senses, to his body and to the world. One which had been completely full of Lantern Horns. If Orberesis already thought they were many before, it was something else now. There were simply too many of them coming out of the rift, of all shapes and sizes, endless flashing lights going on and off from the horns in their heads.

"Are you happy now?" Orberesis asked. He had no idea what his parasite wanted. Was there more?

The Old One chuckled again. *Of course I am. But we get bored after a while. I'll be paying close attention to the Lantern Horns and see how they rule themselves. How they rule over humanity.*

Orberesis scowled. He didn't need to be an educated man to know exactly how they'd rule. All it took was a glance at their imposing bodies, their claws, maws, and long fangs. If humans had survived the ageing, they'd soon face something far, far darker.

Darkness enveloped Solvi. Everything seemed heavier as she opened her eyes and tried to move. Others around her were doing the same. Occasional shouts and screams in the background forced her back to reality. Her son! She blinked a few times to clear her eyes and horror filled her mind as she found a toddler in her arms instead of a newborn. The child had brown skin and lengthy dark hair.

He looked like Orberesis.

Solvi wanted to scream. Was it madness? She tried not to move as not to wake the child. Glancing all around, hoping she would find some comfort, but ended up finding none. Not too far from her, a woman she had seen earlier looked like she had aged quite a lot as well. A younger one now had grey hair. She wasn't the only one with a racing heart and a desperate mind.

A hand fell on her shoulder. Her instinct was to shrug it off, but she noticed it was Nosema. "Are you alright?"

Her eyes widened. The man looked much older too. His hair was longer and had white strands in it. The roots of his beard were peppered in white around his chin. The ageing had made him slimmer, his cheek bones more prominent and his eyes deeper. She struggled to respond, immediately wondering if the same had happened to her. All she could do was nod before she eyed the child again, still asleep in her arms. She had barely been prepared to take care of a new-born son, but she definitely wasn't prepared to care for a child that looked three or four winters old.

"What's happening to us?" she asked in a trembling voice.

Nosema squeezed her shoulder and swallowed. "Orberesis' doing. I think Rednow managed to protect us, but not entirely, as you can see. We've all aged a fair bit. Those outside Rednow's protection must have fared worse. Have you seen it?"

There was a sadness in Nosema's voice.

"Seen what?"

"The land. Come."

Solvi's heart was still racing as fast as it ever had. She didn't know what she expected to find as she held the child in her arms while getting up. Following Nosema's pointing finger, she glanced beyond the base camp.

Death. Desolation.

Where trees used to be were now only ashes and dirt. Rivers had dried up and mountains turned to sand. There was no longer any green, and a thick layer of dust covered the horizon. It was like a desert.

Her eyes widened.

"He's lost his mind," she muttered.

"Perhaps in more ways than one. They were saying he seemed possessed just before he struck."

Solvi glanced at the child, a miniature version of his father, and swallowed. That was something she needed to prepare for. There was barely any time to rest, to get her wits together. Rednow had lost, and Orberesis had won. She had picked the losing side.

"We must go."

Solvi eyed Nosema, frowning. "Go where? It's over. They won."

"The shadowlings are coming," Nosema shook his head. "Look, it's never over until its over. See all these people? We need to find shelter. Safety. The shadowlings will come and kill everyone, so we need to go somewhere they'll struggle to get to."

Solvi had no idea what place that could be.

She was weaker as she had aged years in minutes. She had only been trying to take care of her baby, and now everything was upside down. Somehow, she couldn't shake the feeling that some of this was her fault.

"I could have stopped him," it dawned on her. "I could have made him see reason. What an utter fool."

Nosema patted her back. "I doubt it. And even if that's true, it doesn't matter. We all make mistakes. You've suffered plenty for yours. Now it's time to look forward. No one will blame you for this, so don't you do it to yourself either. Come on, let's go."

No one will blame me for this?

Solvi wasn't so sure. She thought quite a few of them surely would.

FORTY-TWO
LOSS AND GRATITUDE

GIMLORE - KERYON

"Let's move!" Gimlore shouted at a group of folks who were cowering behind a rock. "You'll be in the belly of the beasts in no time if you just sit there crying."

A woman wiped off her tears, took Gimlore's hand, and started moving, the others following. Everything in the base camp was gone, and being on the run with that many people and no supplies was a complete disaster in the making.

The shadowlings were bigger, stronger, and faster. She wouldn't be surprised if they caught up with her any minute now. All the survivors were on borrowed time. Whatever it was that Rednow had done, it had saved them. Or at least given them enough time to seek some kind of safety or shelter.

What happened to him?

She tried running, but everything took more effort, not just because she had been aged but because she had been on the battlefield for much longer than anyone her age should have.

"Mother, where are we going?" Tinko asked.

Gimlore still had trouble understanding they were her child. No longer a child, taller than her, with a defined jaw and high cheekbones, as though she was looking at a copy of her younger self. Instead of responding, she felt an urge to hug Tinko and never let go again, but that couldn't be. There were enemies after everyone. She was a survivor once again, and that meant going back to doing whatever she had always done.

"We're going as far north as possible. Merey and Tellwoon said they have their base camp in the mountains somewhere. Far from here, so it will be weeks, perhaps months with a crowd like this. But we can't leave anyone behind."

Tinko's face soured. "I see."

"What is it?" she asked as they kept moving behind a small cart pulled by a shadesgrowl.

"I was hoping to go back to Heleronde and say goodbye to Thata. The proper way."

Gimlore's heart sank. They were going the absolute opposite way.

How could she reply to this? "Thata will never be forgotten. We will not let it happen."

She needed to think of something they could do, but nothing came to mind. Perhaps a little white lie wouldn't hurt.

"Listen," she said as she tore part of her sleeve off, and then tore that one in half. "When I was in the steppes during the Crimson Wars, we would lose comrades every day, some weeks. We refused to let them perish without a proper goodbye, so we tore part of our clothes and burned them. That fire, that light, would vanish as the cloth burned, but until it did, it we had just enough time to remember what they meant to us, to say goodbye, and send them off to the underworld."

Gimlore looked at Tinko and handed them one of the pieces of cloth. "Take it and burn it. Then close your eyes and pretend that Thata is here with you. It won't be a long time, but if you feel the fire's heat, you can grieve. You can cry or laugh, or whatever it is you need to do to say goodbye."

Tinko reluctantly picked up the cloth and gave her a nod. "What about you, Mother?"

Gimlore lifted the other piece of cloth. "I'll be right by your side."

She borrowed a torch from one of the smithies, who was now fully grey-haired, and lit up the cloths. First Tinko's, then hers. They both took a step away from the crowd's steadfast march toward the north. Gimlore had never done this in the Crimson Wars, but Tinko needed closure. If she was really honest with herself, so did she. Maybe she should even believe her own lies.

She closed her eyes, and tears immediately built up, rapidly flowing down, her nose immediately clogging.

I'm sorry. I'm sorry for everything. I failed you. It's always going to be my fault. But I can promise I'll protect Tinko as I should have protected you. Rest easy, my child.

The fire stopped burning and Gimlore opened her eyes, then glanced at Tinko as they opened theirs. "All done?"

Tinko wiped their eyes. "Yes. Let's go. Better not get left behind."

Gimlore was the one struggling to leave. Her hands shook and her legs trembled.

"Mother? Let's go," Tinko said, placing an arm around Gimlore's shoulders. "We'll figure it out."

Gimlore swallowed and took a deep breath.

"Yes, yes. Of course." They walked towards the march. "Where's Keryon?"

Tinko shrugged.

Gimlore hadn't seen him in a while, but if she knew the man, he'd be helping someone or doing his best to cheer them up. And they all needed some proper cheering. Most people faced the ground as they marched, all life gone from their eyes, old wounds and scars made new. They had done their part and won the bloody battle only to suffer defeat in the end by some kind of being much more powerful than they had even thought. And now the entire world would change because of it.

"Come," she said. "I must speak with Merey."

Gimlore hurried to the front of the convoy. People cried and whimpered as they limped along. The march was slower than it should ever be when there were monsters in pursuit. It all reminded her of the Crimson Wars. People had the same eyes she'd seen in many who had first arrived in Heleronde. Except now they didn't have Heleronde either. They didn't even have cities to be beggars in. All they had was an uncertain future in a desolate land that was about to be razed by creatures of the underworld.

"What will happen to us, Mother? To all these people?" Tinko's determined face still showed a hint of fear and uncertainty.

"They will all be dead before sunset if they don't hurry. It seems the shadowlings aren't chasing, but they won't hesitate to attack if they find us. We're on borrowed time."

Tinko swallowed and quieted as they pressed on through the cold air of the Thousand Hills. Through the corner of her eye, she observed her child. The growth was immense, almost unrecognisable. The mischief was all gone, replaced by a relentless sense of duty and a need to protect others. They had been forced to grow faster than normal, even before the forced ageing. Hope, too, had grown into a scrawny woman instead of the bony little girl, but she still had the wide eyes of a lost puppy.

Ahead in the convoy, Merey was conferring with Tellwoon and others. Arkan was there, but he looked defeated, as though they had all indeed been wiped from the face of the world. Fatuna and Pinesy were there too. Nork and Nosema. Solvi. Even the Tooth stood there, next to the twins. Every single one of them looked like age had not been kind. White hair, sunken faces and dark rings around their eyes were common features between them now. Keryon was the only one missing.

"We were going to call you," Merey said, then looked at Tinko.

Gimlore nodded. "Tinko has seen much. Speak freely. What are our current plans?"

Merey nodded. "We're marching towards the Benaven mountains. Benaven did not take part in the battle, and we know how to cross their borders without being noticed by the kingdom's soldiers."

"And then?"

"I guess it's no longer a secret we can afford to keep, but our base camp is up in the Seven Peaks," Tellwoon added. "It's rough up there. Dangerous on many levels. But we should be safe from the shadowlings."

Gimlore frowned. "Do you all agree with this?"

No one dared speak, but no one denied it either.

"Even if we can all stay in your base camp, we can't all live there year-long. We must find a solution. Something more sustainable. Anything, really." Gimlore only saw defeat in their faces. They were prepared to give up, weren't they?

She gritted her teeth. "Are you fucking kidding me? Are we all going to hide in the world's most remote place and just give up the rest of the world to those slimy fuckers?"

"What else is there to do?" Fatuna asked. "You saw his power with your own eyes. Humanity is doomed and that's all there is to it."

Gimlore scowled. "Doomed? Doomed are those who sit and wait for tragedy. We should march north, even further than the Seven Peaks."

"To the Barren North? The tribes there will never accept us," Merey said. "You don't know them like we do. They're constantly at war with each other. They won't ever unite, and the chances of them fighting on our behalf are null. We're dead as soon as we step foot onto their land."

"Doesn't sound worse than sitting idly on the mountain top and waiting for time to pass," Gimlore said. "Perhaps we should give people a chance to choose. Whoever wants to go to the Seven Peaks can follow you. Those who do not can follow me to the northern fiefdoms."

They exchanged looks. Nork and Nosema nodded. They'd follow her everywhere, no words needed to be exchanged.

"A vote, eh?" Merey asked, scratching her head. "I'm not opposed to that."

Gimlore nodded. "What about you, Arkan? Do you speak for your people?"

The pain in Arkan's eyes was almost palpable. "The Builders are dead. Our cove is destroyed. We're just a few hundred now, nomads again after all these years. I can't feel the Essence any longer. Can you?"

Pinesy shook his head, a look of concern plastered on his face.

"Let's find help. Settle down, heal our wounds, grieve, and come back stronger and with a plan," Gimlore said.

The Tooth waved his fist in the air. "The gutter kids and I will follow you north as long as we can get some proper clothes. This is already as cold as I've ever been and I don't fancy it's going to get any warmer from here."

Gimlore nodded. After all this time, and all her failures, they still relied on her for help and guidance. She clasped the hammer in her belt more by instinct than anything. She couldn't fail them this time.

What had happened to Rednow? No one had seen him yet, and a body had not been found, but he had already been half-dead. Without the Essence flowing within him, he could only be dead.

Thank you for everything, old man.

Keryon dragged himself through the convoy. His legs were heavy, and every inch of his body ached. Every breath he took—even the soft ones—left him with the sense he was breathing blood, and that it was soaking his lungs. Doig was much worse, though, being carried in a cart, pulled by shades-growls. Still hadn't woken up.

He continued to limp forward, a sharp pain in his right leg. Something must be broken. Besides the burn in his face, he had also gained a new collection of scars in his arms and face. His clothes were completely ragged and charred from the fire, and some more burn marks had even made it all the way to his arms and legs.

He should be with Gimlore, helping her lead the convoy, looking after the child. But he couldn't leave Doig. The man had been his salvation. They were smokesmith brethren, after all.

"Do you need help?" a familiar voice asked from behind.

He turned and saw Solvi smiling at him. She was older just like the rest of them, a few strands of white hair rooted in with the blonde. She carried a young child in her arms. The little child held on to her staunchly and looked to be on the verge of crying.

Keryon stopped where he was, and almost let Doig's cart continue in the convoy as people passed by him. He then smiled and shook his head. "No. But will you walk alongside me?"

Solvi nodded and joined him in the march. The ageing had done her good. Last time Keryon had seen her, she had looked like a wild, caged animal ready to strike. Now, after they had lost everything, she almost looked to be at peace. "Is it too late to thank you?"

"Thank me?" He didn't look at her. Too many emotions. There was too much he wanted to say. How proud he was. How he had known all along she could make amends. He stayed silent instead. "For what?"

Solvi smiled. It was a smile whose meaning they both understood. She knew he was playing humble, and he knew exactly what she was thanking him for. "For everything," she said.

Keryon nodded as his eyes found the child's large eyes staring at him. "I'm glad he is a healthy one. That's not thanks to me."

Solvi shook her head. "You helped me see right from wrong. You and Gimlore showed me a better way of living. And thanks to you two, the child is safe."

Keryon nodded, looking away from them. He hoped the child would live a long and healthy life, but the odds were not in their favour. "What will you do now?"

Solvi snorted. "Survive. And maybe live a little, if I'm lucky."

"That's a good answer."

Solvi cleared her throat. "I've been thinking. Now that the child has aged quite a bit, I can't wait much longer to give him a proper name. I was thinking about naming him Ker. You don't mind, do you?"

Keryon nearly choked. *What?* It was as though his lungs had emptied themselves and he couldn't take any more air. The surprise was followed by an opening of the floodgates of pride. "Are you serious?"

Solvi smiled and nodded. "Of course. One day I'll tell him the story of his name, and the man who saved his mother when she didn't even want to be saved."

THE END

EPILOGUE

From the silence came a persistent scratching sound. It could be anything. The darkness was overwhelming and Rednow could only hear that scratch. No movement. No other sound. He couldn't say if it was hot or cold. His sense of time and consciousness had faded. Ten years? Five seconds?

Nothing but darkness.

I'm on my way to the underworld. He knew that for certain.

The scratching sound continued. *Srrrrt. Srrrrt.* Like an annoying insect buzzing around one's ear. The scratch became everything. *But if I'm going to the underworld, then why do I still think?* He was dead twice over. Strangely enough, he remembered very little from the world of the living. He knew who he was, but concrete memories were... a blur.

It didn't matter. He would soon find his ma and pa. Spend time with them in the underworld. Rebma. Thata. They were there, along with everybody else he had killed.

Srrrrt. Srrrrt.

"What have we got here?" an echoing baritone asked. It was loud, and nauseating, unnatural and inhuman. "Another one, is it? Someone's been busy up there. Welcome to the underworld, Rednow."

THANK YOU! PLEASE READ!

You've made it!

Thank you so much for dedicating your precious time and love for the genre to Thorns *of War*. Without readers, there would be no point in telling stories. It is only with your support that I carry on with *The Smokesmiths* series.

So, if you enjoyed *Thorns of War*, please leave a rating or a review on Amazonand on Goodreads. Please. Thousands of books are published every day, millions every year. For *Thorns of War* to have a fighting chance among them, it needs all the help it can get. That means ratings and reviews from readers like you. Leaving a review is one of the best things a reader can do.

Writing *Thorns* was quite the journey. This was the continuation of a story I've wanted to tell for a long time. I've tinkered with parts of it in my mind for years and some bits even came from unfinished manuscripts. I've always wanted to tell stories about non-conventional families and single parents who thrive on their own despite everything thrown at them. About older people, who are often told to stay in their lane. I also wanted to tell stories of displacement and the feelings that come from being forced out of your reality one way or another.

Writing is my passion. I intend to do it forever, and count on you for support. It truly means everything to me!

I promise I'll keep writing and always sharpening the writing tools in my satchel.

Stay strong and persevere,
João F. Silva

Join the Smokesmiths

Sign up to João F. Silva's mailing list and read his prequel novella 'Ruins of Smoke' for FREE. You'll be the first to receive all the news, writing updates regarding *The Smokesmiths* series, any other projects or special offers and discounts.

ACKNOWLEDGMENTS

This book is for all the writers and authors grinding to make their dreams a reality.

Many of us were never told we can have dreams, that it is alright to dreams, yet we dared to dream anyway: against all reason. Because dreams aren't reasonable or rational, because we wouldn't have it any other way.

I had a much easier time writing *Thorns of War* than *Seeds* because I already knew the characters and the world inside and out, but also because I was lucky enough to have the insane and sometimes unreasonable support of an amazing group of people. Ever since I published *Seeds*, there has been a small group of loyal, staunch supportive readers who never fail to amaze me. They are my online champions: always promoting my book, active on my Discord. They are some of the most uplifting people I know. I don't think I could have done this without them, as they are the fuel that keeps my motivation engine running without fail.

Publishing *Seeds* opened many doors, but perhaps none as important as one to the writing community. Without the support of fellow authors, the journey here would have been far harder. Special shoutouts to Joe Lee, Gregory Kontaxis, Mitriel

Faywood, Michael R. Miller, LL MacRae, and Jacob Sannox, who I've had the pleasure to meet in person and have been lovely people. Another special shoutout to my fellow authors Sadir Samir, Michael Michel, Luke Shulz, James Dulin, Bethany Garcia, Katie Andrews, Joe Berne, HC Newell, and Morgan Shank for the comradery and support.

Massive thanks to my editor Sarah Chorn and my proofreader Edward Crocker, both amazing writers in their own right who truly understand what I'm trying to do with this series and help me make it the best it can possibly be.

Massive thanks to all the amazing beta readers whose feedback helped shape this book into its final form: Kris, Lena, BK, Max, Kavga, Haney, Graham, and Danielle,

And of course, I had the support and encouragement of my wife, W, who has long been the rock that keeps me grounded when my mind is plotting imagined worlds and creatures. I'm lucky to have someone like you in my life.

Watch out for what is to come next!

ABOUT THE AUTHOR

João F. Silva was born in a small town in Portugal but now lives in the UK with his feline co-workers/bosses. His debut novel Seeds of War won the Best Indie Debut of 2023 at the FanFi-Addict Awards. His short fiction was published in Grimdark Magazine and Haven Speculative. He has been on the jury for the 2020 and 2022 editions of the "Best Newcomer" Award at the British Fantasy Awards.

Get in touch by filling in the form on his website, by emailing him at joao@joaofsilva.net or by following him on social media.

Goodreads

Twitter

Facebook

Instagram

GLOSSARY

Alarkan – A newly-discovered continent, emerged from the depths of the ocean.

Ancient Ones – Ancient Lost Civilisation which disappeared without a trace.

Belleaf Oil – Highly flammable oil extracted from belleaf flowers. Doesn't require a spark to start burning. Often used by smokesmiths.

Bloodsleuth – Blind reptilian hound with a three-way muzzle with a keen sense of smell for blood.

Cerro – Fruit tree which produces bittersweet berries.

Crimson Wars – A bloody period that lasted years and during which humanity was plagued by hordes of monstruous creatures like bloodsleuths.

Floating City Fleet – A fleet of hundreds of massive-sized maritime vessels owned by the Two Kingdoms of Sirestir and Yab.

Greasy Bomb – Explosive consisting of a sack of black powder doused in belleaf oil. Thrown at enemies like a knife.

Hearthspear – Agile, reptilian creatures used as mount.

Heleronde – The busiest settlement in all of Alarkan.

Marcruncher – Furry carnivorous mammal. Inhabits cold areas.

Mossback – Reptilian creatures found in Alarkan. They produce a coveted liver elixir.

Ominous Kas – A rare herb that grants ability to smokesmiths when burned.

Leeth – Legendary and covert mercenary group.

Pinehead – Sentient humanoid species with a child-like appearance and size.

Puncturing Ceremony – Tradition in Gasho during which a member of nobility pierces their face dozens of times as a symbol of power and wealth.

Smokesmith – Person who is able to breathe smoke and has the ability to manipulate it.

Shadesgrowl – Large yet slow herbivore creature used as a mount in cold climates.

The Miracle – The event during which Orberesis broke the world, slayed the monsters that plagued humanity and ended the Crimson Wars.

The Two Nations – A political alliance between the kingdoms of Sirestir and Yab.

Twisted Twins – A rare herb that grants ability to smokesmiths when burned.

Wickplate – Giant maritime creatures with durable scales. They are fished and their scales are used to build breastplates.

DRAMATIS PERSONAE

Doi "Orberesis" Sonoda – Cult leader who goes by the moniker 'God Himself'

Gimlore – Businesswoman, owner of the Maiden's Hall and de facto ruler of Heleronde

Rednow – Leader of the Leeth, brother to Rebma. Known as the Blood Collector

Keryon – Former lawman and smokesmith.

Solvi – Orberesis' most trusted aide and protector

Edmir – Gimlore's most trusted companion (deceased)

Rebma – Rednow's younger sister (deceased)

Merey – Brash and confident general of the Leeth

Tellwoon – Thoughtful general of the Leeth

Tavanar – Orberesis' oldest friend and confidant

Foloi – Big and strong cage fighter. Gimlore's former lover (deceased)

Nork – Gimlore's henchman

Nosema – Gimlore's henchman

Zatak – Lead houndsman of the Leeth

Piesym – Keryon's business partner and shopkeeper (deceased)

Doemus – King of the Two Nations

Arkan – Leader of the Builders

Ferkin – Exiled smokesmith

Chona – Exiled smokesmith

Fatuna – Exiled smokesmith

Thura – Queen of the Two Nations (deceased)

Taishay – Main Political advisor of the Two Nations

Pinesy – Pinehead in Gimlore's crew

Tinko – Gimlore's infant child

Thata – Gimlore's infant child (deceased)

Eshof – Old woman, citizen of Heleronde (deceased)

Basa Akan – Herald from Sirestir sent to Heleronde (deceased)

Rednalf – Rednow's long-deceased nephew (deceased)